BELOW THE
SURFACE

KAREN
HARPER

BELOW THE
SURFACE

**Doubleday Large Print
Home Library Edition**

MIRA®

MIRA

ISBN-13: 978-0-7394-9136-2

BELOW THE SURFACE

LP.
fic
Har

Sept 20.80

**This Large Print Book carries the
Seal of Approval of N.A.V.H.**

Thanks to my great MIRA Books team.
I value your expertise and support:

Miranda Stecyk
Margaret O'Neill Marbury
Dianne Moggy
Donna Hayes
Craig Swinwood
Katherine Orr, Marleah Stout
and their great staff,
including Maureen Stead
and especially all the dynamic MIRA Books
sales staff!
And, as ever, to my greatest supporter, Don.

1

The Gulf of Mexico off South Florida
September 12, 2006

When Briana Devon surfaced, her boat was gone. Something—besides the fact that the gulf had gone rough since she'd begun her dive—was terribly wrong.

She struggled to keep her underwater camera and strobe from being ripped away by the waves. Her tethered plastic slate with its latex rubber pencil she used to make notes underwater smacked her face; she thrust it behind her.

She kept the regulator in her mouth, clenched between her teeth. Still sucking in the air from her tank, she heard the hiss of her more rapid breathing mingled with the howl of the increasing wind. Since she was fairly low on air, her single tank yanked back and forth on her BC, the vest-style buoyancy compensator that supported her in the water.

This was impossible! Had she come up in the wrong place? No, the pelican float she'd deployed bobbed wildly, riding the waves. She was where she meant to be, but where was Daria and their dive boat? And how fast the distant storm had come up.

Holding on to her gear and using her flippers, she spun in a circle. Maybe the *Mermaids II* was just blurred by the darkening horizon. No, all she saw were clumps of clouds, not even other boats, with that storm coming in much faster than the weatherman had predicted. But Daria would never have left her out here.

Despite being a veteran diver, panic pulsed through Briana for herself and her sister. Bree and Daria Devon were not only twin sisters but had been best friends since they could remember.

Bree put more air in her BC to keep afloat and fought to calm herself. After all, she'd been diving for twenty of her twenty-eight years and swimming these waters even longer. Every week, she and Daria dived the artificial reef made by the wreck of an old trading boat to check on the growth of pollutant-endangered sea grass and marine life. The grass was a bellwether for the health of the gulf waters in general. It had all been routine until now.

Bree had not noticed whether the anchor had been pulled up. She'd only been intent on doing her work well and quickly. Just take the photos, make the notes, get proof. The results were bad news that was going to upset a lot of powerful people. She'd only come up early because visibility was lessening, and that meant the waves were kicking up. But she'd never imagined this churning, gray sea and gathering storm.

The twins had always buddy-dived unless they were just scraping barnacles off hulls at the marina, but there were two reasons Daria hadn't made the dive with her today. She'd suddenly developed a bad toothache, which would have made the underwater pressure excruciating for her. And someone had to stay with their dive boat: Daria had given Manny, their only employee at their search-and-salvage shop, the afternoon off since he'd been having so much trouble with his daughter. Actually, Daria hadn't been diving much this past month anyway, since she'd been so busy concentrating on her accounting class.

Bree's arms ached from trying to hang on to her camera and strobe in the increasing turbulence. She had never feared this vast stretch of water, only respected it, but now terror immobilized her. Alone. Abandoned? She should probably start swimming in, but she was over four miles out and she'd have to ditch her precious gear. She should have taken it as a bad sign when she saw that bull shark cruising past the reef instead of the usual resident grouper. Bulls became disturbed whenever the water was riled, and they were known to attack humans. How many times had she warned someone not to swim alone or far from shore, and to avoid splashing?

Bree had a whistle to summon help, but there was no one in range to hear it. She could set off her strobe to try to attract attention, but holding it above the waves would wear her out. Reluctantly she let her strobe lights and camera drop, hoping they would snag somewhere near the wreck and she— they—could retrieve them later. The camera was worth big bucks; they'd scraped a lot of barnacles off yachts to buy it.

The twins' co-owned marine search-and-salvage shop had been struggling, but things were on the upswing lately. They did everything from underwater surveys to hull maintenance to retrieval of lost items or sunken vessels. It could be dirty, hard, even dangerous work, but they both loved it. They knew what was below the surface of the gulf off southwest Florida almost as well as they knew each other.

It had been a surprise and a thrill when the prestigious Clear the Gulf Commission had hired them—not their larger rival across the bay—to record the difficult comeback of off-the-coast marine life under siege from toxic runoff. The whole local ecosystem was being poisoned by fertilizers from sugarcane fields, golf course fairways, and polluted water releases from just too many people.

To save her strength, Bree decided to dive again and get as far as she could underwater before she'd have to ditch her tanks and weight belt to swim in. Though she saw no watercraft, perhaps one would be heading for safe harbor and she could hail it. She

upended and kicked down until the turbulence seemed to lessen.

The Gulf of Mexico, off Naples, Marco
Island and Turtle Bay, was a shallow body of
water, at least compared to the Atlantic. The
bottom was fairly flat for a long way out: after an initial drop-off, it deepened about two
feet per mile and was broken only by small
ledges and man-made reefs. But because
the depth was fairly shallow, the gulf could
get violent fast. It was the underwater storm
of sand and silt that had tipped her off to the
one above. Though she did a lot of close-up,
well-lit macrophotography, even that was
looking grainy today.

Most people—especially tourist divers from
"the frozen North," as their dive friends called
it—thought the water off Naples was not great
dive territory. But the twins had always loved it
more than the glamour spots of the Keys or
even the Caribbean. Fifteen feet of visibility in
this part of the world was a great disappoint-
ment to some, but in the summers, the sea often went flat and turbulence was minimal. This
part of the gulf was not crowded with divers,
so it seemed pristine, with an abundance of
wildlife like grouper, tarpon, rays, sea turtles,
beautiful shells and, unfortunately at times,

sharks. They also loved the gulf because that's where they'd learned to dive. It seemed so untouched, with the exception of the fact the reefs were man-made. But then, the natural coral reefs on the other coast were as endangered as the sea life would soon be here, if their project didn't help turn things around.

As she swam toward shore, roiling sand and silt and the thickening clouds made it too dark for her to be certain in what direction she was heading. Mostly, she went with the surge of the waves, which should take her in. Unfortunately, the tide was flowing out and the wind was fighting that, churning the water into a soupy maelstrom. She couldn't even read the luminous dial of the compass dive watch Daria had given her for their birthday last month. Daria and the boat. . . She could not imagine what might have happened, why her sister would desert her during a dive.

Surely nothing could have capsized *Mermaids II,* not a twenty-four-foot skiff with a flat bottom. There was no so-called Bermuda Triangle on this side of Florida. Yacht pirates and drug dealers wouldn't want a slow diver's boat. Smugglers had begun to bring in desperate refugees fleeing Cuba, and boats involved in the horrible human trafficking trade imported poverty-stricken Guatemalan women as domestic drudges or even sex slaves on both sides of the state. But those boats sneaked in at night to avoid being spotted or caught. Even if Daria had become ill, she wouldn't leave her. Nothing made sense.

In the murky water Bree could not read her air-pressure gauge, but she could feel the air through her mouthpiece becoming more difficult to breathe. Realizing her air was quickly running out, she surfaced. The waves were four feet now; she rode them up, down, sliding with their strength. It had started to rain. Which way was the shore?

She accidentally took in a mouthful of water, then spit it out. Swallowing salt water always made her nauseous. She was getting sick to her stomach anyway, furious and fearful. Dad had always said never to let your emotions rule your head, not when diving. In a way, after Mother died, that had become his credo for life. Just keep busy, so busy you don't have time for feelings, suffocating, desperate, drowning feelings . . .

Bree dropped her weight belt, ditched her tank with the quick-release straps and began breathing through her snorkel. The tank went

under with a loud gurgle. She felt lighter—
better, she tried to buck herself up. She could
make it in. Keewadin Island, long and narrow,
must be ahead somewhere, maybe three
miles or so. Thank God, she hadn't been at
some of the more distant dive sites like Black
Hole Sink or Naples Ledges, which were
around thirty miles out.

She tried to convince herself that this was
only the usual, quick afternoon summer
storm, which would pepper the gulf, bathe
the Everglades, then depart to leave a warm,
humid evening. When would this summer
weather break? Was she going to break?

Bree tried not to swallow water. Swimming
was suddenly exhausting; despite her desperation to get ashore, she had to pace
herself more. She slowed her strokes and
kicks toward what she was certain must be
land.

Stroke, stroke, stroke, breathe. Despite
the outgoing tide, she was certain the waves
must be pushing her along. But it was so far
in. Hard to get good breaths. And then she
heard it, the thing she feared most.

Thunder rumbling, coming. And that
meant lightning.

Oh, no. Oh, no. Just last week, she had

sat on their veranda at Turtle Bay and watched a storm like this. Forks of lightning had stabbed the gulf and then the bay just beyond the docks, coming closer, closer. As usual, the power had gone off for a while, but the twins weren't air-conditioner addicts like their older sister. Amelia almost never opened her windows, even in good weather. That would make her house dusty. Her poor kids, whom she kept so clean, could use a little dust and dirt.

Bree's muscles began to burn. She could hear Dad's voice telling her and Daria, "When in doubt, get out." Out, she wanted out. She wanted to be on the *Mermaids II* with Daria. She wanted to be home, safe and dry. She loved the water, loved the gulf, but not out here alone, tiring, so exhausted. *Lord, please keep me safe. Daria, too. What happened? Daria, where are you?*

A wave took one of her fins, and she had to kick the other off to avoid swimming askew. On, on, pull, pull, breathe, flee the thunder and lightning coming closer. She was starting to feel in the zone, like when she jogged several miles, but she was getting light-headed, dizzy, too.

The first distinct crack of lightning struck

so close she flinched and shrieked into the mouthpiece of her snorkel. And then she saw another reason to scream. A big bull shark was swimming with her.

Cole DeRoca was shocked by how fast the storm came up. Usually, you could set your watch by the afternoon storms off the gulf, but this one was early, fierce and dangerous. Though his custom-made sloop was all wood, he wasn't about to have his single mast be the tallest thing in the area. After all, *Streamin'* had copper and brass fittings, and sailors knew lightning could be erratic and deadly.

It would be crazy to try to make it back to the mainland. He'd have to beach the sloop on Keewadin Island and hope he could get her off the sand later. The wind was a good twenty-five knots, whistling shrilly in the rigging. Ordinarily, he'd love racing at this speed, but he needed dry land fast.

To his amazement, the boat nearly heeled over on her side and started south. He felt shoved, grasped in a giant's grip. A riptide? Yes, a narrow but deadly one along here, caused by the battle of the waves and wind.

He went with the flow for a little ways, like

they tell you to do when swimming, then fought it to head back north, tacking back and forth. Finally, the long, beige beach of the barrier island of Keewadin appeared through the slate-gray of slanted rain. Cole retracted the centerboard as the sloop neared the shore. With good speed from the driving waves, he released the main and jib sheets, but they began flogging wildly. His primary thought was to save himself and the boat at the likely sacrifice of his nearly new sails.

As he approached the shore, he tripped the jamb cleats to release the halyards and began tugging at the thrashing sails until they both dropped to the deck, finally free from the force of the wind. He felt a wave thrust the bow of *Streamin'* up, then down, as she slammed onto the beach with a thud. Waves pounded the aft of the stranded vessel.

At least it wasn't a deadly riptide this time, just the sweep of surf. He jumped into foaming, waist-deep water and struggled to turn her prow in and get her higher on the shore. Thunder rumbled and lightning crackled. *Get out of the water,* he told himself. *Get out now.*

Cole loved this boat he'd made with his father, the only one he'd helped him build before everything went wrong. Though he was thirty-four now and had been out on his own since he was twenty, sailing still made him feel closer to his dad. Their family tree boasted five generations of boatbuilders, beginning in Portugal, then the Bahamas, onward to Key West, then Sarasota and Naples. Bahamian sloops like this one had once been used throughout the tropics, but now they were like an endangered species. He often dreamed of ditching his luxury yacht interior trade and take a chance on his own boatbuilding. He'd love to build boats like this one again. America had a throwaway culture, but these babies were built to last, even in a storm, though he'd never seen one as quickly fierce as this.

He tried to set the soles of his running shoes firmly in shifting sand. Both hands on the stern, he shoved. *Streamin'* slid her sleek length farther up on the beach. Keeping low, holding the metal anchor by its rope so he didn't have to touch it, he secured the sloop. Then, his shoes filled with water and sand, he slogged behind the line of mangroves and hunched over, crouched on the balls of his feet. He knew not to lie flat, where you'd have more of your body in contact with the ground if it was hit. Thank God, he'd made it safely out of the gulf, because this was one hell of a howler.

Bree wanted to just close her eyes and give up. A countercurrent swept through here, maybe a riptide that would carry her away. Despite her silent fear of her toothy companion, she swam on. She could stop moving to see if the shark would go away and to save her strength, but what if she got pushed farther out? What if lightning . . . or that shark . . .

A fierce, elemental terror flooded her; she wanted to scream and scream.

But then—dear Lord in heaven, was she seeing double? No, there were two of them, two big gray bodies with white underbellies, the dorsal fins knife-edged. The newest bull shark was at least seven feet long, his small, flat eyes staring at her each time he came near the surface. She stopped swimming. Should she just hang still in the water and let herself be taken out to sea? Bulls were aggressive and commotion bothered them.

Maybe the rough water would keep their attention off her.

Was this a sheer, stark nightmare? If lightning or the sharks hit her, they might never even find her body. Had Daria been caught by these devouring depths, too?

Bree let the current take her for what seemed an eternity, then, when its powerful pull seemed to ease, swam on toward shore again—sharks still alongside. Each time she kicked, each time she pulled her arms through the water or even turned her head to breathe, she feared the jaws of her companions, feared being fried by another lightning strike so close.

A blast of something hit her hard, jerked her through the next wave. The riptide again? Shark? Jaws of a lightning bolt? She spit out the mouthpiece of her snorkel and screamed.

Bloodred colors exploded before her eyes, in her head. Something huge lunged at her. Then came only blackness.

2

Cole was soaked to his skin. The wind lashed him, and rain stung his shoulders and back through his sopped shirt. The narrow key seemed to shudder with each roll of thunder. Yet, through it all, he thought he'd heard a shriek.

He lifted his head. It wasn't just the shrill of wind through the boat's rigging. Something almost human . . .

Squinting into the rain, he peered around the thick patch of mangroves to check on his sloop. Though *Streamin'* had listed from the pounding of the surf, she looked all right. But something was sprawled on the beach beside the hull, as if there had been an accident and the prow had hit someone.

Still keeping low, he went to see what had come in. His breath huffed out as if he'd been hit in the gut; his heart pounded even harder. A woman—it looked like a drowned mermaid!

No, no, of course not, he told himself as he bent over the sprawled figure. The short-sleeved, full-length, silvery-green wet suit clung to her curves so tightly it looked painted on. It was designed with a fin-and-scale pattern to look as if she had a tail. Long legs, that was all. Her shoulder-length, auburn hair clung to her head. Her graceful, limp arms were in a ballerina pose, as if she would dance. Was she dead?

Afraid to roll her face up—instinct in case she had spine or head injuries from hitting his boat—he felt for the pulse at the base of her throat. She felt cold and, despite her tan, her cheek and chin looked pale and waxy, almost as if she were a life-size doll. She had a faint pulse, but she was so still he wasn't certain she was breathing. Carefully, he turned her over, faceup.

She had marks on her face from a diving mask, but he knew this woman! Or else he knew her sister. She was one of the twins who owned the Two Mermaids Marine Search and Salvage Shop in Turtle Bay, not far from his own business. He'd had an impromptu lunch with one of them—Briana—the day she'd been scraping the hull of the Richardson yacht when he was paneling the salon with Santos mahogany. He'd been going through the divorce then and was only dating his sloop, or he would have called her. Thank God, she was alive, but she might not be soon if she didn't take a breath.

Ignoring the slashing rain and continued threat of lightning, he pulled her carefully up out of the slosh of the surf. Hunched over her, just beyond the breaking waves, he started mouth-to-mouth resuscitation. He hadn't done that on anyone since he'd tried to save his father when he'd found him on the floor, and that was too late. What had happened to this woman? Surely she hadn't been swimming in the storm.

She seemed slender and small, but he knew she was a vital, strong woman. *Come on, baby. Come on back. Breathe for me. Let my lips warm yours, sweetheart. Come on, come on.*

It had amused him, then impressed him,

that two women would run such a rough-and-tumble business, especially when their competition across the bay was a gruff, tough guy who pretty much had a monopoly on search and salvage in the area. The women mostly did light salvage, none of the heavy stuff with dredging and demolition like Sam Travers, but search and salvage was always a risky business.

Come on, baby, I know you're spunky. Take my breath. Come on, you beautiful little mermaid!

He started to panic, his sweat mingling with the rain, even in the cool rush of wind. After what seemed an eternity, her mouth moved against his. He stopped and looked down into her face, glazed by rain and gulf water. Her thick eyelashes, plastered to her ashen cheeks, flickered. She frowned and moaned.

"Hey, mermaid!" he said, feeling like a fool, but he couldn't remember her last name and wasn't sure which twin this was. Still, he used the name he knew, one he'd remembered for months now because it had seemed to suit her. It had reminded him of the word *brio,* for her enthusiasm and verve that time they'd talked and eaten together.

He'd felt an instant attraction to her, a surge of desire that he'd tried to control by being overly polite and teasing that day. "Briana?" he said, his voice shaking. "Briana!"

She slitted her eyes open. "Daria?" she said, and started to cough up water.

He rolled her over slightly and braced her with one arm around her. One hand held her forehead steady like his mother used to do for him years ago when he threw up. It wasn't until he saw the burn marks on her limp left wrist, like a big bracelet around her dive watch, that he realized she might have been hit by lightning. He laid her back down on the sand, leaning over her, trying to keep the rain and wind off her with his body.

"Where's Daria?" he asked. "What happened?"

No answer. He gasped when he saw her eyes were dilated, the huge, black pupils eating up the gray-green of the irises, the color of the sea. He had to get her medical help—now. He couldn't wait for the storm to end. But there was no way to get an EMS vehicle out here, and a medical chopper couldn't fly in this mess. He could get on his radio and Mayday the coast guard, but it would take them time to get out here and he could have her into Naples by then—if all went well.

He had to hurry. His mermaid had evidently fainted or gone comatose at his feet.

He put his hand on her chest to be sure she was still breathing. Yes, shallow but steady. Though he hated to take the chance with the sloop, he had to risk sailing in with her right now. At least in an all-wooden boat—if he could get it off the beach—they might be able to escape the lightning. It would be rough going, but he had to try.

Praying she had no broken bones or internal injuries, he lifted her into the sloop and gently lashed her down. He stripped off his polo shirt and, though it was soaked, too, laid it over her upper torso. One of his customers had been hit by lightning on a golf course, and his doctor had told him that fast medical help had saved him from severe complications. He could not bear it if this beautiful, bold woman were permanently hurt. That old adage about being responsible for someone if you saved their life hit him hard, but he hadn't saved her yet.

Straining every muscle in his body to get some lift for *Streamin',* Cole tried to time pushing the sloop off the sand with the roll of the surf, but the power of the waves and wind beat it back. Waves could easily swamp or capsize a boat leaving a beach. His fourteen-foot sloop, which he knew more intimately than he knew any woman right now, fought him hard.

But he saw the wind had clocked around to the north. He could use the power of the sails to propel the sloop off the beach. In a hand-over-hand effort, he pulled the main halyard until the sail had reached the top of the mast. Then with a grunting, grinding heave, Cole pushed the bow of the boat off the beach toward the pounding surf. As the little sloop swung her bow through the wind, the sails filled, and she moved into deeper water. He pulled himself into the cockpit and grabbed the tiller in one hand while securing the mainsheet with the other. As he lowered the centerboard, the sloop began to feel her sea legs. She quickly picked up speed on a beam reach and cut through the water like a race car.

But it was brutal sailing. He had to step over his mermaid when he played the main-sheet and sit outboard to balance the heavy heeling. He feared a broach roll and had to adjust the tiller constantly. Every time the boat heeled, water sloshed over the side to soak Briana. She came to again, shoved her head and shoulder up by one elbow and screamed, "Sharks! Daria, sharks!"

"Lie down!" Cole shouted. "Down or the boom will get you when we tack. You're with me, you're all right. Lie down! There are no sharks. I won't let them get you or Daria!"

That seemed to calm her, and that trust clenched at his heart. He had to get her to safety, see that she was taken care of. She was out of her head, and his friend had said amnesia and brain damage could be some of the aftereffects of a lightning strike. If he could just let go of the tiller and sit still a second in this raging chaos, he could call for help, have someone meet him at the marina with a squad for her. But he couldn't tell where he was. To the pier yet? He didn't want to hit the pier.

As for the sharks, she could not possibly have seen them just now, but she was dead on: he glanced ahead and saw several bull sharks racing right with them, just like the ones in the picture in his office. The Winslow

Homer painting called *The Gulf Stream* was the reason he'd named his company Gulf Stream Yacht Interiors, the reason he'd named this sloop *Streamin'*. But these sharks almost bumping the boat were no work of art—this race was life and death for real.

3

"Mayday! Mayday! Mayday! This is the sloop *Streamin'!*"

Cole never took his cell phone out sailing with him since he kept a two-way radio on board. More than once, he'd lost his cell in the gulf or gotten it soaked. His handheld radio was waterproof, and he managed it one-handed. Finally, someone answered his call for help.

"*Streamin', Streamin',* this is the U.S. Coast Guard Station, Naples Harbor. I read you, sloop *Streamin'*. Say your location. Over."

"U.S. Coast Guard, this is the sloop

Streamin'. This is Cole DeRoca sailing solo out of Turtle Bay. I put in on Keewadin during the storm, but I'm heading for Naples—Port Royal, I think." Adrenaline poured through him; he hoped to hell he was making sense. "I have a half-drowned passenger who washed in or swam in on Keewadin. She may have been hit by lightning, too—in and out of consciousness."

"*Streamin',* do you have a GPS on board?"

"No GPS, it's still thick as pea soup out here. Wait—I see the seawall at Gordon Pass, the rock wall to the south—"

"Put in just north of the pass. We'll send an E.R. squad . . . ."

Cole dropped the radio and slammed both hands back on the tiller. He fought the rush of inward tide that was trying to smash them into the stone break wall of the pass he'd navigated so many times. The outward flow of the Gordon River here crashed into the rising tide. With the wind, it almost capsized them.

He leaned out, away from the hull, using his weight against the lunge and roll of the vessel, wishing he'd had time to get in a trapeze harness. "Come on, baby!" he shouted.

His mermaid stirred again, cried out something, but the sloop had to come first now. In these crazy crosscurrents, one wrong move and they'd both be fighting for their lives in the surf. It would be doubtful that he would survive, but Briana would never make it. Above all else, he was desperate to save her.

Cole gritted his teeth and strained to counterbalance the weight of wind and sail. For one terrifying moment, he actually had to steer the tiller with his foot as he hung on to the wire rigging and mainsheet with his hands. The rope cut into his flesh and made his hand go numb. He felt the cords stand out on the sides of his neck; every bone and sinew and muscle screamed at him as he strained to keep the sloop from making a death roll.

Yes! The hull cleared the rocks by about ten yards! He swung *Streamin'* toward the shore, scrambling back into the boat, and readied himself for the crunch of her prow on sand and shells. He threw himself next to Briana and held her to him as the sloop came to a precarious, jerking halt. Her body hit against his, but he braced them both.

Miraculously, as he clambered out, it

seemed the storm had lessened. Maybe he
was just getting used to the deluge of stinging rain. No, it seemed to be letting up, the
lightning and thunder rolling away inland
over the bay and the Glades. It was like being given a prize for surviving his struggle
with the sea.

He reached over the woman's prone form
and retrieved his radio. It still worked. He
called the coast guard again and told them
his position was about six beachfront
houses north of Gordon Pass. They assured
him they'd called 911 for him and a squad
was on the way.

"One more thing," he told the officer on the
line. "Tell them this woman is Briana—don't
know her last name—who owns the Two
Mermaids Search and Salvage in Turtle Bay,
and she mentioned her sister, Daria. If anyone can locate Daria, please let her know
about Briana's accident. I'm not sure, but
she might have been out in the water with
her."

"If that's the case, that Daria or her craft
are missing, let us know immediately. Over
and out."

"Will do," Cole said, suddenly sounding so
weary to himself. "Will—try to," he muttered

to himself as he snapped the radio off and bent over Briana.

He cradled her in his arms across his lap, trying to keep her warm. She opened her eyes once, those hugely dilated gray-green eyes that didn't seem to see him, and cuddled closer. His insides flip-flopped. It had been a long time since he'd held a woman and longer since she was someone who needed him.

It seemed both an eternity and yet too soon when he heard a siren screaming along Gordon Drive. He did not let go of Briana until the medics appeared between two houses and came down on the sand carrying a stretcher. They bent over her to take her vitals and put a needle for a drip in her arm. Cole moved back, then off the sloop to give them room.

Several people with houses along the stretch of beach came out into the diminishing rain. A short, elderly man swung a too-small windbreaker around Cole's shoulders. It was only then he realized he was shaking.

"If I go to the hospital with her, could you watch my boat?" Cole asked him. His teeth were chattering from the chill, and nerves.

"Sure, sure. What happened to her? She your wife?"

"A friend."

"Sure. Beautiful old boat. Don't worry about a thing. I mean, I'm sure she'll be fine—the girl and the boat."

Manuel Salazar, whom everyone called Manny, slammed the door to his old Ford truck, darted through the last raindrops and unlocked the front door to the Two Mermaids Marine Search and Salvage Shop. His four-teen-year-old daughter, Lucinda, trailed him in, yakking all the way. Lately she talked to her parents only in English. Everyone else in the family was proud to speak in *Español,* but not Lucinda. He'd laid down the law to her that she was having the traditional *quinceañera* celebration for her fifteenth birthday, a huge party which announced to friends and family that she was entering adulthood. Most *chicas* couldn't wait for that celebration, which was better than any American birthday or sweet-sixteen party, but not his daughter. Lucinda had suddenly gone from being his angelic, younger daughter to someone he didn't even know.

He walked to his desk to see if there were

any phone messages. Nada. With this storm, he wondered where the shop's dive boat, *Mermaids II,* had ended up. His stomach knotted.

"But it's so expensive, Papa. Think of all you and Mama could do with the money." Lucinda tried another tack to win her argument. "I overheard you say to her you couldn't afford it, that you'd have to find a way, but why should you?" Dark eyes flashing in her pert, round face, she stood with hands on her hips, glaring at him. She looked so much like his sainted mother sometimes, though his mother would never have been caught dead in torn jeans and skinny-strap top that showed too much skin. "My friends— my American friends—" she plunged on, "think it's really old-fashioned."

"So, they not your friends then, *sí? Caramba,* don't you look down on your Latina friends. I never know a *chica* crazy enough pass up a *quinceañera!* Your Latina friends all happy 'bout their parties, dance with boys, make parents, godparents and *padrinas* happy, *sí?* And you just ask your Americana friends, what 'bout ethnic diversity and all that?"

"Man, you go from sounding like a shrink

to priest to politician, Papa. I'm an American teenager, and they have some say in their lives. Sure, most *chicas* want a *quinceañera* party, but not me! You want to spend some money for me you don't have, how 'bout a new car I could use to get a job in town when I'm sixteen—that's the age Americans look forward to."

"No car! Tell your American friends don't come if they don't want a good time with Mexican dancing and food and—"

"I can't even talk to you and Mama anymore!" she exploded, smacking her hands on her thighs. "Carianna didn't have to have one!"

"*Have* to have one? Your older sister give anything, if we could have pay for party for her, invite all our friends and family. But now I got this job with Briana and Daria. They even be *padrinas,* help us pay for things—"

"So it's a party for them? No, this whole thing's for you and Mama, even Carianna and Grandmama Rosa, not for me!"

"Me, me, me!" he mocked, throwing up his hands. "Now that what an American teenager all about! When your mama and I was your age—"

"I'm not you and Mama, and I don't still

have one foot in the great country of Mexico where we were all starving! Why can't you just listen?"

"You shut your mouth, American girl! You gonna have *quinceañera,* honor your mama and grandmama. You make your family proud or you gonna find a new family. Now sit there till I find that video camera."

She turned her back and flopped into the padded chair at Bree's desk. Muttering under his breath, Manny walked out of the small office space into the large, concrete-floored back room where dive and rescue gear was stored. A sign over the doorway read The Water is Our Office, and on the far wall hung a blown-up poster of the twins in their mermaid wet suits with scuba tanks at their feet and the words Love That Bottled Air! Another large picture at the back of the room showed only the twins' mermaid tails as they dove below the surface and read, Bottoms Up!

Wall Peg-Boards displayed depth charts, diagrams of the various artificial wrecks in this area of the gulf, and handmade drawings of the precious turtle sea grass the twins tended out by the Trade Wreck. On the floor, separated by aisles to walk between, were gears, winches, capstans, marker buoys, metal detectors, lift bags, underwater lights, pelican floats, wreck reels, cutting tools and cameras.

His area was toward the back of the shop, where the heaviest equipment—especially anything to do with motors—was stored. Manny also handled in-water ship repairs and serviced dive equipment. He had a deal with the twins that he didn't dive with tanks, only shallow stuff with a snorkel. Too far under water and he went nuts—"claustro-hydro-phobic," Daria had labeled it. Still, he loved the look of this place, the very smell of it. His greatest goal in life was to own the business someday and run it his way. He'd take on the rival salvage company across the bay and, once and for all, shut up its big brute of an owner, Sam Travers. You'd think that since Travers also did industrial dredging, demolition and pile driving, he'd leave the lighter stuff to Two Mermaids, but Sam resented the twins, especially Bree.

This big back room always looked like organized confusion, much, Manny thought, like his employers' busy lives. How he envied them for building this business, though he'd helped too and thought he was worth more than they paid him. But he'd recently found out that he would inherit half of the shop if anything happened to either of them, and since then, he'd made some big, hard decisions.

Caramba, he might even have to force himself to dive to get what he wanted, instead of just operating on the surface. He grunted as his eyes searched for the camera to film the inside of the big, fancy Garcia Party House he had rented for the *quinceañera.* He wanted to show his *madre* how good things were going before cancer took her. She'd given up so much for him. He had to make her proud of him before she died, whatever it cost.

He found the camera and took it out of its plastic underwater casing and rejoined Lucinda, who was twirling herself dizzy in Bree's chair. Finally, his *chica* had shut her mouth. But in a way, the silence got to him, because he had to be doing something to keep himself from going loco waiting to hear about Bree and Daria.

For once, Amelia Westcott was glad to see her own driveway. She hated driving in the rain, hated these months of weather so hot and humid you had to run from AC to AC. At least her sons would not be home from Cub Scouts yet and she could take a cool shower and calm down before they showed up. Her meeting with Daria had been disastrous; later, the docent's tea at the art gallery had gone on much longer than she'd expected, partly because the lights had gone out from that boomer of a storm. Ah, sometime this month or next, the weather would clear and she could breathe again.

If she hadn't married Ben, who was now the prominent and very busy prosecuting attorney of Collier County, she probably would have moved north to the Carolinas. It might have helped her escape painful memories of her youth in this area. She did love Ben and their lifestyle here, and she was very proud of her husband, although sometimes she wished she had a career—a cause—of her own that would *really* help other people, something that mattered more than her committees, however philanthropic their purposes and however much they helped promote Ben's career. Then she could look beyond these very luxurious four walls and the messes her boys made. A stay-at-home mom who didn't want to stay at home, that was her.

The moment Amelia closed the garage door and went into the house, she heard her message-waiting beeper. Maybe the day had been changed for the Clear the Gulf Commission meeting tomorrow. At least her membership on that had made Bree and Daria admit she was good for something, though it was Florida Congressman Josh Austin who had suggested them for oversight of the sea grass and marine life report.

"You have one messages," the recorded voice told her when she pressed the play button. With all the world's modern technology, why couldn't they teach a digital chip good grammar? Heaven knows, her laptop underlined every darn spelling and grammar error she made in the numerous letters to the editor she wrote.

"This important message is for Amelia Devon Westcott," the recorded woman's voice said. Amelia's stomach went into free fall. She never used her maiden name. "One of our E.R. doctors mentioned you're on our fund-raising guild committee here at the hospital, so that's how we traced you. Mrs.

Westcott, I'm calling because your sister—
we believe it is Briana Devon . . ."

Briana, Amelia thought. *Not Daria?*

". . . has been brought by emergency
squad to Naples Hospital from an accident
out in the gulf, and we're hoping you could
come into the E.R. to identify her and be with
her."

Bree! Bree? An accident? Identify her?
Were they trying to break the news to her
that Bree was dead? It couldn't be—couldn't
be Bree!

The voice went on, "We have been informed that she lives with another sister, but
no one at Briana and Daria Devon's place of
employment and residence knows where
Daria is, so we have been unable to reach
her."

As if she were speaking to a real woman,
Amelia whispered, "I've never been able to
reach either of them, no matter how hard—
how *desperately*—I tried."

Cole paced the E.R. waiting room like an
expectant father. He knew he looked like
hell, still in soaked shorts, sopping shoes
that squeaked when he walked and a bor-
rowed windbreaker that was so small he

couldn't even zip it. The distractions of people in trouble here unnerved him, too: a distraught mother with a kid who'd swallowed a quarter; a young man in terrible pain evidently waiting to be admitted to pass a kidney stone; elderly people who looked like death warmed over. The place was packed, but at least they'd taken Briana back through the swinging doors into the depths of curtained alcoves right away. He'd already bugged the triage nurse more than once. Why didn't they come tell him something?

This sent him back to the terrible night of his dad's sudden heart attack. He'd known his father was dead, but he'd called an ambulance. Rather than pronounce him dead at home, they'd done CPR and rushed him to the E.R. in Sarasota, only to tell Cole what he already knew. But Briana had to be all right. She was strong to have lasted out in that brutal gulf, evidently swimming with sharks, too. Cole had practically forced his way into the E.R. vehicle, but they'd shut him out here.

Shut out—the story of his life since his divorce last year from Jillian. He hadn't realized until she cut him off from their friends—or those he thought were their friends, but were really hers—that he'd given up too much of his own world for hers. It hadn't helped his client list to have his social contacts shrink like that. At least it had given him an excuse to quit playing country club games. But what he'd learned most from the biggest mistake of his life was that, after two years of their marriage, Jillian had not really been an integral part of him. He just didn't miss her. He felt sad and bad their marriage had failed, but he didn't feel her loss. Strangely, he'd feel worse if Briana were lost, and he'd only spent one lunch months ago and then this horrible day with her.

He was surprised to see Amelia Westcott, a woman he served with on the Clear the Gulf Commission, rush in the double glass doors and head for the triage nurse at the front desk.

"You called and told me to come right in," Amelia said. She was out of breath, but her voice carried clearly. "I'm Briana Devon's sister. But is her other sister, her twin Daria, here yet?"

Cole went over. "Amelia, I didn't know you were Briana's sister—I mean I don't know why I would—but I'm the one who found her half-drowned on the beach at Keewadin Island and brought her in—"

"Half-drowned? I'll bet she was with Daria. She's always with Daria on some sea search, some underwater mission. I can't believe they were out in that storm."

Though he could tell she was concerned, she spoke with an undercurrent of bitterness. The older he got, the more he saw family problems everywhere, though most simmered just below the surface of people's daily lives. He used to think his messed-up family was unique, but now he knew it was almost normal.

The triage nurse was on the phone, checking on Briana's status. Finally, some answers, Cole thought. He stuck tight to Amelia while she folded her arms and seemed to collapse within herself. She was a good-looking woman, a platinum blonde with every hair in place and icy blue eyes, in contrast to Briana's natural auburn hair and gray-green eyes. Even now, Amelia looked perfectly put together, with makeup worthy of a photo shoot, while the few times he'd seen the twins around they'd seemed windblown and often wet—a sexy combination. Amelia was obviously older than the twins and, he guessed, uptight by nature as well as from the situation. Rather than taking a deep breath, even when he urged her to, Amelia narrowed her eyes and breathed out through flared nostrils as if she were a bull waiting to charge. That reminded him about the bull sharks, but he decided not to spring that on her, at least not yet.

It wasn't long before a thin, balding doctor came out and went straight for Amelia. The man—his badge said Dr. Micah Hawkins—flipped through papers on his clipboard and asked, "Mrs. Westcott, you are next of kin for Briana Devon?"

Cole felt his knees go weak. Had Briana died? She couldn't have died!

"Yes, her sister—one of them," Amelia said as the doctor gestured her to walk with him. Cole kept right up.

"She swallowed a lot of water, but worse, we believe she's been struck by lightning while in the gulf and that can lead to complications. And you are?" Dr. Hawkins asked, squinting at Cole.

"Cole DeRoca, the friend who found her and brought her in. I gave her mouth-to-mouth and got her breathing again. She's going to be all right?"

"You are to be commended, Mr. DeRoca—you probably saved her life. If Mrs. Westcott doesn't mind, you can come along. We'll need to run a battery of tests, call in a neuropsychologist. She keeps slipping in and out of consciousness and asking for Daria."

"Oh, she would," Amelia said. "But, you mean Daria hasn't been found?"

"That's her twin sister. Briana was evidently out in a boat with her," Cole explained to the doctor. "But Briana must have fallen in."

"Dear God, Daria can't be missing—out there, too," Amelia cried, gripping Dr. Hawkins's wrist. "Doctor, call in whatever specialists you need. I'm not sure about Briana's insurance, but I'll take care of all that."

Cole's dislike for Amelia softened a bit. But when she said nothing else, as he followed the two of them deeper into the maze of curtained cubicles, he asked, "But if Briana was out in the gulf with Daria, where is Daria now?"

Was she dead? Briana wondered. She slitted her eyes open, just barely, trying to keep the bright lights out of her dark brain. She felt loggy, helpless, at the mercy of the sliding, shifting sea. Up, down, all around . . . But the sky looked whiter now, too bright, one big cloud floating over her with more than one sun in it. *Ceiling lights.* They hurt her eyes, and even when people spoke across the room, it seemed they shouted at her.

People's faces, unfamiliar, swam in and out above her. The sharks were gone. Had they been real? Daria, her mirror image, where was she? She didn't like to dive alone, she wanted Daria, her other self, there when they stepped together through the looking glass into the wonderland of the deep.

Someone forced her eyelids apart and shone a bright light into the depths of her brain. She jerked away. She tried to lift her hands to shield her face, but one of her arms was heavy with tubes and the other was bandaged and hurt like heck. A man—a doctor—leaned over her. Oh, Amelia was standing beside him. Why was Amelia here? And who was the tall, handsome man with dark eyes and black hair, his face so worried as he looked her over? His clothes showed he was not another doctor. Had he been swimming with her?

"What happened?" she tried to ask, but she didn't sound like herself and no one answered. What was the matter with these people? And where was Daria?

"She sustained no burns except on her left wrist, where she wore a stainless-steel dive watch," the doctor was telling Amelia and the man. "Actually, it's probably a skin lesion—an inflammatory response—which may disappear in a few days. I've already ordered a CT scan and an MRI, and we'll have her in a room as soon as possible, so we can monitor her better. We'll do some functional scans but call in a specialist for that."

"Functional—function of the brain?" the man asked, his deep voice a soothing whisper compared to the others.

"Precisely. Aftereffects can vary widely. And although her pupils are dilated, I want to assure you that does not necessarily mean brain injury, Mrs. Westcott." He leaned closer, very close. "Briana, I'm Dr. Hawkins. Can you hear me?"

She could hear him, all right. She heard every sound in this place, even the dripping of that bag above into her tube. "Yes," she said with great effort, because she didn't think she had the strength to nod. Her lips felt stiff and cracked. "Where's Daria?"

The tall man spoke again. "Brianna, can you tell us where you last saw Daria?"

She fought to form her words. They had to help find Daria.

"When I dove—off our boat—at Trade Wreck—before the storm."

Amelia gasped, a sound that pierced Bree's eardrums. "You mean she could be lost at sea?" her sister demanded, but the man put his hand on Amelia's arm to keep her quiet.

"Was she still on the boat when you saw her last?" he asked.

"Yes. Yes!"

"Then she'll be all right," Amelia said. "She probably had to ride out the storm, or put in somewhere else." She squeezed Bree's shoulder and moved away with the doctor.

No, Bree wanted to scream. Didn't they know Daria never would have left her? Not of her own accord.

"We'll look for her and find her," the tall man said, and put his big hand lightly on her shoulder where Amelia's had just been. His hand was warm, solid. Where had she seen him before? "Just try to rest now," he said.

If Amelia and the doctor thought they were whispering when they moved away, she heard them anyway. The doctor was saying that a lightning strike near her in the water—a side flash—must have given her a concussion. He told Amelia she might have sporadic amnesia or become moody, distracted, irritable or forgetful.

Exhausted as she was, Bree vowed never to forget what had happened to Daria. But what *had* happened? At least that man said he would help. He said "we" would find Daria. She should know who he was, but she could not recall. She felt both fearful and furious, so the doctor must be right about her moods, but she could not have amnesia, not about Daria.

Though Bree was afraid if she closed her eyes again she'd see the horror of the sea, the sharks, she pressed her eyelids tightly closed. Amazing how these bright lights hurt her eyes and how she could hear even the shuffle of the nurses' feet on the floors. Other people's voices and moans, cries of pain. Was she really hearing those or were they deep inside her?

The occasional screech of the curtains' rings across the metal rods almost deafened her. She could hear the man ask Amelia for her cell phone and then take it outside the curtain to make a call to the coast guard to tell them about Daria and their dive boat.

Exhausted, sick, she felt so strange, but Bree knew then what she had to do, even if that man had promised to look for Daria, even if he was calling for help. When Amelia and the doctor weren't looking, she had to get out of this bed, get another boat and go find her sister somewhere out on the dark, devouring sea.

4

It seemed to Bree that the nurses tried to keep her awake all night, not that she had time to sleep anyway. She wanted to get out of bed, find her clothes and find Daria. But nurses came in to check her eyes, shining pinpoints of light into them. They took her blood pressure and checked her drips. She heard them come and go, heard one chewing gum. And always, she thought she heard the roar of the wind and waves.

Despite her desire to stay awake and get up, each time they walked away, Bree slept the sleep of the dead. Had they drugged her? Had someone drugged Daria, too?

Had she seen drug dealers trying to make a drop and they knew they had to silence her? Had the horrible people who brought in women for the twentieth-century slave trade called human trafficking come upon her and taken her prisoner, too? Daria would never desert her. Bree knew Daria as well as she knew herself, didn't she?

Fighting a riptide of fear, she swam from nightmare to nightmare, but was suddenly aware that someone sat by her side. A woman. Amelia, when Bree wanted it desperately to be Daria.

"So strong, the water," she said, once in the midst of a waking dream in which she was trying to tell her handsome rescuer what had happened. She was safe in his arms, huddled against him for protection. She never thought she'd need or want a man that way. Who was he? Shouldn't she remember?

"Just a minute. I'll get you some water," Amelia said, evidently thinking she'd asked for a drink. She held up a glass with a straw to her lips. Bree saw that it was barely dawn and she was in a private room. Light poured through the window as bright as noon sun.

"Any news? Did they find her?" she asked, then drank greedily. She knew one of the tubes in her arm was to hydrate her, but her throat was so dry.

"They're going to do a wide search at first light, so that's right now. The coast guard's starting with the coordinates your boatman gave them and did an initial sweep of the area last night."

Manny. If only Manny had been with them as usual, this never would have happened . . . and then Daria's sudden toothache . . . Bree ached all over.

"My boatman's name," she told Amelia, exhausted from the little effort of drinking, "is Manuel Salazar—Manny. Please call and tell him I'm okay."

But what was the name of that other boatman, the sailor? She felt she should know him—wanted to know him.

"They're going to do an air search, too," Amelia went on, hovering over her. "I'm sure they'll find Daria with your boat. I'll bet the motor didn't work, the anchor line broke and the storm drove her into the Ten Thousand Islands. They'll find her."

"Thanks for being here with me."

"Where else would I be when you or Daria need me? I'm sorry if it took this accident for you to realize that."

That edge to her voice, so familiar. When it came to Amelia, Bree remembered too much she'd like to forget. Amelia was six when their mother died of eclampsia in child-birth, delivering her twins. Now, as adults, they understood how their older sister could dislike them, even blame them. Their wid-owed father had thrown himself into rearing his twins, whom everyone oohed and aahed over. Amelia, a timid soul and a real little lady at heart, though she could be snippy, felt left out when Dad took the younger girls fishing and taught them to swim and dive. He'd always tried to include Amelia, but she'd have no part of it and ended up spending a lot of time with her maternal grandmother while the tomboy twins went to sporting events or dived with Dad.

"Amelia, what's the name of that man who helped me? I know I've met him. I'm just a little foggy on some things—a few recent things."

"You may have a concussion, or maybe that lightning did scramble your internal wires a bit. You've just got to relax or they'll have to give you a sedative, as soon as they rule out a concussion. That will calm your anxiety and make you forget how traumatic it must have been to—"

"I don't want to forget! Of course, I'm anxious, because we've got to find Daria! I've got to go help find her!"

"You're not going anywhere," Amelia told her, gently patting her arm as if she were a child. "They're going to run some brain function tests today with a specialist from Fort Myers before you can be released. But the knight in shining sailboat who rescued you is Cole DeRoca, who serves on the Clear the Gulf Commission with me."

Amelia went on, explaining that the commission was meeting today and that the twins' accident would be the talk of the group and she wouldn't be there to answer their questions.

Yes, Bree thought with a little flutter in her belly. Cole DeRoca, the guy who worked with rare woods and specialized in installing custom-made yacht interiors. Bree had been scraping barnacles off a hull in the marina when he'd been working on the same huge yacht, and he'd shared a sandwich and some wine from the galley with her.

She'd found him shockingly handsome in

a rugged way. His deep voice had seemed to vibrate into the very core of her being. When she was working, Bree usually gave little thought to clothes, hair or makeup, but she'd wished that day she'd done better than an old, tight wet suit and saltwater-soaked hair yanked back in a ponytail. Cole had worn faded jeans and a black, sawdust-speckled T-shirt but still managed to look like an ad for owning a yacht, not working on one. His angular, hard body was sun-bronzed; he made her perpetual tan look pale. When he smiled or laughed, he got a cheek dimple and narrowed his dark eyes under thick but sleek eyebrows. Even as he'd chatted amiably, he'd managed to look her over thoroughly and she could still feel the impact of that down to her toes. If she could recall all that and Cole's initial impact on her, didn't that prove her head and body were still working well?

Other details of their brief time together came cascading back. He'd said he worked alone, measuring, ordering, cutting and fitting the imported woods. He loved being hands-on, he'd told her with a devilish grin. He'd told her his wife hadn't wanted him to work with his hands and had a fit at a party

when he called himself a carpenter instead
of a yacht interior designer. And he'd said he
was getting divorced, didn't he?

"I already talked to Manny at your shop,"
Amelia was saying, "but I had some trouble
understanding him. He has a really thick accent. No wonder you took all those Spanish
classes. You and your Hispanics."

"If you're including Cole, his grandfather
was a boatbuilder from Portugal," Bree told
her as even more images and snatches of
their conversation came back to her from that
hour they'd spent together months ago. Yes,
she was remembering him so distinctly that
there was no way her brain could have been
short-circuited by a lightning strike. But why
hadn't she placed him instantly when she
saw him yesterday?

Granted, she was perceiving light and
sound more strongly than was normal, but
surely she could handle that. She didn't intend to share those concerns or her erratic
memory with anyone right now, because she
had to get out of here and help look for
Daria. She needed to speak to the coast
guard and the civil air patrol in person. She
had a friend who flew for the volunteer patrol, and she wanted to call him. She had

some ideas about where to look for the *Mermaids II.* But what terrified her was that some of those sites were underwater.

After being taken—in a wheelchair, no less—for a battery of neurocognitive tests early the next morning, Bree lay back in her hospital bed, her eyes closed, even more exhausted. The specialist was to be in soon with the results.

"Your knight in shining sailboat brought you this," Amelia told her, "but they didn't let him get farther than the nurses' station on this floor—family only now, especially since there are reporters downstairs who would swarm you." Bree turned her head to see a beautiful, orange-hued orchid plant. Tears filled her eyes at Cole's kindness. In the midst of dreadful memories of storm and sharks and the fear of loss, the blooms looked like small, hovering butterflies. Hope—they reminded her of hope. And the plant was in a stunning, striped, dark and light box, made of a kind of wood she'd never seen.

"He's divorced now, you know, and quite a catch, if you ask me," Amelia said, smoothing the bedsheets as if she'd remake the bed with Bree in it.

"I'm not looking for a man, but for Daria!"

"Of course—I know. It's just you haven't had anyone serious since Ted. Since before Ted died, even. Darn, sorry to have brought that up."

"It's all right," Bree told her, though she would have liked to bandage Amelia's mouth shut before she stuck her foot in it again. "Just don't ever bring him up around Sam Travers, because he still blames me for his Ted's enlisting and his death."

"As if I'd ever be around Sam Travers," Amelia muttered, perching on the chair next to the bed. "And how ridiculous to hold it over you just because you broke up with his son and he enlisted and died. But then, people do hold grudges for years when someone or something dear is lost. I can sympathize with that."

Summoning up what little strength she had, Bree worked the controls to elevate the back of the bed, then got the TV remote from the bedside table. Talking about loss or death right now was the last thing she could bear. As ever, despite how kind Amelia was trying to be, she was getting on Bree's nerves.

Bree switched on the TV, which sat high on a narrow, suspended shelf across from the foot of her bed. It was almost noon, and the local stations always covered search-and-rescue efforts in the gulf. Search and salvage. If only she could go search for her sister and salvage her from any possible harm right now.

The TV came on with a political commercial, the kind everyone was sick of already, and the election was still almost two months away. This one was for Marla Sherborne, the incumbent, conservative U.S. congresswoman who was adamantly antigambling. The ad, like most of hers, warned against the dangers of letting casino boats into the area, because it would open the doors to "unbridled outside control of huge amounts of dirty money." A wealthy Miami businessman named Dom Verdugo was trying to bring a casino boat into Turtle Bay, but it hadn't been approved yet and everyone was arguing about it. A gambling boat would bring more business to local restaurants and shops, but hordes of outsiders could run up property prices and ruin the already endangered old Florida ambience, not to mention create more abuse of the gulf itself. The visuals on this ad even tried to tie the casino boat to water pollution that had endangered marine and plant life below the glittering gulf.

Ironically, there was a tenuous—and doubly tension-filled—relationship between Marla and her opposing candidate in the U.S. senate race, Josh Austin. The scuttlebutt was that Josh Austin's wealthy sugarcane-baron father-in-law, a longtime widower, was having an affair with Marla. If anything came of the relationship, Josh could be trying to unseat his step-mother-in-law.

See, Bree tried to encourage herself, her brain was working great, filled with names and details from days, weeks, months— years ago. So why couldn't she summon up much of what happened during her own rescue by Cole? Could they be giving her that sedative already? She had to remember everything to help find Daria.

"The commission doesn't completely trust Marla Sherborne's claims of being so gung ho about the environment," Amelia put in, pointing at the TV. "Not since everyone says she's literally in bed with that sugarcane baron, Cory Grann, and the fertilizer run-off from their fields is such a problem."

There was a quick knock on the open door followed by a voice Bree recognized instantly, though he still stood out in the hall. "Do I hear my father-in-law's name being taken in vain?" a jaunty voice asked. "They're not letting even the press in to see you, but I pulled a few strings."

"Josh!" Bree cried as he popped his head around the door and came in. She was so glad to see their old friend. A politician one could trust, Josh Austin had the ways and means to solve any problem. She felt better already.

"I hope you didn't hear what we think of all these ads, because yours will probably be on next," Amelia told him. Both sisters knew Josh from years back, when he had dated Daria. Even when Daria and Josh had split up—definitely Josh's decision—all three sisters had wished him well, though they had seldom seen him in person over the years since. But all the locals were proud of Josh Austin.

"Hey, I have no choice," he said, his voice still upbeat. "A necessary evil, a sign of the times. I hate the damn things, too."

"It's good to see you, but we need your pull to make something happen for Daria," Bree told him. "We've got to find her."

"That's why I'm here. I'm doing everything I can. I've already made some this-is-top-priority calls to the guard and the air patrol."

He shook hands with Amelia, then strode toward the bed and bent to kiss Bree's cheek. Indeed, one of his campaign ads ran in the background, touting his views that, with stringent oversight, a clean gulf could coexist with controlled gambling to pour more jobs and money into the local economy. And *that* meant more money for environmental protection. The ad ended with a shot of him and his beautiful wife, Nicole, also a lawyer, holding hands and walking toward the camera on the beach. They had no children, or they would certainly have been in the ad. Daria had said she'd heard that Nicole, whom Josh called Nikki, had suffered two miscarriages.

"I had to see you when I heard," he said, putting his hand on her shoulder. "Nikki sends her love. She's down giving the reporters lying in wait for you a sound bite or two about me so they'll leave you alone."

"I'd talk to them if I thought it would help find Daria. Be sure to thank her for me."

"She's being a real trouper right now. Just between us," he said, whispering now but shaking his head, "she thinks once I'm in congress, the White House is a small step, and that's her idea of a dream home. But enough about that. I'm sure they'll find Daria. Oh, here, I brought you the morning paper about your rescue," he said, producing a folded copy of the *Naples Daily News* from under his arm and handing it to Amelia. "You and DeRoca both did what you had to do. I admire both of you for your courage."

Josh Austin was a wonder, and not just because of his vitality and boyish good looks that never seemed to change. He had always amazed Bree and absolutely awed Daria, who had dated him three years in high school, long before his statewide glory days. In high school he'd been in charge of everything and was voted most likely to succeed. He had, too, leaving everyone behind in his stardust as he married a wealthy man's daughter whom he met at Florida State, became a successful businessman and the youngest state representative in Tallahassee. He was now in a neck-and-neck race to unseat Marla Sherborne for her U.S. senate seat. Everyone in the area liked Josh, including Daria, even though he'd broken up with her before he'd left for college, long before Ted and Bree had split up. But what a fun foursome they had been years ago. Ted was gone now, but not, she prayed, Daria, too.

The three of them watched silently when the coverage of the search for Daria and their dive boat came up as the lead story. An interview with a coast guard spokesman led, then a sound bite from a member of the civil air patrol, who had been flying the coastal islands all morning and found nothing but normal storm debris on various beaches. And then an interview with Cole.

She hadn't realized he was so tall, but he made the reporter look like a shrimp. He wore swim trunks and a black T-shirt that showed how muscular he was. It was obvious he hadn't shaved or slept. It made Bree mad that the hospital staff had turned him away from seeing her, for she owed him her life. If he could only locate Daria, she'd owe him for both of them.

Cole's thick, swept-back hair shone dark in the sun, and his narrowed eyes looked almost black under his arched brows. His chiseled features were half-handsome, half-craggy, almost foreboding when he frowned. Bree shifted her legs under the sheet. As weak as she felt, the mere look and thought of him poured adrenaline through her body.

Cole and the reporter were standing on the dock of the Turtle Bay Marina. "I've been out with friends looking for Daria Devon and her scuba-dive boat," he said into the mike thrust at him. "Especially near Keewadin Island, where Briana Devon was swept in, though she evidently swam a long way to get there."

"Do you consider yourself a hero for saving Briana Devon?"

"She saved herself by managing to swim in during that sudden storm. I'm no hero, just someone deeply concerned and trying to help."

Bree's heart went out to him. He was on edge, frustrated and worried, she could tell.

"Quite a guy." Josh's voice interrupted her agonizing. "His ex-wife was on my initial feasibility/exploratory committee. Bree, how are you doing, really?" he asked, turning to her when the coverage ended. He leaned against the edge of the bed and bent down to take her hand in his. "Your inner strength, I mean, your ability to face all this. I know how close you are to Daria."

"I'll be all right," she vowed, blinking back tears and gripping his hand harder than she meant to. "The doctor will be in with a report soon. They think a lightning strike might have scrambled my thinking some, but that's not true. I'm fine! I'll be fine if we find her."

Now he held her hand in both of his. "Just stay out of it and let the authorities do their thing, both of you," he said, glancing at Amelia. "I promise you, I'll pull all the strings I can and I'll stay in touch." He bent to kiss her cheek again. As he moved away, Bree saw his wife out in the hall, looking in. Before she could tell Josh, he hurried out. The room suddenly seemed silent and small again. Then Josh popped back in, pulling his wife behind him. Obviously, Nikki Austin had more influence getting where she wanted to go in the hospital than Cole did.

Nicole Grann Austin was even more striking in person than on TV, in the newspapers or on the glossy brochures the postal carriers delivered in droves these days. Her long, honey-hued hair framed her heart-shaped face, her teeth looked like an ad for whitening strips, and, even now, she looked dressed to kill.

"Nikki says the press in the lobby are really getting restless," Josh said. "Bree and Amelia, I don't believe you've met Nikki," he added, making introductions all around. Nikki whispered something to him. "Yeah, good," he told her, then turned to Bree again. "Look, we have a friend who does a lot of PR for us and pilots our plane. He's a triple-threat man, because the truth is, he's also a bodyguard. With this tough race and in this day and age, you just never know. Mark Denton is out in the hall waiting for us, and I'd be glad to loan him to you for a while to keep the media at bay, if you'd like. We're staying in town tonight and don't need him to fly us back to Tallahassee until tomorrow."

"That's really kind of you, but that's okay," Bree said. "I certainly don't need a bodyguard." She thought of Cole again. If he would just be willing to help her . . .

"You call us, if you do," Nikki put in. Bree saw that the woman was studying her avidly. Maybe she was curious about what someone who had been hit by lightning looked like. Yet there was an edginess about her, or was that just energy and excitement in her big, blue eyes? "Here," Nikki went on, "I'm going to write down both of our cell-phone

numbers for you in case. And I'm a lot easier to reach than 'the man' here, if you need
anything at all."

Bree took the piece of paper from her, despite the fact Amelia also reached for it. With
more good wishes and promises of help,
they were gone. Bree caught a glimpse of
their companion, Mark Denton, who reminded her of those buff, secret-service
types who hovered around the president.
That joke Josh had made about the White
House—she didn't put it past him or Nikki either.

"Now you just take his advice and get
some rest, because I'm sure he'll help us,"
Amelia said as she opened the folded newspaper he'd brought and a glossy You Can
Trust Josh Austin brochure spilled out on the
bed. "See?" she said, pointing at it. "For
once, truth in advertising."

Finally, Bree was alone. After a detailed,
positive report from the Fort Myers's neuropsychologist about her tests, which had in-
cluded simple memory quizzes, an IQ and
an organizational-ability puzzle, no medical
personnel were in the room. Amelia had
gone to meet her boys, six-year-old Jordan

and eight-year-old James, when they got home from school and take them to a neighbor's before she came back.

Amelia had washed her salt-water-stiffened hair for her, chattering about how she used to wash her and Daria's hair when they were little. The dressing on Bree's wrist burn had been changed and the nurse had taught her how to tape a plastic sleeve around her arm so that she could take a shower, which she'd done before Amelia left. Actually, Bree had lifted several other plastic sleeves off the nurse's cart, because she was going to need them.

She had to get out of here. Forget this staying in for further observation. She was the one who needed to do observation of the entire gulf if she had to. She was going to get Manny to take her out to the Trade Wreck so she and one of her scuba-diving friends could start to trace Daria.

Bree hated to be sneaking out, but she was certain, except for her strange perceptions of light and sound, that she was all right. Dr. Hawkins had said if she had any ringing in her ears, it would probably lessen, so she expected her other problems would end soon, too. He had insisted she needed at least another day of observation and then several days of rest, so Amelia was determined to have Bree go home with her.

Since she was not only burned but burned-out, Bree knew full well the doctor and Amelia would try to stop her from diving. She'd probably have to lie to Manny and whomever she called to help her dive about being given a clean bill of health, but she would do whatever it took to find her sister. What could they do? Arrest her? Lock her up? Nothing mattered but finding Daria. No way could she wait for the possibility of being released tomorrow. That might be too late; it might already be too late.

Bree had racked her brain for clues to what might have happened to her twin. The first thing she could think of to do was to learn whether the boat's anchor chain was still planted near the Trade Wreck. Had it been pulled up or thrown over? Second, she had to find and salvage her camera. While Bree suited up, Daria had shot some sample pics off the side of the ship. What if there was some hint on that camera, maybe of another watercraft lurking nearby? And she had to call her civil air patrol friend, Dave Mangold. She needed a clue, any clue!

Even though Sam Travers hated her, she was going to ask him to use his large search-and-salvage vessel to look for Daria. She'd hire him if she had to. The coast guard and the civil air patrol obviously could use the help. Sam had that expensive echo sounder, too. If it could spot schools of fish and find anomalies, even wrecks on the bottom of the gulf . . .

She covered her face with her hands and sucked in a sob. It horrified her even to consider that *Mermaids II* might have actually gone down in the storm. It couldn't be, but she had to try everything, had to get the answers no one else was giving her. Losing Daria would be almost like losing herself.

She got out of bed slowly. A bit light-headed, not really dizzy. Man, she hated these hospital gowns. At least they'd untethered her from those hanging tubes. She'd forced herself to eat lunch, tomato soup and half a grilled cheese sandwich, to get some strength and convince Amelia and the nurses she was recovering physically from her ordeal.

Bree shuffled over and closed the door to the hall, hoping that might signal she was sleeping. She knew where the street clothes were that Amelia had brought. She'd be crazy to try walking out of here in her mermaid wet suit. In the tiny bathroom, she put slacks, shoes, a blouse and matching jacket on—you might know Amelia wouldn't bring any of her more casual work clothes—when the phone on her bedside table rang. She'd have to answer it. Besides, it might be the coast guard or air patrol.

She picked up the phone on its fourth ring. "Briana Devon."

"Briana! Cole DeRoca. I'm down in the lobby with a friend of yours who heard me ask if you could have visitors this afternoon, a guy named Manny. They say you can't and that they can't even release how you're doing because of privacy laws."

Her heartbeat kicked up. Her prayers—some of them, at least—were being answered.

"Cole," she said, trying to keep from crying in relief. This was obviously a sign she should forge ahead with her plans. "You're a godsend, because I'm leaving and I'd appreciate a ride home. Amelia's not here right now. I'll be down in a minute, but ask Manny to hang around, would you? And if there are reporters in the lobby—"

"Three of them, two with camermen."

"In that case, get Manny to meet us at the shop in Turtle Bay and wait for me by the E.R. entrance, okay?"

"Will do, but are you sure you're strong enough?"

"Strong enough to do whatever it takes to find my sister," she said, and hung up before he could question her more about her sudden release.

Making for the door, Bree felt like a felon escaping from the penitentiary. At the last minute, she turned back and scribbled her nurse a note, telling her she was fine and had gone for a walk. That was true enough; somehow, she was going for a dive, too.

As she peeked into the hall, then strode out nonchalantly, she carried Cole's gift of the orange orchid in her arms.

5

—

"Is Amelia coming to your place to stay with you?" Cole asked as he drove her away from the hospital. They turned onto the busy Tamiami Trail and headed south toward Turtle Bay. She wanted to recline the seat and go to sleep, but she sat erect, cursing the fact Amelia hadn't brought her sunglasses. The light, the sounds of traffic—too bright, too much.

"She's with her two little boys right now," she told him, pulling down the sun visor on her side. "I'm sure she'll be over soon." She couldn't decide whether to just level with Cole or to get home first before she sprang her desperate plan on him and Manny. Cole had helped her before, but would he help her now? Besides, just his presence, his closeness, was making her even more nervous than she already was.

"Have you ever scuba dived?" she asked.

"Strictly for recreation, but I can hold my own. The last time was in Tahiti for a wedding anniversary. I'm single now."

"Sorry." She wasn't sorry, but she had no time for such thoughts.

"Don't be. Definitely the best for me and her, too, since she left me."

A woman had left this man? The entire world was crazy.

"Briana, you look shaky. You aren't going to be sick?"

"Sick at heart. I'd warn you before I'd upchuck in this beautiful car."

He was driving a big burgundy sedan, probably one he used to impress his clients, because it didn't seem like him and it certainly didn't seem like Turtle Bay. This was a man she didn't really know.

The village of Turtle Bay was a fairly secluded enclave between the Tamiami Trail on the east, the Gulf of Mexico on the west, the city of Naples to its north and Marco Island to its south. Turtle Bay had been built up years ago, with two clam-canning factories that were now defunct, and the usual condos and luxury waterfront homes had not intruded yet. A lot of locals feared the proposed gambling casino boat here could change all that. One of the old canneries was now quaint shops and seafood restaurants; the other had been converted to Sam Travers's Search and Salvage. Tourists and fishermen came and went daily in Turtle Bay, but returned to their luxe hotels in Naples when the day's jaunt was over. It was a tidal bay, so the main marina was built up on high posts, as were some of the modest houses, even those built farther back off the waterfront. Everything from dinghies to yachts and all sizes of sailboats bobbed in the bay.

Manny was waiting for them at the Two Mermaids with the door open. Thank heavens, no reporters were in sight. "Let's go upstairs," she told the men and, though every muscle of her body ached, she tried to lead them upstairs gracefully.

Her and Daria's two-bedroom apartment above the shop was a light, airy and pleasant place with white wicker furniture, bright floral pillows and open vistas of the marina, bay and gulf. Without Daria, it seemed oppressive, so she was glad to have their company.

She took the orchid Cole had carried up for her and put it on the glass-topped coffee table, which was cluttered with the books Daria had been studying for her accounting class. They'd finally admitted they'd been too careless with the financial end of their business. Manny had volunteered to handle that, but they'd decided one of them should specialize in it, and Daria had cheerfully volunteered. She'd seemed obsessed with the course work ever since. In college—Dad had insisted they go to his alma mater in Miami—neither of them had taken courses in anything like accounting or business. Bree had studied languages, and Daria was a philosophy major. The truth was, both of them had majored in giving scuba lessons and getting a tan on trendy South Beach.

"Please sit, both of you," Bree said, and went into the small galley kitchen. When she was certain they couldn't see her, she grasped the edge of the countertop and leaned against it, stiff armed, staring at Daria's latest note—dated last Friday—on the bulletin board over the sink: *Don't worry about me. Going to study w/ friends after class and might be in late.*

She could not cry, Bree told herself, could not dissolve in frustration or fear. She must find strength she did not have, courage she did not feel. However hurting and exhausted, she had to get moving.

She gulped a glass of orange juice, then poured Coke into three glasses, dumped a bag of taco chips into a bowl and carried all that in on a tray. She wanted desperately for these men to see her in control. Cole sat on the sofa, and Manny had taken her rocking chair, so she sat in Daria's. They were talking about how Manny never dived but oversaw the shop, their two boats—the larger of which was now missing—and the heavy equipment. Man, Bree thought as she drank down half of her soda, but she needed this sugar and caffeine to stoke her strength.

"So, what you planning?" Manny asked her. "I know you. Want me to get the coast guard and the air patrol on the phone?"

"I'm going to call them, but I want to talk to both of you first."

She forced herself to look directly into Cole's narrowed eyes, because she figured she could get Manny to do what she wanted.

Yes, despite the dire situation, the instant arc of energy and tension crackled between them as fiercely as it had the day they'd had that impromptu lunch on the yacht months ago. She had to admit that Cole DeRoca was still the great unknown, deeper than the sea. He had been nothing but kind and caring, but she well knew there could be unknown fathoms beneath. She felt so intensely drawn to the man that she feared her spinning senses could too easily swamp her usually sensible nature. She couldn't afford a distraction right now when she needed to be self-disciplined. She needed the man to help her and had to shut everything else out.

"To try to find Daria," she told them, gripping her sweating glass hard in both hands, "I need to figure out if she left the dive site of her own accord or unwillingly."

"Caramba," Manny exclaimed, flinging gestures, "for sure, it was unwilling."

"So you plan to do what?" Cole asked, putting down his glass and leaning forward with his wrists on his knees.

"I need to see if our boat's anchor is missing from the seabed near the turtle grass meadow. I dived down the anchor line as usual. But when I was ready to go up, I didn't even look for it and just made the ascent from where I was."

"Yeah, you done that before," Manny put in.

"But was the anchor there," she went on, "and I just didn't see it in the increasing turbulence and lessening visibility? Is it still there? And if so, was the anchor chain hauled up properly or shoved off in a hurry? We paid good money for that new anchor and chain, because we've had them pull loose, and twice our rope was cut on something. If Daria didn't leave under duress, she would have hauled it in."

"What you thinking?" Manny demanded. "That more than a storm made her leave you there?"

"Of course it was more than a storm that made her leave me there!" Bree exploded. "That was bad, but it wasn't a hurricane! Sorry," she added more quietly, covering her eyes with one hand. "I'm just on edge, and I know you've been, too, Manny, trying to handle your mother's illness, Lucinda's attitude and everything."

As she lowered her hand and looked at him, he shook his head. "Lucinda's craziness *nada* compared to this," he said. "Anyhow I can help, I help."

"Good," she said. "I'd like you to go down to our slip at the marina and make sure *Mermaid I* is ready to go and that scuba tanks are filled—for two divers, if Cole will come along. It still stays light pretty late. At least the storms missed us today, so maybe the underwater visibility will be better."

"You're going diving *now?*" Cole demanded. "Look, Briana, I'm sure you know a lot of local divers who could search for—"

"I need to do it! I know the area. Besides, if I could just retrieve my camera, it could have something on it. I had to let it go in the storm."

"You got photos of something strange?" Manny asked. He clenched both fists. Even with his brown skin, Bree could tell he was flushing. His voice rose as he got up from the couch and took a step toward the door. "You really thinking someone did something dirty?"

"I don't want to think that, but I know she wouldn't just leave, storm or not, toothache or not. I know Daria as well as I know myself!"

Manny bent to swig the rest of his soda and went out. She could hear him thudding down the stairs, muttering to himself.

"Briana—"

"You can call me Bree if you want."

"The thing is," Cole went on, "even if the doctor cleared you to leave the hospital, that hardly meant you could go diving right away."

"He didn't clear me," she blurted. "I cleared myself and cleared out. I have to do this!"

She jumped up, making Daria's chair rock back and forth on its own as if a ghost sat there. With a shiver snaking up her spine, she moved to the French doors, which had a view of the bay. The sight of the sunlit marina and the gulf beyond almost blinded her. Pushing the double doors open, she stepped out onto the veranda where they kept a wrought-iron table and two chairs. She grabbed sunglasses Daria had left there and shoved them on to mute the slant of late-afternoon sun. Not only had her heightened perception of light not worn off, but she was certain that, beyond the normal bustle of the marina, she could hear the seductive sounds of the sea.

Bree decided she'd need to start wearing earplugs, not when she dove, but when she was on terra firma. She'd often had to wear them to sleep. Unlike Daria, she couldn't fall asleep anywhere. On their overnight flight to Greece for their college-graduation gift, Daria had conked out right away and arrived raring to go, while Bree had wasted an entire night's sleep just being annoyed that Daria was lost in sweet dreams. Daria . . . lost . . . in dreams that were really nightmares . . .

"Bree," Cole said, following her out and putting his big hands gently on her shoulders from behind, "under ordinary circumstances, I'd tell you you're nuts. You've got a lot of professional people looking for her. Besides, the police have a dive team—though, I suppose, they won't deploy it until they're convinced of foul play, even if we ask . . ." His deep voice trailed off.

She turned to face him and found herself staring at the beating pulse in his strong, bronzed throat. He was half a head taller than she, but his broad shoulders made him seem larger than that. His eyes were a rich mahogany hue, framed by long, thick lashes. She could see her reflection there, could almost drown in their depths.

For one crazed instant, she longed to throw herself into his arms and just hold tight, to beg him to take this burden from her, comfort her, let her hide in his strength. But she did none of those things. Tackle a problem head-on, Dad would have said. It was the way she was and Daria, too. But had Daria, out on that boat in those rough waves, tried to take on something—or someone— she could not handle?

"Cole, I know that area and the currents like the back of my hand. I have to do this or I'll never forgive myself. I'm certain I would feel something if she weren't . . . weren't alive. But I do sense she's in danger. Call it women's intuition or a sister's sixth sense. I just have to go check the dive site."

"Then I'll go with you—on one condition. If you begin to feel ill down there or I see anything I don't like, that's it, we're out. And we're not going to do any kind of wide sweep for the camera if it's not near the dive site. Promise me," he said, gripping her upper arms, "because I mean it. I'll pull you right out of there—again."

"Yes, all right, I promise. I owe you doubly. I really think God sent you to find me, and to help find Daria."

"Then I just pray I'm up to pleasing all three of you," he said and surprised her with a hard hug before he let her go.

While Manny was preparing the skiff and putting air in their tanks and Cole drove to his workshop where he kept his own diving gear, Bree made four quick calls. She phoned the hospital main desk to officially check herself out. They were very upset and said they'd inform Dr. Hawkins immediately, but she hung up before they could page him. Bree knew Amelia would try to stop her from diving, so she called her at home and got her answering machine. That was what she'd hoped for, since Amelia should be picking up Jordan and James from their private elementary school about now. She left her a message that she was feeling much stronger and had decided to come home.

She then phoned the coast guard emergency contact number and, after no news there, the civil air patrol information line. She was disappointed and dismayed to learn her pilot friend, Dave Mangold, was out of town and had not participated in the air search. There was no sign of Daria or their boat, but both organizations would keep her informed.

Informed. She was terrified to get a call from either of them.

Realizing she'd left her mermaid diving suit at the hospital, she donned an old pink spandex wet suit and hurried downstairs. Though she didn't intend to tell Cole, she felt strange, kind of floaty, but she had to do this and now. Surely, this almost out-of-body feeling was not related to Daria's fate.

Dad had told them once that, even though he was outside in the waiting room when their mother died in the delivery room, he knew the exact moment when she'd gone because he felt kind of like he'd taken off from the ground. It was so bizarre, he'd said, like the feeling when you ride a roller coaster and go over the highest drop. There was no thrill, only an awed sense of doom. But Bree didn't want to remember all that, didn't want to think of that.

As she went to check her desk phone for messages, she heard heavy footsteps and turned to see if Manny or Cole were back. Big, burly Sam Travers, who ran the rival business across the bay, stood in the doorway, not in, not out. He seemed to block out the light and air.

With a bulky build and a face and body hardened by years of physical labor, Sam stood slightly over six feet tall. His hair had been gray for years, and he wore it cut tight to his head, which emphasized his prominent ears and narrowed eyes. Crow's feet perched at the corners, matching his deep frown lines.

Sam had never given in to wearing sunglasses or caps.

Bree recalled from years ago when she
and Ted used to hang out together all the
time, that his father, now a sixty-four-year-
old proud Vietnam War vet, looked angry
even when he wasn't. Since she'd broken up
with Ted, though, anger was his perpetual
mood around her.

Sam had never been able to forget or forgive that she had broken up with his only
child after going steady with him for almost
five years, two and a half in high school and
then the first two of college. That had started
what Sam called a fatal chain of events. But
once she was away from Turtle Bay, even
though she and Ted were at college just
across the state, her world had expanded
and Ted's had not.

He'd been jealous of her new friends and
her snorkeling and scuba students, even of
the time she spent with Daria. He'd wanted
to drive home most weekends, when she
had things to do in Miami. He hadn't really
liked college, and she'd thrived there. Maybe
he'd become so stridently possessive because his mother had deserted him and
Sam while Ted was still in elementary school,

but it didn't do any good to try to analyze him. It just wasn't working for Bree anymore, but when she'd tried to reason with him, tried to back away, he'd stormed out and joined the marines—the foreign legion, Daria had called it—without even telling Sam.

So while Ted had gone through basic battle training at Paris Island, South Carolina, Sam Travers had begun his war with Bree. He'd blamed her entirely when Ted was killed by a roadside bomb thousands of miles away in Iraq last year. And when he'd been buried with military honors, Sam had exploded at her, telling her to stay away from the funeral, and Daria had gone alone. Things certainly had not gotten better when she and Daria had opened a competitive search-and-salvage shop, though much smaller and more specialized, on Sam's turf.

Now he stood in her doorway, glaring at her. Ordinarily, she'd be only too happy if she never saw Sam Travers again, but she needed his help.

"Yo," he said in his usual strident voice, which seemed even louder now. "I was looking for Manny the man, 'cause the TV says you're still in the hospital. Just wanted to tell him I been out looking for Daria."

Bree stayed behind her desk. "Thanks for anything you can do. I was going to call you, but I've been talking to the coast guard and the air patrol about the rescue efforts."

"They're good at talk. You want to find something—in this case, someone—you call Sam. You and I had some bad spots, but I got nothing 'gainst her. I'm going out again."

Bad spots? she thought. During these past three years after Ted enlisted, Sam had ranted at her, especially when he was drinking, and she'd come to fear him. However much she sympathized with his loss and grieved Ted's death, she'd even considered getting a restraining order. Ben, her prosecutor brother-in-law, had suggested it, but she didn't want to admit weakness to Sam, who sometimes seemed right on the edge of becoming a stalker. There were times when she and Daria thought he turned up everywhere.

"I can't thank you enough for helping," Bree brazened, though her voice shook. "I know if anyone can find Daria and *Mermaids II,* it's you."

"Yeah, well, bodies might not surface for over a week, but wrecks only give up a trail of bubbles for about twenty-four hours.

Time's awastin'. You facing up to the fact I been using my echo sounder?"

"I'm sure she's all right . . . not—the skiff's not sunk. She put in somewhere. She's safe, I can feel it."

"Yeah, I was sure Ted would be all right, too, big guy like that, body armor and all. A well-trained, gung ho marine riding shotgun on an armored tank. Maybe I'm doing this for him, huh, since Daria was his friend, even if you never really were."

He went out and slammed the door.

6

___

On the way out to the dive site in the boat, *Mermaids I,* with Manny at the wheel, Cole's thoughts were flying as fast as the white wake they left behind. He'd been trying to come up with additional arguments for why this dive was a bad idea, but he knew he'd do the same thing in Bree's place. Unless he tied her up, he figured he couldn't stop her, so he had to go along to be certain nothing happened to her. He knew she was going, with or without him.

Then, too, she'd convinced him that she could sense that Daria was alive. He knew nothing firsthand about that intense kind of simpatico relationship with another person, but he'd read identical twins could be that way, and he'd never seen twins who were more mirror images of each other. He'd studied a framed photo of them in their apartment, a formal, posed picture where they were evidently bridesmaids at someone's wedding. They were beautiful women. If he ever saw Briana smile, he could probably tell one from the other, because one of them had a slightly lopsided grin, with a sort of bet-you-can't-guess-what-I'm-thinking look.

He was coming to know Briana, and he figured he knew Daria a bit, too, so this felt doubly personal to him. Another reason that he was literally along for the ride, even though he should have been installing Brazilian cherry in the salon on a big yacht in Naples today, was that he'd quickly come to admire Bree so much. She had not gotten hysterical and had seemed in control, when most women he knew would be frantic wrecks by now. Jillian's first response to any trauma had been tears and tantrums, so he was totally impressed with this woman. Impressed and just plain turned-on, even in these terrible circumstances.

Cole tried to listen carefully as Bree told

him things he should know about the dive. Though she was speaking over the roar of the motor, she wasn't talking loudly enough, and sometimes he had to almost read her lips. Like Cole, Manny seemed to be straining forward to hear her. Instead of facing her, Cole moved to sit beside her, edging her over a bit.

"Motor's too loud to hear you!" he told her, only to see her cringe. "What is it? What's the matter?"

"I agree about the motor. Your voice—I'm hearing sounds sharper than I did before, that's all. It's nothing. Okay, I'll start over. First off, if you're used to diving in the Caribbean or even in the Keys, the water's going to look really different here, not so clear. We'll both take dive lights. Manny brought two dive lights along, didn't you, Manny?" she asked, craning around toward the back of the boat so he could hear her.

She almost bumped noses with Manny since he was leaning so close to her. "Always got two of everything on board," Manny told her, sitting up straighter. "Usually for you and Daria."

Bree just nodded. When she turned back

toward him, Cole saw she had tears in her eyes.

"Go on," he prompted. He was grateful she seemed to be thinking clearly, despite the fact her emotions were right on the edge.

"We're only going down to thirty feet," she explained, "so we won't have to decompress, but we'll take a three-minute safety stop at fifteen feet, both entering and ascending. The wreck lies in a small, natural trough."

"What's the visibility at that depth?"

"Vis varies a lot out here, from six inches to sixty feet, but since we evidently aren't getting a storm today, it could have settled down to ten or twelve, especially since the incoming tide will bring in clearer water. I've got to find that camera."

"Let's just say we'll check for the anchor today. Set reasonable goals. We can't search a vast area on this dive."

As if she didn't hear that, when he knew she did, she continued. "The camera's in a plastic housing, which mutes the red color I've painted it, especially since all reds disappear about fifteen feet down. At the depth we're diving, everything will look green, yellow or blue."

"I remember. Bree, we should keep this dive short."

"We need to cover a certain area," she countered.

Cole was not used to being told what to do. Damn, this woman was stubborn, but maybe that came with being strong.

"I never would have done a dive alone that day," she admitted, suddenly changing the topic. She kept fussing with her mask she held in her lap. "But Manny needed time to patch up the generation gap with his daughter and couldn't go. It was the fifty-seventh dive we'd made at the Trade Wreck without incident, photographing and recording the growth of the turtle grass there. Daria had a really bad toothache that came on fast, so I said I'd go down alone. It only takes about twenty-five minutes. The storm was a distant line on the horizon, and the marine weather forecast hadn't mentioned it could come in so fast or hard."

"I know. So you anchored nearby but not where the anchor could disturb the site," Cole said, when she frowned out over the water.

"Right. The submerged aquatic vegetation—SAV—is very delicate and not doing well. We always joked that our motto for this Clear the Gulf Commission project would be Save Our SAV."

Her voice trailed off and her eyes took on a faraway look. Was she seeing a scene with her sister? He bumped her shoulder gently, and she seemed to come back from wherever she'd been. He was going to have to stick close to her down there, though she was obviously the more skilled diver.

She went on. "The report we were preparing to give the commission—and the media—next week would not be good news. The poor and declining quantity and quality of the sea grass indicates that the whole marine ecosystem here is still struggling from the increasing industrial and toxic runoff. Too many people means too much pollution, and that extends to the Trade Wreck sea grass meadow, which we're using as a sort of touchstone and symbol for the health of this entire area of the gulf. And it's sick."

"A dire report could mean cutbacks, penalties and political fallout for lots of important people. When the foundation of the marine food chain is screwed up, it's trouble for every living organism all the way up to humans, and that equates to millions of dollars in fishing, real estate and the tourist trade. Had you told anybody about your findings already?" he asked.

"We weren't keeping it a secret," she admitted. "You're thinking someone might want to warn us or stop us from releasing that? But everyone with interests in those things you just mentioned would want the environment to stay safe. They'd want to know what our report says so the situation can be fixed by concerned citizens, environmentalists, scientists, politicians—everyone."

"Back to our dive. We can't search the entire area for a camera."

"I'm hoping it snagged on either the Trade Wreck or another artificial reef nearby."

He nodded. "I heard there's one about three miles off Keewadin, where you came in."

"Right, the Stone Reef. That one's not a wreck but limestone boulders. I don't know if the camera would just go to the smooth, sandy bottom and stay put, or if the tides and currents would move it south until it snagged in one reef or the other."

"So what's the Trade Wreck like?"

"It's a supply ship sunk in the late 1930s,

made of wood and metal. It broke apart but what's there is pretty well preserved."

"Do you use GPS coordinates to locate the site? I don't see that equipment on board."

"Our only GPS is on the bigger boat, but we've been out here so much, it's half instinct and half compass coordinates. You'll be glad to know it's ordinarily a safe dive, with no sharks out here. I think the rough water or sudden change in barometric pressure from the storm yesterday stirred them up."

"I was wondering if you still remembered the sharks. You must have swum with them. Some followed us into shore in the sloop."

"I don't want to think about that," she said, shaking her head. "At least the only big fish usually around the Trade Wreck is a resident grouper Daria and I named Gertie . . ."

She sniffed hard. Tears welled up in her eyes again, and she bit her lower lip. He wanted to put his arm around her, but he just held on to the rail tight as Manny turned them in a slow circle and killed the motor.

Bree usually felt at one with the sea and completely relaxed during her dives. But not today. She wore a high-volume mask that had more airspace and side ports so she could see sideways without turning her head. She'd worn this old day-Glo-pink wet suit partly because it had a pocket on both upper thighs for a dive knife. She carried two knives, hoping Cole didn't find that strange and that Manny would keep quiet about how abnormal it was.

But *everything* was abnormal. She had the worst feeling something evil was lurking underwater. At least she had Cole along. Though she didn't like to think of Cole as a bodyguard, she felt much safer near him. It was obvious that Josh and Nikki Austin felt that way with their pilot-PR man-bodyguard, so why shouldn't she admit the same to herself? In ordinary circumstance, the idea of this compelling, virile man guarding her body would be to die for—damn, why had she thought of it that way?

She'd used a plastic sleeve to cover the bandage over her burn and wore her old dive watch on her right wrist. She'd have to call the hospital to ask where the one Daria gave her went, because it might be the last gift . . . the last . . .

She turned back to her preparations. They screwed on their pressure gauges and checked the air fill, then hooked up their regulators and sucked on them. Bree heard the familiar hissing of gas and the click of the valves, but so much louder than usual.

They back-rolled over the boat rail and went under in a rising blur of silver bubbles. When the cloud cleared, Bree looked for Cole and saw he was above her with only his big body visible, as if he had been decapitated. He must have stuck his head out of the water to say something to Manny.

Waiting for him to join her, Bree racked her brain to recall if she had looked up at the surface or even over at the anchor yesterday while she took photos, made measurements and took notes. When had *Mermaids II* left? If a second hull had loomed above, she would not have seen it in the low vis and increasing turbulence, but she should have heard an unfamiliar motor. Or had she been too rushed, too intent and busy to note sounds? Usually, even the bothersome little wave runners zipping here and there made a distinctive sound, and she was good at differentiating motor reverberations, from buzz to hum to roar, depending on the size of the vessel.

Cole upended and kicked down to join her

at fifteen feet for their safety stop. They were diving the anchor line, but didn't hang on to it, just near it. From watching him come down and reverse his position to stay stationary beside her, she could tell he was a good diver.

They hung suspended, facing each other, kicking slowly in unison, barely moving but nearly touching. There was something intriguing and intimate about being here like this with him, hidden, close, almost motionless, suspended as if they lay side by side. Although the vastness of the sea was her favorite place to be, Cole DeRoca made her feel small. She wanted his protection, but the turbulent sensations he stirred in her made her also feel out of control and she could not afford that, especially not now. Find clues, she told herself. Find clues to find Daria.

Through their masks, they looked below toward the two gray, shadowy, separate sections of the fifty-foot wreck. Yet their gazes returned to hold each other. Bree forced herself out of the deceptively peaceful lull. She nodded and they swam down toward the wreck with her leading.

The supply boat, named the *Charlotte G.*

Loher but referred to by most local divers as the Trade Wreck, had sailed out of Tampa bound for Key West with cattle in the pre-highway days of southwest Florida. Caught in a hurricane, it had broken into two sections. The stern had settled on its hull, but the midship and the prow lay on its port side. With several entrances into the interior of the ship, it had long been an attraction for divers, though it was labeled a hazard dive now for its rusted, jagged edges and unstable structure. The twins had a theory that the increasing pollution in the gulf had accelerated the disintegration of its wood and metal. One of the wreck's bizarre attractions was that occasionally, even now, the skull of a steer would float loose from the innards of the ship to gape eyeless out a porthole in the hull or emerge from the dark entry to a mazelike corridor. The twins had never taken one for a dive trophy, but they knew more than one bar or family room that boasted a skull from the Trade Wreck. Bree realized, too late, that she had forgotten to mention that to Cole.

As the wreck loomed closer in the shifting soup of the sea, they clicked on their lights. Bree startled. She was used to things looking twenty-five per cent larger underwater, but she hadn't been prepared for the increased brightness even here. Perhaps her heightened perceptivity of sound and light could be a blessing. The backscatter of tiny, drifting marine organisms stood out brilliantly. Their slow, swirling movement made her dizzy, but she shook that off. Anyway, this close to possible answers, she was not turning back.

A three-foot sea turtle swimming above the debris eyed them, then glided away. When they swam over and hovered above the sparse sea grass meadow, tiny, spidery arrow crabs with fuzzy topknots seemed to stare at them, but they saw no Gertie the grouper and no camera snagged anywhere here or on the sand flats.

Bree noted that the storm had pulled a few strands of grass loose. Of the fifty-two species of marine sea grass worldwide, only about four of those were widespread in Florida. Her precious turtle grass—fancy biological name *Thalassia testudinum*—was the most hardy, with its deep root system and sturdy runners from which grew blades of graceful, bright green grass. Most of the sea grass meadow stood about fourteen inches tall and shifted its gentle, ribbonlike blades in harmony with the currents. It should love the relatively shallow waters here but, as she'd told Cole, it was struggling to survive here—just as she was, she thought.

But she had no time for her beloved project right now. They swam back toward the wreck, playing their yellow beams ahead of them. Sometimes Cole's shaft of light seemed to dance with hers. If only her camera had caught here on the exterior of the ship, and if only it had captured some clue to what happened on the surface.

Bree motioned to Cole, and they swam the area around the wreck in broadening circles, searching for the camera and the anchor. Cole was not letting her out of his sight. When she motioned he could go one way and she the other, he shook his head and swam right on her tail.

And then they saw something. Both their beams shone dully off the links of a chain, which they followed to the half-buried anchor itself. Yes, their new anchor and chain! It was at least thirty feet from the position of the anchor and rope from their smaller skiff today. When Cole held his hands up in a questioning gesture as if to ask her if that was her anchor, she nodded, but her heart sank.

Daria never would have thrown the entire chain overboard, not unless something terrible—more than an approaching storm—had made her flee fast. Or had someone else thrown it over? And if that someone had wanted the *Mermaids II,* would they have also thrown Daria overboard?

The find filled her with frustration and fury. She had to locate that camera now at all costs, even if it meant going a ways into that broken, rusting old wreck.

She led Cole back in that direction, and they swam the entire length of where the camera might have drifted down or been snagged against the ship by the incoming tide. It was just over twenty-four hours ago now. How could so much have happened so fast? Twenty-four hours—like Sam had said, a new wreck only released a trail of bubbles for that long. *Daria, even if the boat went down, tell me you didn't go with it! I made it in. You must have, too!*

They saw no sign of the camera, so they started back, this time peering into nooks and crannies where it might have caught. Bree berated herself that she hadn't somehow kept the camera with her in the storm, how-

ever heavy and bulky. Using both their lights, they illumined each dark entry spot until—

Bree jerked back. Oh, it was just one of those cow skulls, bobbing on the other side of a thick glass porthole. When they'd first dived this wreck with their father years ago, the portholes had been covered with algae, but that, too, had been done in by the lack of oxygen in what some called dead water.

She tried to fight off the images that being this close to the wreck often triggered in her. Whenever she could, she ignored the ship's ruins and just concentrated on the sea grass meadow. She and Ted had dived this wreck just before they'd broken up, the summer before their junior year of college. The two of them had always called this wreck the *Titanic,* not because of its size, but because they'd seen the movie just before they'd first dived it together.

As bold as Bree was underwater, that movie had shaken her to her core. The scene where Kate Winslet and Leonardo DiCaprio had stood together at the top of the ship as it was sinking into the cold Atlantic had not just scared her but haunted her ever since. The first time Sam berated her for being the

reason Ted enlisted and died, he'd said she'd *scuttled* and *wrecked* his son's life. And in her nightmares about Ted's death, he wasn't killed by an improvised incendiary device in Iraq but was sent down to his death on a sinking ship, while—like the woman in the movie—Bree survived and lived her life. Then guilt hung heavy in her heart, until she could convince herself once again that Ted had made his own choices and that his loss—like her mother's death—was not her fault.

Now . . . now, when that nightmare stalked her, in sleep or awake, would she see Daria going down with the ship? While Bree still lived and breathed and walked and swam, would it be Daria she saw, doomed and clinging to *Mermaids II* while it slipped into the dreadful depths.

Cole tapped on his tank and gestured about the skull. She tried to motion back to him that cows had been the cargo. He nodded, and they went on, swimming about five feet apart, peering as far as they could see into entries of the wreck. It didn't take long to determine that the camera was not snagged against the upright stern, but she knew it could have settled into numerous nooks in the tipped fore parts of the ship.

And then Bree saw it! A glint of new metal! It was lodged in a small cranny that had once been clearly marked but was now faded: Fire Ax and Hose—Break Glass. No glass now, and someone might have taken the ax head for a souvenir, but the ragged remains of an old fire hose hung there below the rotting ax handle. It looked like the plastic housing had come off the corner of the camera, but she reached for the piece of metal she could see.

And yanked her arm back. From behind the remnants of the hose, a moray eel lunged at her, barely missing her hand. Bree backed away fast; the eel retreated partly into its lair. Her heart was thudding so hard it sounded like a bass drum was in her mask.

Morays loved to hide in rocks, tall grass or small crevasses to wait for their prey. Frightening in appearance, they had small eyes and a protruding snout, but worse was their always-open mouth, with their powerful jaws and long, sharp teeth. Their skin was scaleless and they had thick, mucous-covered, patterned bodies so they could hide from their prey. This one looked about four feet long, dangerous and hidden . . . like someone who may have hurt Daria.

Cole took her elbow and pulled her farther away. She pointed at the edge of the camera and he nodded. He swam over the moray's lair and carefully retrieved the half-rotted wooden ax handle. With it, he hooked the edge of the camera and pulled it out. The eel lunged at the metal, then retreated once again to protect his piece of property.

Bree was relieved until she saw that what had lodged there was the strobe lights she had released and not the camera.

She held the strobe up and shook her head. Cole squeezed her shoulder. *Is that yours?* he gestured, and she nodded. Their eyes met through their masks. Bree fought back tears. She did not dare cry or the mask would be a mess. She motioned to him that if the strobe was snagged on the wreck, the camera could well be, too. He shook his head and pointed to his watch, though she saw they'd only been down twenty minutes and they had much more air. When he pointed toward the surface, she shook her head and gestured with both hands and her fingers spread: just ten more minutes to peek inside the open entryways.

Another of the common safety sayings about diving, one her dad had stressed, popped into her head. *Only fools break the rules.* She was not a wreck diver and she hadn't brought either a wreck reel or a penetration line to help find her way out once she was inside the decaying wreck, where pieces could be loose or block an exit. These lights were good for a thirty-foot dive but not for diving blind inside a wreck—another rule about taboos. Still, when she hit the button on the strobe, it flashed its nearly blinding light. That would have to do to guide her just a little way, to find the camera, which she'd let go of in the same spot she'd dropped the strobe. The risk of moray eels be damned.

She gestured for Cole to follow and swam quickly toward the Trade Wreck with her strobe in one hand and her flashlight in the other. She did not look back. Just a short glimpse inside this corridor and then she'd quickly back out when she was sure the camera could not have been swept farther in.

She heard not only her dad's words this time, but his voice, too, loud over the hiss-hiss of her own breath in her ears. *Only fools stretch the rules.* She was a fool, then, a frenzied fool. But if Dad were here, he'd understand why she had to find the camera, find any clue to find Daria. He'd agree that the motto for now was *Daria's lost, and must be found at any cost.*

Cole was quick. Bree felt him make a grab for her ankle, but she kept kicking. She shot the strobe off repeatedly to see as she swam inside the sunken ship.

7

Bree was desperate to find the camera, and it was too narrow and too late to back out now. In and down she swam, headfirst into the rabbit hole of a dangerous wonderland. Everything seemed alien, even when she lit the dimness only by her single shaft of flashlight beam. Each time the blinding strobe flashed, the rust-encrusted depths of the long-sunken ship made it seem as if its metal skin was bleeding. The dizzying whirl of floating particles caught in the weird currents toyed with her equilibrium.

In this section of the ship, the port-side wall was the floor of the wreck, so the vessel's ceiling swirled past on her left and its floor on her right, making her feel even more disoriented. She swam over portholes that living souls had once peered out on their fateful voyage. This world—her entire world—had gone topsy-turvy. Had any of the crew's bones been trapped here like their living cargo's? Had something or someone sunk *Mermaids II?*

Bree saw no more cattle skulls, though several strange sea creatures peered at her and a small lobster scuttled away. But there was no camera. When the corridor turned and she peered beyond to some sort of galley, she maneuvered around to go back out and was amazed to see Cole, so close that she jerked back and clunked her tank into a bulkhead.

In the small, enclosed space, Cole seized her wrist and pulled her toward him. *Out of here and up to the surface,* he motioned, shining his light on his gestures. Shadows from his hands leaped across his face mask; with his beam at that sharp angle on his strong, sculpted features, he seemed to wear a fright mask. It made her think she really didn't know this man, yet she needed him badly.

Bree knew he was right to make her get out; she'd decided to leave anyway, now that she'd checked for the camera here. But, as if in protest, she accidentally hit the strobe button again. It flashed close in his face. His grip on her tightened, powerful, determined, and he took the strobe from her. Using only his flashlight beam, he gestured, *Out! You first.* She nodded and started out, using her light again. When they emerged into the relatively brighter water outside the Trade Wreck, she saw he had cut his wrist and was bleeding green blood, because at this depth, crimson always looked green.

She tried to motion that she hadn't known he was cut and hadn't meant to flash the strobe in his face. He just jerked his thumb up again. She took the strobe from him so he could stem the blood—she could not tell how bad the cut was—and they quickly ascended with no rest stop and no more communication. They both knew what a tiny bit of blood diffused in a vast stretch of the water could mean, and they didn't want those bull sharks back.

Bree felt light-headed. Those sharks . . . could they have attacked Daria if she had fallen in or been pushed off *Mermaids*

II? Bull sharks . . . the bones of bulls, the skulls of steers caught inside the Trade Wreck . . . Bree's life, wrecked without Daria . . . Daria trapped, her life maybe ruined, sunk . . . gone.

In a whoosh of foam and bubbles, they broke the surface together and swam to the skiff's ladder. Manny hurried over to meet them. Cole surprised her by giving her a one-handed boost on her bottom. She spit out her regulator and shoved her mask up on her head. "No, you're hurt. You first!"

"Get up there!" he ordered, his deep voice rough. "From now on, if we dive together looking for clues, I'm the dive boss. I don't care if you're the better diver! You're distraught right now, so I'm giving you a pass, but you're not going down there again without someone else in charge and you following orders!"

She climbed out with him right behind her. "How did you get cut?"

"Following you into that rusted bucket of bolts!"

"Since the strobe was there, I just had to look a littler farther in."

Trying to get a word in, Manny bent over them as they collapsed to sit side by side on the deck. "You find the camera?" Manny asked. "What 'bout the new anchor and chain? You find anything suspicious, any clues at all?"

Briefly, Bree updated him as she worked on Cole's cut with disinfectant from the first-aid kit. "I think you'll need a few stitches. I hope you've had a tetanus shot," she told him.

"Working with hammers and nails—and a crazed female diver—I'd better."

"I'm sorry this happened while you were trying to help me again. I can drive you into an urgent-care clinic if you need stitches. I'd rather not face the E.R. at the hospital again right now."

"Yeah, it needs a couple of stitches, but I'll take care of it. Your burned wrist and now this," he muttered. "We're a pair."

We're a pair.

He'd said it quietly, but she heard him clearly. She looked into his dark eyes, so close, with the bright, setting sun on the gently rocking boat. Manny still hovered, asking more questions, but none of that registered as the physical and emotional impact of the man she tended hit her hard. She barely knew Cole DeRoca, her hero and rescuer, yet he cared about her and she for him.

We're a pair. That was a cliché she and Daria had used more than once, but now the words meant something different. This sweeping sensation hardly resembled the bond of empathy and synergy she and Daria shared. This was raw energy and power—a fierce magnetism—something she had never felt before, even with Ted, with whom she'd once been so infatuated. This was deeper, almost dangerous. But the timing was terrible, when she had to use anything and anyone, including Cole, to find her sister.

"I'll ask some local divers to help search," she said, when the silence between them turned awkward. "But if you could continue to help, I'd be so grateful. I have a supply of plastic sleeves to cover a hurt wrist." She finished daubing the antibacterial cream on the jagged inch-long cut. Maybe it wasn't as deep as it had looked at first. Thank God, it was on the side of his wrist and not the soft, inner skin, where he would bleed a lot harder.

Bree jumped when Manny started the motor. She'd been so intent on Cole she hadn't realized Manny had moved away; she'd forgotten he was even here. Looking away again, out over the gulf that held sacred secrets, Bree pressed her lips tight together. Again she longed to throw herself into Cole's arms, but then she would explode in the hysteria she felt pressing down on her like the weight of water.

"When Daria and I were kids," she told him, raising her voice to be heard over the motor, "we once cut our wrists and swore a blood oath to be friends forever—very childish and very dramatic. Also stupid and dangerous, though we didn't know that. We were only about eight. We got in all kinds of trouble for it, and Amelia told her friends we were total flakes who didn't know you were only supposed to prick fingers."

Her voice broke, and she cleared her throat. She blinked back tears as she smoothed the edges of the big bandage onto his skin, tanned and flecked with crisp black hair. They were kneeling now, face-to-face, their hips and shoulders steadied against the rail by the ladder to keep from bouncing against each other as Manny headed the ship toward shore.

"Cole, I'll never be able to pay you back—I can't thank you enough for everything," she blurted, then scrambled to her feet and turned away to pick up some of her gear. Her emotions were so jumbled she was afraid she was going to burst into tears. She sat on the front seat, facing away from him, hunched over the strobe she held across her lap.

Cole came to sit beside her as they sped back toward Turtle Bay. "When this is all over and we've found Daria," he said, bending toward her so only she could hear, "we'll think of some way you can thank me."

At dusk that evening, Bree sat at the table in the apartment, poring over a marine map that detailed every reef, contour and cranny offshore in this area of the gulf. As she'd promised Cole, she'd made numerous calls to diving friends for help to search the gulf underwater tomorrow. Everyone—some were even taking personal days off from work to help—was going to assemble at her shop at nine in the morning. She jolted when her doorbell rang. Probably someone else from the media, she thought.

She almost wished she'd taken Josh and Nikki up on their loan of Mark Denton for a while. He was evidently good not only at protection but at handling press releases. Bree had given a brief statement to the man from the *Naples Daily News* and the Fort Myers ABC-TV reporter when they'd caught up with her earlier at the marina, but she wasn't going to answer the doorbell if it was more of the same.

Yet, what if there was word from the search teams—good news? Sometimes the media caught wind of things before those who should have been told first. Or what if Cole had returned? He'd said he would go have his wrist cared for, though, and wouldn't be back until tomorrow morning, unless she wanted him to sleep on her sofa tonight. She had wanted him to, but she'd told him she was all right. Several times today, in her desperation, she had done things she shouldn't have and she was afraid of what she might do if she could cling to Cole.

Bree peered out the side window that looked down onto the street to see if she could spot a TV van. There stood her brother-in-law, Ben, looking up with his arms crossed over his chest. His premature silver hair and white, long-sleeved shirt folded up at the elbows seemed to glow in the dusk. As usual, his edgy, stiff body language said everything about his steely backbone. Bree waved at him and hurried down to let him in.

She was proud he was such an upright, unbending county prosecutor, but she thought he too often brought an adversarial stance home from the office and courtroom with him. Ben was up for election in November, just like Josh, and had been bemoaning the fact there had been no high-profile cases to keep him in the public eye lately. Unlike other elected officials, he seldom paid for campaign ads—name recognition and frequent sound bites for the media seemed to be all he needed.

No doubt Amelia had sent him, though he'd probably be happy to lecture his maverick sister-in-law on his own.

"You didn't need to come all this way," she greeted him as she let him in. "I'm hanging in. You could have called me."

"Your cell was busy for hours. Besides, I had to see someone nearby—actually, our casino mover and shaker, Dom Verdugo. All we need is the whiff of organized crime around him, and he'll be on *my* hit list. I wanted to tell him privately to keep his nose clean. He invited me to go along on the casino boat's first cruise to show me he's on the up-and-up. But I wanted to see *you,* not only for your and Daria's sake but Amelia's, too."

He gave her a quick hug, then released her to close and lock the door behind him. "Bree, I realize you're upset and anxious, but you really distressed your older sister by just leaving the hospital today."

"Come on up, then you can call her to say I'm okay," she suggested, and motioned him toward the stairs. With a barely perceptible grimace toward the shop, he followed her.

Ben had ditched his usual suit coat and his tie was gone for once. His leather briefcase, too. Still, he managed to look like a ritzy real estate ad from *Gulfshore Life* magazine, whether he was garbed for the courthouse or his own house. He was a driven man, talented and ambitious, a crusader against breakers of the letter of the law. The more high-profile and gruesome the case, the better. It terrified Bree to think that might come in handy if they didn't find Daria safe and sound.

"This is exactly the kind of thing I'd warned both of you about," he went on, sitting upright on the edge of the sofa. "Something was bound to go wrong with all the risks you take."

"You warned us that Daria and our newest boat might go missing in a storm sometime?" she countered sarcastically, propping her hands on her hips and still standing so as not to feel at a disadvantage to him. With Ben, she always felt she was being grilled on the witness stand, and she'd found the best defense was to be a bit offensive.

"Not precisely," he admitted, frowning, "but I've warned both of you about behavior unbecoming of your brains and beauty."

"Thanks for the backhanded compliment."

"Hate to put it this way, Bree, but you're in too deep. You needed a couple more days under doctors' care, and you shouldn't be on your own right now. You should never have chosen to get into a business with so much danger involved."

"There was nothing dangerous about checking the sea grass meadow for the fifty-eighth time!" she exploded. "I appreciate Amelia's help in the hospital and your continued concern, but—"

"Just listen for a second. You need a level head here, so I called both the coast guard and the air patrol and told them to report to me if they learned anything."

"Oh, no . . . oh, no!" she cried, and collapsed onto the sofa with her head in her hands. "And they called you? Did they find her? The boat?"

"No, but the fact they didn't isn't good news either. Calm down," he went on, turning toward her and putting a hand on her slumped shoulder. "Amelia and I just want to help. This pipe dream, this search-and-salvage endeavor of yours, should be left to the likes of Sam Travers. You know he contacted me last year about buying you out, and I counseled you to take the offer."

She was angry now. Not only had Ben scared her, maybe intentionally, but he was still doling out advice she—they—didn't need or want. And now he was trying to become the kingpin in the search for Daria, taking over like he did everything and everyone.

She forced herself to inhale deeply, slowly.

"Ben, I know you don't approve of what Daria and I chose to do, and that's your business. But this search-and-salvage shop and finding Daria is *my* business, though I thank you for sideline support."

He leaned back on the sofa, one bouncing ankle crossed over his other knee as if he hadn't heard or heeded a thing she'd said. His voice was soothing, as if he spoke to a child, and that grated on her already raw nerves.

"Come on now, Bree. Why don't you get some things together and come on home with me for a couple of days? It would do you and Amelia both good, and the boys would love to see you, though I'd appreciate it if you wouldn't tell them all those deep-dive stories or promise them scuba lessons again—not until they're ready."

"Which won't be until you and Amelia are ready and that might be never. I know you have friends in high places, so I repeat, any support you can lend to keep the search going is much appreciated, but I will be the contact and the spokesperson. Now, can I get you some coffee? It's all ready," she said, standing.

"Have you been drinking it to stay up? You need your sleep? You look like hell."

Bree spun back to face him. "That's because I'm in hell on earth until I can find my sister!"

"*You* can find her?" He sat up straight again. "That's exactly what Amelia's worried about."

"It's not just me. I've got volunteers who are coming to help tomorrow."

"You'd better not get in the way of the professional searchers. I've seen a lot of missing persons cases, and the best advice I can give you is to keep calm and keep out of it. Sure, stay informed, but let the authorities—"

"The authorities need my help. I know that gulf out there, and I know Daria as well as I know myself. I realize you've seen a lot of dire situations, and if someone has deliberately harmed her, you'll be the first person I'll ask for advice. I know you're the prosecutor for the entire county. You do realize I'd think of that, at least?"

"Fine, I hear you. If that turns out to be the case, all I can promise is that we'll find whoever's to blame and prosecute him or her to the full extent of the law. And Amelia and I will keep in constant touch."

Bree nodded, but she wanted to scream at him that she didn't care about the law, or his levelheaded rules, only about finding Daria any way she could.

It was nearly nine at night by the time Cole had six stitches in his wrist and got home to shower and chow down a hamburger. Despite that, he drove back to the Turtle Bay Marina. He parked along the dock and glanced up at Bree's lighted apartment. He was totally tempted to see how she was doing, but he hesitated. He'd called her from the urgent-care clinic, and it might be overkill to stop by like this so late. She needed sleep, though he figured she'd be hard-pressed to get any.

He leaned against the wrought-iron lamppost, then squinted up at the second-floor veranda and double doors. Two figures stood within the apartment—Bree and a silver-haired man.

"And why not?" he muttered to himself, and shoved away from the pole. "She has friends and needs them now." He knew that she'd arranged a search of other possible spots in the gulf by local divers tomorrow, and he and Manny were going to be there at the crack of dawn to help. But it bothered him that another man was with her tonight.

Besides, Cole told himself, he had come to talk to Dom Verdugo, not Bree. Although "the godfather of offshore gambling," as the local paper had dubbed him, had not dared to bring his one-hundred-eighty-foot floating casino into its berth at the end of the main marina dock yet. He kept his private yacht, the *Xanadu,* there. Just as Cole had noted before, the sleek ship seemed to sprout its own bodyguards.

"Hey, how ya doing?" the stocky young man who was obviously standing sentinel near the gangway asked as Cole approached. He had a shaved head, which seemed planted directly on his shoulders with no neck. His black T-shirt and dark pants made him almost blend with the night.

"Not doing too bad," he told the guy. "I'm Cole DeRoca. Mr. Verdugo asked me to panel the main salon of the casino boat, so I thought I'd have a word with him about it. It's after office hours, but I figured it was worth a try."

A second man, who looked like a clone of this one, materialized from down the dock. With a nod to his friend but his eyes assessing Cole, the first man said, "I'll check."

Cole tried not to judge the situation in a negative way. The anti-casino-boat locals insisted a flock of security people reeked of organized crime, but those who were pro offshore gambling argued that any rich man with an expensive yacht would want some protection these days.

Personally, but privately, Cole was anti-gambling, because he'd seen how it could ruin a family—his own. He used to hate his mother because she'd gambled so much of their lives and happiness away, but ever since she'd died, several years before his father had, he regretted he'd shown her anger and not understanding and love.

Cole was an only child, and he'd once adored his beautiful, vibrant mother. Still, he'd never been able to forgive her for her lies and deceit over her gambling addiction. Time after time she'd sworn she wouldn't squander family funds again, get them in debt, or hang out with people who only wanted her money. She'd drunk too much, too, and had been drunk when she'd gone swimming late at night and accidentally drowned—at least, Cole and his father had told themselves it had been an accident. Surely, she would not have taken her own life, no matter how guilty she'd felt—and how upset she was they could not understand the sickness that made her risk all her husband had worked for and continually gamble away her only son's esteem and maybe his financial future, too.

But it was not the promise of money that

brought Cole here today, considering a job from a man whose glittering gambling empire could ruin people's lives. His offer from the Miami business mogul was to panel the large central gambling salon of the casino yacht with Caribbean rosewood. Though the job was worth big bucks, Cole had planned to turn it down in protest of Verdugo's hellbent push to bring gambling into the Turtle Bay area, one of the few regions left with old-Florida ambience.

But because of Cole's feelings for Bree, he was considering giving this a try, however much it went against his grain to deal with the devil. If there was anyone Cole could think of who might have the means, the might and maybe the motive to keep the Devon sisters' dire ecological report from being released next week, it was Verdugo. The man had been pouring money into promoting the new jobs and tourist benefits that would come from voting his way. But if the twins and the Clear the Gulf Commission made a big deal about the gulf waters not recovering from pollution, the swing vote might turn against a big gambling cruise boat making numerous trips in and out of Turtle Bay.

As Marla Sherborne, one of the candidates for the U.S. Senate, had put it in a brochure he'd read, "Verdugo's Fun 'n' Sun Cruises are unregulated, and such ships dump waste right off Florida's pristine shores."

Besides helping Bree by keeping an eye on Verdugo, it perversely pleased Cole to think a gambler would be paying him. He could use the money from this lucrative job. He wanted desperately to set up a sailboat-building business and get out of doing luxury yacht interiors. Florida was the center of the universe for handcrafted wooden boats. Since net fishing was illegal now, the sloops he'd make would be strictly for pleasure. For years, far too much of his own money had gone down the sewer hole of paying off his mother's massive gambling debts.

"Okay, he'll see you now," the first guard called from behind the polished mahogany rail of the main deck. "Mr. Verdugo's having a drink and says come join him."

The second, silent man gestured he should board. As Cole walked up the gangway and followed the first guard to the stern stateroom, he heard a woman's whining voice on board somewhere aft. He'd seen bigger, plusher yachts, but not in Turtle Bay. The *Xanadu* stuck out like a manicured thumb in a handful of unpolished nails compared to the other vintage craft moored nearby.

As he entered the golden glow of the stateroom, Cole recognized Verdugo from newspaper photos, though they'd managed to obscure his stature, perhaps intentionally. Short and portly, the fifty-something entrepreneur greeted him with an outstretched hand. "I hear you're the hero of the hour, DeRoca."

"For rare woodworking or breaking news?"

He followed his host into a room larger than most landlocked living rooms. A huge horseshoe couch of ivory leather arched around a freeform glass-topped table; what appeared to be two authentic Picassos overlooked a grand piano. The paintings, a scattering of throw pillows and a large aquarium built into one wall were the only real color in the room of ecru and white with metallic touches. A round area rug muted footsteps. Soft music—an opera?—played in some sort of surround sound.

"You bet, the rescue of that woman—what

did I hear she was? Oh, yeah, the ecology photographer," Verdugo said, his voice naturally gruff but bearing no foreign accent as Cole had expected. "Any word of her sister or the missing boat yet?"

"Unfortunately, no," Cole said, noting that Verdugo had twice said he'd "heard" something, as if he had eyes and ears out getting information for him. Did the man watch TV, or did his lackeys keep him informed? Or did he somehow know things firsthand?

"I woulda volunteered this boat, but I didn't want to get in the way of the official search. That storm must have capsized the other sister. Man, can you imagine surfacing from a routine dive and you're all alone? Is Scotch all right? Neat or on the rocks?"

"Rocks would be fine." Cole was going to ask him where he'd heard the twins were out on a routine dive, since he hadn't heard or seen that in the media, but Verdugo pointed at a huge metal bowl and spoke again.

"Have some caramel popcorn with it. People think I'm nuts, but they go together great. Love this stuff," he added, and grinned to show perfect teeth—probably perfectly false—as he tossed some popcorn in the air and adeptly caught it with his mouth.

"So look," he went on, pouring drinks behind a metal and white leather bar, "I assume you've decided to take my offer to panel the casino ship, or you surely would not be here. Right?"

"I'm here to discuss the possibility."

"Okay, then," Verdugo said, and pointed again to the bowl of popcorn as he carried the drinks toward the couch. Cole leaned over, took a small handful of the popcorn and ate some. He studied Dom Verdugo as he handed him a drink and sat on the curved couch, facing him across the glass table.

The man wore tailored Bermuda shorts and a muted silk print shirt, tails out. He was barefooted and deeply tanned, perhaps not as much from the sun as from his obvious Latin heritage; his hooked nose looked Italian and his narrowed, deep-set eyes were just plain hawk-like. He led some small talk, mostly about Cole's work. The guy was as smooth as the Scotch, and Cole had to remind himself that Verdugo bore watching. He wondered if he had been watching—or "hearing about"—the twins and knew about their coming report, but he couldn't figure out a way to broach that subject without giving his intentions away. He was probably just overly suspicious, since he'd become so attached to Briana so quickly and, damn it, deeply.

After his first sip, he swirled the Scotch in his glass, chewed on his popcorn and tried not to stare at the beautiful wood paneling on the grand piano. From here it looked like Mexican cocobolo wood, and that stuff was difficult to harvest. Verdugo's wealth—and the additional fortune he could no doubt make from getting a toehold in southwest Florida with lucrative gambling cruises—made Cole realize he'd probably never harm anyone directly. He'd just have one of his hey-boys do it.

"Actually, I'd like a chance to see the cruise-ship salon before I accept your offer," he told Verdugo, since the other man had started to talk as if Cole's employment was a done deal.

"Money's not an issue."

Cole swallowed hard at that thought. "But my doing an excellent job for you is. I can see from the stunning surroundings here you have excellent taste."

"Nothing but the best," he said, and lifted his glass as if in toast to Cole. "And that's what the Fun 'n' Sun Casino Cruises will

bring to this area—jobs, the best new restaurants and upscale stores, even more luxury yachts that need rare wood paneling,
eh? Our critics call my other floating casinos
'pay for play' boats and 'cruises to nowhere,'
but I beg to differ. We give the customer what
he or she wants—craps, blackjack, slots,
booze, live entertainment, lots of laughs, you
name it. It's not a cruise to nowhere, no way,
but a cruise to fun and profit for everyone."

You name it . . . a cruise to nowhere. The
words caught in Cole's mind. He agreed to
drive to Miami by Monday to see the cruise
ship's salon and decide whether or not to
take the job. If Dom Verdugo could give his
customers anything they wanted, he could
surely give himself the same. How badly did
this man want to stop a negative report on
the local environment from coming out?
Cole wondered. He'd never tell Bree, but
since Daria and *Mermaids II* were still missing from a storm they should have been able
to ride out, he expected the worst. At any
rate, if he took the job, he planned to keep
his eyes and ears open around Verdugo.

As he reached his car, he saw Bree's lights
were still on. Surely her visitor had left by
now. Cole leaned his arms on the top of his

car and gazed out over the sailboats and motor craft nodding from their perches on the inky bay. A single small vessel was heading out past the lighted buoys with its fore and aft lights glowing until the blackness of the gulf devoured it.

Cole shook his head and shuddered. Had Daria Devon somehow taken a cruise to nowhere?

It was almost ten-thirty when Amelia heard Ben drive into the garage. She met him in her nightgown the minute he came in through the laundry room.

"She's not with you," she greeted him. "I knew she wouldn't want to come stay with me—even now."

"I tried, but I guess my powers of persuasion only work in a courtroom. She's obsessed with finding Daria, and I can't blame her for that, at least." He walked into the kitchen. Amelia hurried barefoot behind him. Flopping his briefcase on the counter, he kissed her cheek. "You've been crying again."

"Of course I've been crying. Daria's my sister, too, not just Briana's. I should go to her, sleep on her sofa, keep an eye on her.

I've got to know what she's planning. You never know what she'll do."

"She seemed totally distraught one minute, but full steam ahead the next. When I was leaving, she told me the guy who picked her up in his sailboat is going to help her run a search with other divers tomorrow. It sounds to me as if he's keeping close tabs on her. I thought they didn't really know each other before the storm, but they sound . . . close."

"Actually, they had met once briefly," she said. "He's her rescuing angel," she muttered, "and I hope not her avenging angel."

"What's that about revenge?"

"I didn't say revenge. It's nothing."

Ben reached for the door of the fridge but turned back and put his hands gently on her shoulders. "Bree's really going to need you when they find Daria."

"Find her body, you mean."

Her stomach cramped. Tears blurred Ben to make two of him—like the two of them, little Bree and Daria, always the center of attention, of Dad's world, of everything in the damned universe. Even her boys were ecstatic when her sisters came over—no doubt to see them, not her—as if Santa and the

Easter Bunny and every *Star Wars* character they adored had all rolled into one and come to visit.

"Yeah, I'm afraid I do mean find her body," he said with a sigh as he pulled her into his arms. "The odds aren't good they'll find Daria afloat on a piece of board or shipwrecked on one of the Ten Thousand Islands."

"I've been racking my brain for what could have happened to her," she said, leaning against him with her head turned on his shoulder. "Even crazy thoughts like maybe someone found her on the boat alone and kidnapped her, but then wouldn't we have received a call about ransom? Or what if those horrible people who steal those poor women for labor and sex—"

"Human traffickers?" he interrupted. "Hell, I'd love to prosecute one of those modern-day slave traders who import girls from South America and force them into labor or prostitution. That's been growing in Miami, and now they're avoiding law enforcement across the state by coming in here at night, since this coast is darker and less populated. No, I don't think those boats come in during the day."

"But if they were waiting offshore to land and then the storm was so bad . . ."

"That's too much of a long shot, honey," he said, hugging her tight. "I'll bet if there's a culprit, it's the storm. Still, we've got to hold out hope with Bree. She's tough and she's determined."

"Oh, yes," she said, pulling away to get a tissue to wipe her eyes and blow her nose. "She's that and more. You admire her— everyone does. Daria was even more willful, just for the heck of it, but Bree always had some burning purpose. They were—are— different, as well as being like the two peas in the proverbial pod."

When he stood there, staring at her and frowning as if she were a defendant who would blurt out her guilt to him à la Perry Mason, she pushed past him to open the fridge and take out a carton of orange juice for him.

"Not that," he said.

"You want some fresh squeezed?"

"Just hand me the soda. I need something a little stiffer than a jolt of Vitamin C."

"You've been busy at work," she said, trying to change the subject so she could get hold of her emotions.

"Actually, it's been deadly dull. I could use some face time on TV and some coverage in the papers. Hate to think I'm going to have to pay for all that this time around in the election."

"Your name is well-known. People respect you, and they'll vote what they trust."

"What they trust?" he said almost bitterly as he got a bottle of whiskey from the top cupboard above the fridge. "I don't think most people trust anyone on a ballot anymore, so I hope and pray they don't put me in the politician category. Let Josh Austin and Marla Sherborne fight that stigma as well as each other. Prosecutors are public servants. Hell, I could make ten times as much in private practice."

"I know you could, but we do just fine. You love what you're doing. It's your calling in life."

"You and the kids come first," he corrected her, but she wasn't certain she believed him. If her own father hadn't really loved her, how could Ben?

He mixed himself a stiff drink while she stared at herself in the window above the sink with only dark night beyond. It was like looking at her reflection in a black mirror. She did resemble the twins somewhat. If she'd let her hair go natural, she'd look even more like them. But she looked worn down by worry: guilt weighed heavy on her heart and mind and soul. She felt she was in a stupor, like she was slogging through water—damn, why did she have to think of it that way? She should never have gone to see Daria alone, thinking she could divide and conquer the two of them. And then it had suddenly gone so, so bad.

more like him. But she looked well. Her
body no duit weighed heavy on her bed
and mind soul. She felt the weight of the
pillow sheets, fabric and rough water
filling, and she have to think that that
weight was sufficient. Have done these
Daria alone thinking she could divide and
span just life, two of them. Are they it had
thinking g his so much bed.

8

Early the next morning in the office of the
Two Mermaids Search and Salvage Shop,
Briana stood in the circle of her diving
friends and acquaintances, fourteen at last
count. Most already wore wet suits. Some
had dragged in their gear, though others
would have to go back to their cars or boats
to get suited up.

Manny sat on Daria's desk, hunched over,
elbows on knees, staring at his feet. Behind
her guests, Cole leaned next to the closed
front door with his arms crossed as if to keep
any reporters from getting in. A TV van with
a satellite dish on top was already parked

down the street, so they must have somehow gotten word of this hastily called meeting.

"I can't thank all of you enough for coming
to help on such short notice," Bree told them.
"As you have heard, this may indeed be a
life-and-death search." Her voice shook, but
she went on. "Manny has already handed
out the diagrams with coordinates of underwater sites we would like to have searched
for any signs of our dive boat, in case it
broke apart in the storm. I'll let you decide
among yourselves which site you'd like to
check for possible . . ." Her voice caught,
and she cleared her throat. "For possible debris since you may have places you're more
familiar with than others. Many of you know
what the *Mermaids II* looks like, but just in
case—" she held up a piece of paper "—this
is a photo of it you can pass around. We've
already had an extensive official search
which, unfortunately, I've been informed will
be called off at noon today. But the coast
guard and civilian air patrol have obviously
not been looking under—"

Biting her lower lip, she blinked back tears
behind her dark sunglasses. She felt weird
wearing them inside, but her eyes were

bloodshot and any sort of light bothered her. When she saw Cole leave his post to come forward as if to take over, she cleared her throat again. "Although Sam Travers has used his boat's echo sounder, no one has actually done an extensive search underwater."

As if just saying his name could summon him up like some evil spell, the bell attached to the front door rang and Sam and two of his divers stepped in to join the group. When Bree nodded her silent thanks, several heads turned Sam's way. He glowered at her, but she was still glad to have his help. Manny saw him come in, too. Like a loyal watchdog, he stood with his arms crossed over his big chest, glaring back at Sam.

"I hate to admit it," Bree told everyone, "but it is possible the ship broke up or sank in the storm and my sister is afloat on a piece of it somewhere. So if you should find any signs of the *Mermaids II,* please let us know here right away, even if you do contact the coast guard, or—or the police."

Again, through her sunglasses, her eyes met Cole's intense gaze. He'd come even closer, next to her desk, as if he and Manny stood sentinel on either side of her. In a way, this search was Cole's doing, because he'd made her promise she wouldn't dive again unless she had some sort of lead. She was praying these people would give her that— anything to go on.

"And last but not least," she said, picking up her old camera in its plastic housing. "When I swam back in from the Trade Wreck in the storm, I had to drop a camera much like this one in the water. It's painted red inside the housing and is quite new. If anyone sees it, please retrieve it for me. Daria took some shots on it before I dived, and I'd like those back." Bree had decided not to share her fears of foul play. Besides, she couldn't bear to believe it herself, so she just concluded with, "On the back, the camera's etched with the initials B & D D.

"I guess that's it," she told them as they circulated the picture of the missing vessel and heads bent briefly over it. She could hear individuals whispering. Someone near the back of the room murmured, "Like a needle in a very big, wet haystack."

"Again," Bree said, "I'm so thankful for your help. For those of you who just arrived, we're using this office as a command post. Cole, Manny and I will be here monitoring the radio frequency and the cell-phone number we've written down on the dive sites handouts. Any questions?"

Guy Russel, a friend of a friend she'd never seen before today, asked, "I know you were twins, but did she look like you?"

The man's use of the past tense jolted her. She wanted to scream at him, but she said calmly, "This is still a search mission, not a recovery one. Yes, Daria does look like me, except for little things such as her hair's a bit longer and parted on the other side— my mirror image."

With a hard sniff, she gestured that they could get started. After they'd left with encouraging words or a hug—except for Sam and his duo of divers, who just walked out—Cole put one arm around her waist. He felt so warm and strong when she was cold and shaky.

"That guy who made it sound as if Daria was permanently gone didn't mean it that way," he whispered. "He wasn't thinking."

"It's all I've been thinking," she told him, shoving her sunglasses up on her head and pressing her palms over her aching eyes. She leaned back into him, her head resting against his rock-hard shoulder. "Let's face it, if we're desperate enough to look for the boat underwater and no one's found Daria by now, washed ashore in the way you found me . . ."

Cole gave her a sharp hug. "Stop thinking that way until you absolutely have to."

"We should contact the border patrol." Manny had suddenly come so close that Bree thought at first he meant to push Cole away from her. His body language said he was angry. He didn't look either of them in the eyes but stared at Cole's arm around her. "They track down illegal aliens," he said, "so how 'bout they can help track down Daria, no? What if she got in the way of those bastards smuggling in Cubans, or she see something she shouldn't? Big money, so smugglers get more dangerous 'round here. We got a few border patrol agents on this coast now. How 'bout we call them, get more help, yes?"

"I think," Bree told him, "we have pretty good clout with Josh Austin and Marla Sherborne. Senator Sherborne phoned this morning to say she'd be stopping by. If worse comes to worst, my brother-in-law will help. He stopped by last night."

She heard and felt Cole give a sigh of relief, but when he said nothing, she went on.

"Josh and Senator Sherborne may be fierce political opponents, but I'm willing to play both sides. And, Manny," she added, putting her hand on his arm, "I don't think smugglers—or yacht pirates, if they've been in the area—would want a dive boat like ours."

"Caramba!" he said, shaking off her touch. "What I mean is the storm could have panicked smugglers, they needed a small boat and they play rough."

"I appreciate all your help," Bree said, trying to calm him as well as herself. She stepped away from Cole but turned back to face him. "People like Manny," she told Cole, "who came into this country legally and are willing to do what it takes to make a good life here for their families, are just as upset about illegals as many Anglo citizens are."

"Yet you know desperate people take risks, Manny," Cole put in. "The refugees, I mean, as well as the smugglers."

Manny surprised Bree by smacking his fist into the palm of his other hand. The strain of Daria's plight was rubbing his nerves raw. The poor man had enough trouble, with his adored mother so sick and his daughter's rebellion, none of which Cole knew about.

"Yeah, Manny Salazar—he knows that, all right," Manny muttered, glaring up at Cole.

To Bree's dismay, Manny shoved past them and stalked out into his cluttered realm of the back room.

Sitting at the two desks, Bree and Cole drank coffee all morning and jumped to answer a call whenever one came in. Too many of them were from reporters or well-wishers. Four had come from the groups of divers so far, and the word was that they'd found nothing. Amelia called and was relieved to hear that Bree herself wasn't diving. It annoyed Bree that Amelia still seemed miffed about the fact she'd left the hospital without telling her, when there were so many more important things to focus on right now.

Manny mostly banged around in the back room, but emerged from time to time to get fresh coffee and see what was going on, especially when Cole went to use the bathroom out in the storage area or to make more coffee upstairs.

"Manny, I'm sorry if you felt I didn't listen to you or Cole insulted you," Bree said during one of those times she was there alone.

"I know you're blaming yourself about Daria, too."

"What you mean?" he demanded, crossing his hands over his chest.

"That you weren't on the boat when something terrible must have happened. Ordinarily, you would have been there."

"Yeah, that's true. Sorry I snapping at you. Sometimes, even stuff planned out, it don't go like it should."

They both turned as the bell on the front door rang when it opened. If only it could be good news, or better yet, Daria walking in, a miracle, Bree thought, looking up.

It was a woman about Daria's height and, for one insane moment, Bree's insides cartwheeled before she saw it was Senator Marla Sherborne. No way Daria would ever wear a conservative, gray pantsuit like that or the big gold starfish pin on her shoulder. Gypsy skirts with peasant tops and clunky shell jewelry when she was dressed up, that was Daria.

Bree had met Marla Sherborne at several fund-raisers for various ecological causes, but hadn't seen her since she'd become Josh's opponent for her U.S. senate seat. At forty-seven, Marla was a striking woman, blessed with a beautiful heart-shaped face, gorgeous skin and, evidently, eternal energy. If the rumors about her affair with Cory Grann were true, that certainly added some spice to a rather bland reputation up to now. That would really be sleeping with the enemy, since King Sugar in this state had often been blamed for fertilizer runoff pollution problems, which Marla was always attacking.

"Senator Sherborne," Bree said, rising and coming out from behind her desk to greet her. "I'm very grateful for your concern and anything you can do to keep some sort of official search going. It's being called off right about now."

"Briana, I'm so sorry about everything," she said as they shook hands. "No word yet?"

Bree explained about the dive search they had organized today.

"Then you're facing possible bad news."

"Let's just say, I would never forgive myself if, even underwater, I left any stone unturned."

"Actually, it was Josh Austin who mentioned the tragedy to me. I must admit I get so busy sometimes that I rely on aides to monitor TV news and scan the papers for me. Again, I am so sorry for all you are going through. And you were struck by lightning, Josh said. But there was no real fallout from that, evidently."

Bree didn't mention her acute hearing and sensitivity to light. She'd told no one but Cole. It was amazing how she felt closer to him than to anyone right now, including Amelia. She prayed she wasn't leaning on him because the person she'd always been nearest and dearest to was gone. No, she still felt Daria's presence—didn't she?

To shift the subject, she said, "I'm happy to hear you and Josh are not always in some sort of debate or disagreement."

"Not at all," she said with a decisive nod and a hint of a smile, which lit her blue eyes to make her look even younger. "Both of us are working as best we see fit to help our constituents in this beautiful part of our world, and that certainly includes you and your sister—Turtle Bay's two mermaids and champions of our ecological future. Besides, Josh and I have some very good friends in common, and one can't always legislate one's heart. I understand that Josh once dated your sister."

"He told you that?"

"I believe I overheard his wife mention it. I see her sometimes, since her father's a dear friend of mine. You look surprised I admit that. I supposed you know I mean Cory Grann. He's a longtime widower, you may have heard, and I've always been too busy—and too ambitious, I admit that—to marry, though I don't know what's in the future for either of us. He and I have been at odds in the past over some issues, but in this case, opposites attract. Besides, I don't completely blame big sugar for our pollution problems. It's much more complex than that."

"Yes, I understand. So many things are not all they seem."

"Exactly. The sugar industry has poured money into ecological causes and has greatly cut back on toxic pesticides. But that is a topic for another day and not why I'm here. I just want you to know that the work you and your sister are doing for the Clear the Gulf Commission is important, our linchpin for change. Although finding and returning Daria safe and sound is the top priority for all of us, that Trade Wreck ecological report of yours may be your legacy—both of you. And, I must admit, your plight and hers will draw much more attention to that report."

"I hadn't thought of that," Bree admitted. "Perhaps something good coming out of all this terrible mess."

"Briana," the senator went on, taking one of her hands, "I'm hoping that, whatever happens, you will be willing to stand behind that report, however disheartening its findings. I intend to make it a battle call to action, both here in southwest Florida and on a national level."

As Bree nodded, she noticed Cole had come downstairs, or rather, she felt his presence. As she introduced him to Marla, she couldn't help but wonder if the woman was here because she cared about finding Daria or just about protecting her precious report. Everything she said sounded like a beautifully prepared and written speech.

Bree jerked when the radio static became a voice. "Travers here, Sam Travers, over. Briana, you read?"

She rushed to her desk and bent over it to pick up the mike, then pushed the button to talk back. "Sam, Briana here, over." Her heartbeat accelerated. Of all the searchers who had gone out today, Sam was the least likely to call unless he really had something.

"One of my guys found your camera. They dived the Boulder Reef, and it was there. It's got your initials on the back."

"Sam, thanks! But nothing else?"

Static crackled for a moment. Bree's heart fell to her feet. Was he breaking her in easy? Cole came to stand beside her and put his arm around her again. Manny came charging in from the back room. Marla Sherborne hovered.

"Someone got something?" Manny cried.

"Nothing else," Sam's voice came loud and clear.

Bree didn't know whether she felt relief or grief, but at least she could look at Daria's pictures on that camera now.

Briana's hands shook as she took the camera from Sam's diver, the freckled, red-headed one, at the front door of her shop. "Boss says, let him know if you find anything that helps," he said, and was gone.

Bree cradled the camera in her arms. It looked so normal, so undamaged, even dry. Both she and her gear had been through the ravages of the storm and sea, so maybe it was a sign Daria would soon be home soon, safe and sound, as Senator Sherborne had said. She'd been gone for almost an hour now, promising to keep in touch.

"Let's download whatever this camera holds and have a look at it," she told Cole and Manny. She was heading toward the corner of the office where she kept her computer, scanner and printer when her desk phone rang. She ran to get it. Manny's wife, Juanita, was on the line.

"*Hola,* Briana," she cried, evidently recognizing her voice. "I so sorry 'bout Daria. I been lighting candles at Our Lady of Guadalupe for you get better, her be found."

"Thanks for your support, Juanita," Bree said. Looking instantly more worried than he already was, Manny stepped closer.

"At this time, I hate bother you but Manny there?" Juanita said, her voice breaking. "Our Lucinda—tell him I think she run away!"

"Oh, no. Let us know if we can do anything to help. Here's Manny," she said, and thrust the phone at him.

"My mother worse?" he said into the phone in Spanish, then frowned as he spoke loud and fast.

Bree didn't mean to eavesdrop, but her Spanish was good enough that she could tell what Manny was saying as he raked his hand through his hair. He insisted Lucinda would not dare run away, so had someone taken her? The conversation was all a horrible echo of her own fears for Daria. Juanita was now screaming so loud, Bree could actually hear her through the phone's mouthpiece, telling him something about a note. No, a note from Lucinda, not for ransom, Juanita was shouting as Bree and Cole moved away to give him more privacy.

"*Caramba,*" Manny said. "*Sí,* I told her if she's not proud of us to find a new family, but I didn't really mean run away."

"Manny," Bree told him, "go on home. Tell her you'll be right home."

"I coming home right now, pronto," he told his wife, digging his truck keys out of his jeans pocket.

"And call if you need help," Bree called after him as he raced for the door.

"May *Nuestro Señor* and the Virgin help us all!" he cried, and slammed the door behind him to leave only the jingling of its bell.

In the sudden silence, Bree and Cole stood staring at each other.

"I was going to say," she whispered, "when it rains, it pours, but that seems worse than a cliché right now. Every time I think the nightmare can't get worse, it does."

She realized she still clutched the camera to her. "Let's take a look at these pictures," she told him, anxious to be doing something. "Especially the few Daria shot before I dived."

He followed her over to the computer table. She opened the camera's plastic housing and downloaded the pictures to her desktop PC. In a moment, the screen displayed the array of pictures in three rows.

"Great!" Cole said. "They're in good shape."

All but the first three were underwater close-ups of the turtle grass meadow. But the first three were Daria's shots off the boat before Bree dove.

"I'm going to enlarge those," she said, clicking the zoom icon as Cole leaned over her shoulder. Despite the intensity of the moment—or maybe because of it—she could smell the tang of his aftershave or cologne. She could hear his deep, even breathing. Everything about him emanated strength, and she needed that—needed him.

Taken over the bow of the boat, Daria's

first photo was of the northwest horizon toward the storm.

"The water's still quite calm, and the storm
far off," Cole observed. "The wave height is
what the weather guys call a light chop, two-
to four-foot waves, like what I started sailing
in. Man, that baby came up hard and fast. So
if someone boarded your boat after you were
underwater, he or she—"

"She? Ben said that, too. I guess it could
have been a woman."

"So whoever didn't know the storm would
be that bad, either, that it could cover up a
crime if one was committed. But I see no
other boat on that horizon."

She selected the second picture and en-
larged it as big as she could. "One very distant
boat," she said, squinting at the screen, "but it
seems to be heading southeast—probably toward either Gordon Pass or the Marco River.
And what's that in the sky? A pelican?"

Cole leaned even closer, his brow brushing
her hair. "That or a plane. Can you move the
cursor around and blow up that part more?"

She did but they couldn't tell. A speck,
maybe even a flaw on the camera lens,
though it didn't appear in the next two photos
they examined minutely.

"She was just trying to be sure everything worked before I went down," Bree said, her voice sounding small and shaky again. "If these are the last pics she ever shot, I'll frame them."

Blinking back her tears, she skimmed through the shots she'd made below the surface. Good pictures of a bad result. Even before the storm pulled up some of the turtle grass by its roots and roiled the underwater visibility, the sea grass meadow was sparse, with puny growth and skinny, brown-tinged blades when it should be—used to be— flourishing. Yes, Marla Sherborne would have the explosive, negative report she obviously coveted. But, Bree supposed, a lot of others would be upset. Would their report be enough, as Cole had once implied, to rile some important people?

"I'd just like to rip the whole world apart looking for her," Bree admitted, putting her head in her hands so she didn't have to look at these normal, calm, beautiful pictures anymore.

"Maybe that's it," he said, kneeling by her chair and wheeling her in a half turn to face him. He pulled her hands from her teary face and held her wrists hard.

"What's it?"

"When you said 'rip apart' right now, I thought of something we've both been ignoring. When I tried to make it in to shore in the *Streamin',* I had to fight my way through a riptide the storm and currents had somehow concocted."

"A riptide. I think I swam through one, too. Yes, I remember! It tried to take me south, toward Marco Island. I went with it, then finally found my way out."

"So if Daria and or *Mermaids II* tried to get into shore—or if the boat was even adrift at that point—they could have been caught in the current and taken a lot farther from the area that the authorities and your friends have been searching."

"And that means the Ten Thousand Islands, which are like a jigsaw puzzle."

"Or, if she didn't get taken that far, she'd get caught by those crosscurrents where the Marco River comes out into the gulf."

"Big Marco Pass."

"Can we radio your dive teams to move farther south?"

"Not after the day they've already put in. We agreed their search would be over by one o'clock, and it's almost that now, with nothing found but the camera. But you could be right."

He jumped to his feet, and she leaped out of her chair. "I'll call the coast guard and talk to them about the possibility," he said.

She seized his arm. "Let's do that only if that site pans out. Otherwise, with them calling off the search at noon today, that would be like us immediately crying wolf. Come upstairs and look at an underwater marine map I was studying last night. Maybe the combination of storm and tides made a vicious current that isn't usually there—the perfect riptide."

As they thudded up the stairs to her apartment, she tried to shove away the memory of the tragic scene in the film, *The Perfect Storm.* Everything terrible had converged to sink a sturdy ship with a skilled crew, sink it in towering waves and howling wind.

She seized the map and turned it toward them. They didn't even sit but leaned over the table on their elbows. "See," she said, pointing. "See this trough the Marco River makes at Big Marco Pass? It can be deep and choppy even in normal conditions, but with extra wind and tide . . ."

"A lot of water traffic goes in and out of

Marco Island there. Maybe someone saw something."

"I'm praying that our boat's motor simply stalled and the storm ripped the anchor with its chain off the boat. She was injured or had no way to get to me if the storm shoved her in—maybe to here," she cried, pointing to small outer islands just north of Big Marco Pass. "She could be marooned anywhere here, maybe hurt. Or, like you said, a boat could have capsized right here where a riptide or rogue current shoved it into the battering of river, tide, currents and storm. And there are rock and stone jetties in that area. Cole, we've got to go look, just make a quick dive to be sure, then check islands and beaches."

"Call some divers back, because you're not going down with just me. Call Travers to use his echo sounder."

"He hates me—blames me for his son's death in Iraq," she blurted as she ran into her bedroom to grab some clothes, then continued to talk from her bathroom as she pulled on a one-piece bathing suit, then a spandex dive suit. "We dated for years, high school sweethearts, then went to the same college. But I broke up with him and Ted enlisted!"

she called to him. She tore back out into the living room. He did a double take when he saw she was dressed to dive.

"Bree, I said, call somebody else for help. The riptide—your coordinates—it's just another possibility."

"I'm going. I'm sure our other boat has been returned by now. Just a quick look, then a call to the coast guard and/or the police dive team. They'll really check it out—if I see anything there . . ."

"If you *and* the others you're going to dive with see anything there," he corrected.

He grabbed her by both arms to halt her path toward the door and gave her a little shake. "For starters, we need somebody to man the boat if we're both going down."

"You'll go with me? I promise, no surprises like the dive into the Trade Wreck. But we'll have to get close up to see things, because the vis will be low there."

"I think it's a good place to check, but—I don't care what you say—I'm calling Travers. We need someone to stay on the boat and someone else to go down with us."

"You're right," she said, nodding. Anything to get him to go down with her—to let her go. "My dad used to say only fools break the rules, and I got you cut doing that yesterday. All right, we'll call Sam. However much I used to think I couldn't trust him, he's been helping me now, because he said he didn't blame Daria for what happened to his son."

"Meaning he still blames you." He looked down intently into her eyes. "I guess it's none of my business, but did you really love Ted Travers? That's a lot to handle. His death, now—"

"Now Daria's?" she challenged, hands on hips.

"I didn't say that. I was going to say her being missing."

She gripped his wrists hard, feeling sinews, muscles and bones, so solid in her trembling world. "I keep clinging to the fact we are so close—Daria and I. I'm hoping I'd feel—I'd know—if she were really gone. But she can't be gone. I won't *let* her be gone!"

"Then let's get some help and get going."

"All right—yes," she said, and gave him a quick hug. She started to pull away, but he anchored her hard to him.

They clung full length, both holding tight, Bree standing on tiptoe with her arms clamped around his neck and his around her waist. She turned her face into the side of his throat and felt his pulse pounding there. Her blood pressure was surely off the charts. The top of her head fit perfectly under his chin. Her breasts pressed flat to his hard chest and her thighs to his. She was toned, but his flesh was harder, his entire body like the wood his big hands fashioned. She felt swept away, outside herself.

She had not answered his question about loving Ted. She guessed she had once, an adolescent love, fierce then faded. Although she'd been with Cole only three days now, they'd been in such a seething cauldron it seemed she'd needed and wanted him forever. But it was the impact of her own desire that stunned her. This man, she told herself, as they finally, shakily stepped apart, made that jolt of lightning that had hit her seem like nothing.

9

As they left Turtle Bay in the smaller of Sam's two slow barges, Cole almost wished he hadn't pushed Bree to call Travers for help. It wasn't so much Travers's bleary-eyed employee who captained the sluggish vessel nor the two divers who worked for Sam that worried him, but the spearguns they were cleaning.

Cole had never hunted with spearguns, and these babies looked fierce. "State-of-the-art," one guy boasted, and explained to him how they worked.

The weapons had small carbon-dioxide bottles slung beneath their shafts, so a squeeze of the trigger released a burst of gas and fired the spear with a velocity that could not be matched by older guns. The spearheads were bulky and contained .357 magnum cartridges that would explode on impact, driving the shafts deeper and springing out the prongs they proudly demonstrated to Cole while Bree was talking to the captain in the engine house. They showed him how the shaft clipped to their weight belts.

"You aren't going to dive with those today," Cole said, more a statement than a question.

Ric, who looked like a young Arnold Schwarzenegger, muscles and all, just nodded. Lance, the thin, red-haired guy, said, "Usually do, in case we see something we don't like—or something we do, for dinner."

"With four of us diving in murky water, it doesn't sound safe," Cole countered.

"Nothing too safe about looking for debris in soupy water in a boat channel anyhow," Ric said. "But I guess we can leave the guns on board for once. If we have to pass up a big grouper though, it'd be real nice if you'd spring for a fish dinner."

Cole could not believe they'd consider

fishing on a dive as critical as this one, but it must be just more business to them. "You guys and Sam have been very helpful. Yeah, I'll do just that," he promised.

He was glad Bree hadn't overheard the conversation. She was standing at the stern now, staring into the water, so she didn't hear the divers or his agreeing to their bribe. But then, maybe she did hear, because he was amazed at how acute her listening powers seemed to be. It had worried him when she'd said she'd heard and seen more things than she should after Daria went missing. At first he thought she meant she was seeing ghosts, or some sort of visions of her sister, but that wasn't it—he hoped.

He walked aft and leaned on the taffrail beside her. Partly blocking their view, heavy wire cables and a big hook hung from the winch spool; he wondered how much dead weight this barge could lift out of the water, but he didn't feel like asking Sam's divers. For some reason, Sam had not been able to come along, but said he'd be out in a smaller boat soon to see how they were doing. Cole's protective instincts about Bree made him want to tell Sam he ought to let bygones be just that, where Bree was concerned.

Sam had told his captain to anchor on the north side of the channel and float several dive flags. Hopefully, those would slow boats and Jet Skis coming in and out of the Marco River even more than the No Wake and Slow—Manatee Zone signs already did.

"I'm glad we're in this scow, even if it is a bit slow," Cole told Bree, intentionally trying to lift her spirits. Her fierce determination had ebbed to a quiet moodiness. "In the crosscurrents there, it will give us a stable diving platform."

"Despite its flat bottom," she said with a sigh, "a boat the length of *Mermaids II* would have been anything but stable there in that bad storm."

"Do you sense something?" he asked. "I mean, that we're getting closer to answers—to the boat or Daria?"

"Not exactly that," she said, frowning out at the churning wake of the barge. "It's just that she *has* to be alive. I know she is. I want answers and yet I fear them. This possible scenario seems so possible. I've seen wrecks in the gulf, both ships and airplanes, but it just can't be *my* boat and *my* sister! But then," she said, her voice softer, "I'll bet poor

Manny and Juanita are saying it can't be *their* girl who ran away."

"You don't mean that you think Daria could have run away, staged something . . ."

"No, no!" she said, covering her ears like a child. "She has no reason to. She's not the type to do that. I know my sister like—like the back of my own hand. Except," she added, staring dazedly at the back of her hand in the bright sun, "one of the mirror-image things about us was that I'm right-handed and she's a leftie. Lefties always feel a little different from others. It was the earliest thing that made us feel we weren't one and the same."

He took her hand in his. "Bree, why don't you stay on board with the captain and let me go down alone with Sam's divers?"

"Because having a fourth diver could make a difference in low vis. If you reported nothing was there, I'd have to prove it to myself. And if something is there, I'd have to be on-site, look for clues of how the boat broke up."

She tugged her hand back and hit both fists on the rail, then, obviously fighting tears, whispered, "Cole, I don't know what I would have done without you, even after you got me breathing again and to the hospital. You've been my life preserver in more ways than one, but I know you have a life to go back to."

"I do need to drive to Miami soon to look over a yacht for a big client I might take on. Actually, it's Dom Verdugo's casino cruise boat. I was going to turn him down flat, but I think he bears watching and that would be a good way to keep an eye on him. To tell you the truth, my mother was a gambling addict and ruined her life—and almost Dad's and mine—that way. I'm not sure, but her accidental death may have actually been suicide. Beyond needing this big commission, I'd like to see Verdugo's plans and boat stopped somehow."

"I'm sorry about your mother. I can imagine how terrible that must have been—losing a mother tragically," she whispered, squeezing his hand.

She sniffed hard and abruptly turned away to check her gear, which she had laid out behind her on a metal bench. He raked his fingers through his hair. He was a selfish jerk to bring his own family problems up right now, but that had just spilled out. He'd kept what Dad had called their "dirty linen" secret for years, penned up inside, without even telling his wife much about it, yet here he was sharing it with Bree.

As Cole started to recheck his gear, too, the boat began to rock and roll, as he always called such movement in crosscurrents. On the barge the motion was subtle, not like in a sailboat where the helmsman could feel every shift and shake intimately.

He admitted to himself that he was yearning to be that way with Bree, to be able to read her, to sense her movements and moods like a sleek ship under his command, although he knew he'd never control her any more than he could the sea. Still, like the best sailing on the *Streamin'*, it could be a beautiful union. But the shaky ship that was Briana Devon right now was in rough waters, and he prayed she wouldn't break apart. Cole shook his head to clear it, but Ric's voice cut short his agonizing.

"We're here," he yelled. "Let's dive."

For Bree, it was like being in the storm again.

Even with all the diving she'd done in low-vis water, she was not prepared for the impact of this dive on her body and her brain. She felt the heavy, gray weight of the water and the push and pull of powerful currents as if she swam through an Everglades swamp. All around in the wide channel that was the mouth of the Marco River, where it met the tides and waves of the gulf, eddies of sand and silt shifted and resettled. The dark bottom was like a writhing, living being, devouring things then spitting them back up.

Ordinarily, if a diver stopped kicking and swimming for a minute, low-vis water would clear a bit but not here. She could see only about four feet ahead, even with the high-powered lights Sam's divers had provided. Thank heavens, they each had a writing slate tied to their weight belts, because even hand signals from the others were hard to read.

So she stuck close to Cole, or he to her, she wasn't sure which. The four of them meticulously followed the typical search-and-salvage spiral-pattern grid they had agreed on before they'd left Sam's dock. After marking their starting point on the bottom in the middle of the channel, at two arms' width apart, they swam side by side in a widening circle. Occasionally, they switched positions because the divers to the east and west took the brunt of the buffeting currents.

They also had to swim low because yachts with deep drafts occasionally went overhead, though even with the biggest, the divers had almost fifteen feet of clearance. They'd swum about forty feet from their dive boat to begin; they would have to be even more careful when they surfaced to come up at the site they'd marked.

However much Bree had always loved diving, even under challenging conditions, and despite the fact it was at her insistence this search had been set up, she was suddenly panicked to get out. She should have listened to Cole about not diving. This was a desperate, stupid scheme. The coastal waters of the gulf were huge—as big as the gap between Amelia and the twins, as big as between poor Manny and his daughter right now. Daria and the boat could be anywhere out here.

Bree's acute hearing was bothering her. She should have worn plastic earplugs. The ping-ping or low, reverberating buzz of motors overhead, the occasional clank of a dive knife or gauge into a tank down here, the sound of all their bubbles fighting toward the surface—the shriek of fear in her own head and heart . . .

When someone's dive light accidentally swept her way, it almost blinded her as the glare stabbed deep into her brain. Even the dull reflection of a beam off Lance's face mask was too bright. Yet maybe, since she was seeing better than she would have otherwise, it would help her to find things down here. She forced herself to try to pierce the swirling waters just as they all made a turn to the south.

Her eyes caught the grayish glint of metal. It could be anything thrown over or lost from a boat. But it looked to be a curved aluminum handrail, like the one that led up from the diving platform to the stern deck of *Mermaids II*. She gave a kick away from the men and touched the cold metal, half-buried in sand and silt.

Dented and bent, broken, it seemed to point a bit farther out, luring her on. Cole swam with her, behind her; she wasn't sure where the other two were, only that she had to go on, off their search grid, off the ends of the earth, if she must.

Then she saw a four-foot piece of gleaming white metal, also partly buried, but it looked new or well cared for, like their dive boat had been. She brushed sand away from a part of it and uncovered a jagged piece of what was once the stern of a boat. Her and Daria's boat. She was certain, because part of the name *Mermaids II* was there in the bent and broken metal, painted bold and bright in the beam of her light: *MA D I*

Bree gasped so hard, she choked on her mouthpiece and almost spit it out. Cole grabbed her wrist, but she yanked away and swam on, sweeping her light right and left, down, around, as if something drew her like a powerful magnet. Ahead, looming large, in the deepest part of the channel, at a slight tilt, rested the main deck and wheelhouse of their dive boat. It looked fairly intact.

Good, she told herself. That surely meant Daria could have weathered the worst of the storm and gotten to shore before it went down. But this area was so heavily populated, why hadn't someone found her by now?

But then . . . then . . .

Awed, horrified, Bree swam closer, upward to peer in through the side window of the wheelhouse. Trembling, she trained her light through the glass to look inside.

And there, floating near the top of the ceiling, her hands lifted and her hair shifting in the water as to hide her once beautiful face, her sister, her other self, was trapped inside.

Cole could barely keep up with Bree; for a moment he'd lost sight of her in this thick water. All at once, she'd seemed to know where she was going, kicking hard toward he didn't know what. But he was certain they had found the wreck of the boat.

And then he saw the bulk of the sunken ship. The hull had a huge piece missing, or was just caved in, but the small upright, half-glass wheelhouse looked intact. Intact—and within . . . Daria?

Floating inside, her hair streaming loose and free, was a woman, or what had been a woman before being trapped two days in the graveyard of the sea. Her skin looked loose and greenish, mottled. And he saw Bree meant to go inside to her.

He kicked harder and reached for Bree. She tried to shake him off. She dropped her light and put both hands to the doorknob, braced her fins on the side of the wheelhouse and tried to wrench the door open. Cole seized both her wrists, shoved her feet off the metal, got his mask right next to hers and shook his head, no. No!

He would never forget the look in her wide eyes: shock, terror, fury and tears. *Up!* He pointed. *We go back, get help,* he tried to gesture.

To his surprise, she reached for her slate and scribbled, "Can't leave her here," then shone his light on it.

Without going for his own slate, he wrote on hers, "Crime scene?"

He was grateful when she nodded. Then she broke his heart, going closer to the window of the wheelhouse and putting both her palms against it as if she gave some sort of blessing—or as if she could embrace her sister's body through the barriers of glass and death.

On board, after holding out hope and pushing herself for so long, Bree collapsed in tears. Cole led her into the small supply room aft on the barge and, leaving the door ajar for air and light, sat on a huge coil of ropes next to her. She didn't want to be held, but she kept a tight hold of his hand. She was shaking, in shock, he figured, but he knew she'd never agree to go ashore right now. Besides, until Sam or the authorities showed up, he had no way to get her there.

Sam's men radioed both the coast guard and the Naples Police dive team. The already busy waterway quickly became a hub of activity. Gawkers lined the edge of the river and boats huddled close; the press arrived by boats, trying to get video and interviews. Bree and Cole hid out, but they could hear Ric and Lance answering shouted questions. Finally, Sam arrived.

"Sorry for your loss," he told Bree gruffly as he stood in the doorway of the small supply room, arms crossed over his chest. "Obviously, I know whereof I speak, losing someone nearest to you."

Cole glared at the man. Although they had him to thank for the means to discover and recover the ship, it was hard to feel grateful to him.

Sam plunged on, "Don't know if foul play has a part in this, but there's always something foul about the death of a healthy, vital, young person, especially one dearly loved. In a ways, someone's always to blame. I've known that for years, even if you're just finally learning it."

"Stow it," Cole demanded. "Have a heart, man."

"I had one once, but got it shattered," he said. When Cole made a motion to rise, Sam left them alone again.

"I don't suppose he's right about foul play," Bree said in a monotone, the first time she'd spoken for an hour. "He was probably only trying to make his point about my screwing up Ted's life again. The evidence will probably point to her not handling the storm somehow and the boat going down in it."

"With that storm, it will be hard to convince people of anything else, but I'm sure they'll do an investigation."

"If they don't, I will. She was good with the boat—with swimming, too, you know."

"Of course she was, but you need to concentrate on a funeral and getting your life back together."

"But . . . without her, it may just seem like half a life. I need to call Amelia and Ben. Could you get my cell in my stuff?"

"Sure. Be right back."

When he returned, a Naples Police officer

was talking to her. Though he stood back, Cole overheard what they were telling her, especially the word he'd been afraid to say—*autopsy.*

"I understand," she was saying in a terrible monotone that didn't sound like her. But he remembered mourning, the out-of-body feeling of it where you moved and talked but weren't really there. With a sick-in-the-gut feeling, he pictured again his mother's body, drowned, though she hadn't been in the water as long as Daria was. He and his dad had put their arms around each other and sobbed.

"How long," she was asking the officer, "before I can have her—have her back and we'll know the cause of death?"

"I can't tell for sure, Ms. Devon. It will be up to the coroner, but of course, as soon as possible."

When the man moved away, Cole returned to sit beside her and handed her her cell. The moment she turned it on, it played "Under The Sea," the bouncy tune from a Disney animated movie. For a second, he couldn't recall the movie's name or why he'd seen it. Oh, yeah, he remembered—*The Little Mermaid.* He'd taken a client's kids to see it when the parents had the flu a couple of years ago.

"Lots of missed calls," she told him, swiping at tears on her cheeks. "Can word have spread that fast already? Amelia will hear it from someone else. I should have called her right away, because she's all I have now . . . but I want to go back down to Daria. I want to be with her when they bring her up."

"Sweetheart, you can't. They'll take good care of her, bring her up in a body bag so no one can see. It's out of your hands now—"

"I know. I know."

Suddenly, she exploded into sucking, gasping sobs and threw herself across his lap and clung to him. With his foot, Cole closed the storeroom door and, tears running down his face, held her hard to him.

That night, Bree swam from dark dream to dark dream. She and Ted stood together on the deck of the *Titanic* as it went down into icy waters—no, that was Daria beside her, going down, down under the sea . . . voices somewhere . . . Ben, Amelia. Had they drugged her? Was she back in the hospital. No, this was her own bed.

She dived again, swimming hard to get

to the wreck of her life. The sign with the boat's name was still there, broken, distorted: *MA D I*

Only one mermaid left now, just Bree alone. And she was mad. "I am mad," she changed the sign to say, scribbling on Cole's slate. I am furious and I am crazed with anger and pain. She beat her fists on the glass of the wheelhouse to get Daria's attention. Wake up, wake up! Swimming around inside, she was swimming when she should have been steering the boat. Had the storm killed her? The iceberg? Or something else?

Daria turned to her and waved, mouthing the words, *Come on in. The water's fine . . . .*

Bree tried to pull the wheelhouse door open. Tried and tried, but Cole wouldn't help her, and Daria shook her head and tried to hold it shut.

"No, I have to go to her!" she screamed at Cole. "I have to find her, find out what happened!" Someone shrieked those words so close that it woke Bree up.

It was her own voice. Thank God, just a dream! But waking reality was just as bad.

She sat up amid the sheets she'd churned to huge waves around her. The bedside digital clock read 3:00 a.m. and her bedroom

10

Manny was furious that the police refused to start looking for Lucinda for at least forty-eight hours. They'd said she was just another teenage girl who'd left a note she was running away, and they saw that "all the time." Not with my daughter, Manny had insisted, but he knew this was all Lucinda's fault.

Still, all afternoon, and again when the high school let out, he drove the streets of Immokalee, looking for her. He stared at clumps of kids as they walked home, boarded buses or hung around. Lots of *chicas* resembled his youngest daughter—but none were. Didn't door was ajar. Lights came on in the hall, and Amelia rushed in, wearing silk pajamas. She had huge half circles of black mascara under her eyes.

"I'm here, I'm here," Amelia said, sitting on the bed and reaching out to hug Bree. For one moment, Bree just stared at her.

That's right, Amelia and Ben were here, though Bree had hated to see Cole leave.

"You—are you sleeping in her bed?" Bree stammered.

"No, of course not. On the sofa. Ben said not to touch anything of hers."

Maybe he thought something was strange about Daria's death—or else he was just being himself, a trained criminal lawyer who was now a prosecuting attorney. Amelia kept saying over and over, "Bree, I'm so sorry— so, so sorry! So, so sorry . . ."

So Bree pulled Amelia into her arms and comforted her.

Lucinda know that human trafficking was a growing problem in South Florida? Sure, most of the girls abducted and forced into prostitution were from Guatemala, but it could happen if she was found wandering the streets. She looked as Hispanic as those poor women who were either sold by impoverished families or just plain abducted. Didn't Lucinda know she could ruin her life, much worse than she was ruining his?

When he'd gotten home, he'd learned Juanita had called Lucinda's Latina friends. They weren't sure who her Anglo friends were. Like poor Bree, he was out looking for a lost girl, when the news he'd been expecting and fearing came over his car radio.

"Boat debris and the body of missing Turtle Bay resident, Daria Devon, has been discovered underwater in Big Marco Pass. Although the coast guard and civil air patrol have been searching for her since she disappeared during the storm on Tuesday, the discovery was made by her identical twin sister and business partner, Briana Devon. Authorities, including the county coroner, are now on the scene. Daria and Briana Devon owned and operated the Two Mermaids Search and Salvage Shop, and are sisters-in-law of Ben Westcott, Collier County prosecuting attorney. Daria Devon and her sister were currently overseeing the Save Our Sea Grass project for the Clear the Gulf Commission and . . ."

Manny pulled into the parking lot of Our Lady of Guadalupe Church and, gripping the steering wheel, pressed his forehead to his hands. They—*Bree*—had found the body. Now came worse suspicions and, maybe, accusations. He could only hope it would be ruled an accident to avoid all that.

Despite his trials, Manny hadn't cried for years—not *macho.* But now, tears ran down his wrists; some plopped onto the knees of his jeans. Too much . . . too many things out of his control. He owed it to Bree to be with her, to help comfort her, even though she'd gone starry-eyed over Cole DeRoca. And she had her other sister and her big-man husband to call if she needed them. *Caramba,* if there was any hint of someone hurting Daria . . .

"An autopsy will be performed," the radio voice went on, "to discover the cause of death and rule out any possibility of foul play."

Foul play—foul play! Play was a *stupido* word for such a horrible thing.

Manny jumped when his cell phone rang. He swiped away tears with his sleeve and reached for it on the passenger seat. It would be his wife on the line, probably to tell the bad news about Daria—or, God forbid, something about Lucinda.

"Que pasa?"

"It's Lucinda," Juanita said in her quick Spanish. "She came home because she heard Daria is dead. Did you hear?"

"*Sí. Muy malo!* At least something good can come of that if the news brings Lucinda home. Give her the phone."

"She says she's sorry. She went right into your mama and told her she is very sorry. She's been with friends—her Anglo girl-friends, no boys, she says."

"I'm coming right home, then I have to go see Bree, help if I can, after . . ."

"After what?"

"I'll be right there. And that *chica* better be waiting," he muttered and punched off.

On the short drive home, he berated himself. He'd caused Daria's death, and Bree knew it. If he'd just been there, she'd said. But in a way, it was his defiant daughter and his beloved mother who had caused it. Too much pressure on him. He needed control of his family and he needed money. *Es necesario!* And half of the salvage business was now his. He'd done what he had to do.

Fists clenched, blood pounding, he banged into the house, furious with himself, his daughter and the world. Juanita met him at the door, holding up both hands to halt his steps.

"Get her out here," he ordered, walking past Juanita, then turning back to face her in the small, cluttered kitchen. He lowered his voice. "My sick mother does not need to hear this. Lucinda's not hiding behind her or you. I said, get her out here."

"I said she's very sorry. She learned her lesson," Juanita pleaded. "Don't let your temper get the best of you, because it can be the worst of you."

By the next afternoon, Bree had sobbed herself sick, then gone stoic. When their pastor dropped by, she had asked him if they could use the little Turtle Bay Community Church for the funeral. The twins loved the church, with its seaside ambience. When they stood up to sing a hymn, they could see the bay and God's great sea beyond, and the congregation was so Deep South friendly.

But Pastor Wallace had been right to sug-
gest that, weather willing, they hold the funeral in the back of the church on the lawn,
overlooking the bay. "The family of the bereaved," as he put it, had many friends, and
with the publicity, a lot of strangers might
also come to pay their condolences.

Would someone who wished her or Daria
ill because of their report about the toxic gulf
water be among those strangers? Bree had
wondered silently. Surely, not among those
who knew her.

Bree had put in a few frantic hours. She
had met with her and Daria's lawyer about
Daria's will. Because of the sometimes dangerous work they did, they both had wills with
each other as the beneficiary. If they were
both deceased, there were bequests left for
Amelia's sons. They'd used the only lawyer in
Turtle Bay because they feared Ben would try
to control everything. At Daria's suggestion,
they had recently added a codicil that, should
one of them die or leave the business, Manny
would become a full partner.

After her visit to the lawyer, Bree, Amelia
and Ben picked out a coffin and arranged for
a funeral home and the burial of Daria next to
their parents, though Amelia kept protesting

that she should have her own grave site, even if it was in the same cemetery. The grave site their father had bought when Mother died had a third plot next to her grave, although they weren't sure why. "Maybe the deal was for three plots, so your dad just bought the extra," Ben had said.

All this, and they still didn't have the body released for burial—nor did they have answers, Bree thought. She promised to drive to Ben and Amelia's to have dinner with them and see the boys later, but as soon as they were gone, Cole came over.

"No word on when we'll hear," she blurted when she saw him at the door. They hugged in greeting, and he kissed her cheek. He looked exhausted.

"I probably taste as salty as the gulf from crying," she told him.

"Blood, sweat and tears."

"Something like that."

"How are you holding up?"

Arm in arm, like old friends or contented lovers, they walked toward the sofa. "Cole, I'm just praying the coroner and police come up with a foolproof ruling of accidental death. I—I can't believe it could be anything else." She sat next to him, turning toward him with one leg bent, and hugged a throw pillow to her chest to keep from crawling into his lap as she had on Sam's barge.

"Surely not," he said, covering one hand with his. "Have you been through her things?"

"Ben said not to, in case it does become a criminal investigation. He—it's just that he's trained to think that way. He's seen too many bad situations. I can't be wrong in thinking that this is just a horrible, freak tragedy. I know I was wrong in thinking she was alive all this time when she obviously wasn't, but it's just that I couldn't bear to accept she could be lost—dead."

"I suppose when you've been so close to someone, it's hard to admit that as adults, your connection might not be quite as strong."

She frowned at him. "We may have liked some different things and had some different friends, but we knew all that about each other. It has to be an accident, for heaven's sake! People don't just stroll up and surprise you miles out in the gulf. I still can't recall hearing a boat motor. I didn't even hear her start our boat's motor, and I'm very familiar with its sound, even underwater."

The street doorbell rang, and Bree jumped up as if it had been a fire alarm. "Maybe one of our friends," she said, starting for the stairs. "They've dropped off enough food to feed an army, but Amelia still insists on cooking tonight. If it's another reporter, I'm not opening the door."

She heard Cole come down the steps behind her. It was strange—she'd only known him for three days, but she trusted him completely, just as she did Manny, Amelia and Ben. She crossed the office, running her hand along Daria's desk, and glanced out through the locked door. A good-looking middle-aged couple stood there with serious, almost pained looks on their faces.

"You know them?" Cole asked behind her.

"No."

"I can tell them you're not seeing anyone."

"Since I'm seeing them and vice versa right now, I'll just ask them what they want." She unlocked and opened the door. "May I help you?"

The woman spoke. "We're Vivian and Frank Holliman, friends of Daria's from her accounting class."

"Oh."

"Of course, the entire class and instructor

send their deepest sympathies, and we are so very sorry for your terrible loss. But we're here to speak with you about something that can't wait. Perhaps Daria didn't mention our names to you, but of course, she told you about her plans to be a spokesperson for Shells Eternal."

"No. What is Shells Eternal?"

"Oh, dear," Vivian Holliman said with a roll of her blue eyes. "You see, she made plans for her own burial at sea."

Cole couldn't believe Bree asked the couple upstairs or was listening to them with rapt attention as the Hollimans sat on the sofa and Cole and Bree took the wicker rockers. Bree had hers tipped forward, almost upright. When they'd announced the reason for their visit, Bree had looked completely stunned. She must have thought at first that they meant Daria had planned her funeral ahead, then committed suicide. Now she looked as if she was seething but keeping the lid on her temper. The whole damn thing smelled like a con game to him.

The Hollimans had explained that they represented a business that sank large, sculpted, concrete seashells onto the sandy floor of the gulf. In carefully constructed niches, the shells sheltered the cremated ashes of people. Accompanying plaques served as headstones.

Cole studied them as they did the fast talking. Viv, as she asked to be called, had pure white hair but a young face and a great body for her age; Frank was bald and was the better dresser of the two, including his expensive wristwatch and diamond-and-onyx ring. Bree had started out by demanding how well they knew Daria before they segued smoothly into a well-honed sales pitch.

"We really are an ecology-conscious business, and that appealed to Daria," Frank went on. "As her business partner and a fellow diver, I'm sure it does you, too. And the fact that Daria loved the sea, made promotion for Shells Eternal a perfect match for her. She agreed to be our spokesperson in exchange for a fee and a gratis eternal shells resting place when she passed on."

"Of course," Viv went on as if they were a tag team, "we—and she—didn't expect that she would actually have the need for that for decades. But the point is, she was extremely taken by a photo we showed her of one of our beautiful shells—"

"Offshore at Tampa," Frank put in, "though the next one will be near Naples."

"Our goal is for the shells to be covered with algae, barnacles, soft coral and small sponges, except for the bronze plaques with names and dates of the deceased. Of course, being a diver yourself, you could easily visit the site. A person who loved the water, the gulf, that much should surely have her cremains rest there, even though she can't be our spokesperson now. Actually, we were hoping *you* might consider our offer now—in honor of Daria's wishes."

"Her cremains?" Cole said when Bree just stared at them.

"Cremated remains," Viv explained. "Our ads urge our ecologically minded customers to think outside the box, and Daria did that. I'm so sorry she didn't mention to you that she was interested in a partnership with us."

Cole could almost read Bree's expression. She'd been struggling to smother her emotions since her hysteria in his arms on Travers's barge, but her eyes widened and she looked as if she'd throttle these two. Somehow she managed to unclench her fists and grip her hands together as if in prayer.

"Daria didn't mention it," she told the Hollimans, "but I assure you, your offer is so . . . unusual that she surely would have told me about it. We lived together, we shared our business and—"

"But she took the accounting class alone," Viv put in, starting to look miffed. "We were hoping you would honor her wishes."

"I assume, since this so-called partnership was so far advanced, you have a contract or some sort of written agreement from her you could show me."

"We were preparing one for her to sign," Frank said, sitting forward on the sofa. "We can bring you a copy of that, of course, or amend it to suit you."

"What would suit me is for you to leave now," Bree said, rising. "Our family has already made burial arrangements, and I'm not interested in Shells Eternal."

The couple stood, reluctantly, even angrily, Cole could tell. He couldn't believe their gall.

"It's not unusual, you know," Viv said, "for someone as young as Daria not to want to upset those dear to her by talking about death."

"And I assure you," Frank put in as they moved toward the door of the apartment, with Bree leading and Cole bringing up the rear, "that this is not some sort of scam, though I can tell you think so. You can check our Web site, talk to the families of those who already rest under the sea."

"Our search for Daria, and now her death—" Bree choked on that last word "—have made Daria quite high-profile. Anyone could read about her background."

"I repeat," Viv said, "we are sorry for your loss and deeply regret you cannot honor her wishes. I would have assumed she shared this with you."

Cole figured the Hollimans were lucky Bree didn't just shove them down the stairs.

The bell gave a last jingle as she closed the door to the street firmly behind them and leaned against it.

"Do you believe that?" she asked, smacking her hands on her thighs. "If I wasn't so desperate for any lead about what could have happened to her, I would have thrown them out the moment they said their motto was Think Outside the Box." As they went back upstairs together, she went on. "You don't think those people are bizarre enough that they would harm someone just to get publicity for their concrete shells, do you?"

"I can check them out online. They would hardly have said all that if it was totally bogus. My guess is the business is legit and they just thought they could use a high-profile former scuba-diver to give them sympathy and credibility. And they could get you, Daria's look-alike, to be in their emotion-packed ads."

"They said they were in her accounting class, so that's easy to check." At the top of the stairs, he put his arms around her and felt her shudder. "What scares me," she said as she laid her head against his chest, "is that suspecting those off-the-wall people of harming Daria makes as much sense as suspecting anyone else. I don't think she had an enemy in the world—but if she did and if someone could possibly have hurt her, have I inherited them now?"

Being with her nephews lifted Bree's spirits, though both James and Jordan telling her they were going to miss Aunt Daria pierced her heart. "Now you and Mom get to be best friends, 'stead of you and Aunt Daria," six-year-old Jordan told Bree. Amelia stopped stirring the spaghetti sauce; her eyes met Bree's over the steam.

"Yes, that's right," Bree managed.

"Okay, you two," Amelia told her boys, "go put those *Star Wars* action figures away, wash your hands and come back down for dinner. See if Daddy's off the phone yet, and tell him to wash up, too."

"But we aren't done yet—Anakin is going to turn into Darth Vader and be really bad soon," Jordan, the younger, protested. "See, Anakin used to be good but he's going over to the dark side."

Amelia turned to face the kids. From her seat on a stool at the breakfast bar, Bree thought Amelia looked absolutely stricken by something they'd just said.

"I don't want to hear that kind of thing," she told them, her voice as stern as her face. "Why can't you play with something that has good people in it?"

As if to defend his younger brother, James said, "Luke Skywalker and Yoda are good, and Chewbacca. Sorry, Mom, I know you been crying a lot."

"Yes," Bree said, reaching out to put a hand on each of their heads. "Your mother's tired and sad, so you two go do what she says, all right? And when she works hard on a meal like this, you can both help by eating really well."

"And wash those hands until you've sung all the Birthday Song," Amelia shouted after them.

"The Birthday Song? What's that about?" Bree asked. It felt good to be talking about little, normal things, though her pain and loss sat so heavy on her chest it was an actual physical pain. Surely, that was why Amelia was so strung-out.

"Their idea of washing hands is zip, zip. If they sing 'Happy Birthday To You' all the way through, they get some of the grime gone. Bree, that was really weird about the Eternal Shells stuff—bizarre. Had Daria ever, ever talked about cremation instead of burial?"

"Only in a general way, that for some people it might make more ecological sense, but I don't think she ever felt visiting Mom and Dad's graves was morbid. We always thought it was pretty and peaceful there. We went once in a while and left flowers, tried to concentrate on the good things and happy memories."

Amelia pressed her lips together before she gave the sauce another swift stir and turned back toward the kitchen sink. Bree could see her face only in the reflection of the window. "It's good you two went," she said quietly. "I—I just can't face that place any more than I could being under all that water when you two used to dive with Dad so much."

The front doorbell rang, the chimes beautiful. But then, Bree thought, everything in this house was beautiful and beautifully kept. "Are you expecting anyone?" she asked.

"No, and if it's those Eternal Shells people trying to get to us now, they'll get a sieve of wet pasta dumped on them. Ben will get it. He said he'd man the phones and watch the door. The neighbors have been really nice about dropping things off to eat, but I just needed to make something myself tonight for us, for you. As if there's any such thing as comfort food at a time like this."

Bree heard voices, a man and woman. Surely, the Hollimans had not come here. Ben appeared in the kitchen door, his face solemn.

"What? Who is it?" Amelia asked.

"Josh and Nikki Austin," he said, looking at Bree. "Josh says he's been pushing the coroner for a fast decision and he has something to tell us."

Bree's legs went weak as she followed

Ben into the living room and Amelia followed. She went to the broad staircase and called up it, "You two can play a little longer, and I'll call you when you can come down!"

Bree could not read Josh's expression. All those years she'd known him, and she could not psych out what he was going to say.

Nikki looked as if she hadn't slept, with smudges under her eyes as if she'd been crying. Bree was touched that she was evidently taking a stranger's death so to heart, but then perhaps something else had upset her. Nikki's jaw was set hard, as if to keep herself from dissolving in emotion. Bree empathized with the woman; she felt the same herself.

Josh hugged Bree while Nikki hugged Amelia, then Bree. Nikki smelled of expensive perfume. She hugged quickly and lightly, then stepped back to perch on the edge of the deep leather couch beside her husband.

Some movement outside caught Bree's attention through the window behind the couch. In the gathering dusk, standing beside a dark car by the street curb, waited the Austins' jack-of-all-trades, Mark Denton, whom Bree had briefly glimpsed in the hospital. Was he their chauffeur, as well as PR man, pilot and bodyguard?

"As I told Ben," Josh said, "he's not the only one who's been pulling strings with the coroner for quick answers, for all of your sakes, as well as to just get this settled."

"We're grateful for your concern."

Josh nodded. "At least I have some answers for you. There will probably be a few other results later—blood and toxicology tests, for example."

"She wasn't drinking or on drugs," Bree put in.

To her surprise, Nikki spoke, uncrossing then recrossing her long legs. "Of course, Josh is always concerned for all his constituents, but as Briana and Daria were childhood friends, this is especially important to him."

Daria was much more than a childhood friend to Josh, and Bree recalled that Nikki knew that. Marla Sherborne had said she'd mentioned that Josh had dated Daria.

"I admit," Josh said, "because Briana and Daria have been at the forefront of the efforts to monitor the problems with the gulf water, I've gotten more deeply involved than I might have otherwise. I know you have a key report to unveil soon, Bree, and it would be best to have things settled and Daria at rest before that. And, for your sake, Ben, too. With the election coming up, you need answers and closure."

"We all do," Bree said. "Just tell us the coroner's ruling."

Josh exhaled through flared nostrils. "Accidental death. The autopsy showed she hit her head very hard in the back. The shape of the skull fracture suggests she fell against the steering wheel and was knocked unconscious, perhaps in the rough sea. The medical language says, 'a compression fracture in the occipital region of the skull with internal hemorrhages.' The exact cause of death, though, was drowning, no doubt when the boat drifted ashore, hit the concrete breakwater wall—they think they've found the place—and went down in the choppy channel of Big Marco Pass. They've decided not to raise the wreck, so it will remain there as a memorial of the tragedy. Officially, the wreck of *Mermaids II* is off-limits because of diving dangers in Marco Pass."

Nikki put in, "Of all the terrible, possible

scenarios for the accident, that ruling seems the best, at least."

Nothing was the best, Bree wanted to shout, but at least now, surely, with this accidental ruling, she could put her mind at rest.

11

It was nearly ten o'clock that night when Bree entered Daria's room. She had phoned Cole to tell him the results of the autopsy. He'd told her not to do anything until after the funeral, now scheduled for Monday, and had volunteered to put off driving to Miami to check out Dom Verdugo's casino boat tomorrow so he could be with her.

She had insisted he go ahead with his plans. She knew she had to let him get on with his life, though she didn't want him to go back to a life without her in it. If anything good had come from the tragedy of losing Daria, finding Cole was it. And, perhaps, a better relationship with Amelia down the long, tough road without her twin, her other self.

"I'll see you when you get back. I'll be here and I'll be just fine," Bree had assured Cole, though the truth was that she was anything but fine.

As Bree began to go through her sister's possessions, she felt her presence so strongly it was as if she were in the room. She could almost believe Daria would appear in the mussed bedsheets still shaped to her form. When Bree glanced through the medicine cabinet, she felt as if her sister might emerge from behind the shower curtain, her hair soaked, as if from the sea.

Bree gasped when she caught sight of herself in the bathroom mirror. Her mirror image, indeed! It was as if a distraught Daria stared at her from beyond the fragile barrier of the glass.

She forced herself to look away and put both hands on the washbasin to steady herself. "Dead woman walking," she whispered. A shiver snaked up her spine. She shuddered, recalling the old superstition that people felt a chill when someone walked over their grave. Ridiculous, absolutely crazy and in her own head, she scolded herself. But, in a way, the image of her dead sister would always be with her, aging, changing. What would Daria have looked like at age forty or fifty or sixty? All Bree had to do was glance at her reflection in a mirror or lean down to look at the surface of the water.

She got hold of herself and started in earnest with the dresser drawers. The top one was the catch-all junk drawer and held the usual: extra truck, car and boat keys; some dollar bills; a few old photos, including a faded copy of their parents' wedding picture; a pair of earrings that hadn't made it back into her jewelry box; sunglasses; a few souvenirs of places they'd been; and a coaster advertising an unfamiliar bar, the Gator Watering Hole, a bit north of Turtle Bay on a back road off the Tamiami Trail on the edge of the Glades.

One side of the round cardboard coaster had a dancing alligator wearing sunglasses, with a cigarette in one hand and a beer bottle in the other. The place claimed to have "Great domestic beers, fried grouper and gator sand's, and the Old Florida Laid-back Feel."

Bree pictured Daria's last note. She'd be studying with friends and might be back late. But at a place like this?

Daria had often said she preferred the wine bar scene in Naples to the seedy bars Manny talked about. The Gator Watering Hole sounded like a hangout for Glades fishermen and hunters. Bree looked it up in the phone book; it wasn't even listed. So strange—Daria was gone and it was as if this place no longer existed either. What had the place meant to her that she'd kept this?

Bree flipped the coaster over. A list of beers, all domestic. Scribbled in small print on one side was the message, *"Luv ya,"* and opposite that, written in the other direction, as if each were to be read by a person across a table, *"Ditto, babe!"*

Tears blurred Bree's vision. The *"Luv ya"* was in Daria's writing. It must have been a happy, swiftly forgotten moment of fun in her too-short life. Daria had dated several guys in the last few years, but no one seriously and no one lately. And no one, as far as Bree knew, who she'd write *"Luv ya"* words to, even in fun.

Blinking back tears, she put the coaster back in the drawer and went through the rest of the bureau, including her cluttered jewelry box. Nothing unusual. She looked in Daria's purse and found their dentist's name, number, and an appointment time—the morning after the storm—scribbled on a piece of paper. Since the accident had been so public, evidently the dental receptionist had not phoned to remind her of this appointment nor, afterward, to ask why she had not come.

In Daria's purse she also found a calendar the size of a checkbook, one she hadn't seen before. She flipped through its pages. Blank but for big stars drawn on certain dates—oh, yeah, these were the days she had her accounting classes. Now, why hadn't Daria put her dental appointment in here? Daria had worked really hard at learning the financial ins and outs of keeping small business records, but big stars? And then she noted there were several times scribbled on a couple of the starred pages. Not the time of the classes, though—these were later.

"Oh, probably when she studied with the others after class," she said aloud. Had she met someone from the class she liked—or "luved"—and studied with? But why wouldn't she have mentioned that?

As Bree sat down at Daria's computer, she saw a brochure for Eternal Shells half-hidden by the mousepad.

She gasped. Had the Hollimans been telling the truth? She began to shake again. What else hadn't Daria told her? It was a beautiful glossy brochure. The Hollimans must have indeed assumed that Daria had shown her this.

More frustrated than ever, Bree tried to read Daria's e-mail and check sent and deleted mail, but the password she was sure Daria used—Mermaid2, instead of Mermaid1, because Bree had been born first—didn't work. She'd evidently changed her log-in info and hadn't mentioned that, either. Well, of course, she tried to tell herself, passwords were personal, but even that had not been a secret between her and Daria—until now.

She got off the computer. Maybe she could find a techie who could get around the password. From reading about one of Ben's high-profile prosecutions, she knew that even deleted documents could be recovered. Bree searched the rest of the room, but she was so exhausted she felt near collapse.

She lay down on Daria's bed and stared up at the whirring ceiling fan as her sister must have so often done. Of course, there were probably things she hadn't told Daria, too, but something was very wrong. That Eternal Shells brochure. That coaster from a place she'd never mentioned . . . and those haunting, even if brief, words, *Luv ya.* Those times scribbled down for after class. Bree had prided herself that she'd known her twin sister almost as well as she'd known herself. And now she was supposed to accept that Daria had evidently hit her head, and the storm had taken the boat and crashed it into a concrete breakwater and she'd drowned.

What was true and what wasn't? She should just go on with her life after Daria's burial. Get back to building the business and, hopefully, build a relationship with Cole. Resurrect ties to Amelia. Present that important environmental report and not let dreadful, doubtful thoughts torment her.

But had she really known her sister well? Had Daria died in a freak accident? Am I my sister's keeper? a voice in her head taunted Bree. Am I my dead sister's keeper?

"Yes, I am," she whispered to the cluttered but very empty room. "Yes, I am. Was she seeing someone? Was Daria hiding something? And was her death, for sure, an accident?"

The huge, white canvas sign swagged across the port side of Dom Verdugo's one-hundred-eighty-foot casino boat, *Fun 'n' Sun,* tied up at the Miami marina read, "A fabulous time with great food, entertainment and gambling—You Can Bet On It!"

To Cole's surprise, there were no goons on guard, and Verdugo himself greeted him. Cole had thought Verdugo was over at Turtle Bay, but he'd heard the man owned a private plane that took him coast to coast in a flash. He still could not shake the feeling the man bore watching.

"Hey, Cole, my man," Verdugo said with a firm handshake as he stepped aboard. "Sorry to hear they found the body and boat of that Turtle Bay scuba diver. Please give my regrets to the sister."

Again, Cole thought, Verdugo had *heard something.* It worried him that the man was aware of Briana and seemed to know that Cole would be seeing her.

"Where are your guards?" he asked.

"This is my territory," Verdugo said with a

shrug. "In Turtle Bay, not yet. But I'm fine here with just my onboard staff."

"It will obviously be worth millions if you can get the Turtle Bay venue."

"Oh, yeah, for sure. I make no bones about the fact it's big biz, and I'm glad you are—literally—on board," he said with a tight grin.

"As I said, I'd like to see the extent of the job first."

"Sure, that's partly why I'm here. I'll give you the personal tour. Anyway, you think that girl's death will delay the report on the quality of the gulf water?"

Verdugo was a smart guy and a smart guy wouldn't bring that report up so blatantly if he'd had something to do with Daria's death—would he? Or did he figure he already had Cole in his hip pocket? Probably. Not many people said no to Dom Verdugo. But the whole idea of this man bringing gambling, an addiction that ruined some people's lives, ruined families for years to come, into Turtle Bay sickened him. Hell, panel the luxury gambling salon on board? He'd really like to sabotage the whole boat.

"I'm only asking," Verdugo said, "'cause I hear you're on the Clear the Gulf Commission. I don't want you to think I've offered you a lot of money to do this job as a sort of bribe about how that all comes out. I don't operate that way."

Cole was suddenly more furious with himself than with Verdugo. He'd been so obsessed with helping Bree he hadn't even thought of how it would look for him to take Verdugo's lucrative contract. But even if he turned him down in the end, maybe he could first determine whether Verdugo had had anything to do with scuttling the *Mermaids II* to derail the Devon twins' damaging report. If he could prove that, it would also set back the gambling in Turtle Bay. He was flooded by memories of his parents fighting over his mother's debts, his own struggle to continue to pay them off over the years—

"You still game?" Verdugo interrupted his agonizing as they walked along the deck and turned into the gaming salon.

Cole just nodded. He was game, all right, although he was risking his reputation if he accepted. But strangely, nothing mattered more than trying to help Bree. He must, he figured, either be insane or in love.

Bree was horrified to wake up snuggled in Daria's bed. Light was streaming in the window, and she sat up abruptly. She had so much to do today. If Manny had called about Lucinda, she hadn't heard the phone ring. Or was he downstairs in the shop, waiting for Bree to appear? She'd been so exhausted— how late was it?

She rolled over and groaned to see the bedside digital clock said almost ten o'clock. Though she'd been drained since her swim during the storm, she could not believe she had fallen into a dead sleep. She'd slept almost ten hours!

She rushed into her own room, jumped in the shower, then ran a brush through her hair. Pulling on capris and a *Mermaids II* T-shirt, she called Daria's dentist to explain why Daria had missed her emergency appointment.

"Sorry, Ms. Devon," the receptionist said, after offering her condolences, "but the appointment you're referring to was to get her teeth whitened. It wasn't an emergency appointment, but one she'd had for a while."

"Daria Devon? Teeth whitening?"

"Definitely. I remember the call."

"Thank you," she said, feeling foolish. Perhaps Daria had just decided to use her whitening appointment to get her toothache taken care of, but that wasn't what she'd told Bree. It was so unlike Daria to give a darn about whiter teeth. Besides, both of their smiles looked good—at least, Bree thought so, and Daria had never said any different.

She went downstairs in a daze. Manny was not there. The place was silent, but the message lights on her and Daria's desks were blinking. Her phone said twelve messages; Daria's just one. For a moment, Bree imagined the lone message could be Daria, saying, *Come get me. I want to come home.*

"Are you going nuts?" she scolded herself. "Stop it!"

She punched Play on Daria's answering machine.

"Bree, Manny here. I called in on Daria's line, 'cause I figured my message might get buried on yours with all that's going on, just like on your cell. Didn't want to call the 'partment case you trying to get some sleep. Lucinda came back, says 'cause she heard about Daria. I know we closed the shop till after the funeral, but I'll come in after lunch, try to do what I can to help. Juanita stood up for her, but Lucinda's grounded for the rest of her life, far's I'm concerned. Tell you more later. *Vaya con Dios. Adios.*"

At least, Bree thought, Daria's death had brought Lucinda back. She bent to scribble a note to Manny: *Gone out for a while. Don't worry about me. Take care of your own—life is short. B*

She ran upstairs to grab her truck keys and purse, took a breakfast bar and her water bottle and copied the address to the Gator Watering Hole off the coaster before returning it to the top dresser drawer. She rushed back downstairs. First, she was going to Daria's accounting class. The group met at different flex times, some mornings, some afternoons, some evenings, so working people could attend at least some lectures. She wanted to see what else the Hollimans or anyone else knew about Daria, and then she was going to check out the Gator Watering Hole.

She stood in the doorway and stared outside. She'd been so out of it, she hadn't realized it was starting to rain. The wind had kicked up, which made her uneasy. But nothing was stopping her until she got some answers—and she wasn't even certain of the questions.

To Bree's dismay, the Hollimans were not in Daria's class when she poked her head in the door. She had gotten wet darting into the building from her truck, but even if she'd had an umbrella, it likely would have gotten turned inside out, the wind was gusting so hard. The instructor had evidently dismissed the class a bit early.

Too late, she realized her mistake of showing herself so suddenly. Several of the students gaped at her and one pointed. She couldn't blame them. After all, she had even startled herself looking in the mirror last night.

Loudly enough for everyone to hear, she introduced herself to the instructor. "I'm Briana Devon, Daria Devon's twin sister, and I just wondered if I could talk to you for a minute."

"Of course," the tall, young man said. His crew cut and open face reminded her of the photo she'd seen of Ted in uniform, the one in the paper that went with his obit and the story about him. "We are all very sorry for your loss," he told her. "I'm Seth Johnson."

They shook hands. Several other class members expressed regrets on their way out. "Daria mentioned the Hollimans—Viv and Fred," she told him, surprised she'd lied so smoothly. It was easy when you wanted something badly. Is that why Daria had lied? "I see they aren't here," she added. "I wanted to extend an invitation to the funeral to them."

"They missed today, which is unusual. You know," Seth said, "I can't say the same for your sister."

"What do you mean? Daria attended class religiously. It was very important to her!"

"I'm not criticizing," he said, holding up both palms at her outburst. "After all, this class is set up with flex time, with some on-line assignments, to suit the needs of our busy adult students. But she had conflicts, especially the night classes, which is when most of the students can make the lectures. As she may have told you, we flip-flop key lectures and exams between this hour and two evenings a month to allow people to attend."

"And she—she didn't? I'm not sure what you're saying. Do you keep attendance? I just—" She could not think of a lie to cover this bumbling question. "I just would like to know."

He showed Bree his records. Daria's attendance had been spotty, especially the night classes, always the first and third Tuesdays for the last two months. Damn, Bree thought. Daria was moonlighting to earn more money—for teeth whitening, the new dive watch she gave Bree for their birthday. Or—and this she refused to believe, because they'd always shared girl talk—she was meeting someone. But that must have been it.

Shaken, Bree thanked him and started away, then turned back at the door. "The Hollimans—do you know anything about their Shells Eternal business?"

"Everyone in the class did," Seth told her. "They were like walking, talking advertisements."

She went out into the corridor. Walking, talking advertisements—that's what they had wanted Daria to be for them. Now Daria wasn't walking or talking anymore, and the Hollimans had uncharacteristically missed tonight's class.

Before she went outside, Bree leaned against the thick floor-to-ceiling glass window next to the back door of the school and looked past the puddles in the parking lot. Everything looked wet and gray, almost as if the entire place was underwater. Daria, she agonized silently, why did you lie about these little things? Did you really have a toothache that kept you from diving with me that last day? Manny's not being there would have been reason enough I had to go down alone. Come to think of it, Daria hadn't dived much the last several weeks. Why did she miss classes and not mention something as strange as Shells Eternal? And why hide a new man in her life?

Bree glanced down at her watch. However dark it looked outside, it was not even noon on this Friday yet. TGIF day for many people, and among the laid-back locals, that could start early. The Gator Watering Hole had the *Old Florida Laid-back Feel,* as Daria's souvenir coaster read.

The rain seemed to be letting up a bit, but it was so hot and humid that she'd probably be just as wet as if the rain continued. She'd go to that place in the Glades and ask around to see if Daria had ever been there. And if so, with whom?

12

Amelia knelt on the thick, wet grass with rain and tears dripping off her nose and chin. She bent close to her mother's headstone in the cemetery she had never set foot in since the day of her father's funeral four years ago. The area looked so different now, no tent, no fake grass blankets laid at the lips of the grave, no metal framework holding the coffin before it was lowered.

The cemetery workers had not yet dug Daria's grave. If they had, she might have thrown herself into it, so deep was her despair. She didn't like it that Daria would be buried here on Monday. The twins should be buried somewhere else, together. Since Ben insisted he wanted to be cremated, Amelia wanted her eventual resting place to be here by her mother's.

"Mommy, I think Daria's death is sort of retribution for yours," she said in a trembling voice. She swallowed a sob. It helped to say things out loud where she was certain no one would hear. "I found that medical report about your death years ago Dad had hidden. The fatal cervical rupture was from the birth of the second child, not that Briana wasn't partly to blame. After you died, Dad forgave them, even favored them. It's not my fault they were his favorite. What happened—" here she emphasized each word "—wasn't my fault!"

She gripped her hands together, trying to find the right words to stop her pain. "I thought that when I had my two boys, everything would be better, but it isn't. I try to want to do things with both of them, but they are so loud and get so dirty and they want to swim and snorkel, and you know where that leads. But I didn't mean to shout at Daria and hit her that last day . . ."

She almost choked on those words she hadn't meant to say. Was she sorry? Her guilt was making her physically sick, so didn't that mean she was sorry? At least now, she and Bree would be closer, wouldn't they? That is, if Bree ever got over losing Daria.

It began to pour. Her hair stuck to her head and rain ran down her neck and throat. Bree had said Daria's hair had been streaming loose under all that water, holding her and the boat down, holding it down to drown . . .

Amelia squeezed her eyes tightly shut, but the images of herself trapped underwater wouldn't go away. It was like in the nightmares she'd had since Mommy died, worse when Dad and the twins went scuba diving. Trembling, she forced her eyes open. Tears, rain, deep water, even blood—it was all the same.

"I'm sorry, Mommy. Really sorry . . ." she whispered.

When she heard a low, distant rumble of thunder, she knew she'd better get going. Thunder might mean lightning, and she had no intention of ending up in the hospital like Bree, or worse.

That fear was surely rational. That meant she was coping, that she wasn't clinically depressed, didn't it?

"What happened could have been worse," she whispered to herself as she got to her feet. "Bree could be dead, too."

She bent to stroke her mother's wet, gray marble tombstone in farewell, but she couldn't bear to touch her father's.

Bree drove south on the Tamiami Trail through fitful rain and gusts of wind until she reached the turnoff to Cypress Road, heading east into the Everglades. A small runway with a few prop planes huddled by a single hangar at the intersection. She had to wait before making the turn as a string of cars came at her from the other direction. Although most people drove Alligator Alley to cross the state toward Fort Lauderdale or Miami, traffic was still heavy on this older route linking Tampa and Miami. She glanced across the airport tarmac; even in the rain, one man was working on an airplane. If the Gator Watering Hole wasn't too far down this road, it was possible that pilots stopped for a few drinks there. Now that was a scary thought.

After her turn, the tires crunched wet gravel; she drove slowly on a road barely wide enough to be called double lane. She was immediately on the edge of the Everglades, where shallow water surrounded grass on both sides of the road and cypress trees and their knobby knees poked through the so-called river of grass. She passed some slightly elevated islands called hammocks, from which sprouted pine and palms. Vegetation grew so thick in the heat and humidity here that she felt she was almost driving through the seaweed world on the bottom of the gulf.

She wondered how their—now her—precious turtle grass was doing at the Trade Wreck site. It needed to be monitored and photographed again, but who would be her dive buddy now? She'd have to give the Clear the Gulf Commission their "state of the sea grass" report alone next week. And it was going to be dire enough that all hell could break loose over that, too. She sniffed hard and grabbed a tissue from her purse to wipe her nose.

Although Manny was great with motors, machines and technical problems, he'd never make it as her new diving buddy. If he couldn't see all the way below the surface, he wasn't going down. He couldn't speak for their sea grass project. She might have to hire someone for dives—that is, she and Manny might—but she couldn't bear to think of running Mermaids without Daria. Funny, how she'd hardly given a thought to the business since that fatal day.

If—just if—someone was behind Daria's death, did they assume that, deserted at sea in rough waves and an approaching storm, Daria's twin would die that day, too?

About a mile off the highway, Bree saw a hand-painted sign for the Gator Watering Hole. The actual hole was a water-filled ditch surrounding the building and small parking lot on three sides like a moat. That could indeed hide an alligator or two. In these parts alligators made their way into golf course lakes, ornamental ponds, canals and ditches. People had to keep an eye on pets and children, not to mention themselves.

The tavern or bar—whatever it would dare call itself—looked like a dive out of the backwoods boonies, which it was. Its roof was part sturdy old Florida tin over the main section and part ragged palm thatch over the full-length porch, like the Seminole Indian–style *chickee* huts which had been made fashionable on cabanas and pool bars at ritzy hotels. But there was nothing ritzy about this ramshackle place.

Bree was pretty certain this was a wild-goose chase. Even if it was a short drive from Daria's accounting class, she couldn't fathom her sister meeting someone here. And it would be pitch-dark out here at night. Bree decided she'd have to go back to the next accounting class and ask if the students had gone here as a group. Or else Daria had just found the coaster, it had intrigued her and she'd kept it. But those *Luv ya, babe* notes bothered Bree. Who had written that back to her sister? She needed answers now, before they buried Daria, so that she could go on with her own life. Since she was here, a quick question or two in broad daylight—or cloaking rain—could help to settle her soul.

Three vehicles were parked in front and one in back, all pickup trucks, two in various stages of rusting out. One of them displayed a Confederate flag and a gun rack in its back window, not uncommon in these parts. One had balloon tires like locals used for what they called swamp buggy races through mud-filled obstacle courses. Bree parked off to the side so she could stay away from the other vehicles.

It boosted her courage to see a woman step out onto the porch and light up a cigarette. She had too much hair, too much makeup and too-tight shorts and halter top, but at least it wasn't all good old boys inside. After just a couple of puffs, she tossed the cigarette in a puddle and darted back inside. Maybe she was the cook or waitress.

Bree backed in against the palm tree trunk barrier at the top of the east-side ditch so she was parked heading out. As her wheels bumped against the barrier, something she'd forgotten hit her.

Up until the time they were in their teens, Dad sometimes used to teasingly pronounce Daria's name like *Dare*-i-a, because of the risks she sometimes took. He'd dubbed her his daredevil, "The Evel Knievel of the Deep," known for too fast a descent or too deep a dive. Only when his little daredevil almost choked to death from swallowing chewing gum underwater did she slow down. That's right, Bree thought, *Dare*-i-a had once been so sure that nothing could harm her that she reveled in taking risks.

Bree had always been more circumspect. She wasn't going to take any chances in this place, either. Just a quick question or two and she was out of here.

As she headed toward the building, a quickening breeze shoved clotted clouds overhead, and the rain increased. The wind was coming from the same direction as the storm that had killed Daria.

The rain beat incredibly loudly on the tin roof. Other than that, the place was quiet, the lighting lousy. No TV blaring, no canned music. Stepping into the building was like stepping back in the past. An old jukebox half blocked the entryway but it sat silent. Plain, mismatched wooden tables and chairs were clustered around the edges of the small room; a row of rattan stools lined a long bar. There was a worn-looking pool table in the corner.

The clientele was negligible, as she had hoped. Two guys who looked like denizens of the deep Glades played foosball, and one man hunched over a table, apparently asleep. The woman was not in sight. From behind the bar, through a small opening with a serving counter from what must be the kitchen, drifted the smell of frying burgers. The walls had no neon-lighted beer signs, just some Florida State Seminoles and Miami University Canes football pennants and blow-ups of the stadiums.

Actually, the dominant decor could be called early alligator. At least ten gator skulls, with open jaws flaunting razor-sharp teeth, were nailed high on each of the four walls. They seemed to grin at her.

Suddenly everyone looked at her; the men stopped talking and playing foosball. The only sound was the rattle of rain on the metal roof and the swish of palm fronds against it.

Here we go again, she thought. They think they're seeing a ghost. Her heart careened to her feet. That meant Daria must have been here.

"You're here way off schedule, honey," said the bartender, a tall, gaunt man. "You want the usual?"

Hadn't they heard Daria was dead? She guessed it was possible. Glades guys were not like boaters and divers, totally attuned to what went on in or near the water. In that case, she wouldn't be dead woman walking, but live one talking.

"Sure," she said, deciding to be Daria to see if that got her more info than the way she'd intended to proceed. "Change of plans about my schedule," she told him, and dug in her purse for some money. The foosball game picked up again, along with the other conversations. "When were you expecting me?"

"Next Tuesday, like always," he muttered, slapping down a tall, old-fashioned Coca-Cola glass on the bar.

Bree's eyes widened when he poured it half-full with lemonade and half with foaming beer. Daria loved what the Brits called shandies; she'd learned to drink them when she'd dated a snowbird from Toronto.

"Okay, then, this one's for here, and these beers are for the road," he told her with a smile that was missing two prominent teeth. "Or for the guy you're meetin' out back, like always."

Bree's pulse pounded as he produced two bottles of Mountain Brewed beer. "Tell me what he looks like," she said, trying to sound coy as she put money on the bar. "I just might have the wrong guy in mind."

"Never really seen him, and you know it, but Bess—" he gave a toss of his head to indicate the kitchen "—or a little bird musta told me, well-built, dark hair. Out here it's see no evil, speak none neither. Say, you two goin' parkin' in the Glades in this wet mess, since it's nearly dark as night outside?" he asked with a laugh.

Bree realized her mistake now. She might insult him if she explained who she really

was and started to grill him. Having pre-
tended she was her sister, she could hardly
ask more about the guy she was meeting.
Well-built and dark haired? Someone who
called Daria "babe" and liked Mountain
Brewed Beer? And someone who didn't
come in here for his own drinks?

She drank half of her shandy down, just
because she was suddenly so thirsty, then
spilled most of the rest of it on her wrist
when a clap of thunder sounded. It seemed
to echo off the metal roof and inside her
skull. Lightning! She had to get in the truck
and get out of here.

"Thanks," she said, stuffing the two beers
in her big purse and heading for the door.

"Don't he want them opened this time?"
the bartender called after her.

"No. I'm—we're fine," she said, realizing it
was probably a good thing they thought she
was meeting a man outside.

Even with her sensitivity to light, Bree was
surprised to see how much darker it had become outside in mid-afternoon. She prayed
it would not turn into another one of those
afternoon deluges like the one that had
trapped her and Daria. She had to get home
and think through all she'd learned. She

wanted to come back here with Manny or Cole, maybe even Ben, though she didn't want him to know she was investigating on her own.

Daria obviously did have someone she was meeting secretly. A married man? Had she rekindled a flame with Josh Austin? No way, not with a stunning wife like his and his high profile, not to mention how busy he was.

Holding her big purse over her head for a break in the rain so she could see, Bree ran for her truck.

"You run away like a dog, you spend Saturdays with me on a short leash," Manny told Lucinda as they entered the Two Mermaids. He handed her a broom and pointed toward the back room.

"That's a big place with lots of junk in it!" she dared to protest.

"I don't care. Just do it and not complain— same with that *quinceañera* party. Now that Daria's half of this business come to me, we have more money for a nice one."

"Yeah," she said, taking the broom from him with a frown, "but without Daria to dive with Bree, your profits will be down, won't they?"

"Maybe we hire a part-time diver. When the mourning for Daria is over, we advertise more. But this been a lot of publicity already."

She just shook her head, glared at him and stomped into the back room. The swish, swish of the broom convinced him he'd at least had a small victory with her.

The front doorbell rang, and Manny saw it was one of Sam Travers's workers, the red-haired one named Lance. He carried a pair of green fins. It looked strange to see him alone. He was usually with his diving partner, Ric, a real stud who evidently worked out a lot.

"Your boss left these on Sam's barge," he said without a greeting.

Manny was tempted to tell this man he was partners with Bree now, but it hadn't been announced and he hadn't even reminded Bree of it yet. He didn't want to seem too pushy when she was grieving.

"Thanks," Manny said, taking them and putting them on Bree's desk.

"I can understand why she forgot them," Lance said, folding his arms over his chest. "Hell of a thing—bad enough her sister was dead, but to find her like that? The whole scene was surreal."

Manny wasn't sure what *surreal* meant,

but he could guess. "We are grateful for Sam's help," he told Lance.

"Considering that you're our business ri-vals?" Lance asked, as he headed for the door. He stopped and turned back. "Or that he blames Briana for his son's death?"

"You know that, too?" Manny asked. Lucinda's broom had stopped. He had to check on her.

"Sam hardly makes a secret of it. Man, I'd like to get a glimpse of that attic shrine he's made to his son. Talk about whacked-out . . . The way he really feels about Briana, I wouldn't be surprised if he isn't up there sticking pins in a voodoo doll of her. Know what I mean?"

Manny wasn't clear on what a voodoo doll was, either, but he got the message. And he was going to make sure Bree got that mes-sage when she returned.

Bree ran toward her car so fast that she slipped in the mud and sprawled to both knees and both hands in the mire. Her keys got coated with muck. Cursing but moving carefully, she got to her feet and wiped the keys off on one of the few clean spots on her jeans, then looked around.

For a moment, through the slant of gray rain, she felt disoriented. Was her truck where she had left it?

Of course it was, straight across the tiny parking lot. She'd gotten turned around and was looking the wrong way. Was she losing it?

With a nervous glance, she walked toward it, telling herself to watch her footing. Any thought she'd had of walking around back to talk to Bess in the kitchen or to try to find out why Daria met a man "out back," as the bartender had said, flew right out of her head. She was getting away from here.

In the driving rain, she tried to get her key in the door lock, but she was shaking so hard it didn't go right in. At least the rain cleaned the last of the mud from her keys.

And then—she wasn't sure where he'd come from—she saw a man striding straight for her, as if he'd emerged from the ditch or the swamp. He wore all black, jeans and old running shoes, windbreaker and a billed hat. The neck of a second black T-shirt was pulled up around his face for a mask. And he held a huge, raised wrench in one hand.

13

Bree ducked the man's first swing with his wrench and didn't wait around for a second. Where had he come from? Was he one of the guys inside?

She screamed but a clap of thunder drowned her out. With the rattle of rain on that roof, people inside might not hear. *Save your breath to run. Someone will come out or along the road to help.* Hoping she could beat him to the other door of her truck, Bree dashed around the back with her key out. She and Daria had taken a self-protection class; Ben had insisted on it when they'd moved to the apartment above the marina shop. Hold your car keys between your fingers as a weapon. But nothing she had could take on that wrench.

He was too fast for her. He came around the front end and lunged at her again. Who? Why?

Sidestepping him, she tore for the door of the bar, but he caught up and yanked her back. He didn't swing the wrench this time, but turned her away from him—so strong—and clamped a hard, dirty hand over her mouth. His arm was so tight around her waist she couldn't breathe. She tried to bite his fingers, but he smacked her mouth. Her teeth cut the inside of her lower lip and she tasted blood. When he tried to drag her toward the ditch, she elbowed him in the ribs, then just picked up her feet.

They toppled over, side by side. She screamed, but the rain on the tin roof drowned her out, drowned her . . . Horrid images leaped at her: Daria trapped in that flooded wheelhouse underwater . . . her hair wet and waving . . . her hands upraised, as if for help. Another wayward thought hit her. What if someone—this man?—had tried to hurt Daria? What if her skull had been struck by a wrench and not the boat's steering wheel?

Her attacker half rolled, half jumped to a standing position and dragged her to her feet. She clawed at his wrist with the keys. He let her go but blocked her path toward the bar door. Knowing the woman was out in the back room, Bree tore around that way.

She evidently took him by surprise and got a little lead. Behind the place were picnic tables, two big, shell-shaped planters for cigarette butts, and a crude bridge over the back part of the ditch. Thick, wet vegetation loomed ahead.

Bree heard him coming, his feet fast, his breath loud. She cursed her acute hearing, because her pulse pounded in her ears.

He got to her before she reached the back door. The building had windows here, too, but the louvered wooden shutters were down in the rain.

"Hey, babe," he said, his voice a low rasp, but the words screamed inside her skull and her soul.

Babe? Could this be the man Daria had met here, the one who wrote on the coaster? Had their affair gone wrong, and he'd killed her? And now meant to silence someone who looked like her or someone asking too many questions?

The last thing in the world Bree wanted was to run into the Glades, but he would be slowed by the standing water. She was used to it and could handle it, was more sure-footed, she was certain. Then she could go around toward the road, circle back to her truck, or maybe someone would come by. It was only about a half a mile to that little airport, and she'd seen a man there. And on the highway, there were plenty of people to flag down, people who would never turn down little Cypress Road.

She veered away from him and sprinted toward the bridge. She made it that far. It was the first time it registered that she still had her heavy purse over her shoulder, pressed under her arm and that her cell phone was there. If only she could put a little distance between them, she'd call 911. And she had two beer bottles for weapons.

But out on the rickety bridge, he had her by her wrist. Rain tattooed the water in the ditch and enveloped them in a gray, slanted curtain. Bree reached for one of the bottles and threw it at him. Beer sprayed over both of them as the bottle broke on his head, maybe dazing him, but his cap and the T-shirt that covered his face kept him from getting cut. If she could just yank that mask down! But then, if she knew who he was, he would surely kill her. She was hoping he might only mean to scare her. He'd done that, all right.

But she felt power pump through her. She'd aim her keys for his face this time or swing her purse at him. Moving a little slower, he raised the wrench again.

Bree swung her purse. The wrench went flying into the ditch, but he slammed into her. She opened her mouth to scream again, but they broke through the wooden bridge railing and splashed into the ditch.

Water enveloped her with a surge and a smack. She hit her head against something. Was she diving? She'd gone off the boat backward. But no tanks, no regulator, no mask. She held her breath, so dizzy at first. Under the sea, under the sea, Bree and Daria, under the sea.

But it wasn't deep. Her bottom hit bottom, and she bounced right up for a huge gasp of air. A few feet from her, her attacker was try-ing to stand, sputtering, splashing. Dear God, she prayed, don't let there be gators in here.

She had the choice of either daring to pull down his mask or scrambling out to run.

Clawing her way up the bank, she slid back twice while he reached for her ankles. His fingernails raked her leg. Amazingly, her purse, full of water, was back over her shoulder.

She kicked the man away, lost a shoe, then clambered out and ran, dripping wet, her purse sloshing, her soaked hair flinging water. Gut instinct told her not to run back inside but to get out of here. She had a head start. Beat him to her truck this time!

She glanced back once as she turned the corner of the building. Her attacker's hat but not his mask had come off. He was floundering out of the water, shaking his head and spraying water off dark hair as if he were a dog. She didn't even recognize him bareheaded, but she had water and her own hair in her eyes.

Run!

Gasping, she made it to her truck and steadied her right hand with her other to turn the lock and throw herself in. She slammed the door, locked it, praying he didn't come, hadn't found that wrench to knock out her windows. Could fingerprints be taken from a wet wrench, if it was found later?

Her right hand, which had clutched the keys the entire time, seemed frozen into a claw. She was shaking so hard she almost couldn't shift gears. With a screech, she turned the wheels to roar out onto the small road.

She sped back toward civilization. Throwing water in the rain, the windshield wipers whipped across her vision, *whap-whap, whap-whap.* She should not have tried this alone. She needed Cole or Manny, even Ben.

At the stop sign to the Trail, she didn't see anyone following and had to wait for traffic again. She put her forehead on the steering wheel and sobbed. Maybe Daria, with her good sea legs, had not slipped and hit her head on the boat's steering wheel, no matter how rough the water was. Maybe someone had boarded the boat and hurt her. No matter what Josh Austin reported or the coroner ruled or other people accepted, she had to look into that horrible possibility. Could the storm have cleverly been used to make a murder look like an accident?

After hugging her, then holding her at arm's length, Cole took to furious pacing while she told him everything, starting with the fact Manny had warned her that Sam Travers was as unforgiving as ever and then working up to the worst by blurting out about her attack.

As he walked back and forth, Cole alternated between clamping his hands under his armpits or gripping them on top of his head. Bree could tell he was livid, not only with Sam and the man who'd attacked her, but also with her. She figured he kept his hands constrained so he wouldn't give her a good shaking.

She was just lucky she'd had time to clean up and change out of her wet clothes, so he didn't see what a mess she'd been, but she hadn't had time to shower or wash her hair. She'd toweled it dry but tiny flecks of green algae clung to it, pond scum like the bastard who had attacked her. After she'd dived into the depths of the Trade Wreck with the strobe, she'd seen Cole angry, but he was a lot angrier now. His dark eyes were narrowed; every muscle in his face looked chiseled from stone. A pulse beat at the side of his throat, and his big body seemed coiled tight, ready to strike.

"You said you'd stay here, and that you'd

be fine," he interrupted. "Go ahead, tell me the rest."

"I'm sure I didn't know him," she concluded, still clutching a cushion to her breasts as she sat cross-legged on the sofa.

"He was masked."

"I would recognize you in a mask—or Manny, Sam Travers, Ben, Josh Austin. Lots of people," she protested.

When he finally sat down beside her, his weight toppled her into him. He lifted and turned her chin to make her look at him. The cut inside her mouth made her flinch. That and the scratch on her leg were her only physical injuries, however achy and black-and-blue she might be tomorrow and for the funeral, two days away.

"So," Cole said, "it couldn't have been someone from inside that place because you're sure no one left after you entered."

"Unless he was out in the kitchen with Bess."

"Yeah, I want to talk to her."

"The thing is, my attacker fits the vague description of the man Daria was evidently meeting. He could be the one who wrote on the coaster. He called me 'babe,' too. It's the only thing he said—'Hey, babe.'"

"It could connect, or not. Lots of guys are muscular and dark haired—including yours truly."

"He wasn't as tall as you."

"Great, then it wasn't me," he said, his voice suddenly dripping sarcasm. "We've narrowed the suspect down to someone we know, such as one of Verdugo's guards— they all look like that. Or Ric, Sam's worker, though his choice of weapon seems to be a speargun, not a wrench. Then there's Frank Holliman, for all we know, not to mention a gazillion guys we don't know. And saying *Hey, babe* doesn't mean much. I could say that to you, too, as a come-on and not a threat."

"Why are you tearing down everything I say?" she demanded, and threw the pillow at him. He swatted it away as if it were a mosquito.

"I'm not. I'm just a little upset—you could have gotten yourself killed. And I don't want you jumping to conclusions that just because you were attacked, Daria was, too. Don't assume we have more answers than we do."

He'd said *we* again, she thought. As frustrated as he was making her, she loved that.

"Cole, I admit I shouldn't have gone in there, but you surely shouldn't, either."

"Why the hell not? I'll take Manny with me, talk to the bartender and Bess, check for that wrench, though you're right. It can't have prints on it if it's in the ditch."

"I don't want you to get in trouble over this."

"What's the diff?" he muttered as if to himself, shaking his head. "I'm already in over my head with Verdugo—and you."

"Me?"

"Yeah. I'm furious with you—again—for losing your head, and here I've lost mine over you."

"Oh."

"Oh? Is that the best you can say?"

His hands on her shoulders were more than firm. He bent to nuzzle her cheek, then dipped his head to trail his lips down her throat, which she mindlessly arched back for him. He kissed the hollow between her collarbones, then moved up the side of her neck to her left ear. He nipped at the lobe, then darted his tongue inside the shell of her ear, thoroughly, just once.

Every nerve in her body jumped to attention, screaming for more. She sucked in a sudden breath, teetering on the edge of beautiful oblivion. She was acting like a schoolgirl, she scolded herself, as if she'd never had a man near her before. But this was so different. Cole's merest touch set off a torrent of insane sensations clear down to the pit of her belly.

"I know you hear things too well lately, so I'm whispering now," he said, his mouth moving against her cheek. "And I'll make it quick because, as luscious as the rest of you is, your hair smells like . . . gator water."

She almost laughed. Amidst all this terror, he had the power to take her on a roller-coaster ride of emotions, and that both scared and sobered her.

"Two things," he said, his voice deadly serious. "You stay put until I get back. And, however helpful he's been, stay away from Sam Travers."

"He may come to the funeral. After he helped us look for Daria, I can't tell him to stay away."

"I just mean you don't go near him, okay?" he said, putting her back at arm's length to look hard into her eyes. She wasn't used to taking orders, but from him, she was starting to welcome them.

"All right. I won't go near Sam."

"Meanwhile," he said, releasing her and frowning at his hands while he flexed them, "I'll take Manny to cover my back and you can babysit his daughter. I feel the urge to go order a Mountain Brewed at the old laid-back, good-time Gator Watering Hole."

Bree tried to keep her mind off her own problems by listening to Lucinda's woes, but she was really worried about Cole. With Manny, he was going to do her dirty work, to find out about the man who met Daria on the sly, but also, she feared, to pay someone back for attacking her. She couldn't bear it if he or Manny got hurt.

Lucinda seemed happy to have been res-cued from sweeping the back room down-stairs and from her father's presence. After Bree showered and washed her hair, they sat at the table in the apartment eating shrimp salad and the brownies one of the church people had dropped off. Bree was too uptight to feel hungry, but Lucinda had a good appetite. She was a pretty girl with lively brown eyes, just on the verge of be-coming plump, but that gave her a voluptu-ous figure. No wonder Manny was trying to keep an eye on her. She chattered on about things, then something she said brought Bree back from her agonizing with a jolt.

"Swear you won't tell my dad something, Bree?"

"If it's something bad or dangerous, you really shouldn't put me in a position like that. Manny's an employee but also a friend."

Lucinda's sleek eyebrows lifted. "Yeah, but won't he be a partner now?"

"Yes, when everything is settled. I didn't realize you knew all that."

"A bunch of stuff I overhear—like what that guy who brought your fins back said about you. But yeah, Dad told our whole family all that about the partnership a long time ago. It's really a good thing, too, 'cause we can *so* use the money. Is it okay if I just ask you a general question then, not tell you a secret?"

Bree knew the entire Salazar family. Lucinda was the only one who really sounded Anglo and that bothered Manny. In his opinion, his daughter was too much an American teen and Bree didn't want to interfere with that, not considering how strict Manny was with his family.

"All right, Lucinda, shoot," Bree said, deciding not to quiz the girl about what else Manny might have said about becoming a partner.

"First of all, you can call me Cindi if you want—with an *i* at the end. I like to dot both *i*'s with little hearts or happy faces, know what I mean?"

"Sure. But in front of your dad, I might stick to Lucinda."

"Oh, yeah," she said, rolling her dark eyes. "I mean, it's *so* good to talk to a straight-up adult who understands me. So, let's just say a friend—a Latina—falls for an Anglo guy— I mean, about as American as he could be. This guy is *da bomb*— blond, great body, tall, on the basketball team. A real hottie. Let's say his parents are not real happy either, 'cause they think Hispanics are all a bunch of illegal immigrants—and Catholic, 'stead of Baptist, which is true. Anyway, I'm asking you for her, 'cause I know you dated Sam's son in high school and Sam didn't want you to."

"No, that's not quite it," Bree said, shoving her plate away and leaning back wearily in her chair to rub her eyes. "Sam Travers was all for me dating his son, even marrying him, but I broke it off when we were in college. Ted got really upset and enlisted in the marines and was killed in Iraq. Sam Travers blames me for the fact Ted was there—and got killed."

"Man, that bites," Lucinda whispered, frowning and shaking her head. "You don't blame yourself, do you?"

"Ted Travers made his own choices, but I feel like I've got a big target on my back when I'm around Sam. Listen to me, Lucinda—Cindi," she said, sitting forward and taking the girl's hand across the table. "My sister dated someone in high school for a long time, too, but when he broke up with her, she just went on with her life. No one blamed anyone, ran away from home or did anything crazy. So trust me on this and just tell your friend not to think her relationship with this boy has to be the end of the world. If it works, it will have to take time, patience and understanding. If it doesn't work out, life goes on and maybe there's someone, Anglo or Latino, even better for her a little ways down the road of life."

"So you mean your sister—she got over the guy she dated in high school?"

"Yes, exactly."

"And found someone else to love. She

must have been so hurt by the guy breaking it off—even if she didn't show it."

Bree frowned. Since Josh, Daria had dated several men and had been the one to break it off with every one of them. Was she afraid of commitment, or did she think she'd better break things off before they dumped her? Could that have been the fallout of her loving, then losing, Josh? And why hadn't Bree thought of this when Daria was alive?

"I know," Bree went on, her voice shaky, "it's hard to take advice from older people, especially parents, and especially when they get all upset and yell, but that's only because they care about you so much. Cindi, please try to treasure the time you have with your parents and your sister, because you won't have your family forever. And don't be in too much of a hurry to give your heart—or your body—away. Sometimes, in a way, you might just not get either back."

Bree jumped up and took their dishes to the kitchen before the girl could see she was going to cry. Time with parents didn't last forever, let alone with a sister. Had Daria ever gotten over Josh Austin? Bree thought she had . . . she was *sure* she had. But now she wasn't sure of anything, including the fact that she had known her identical twin sister, the person closest to her in the whole world, at all.

Cole and Manny looked around the property of the Gator Watering Hole before going in. The sun had come out after all the rain, and they felt as if they were in a steam bath.

They saw where Bree and her attacker had fallen through the railing of the bridge. They also saw a couple of gators sunning themselves near another part of the ditch, so they decided to fish around for the wrench later—a lot later. There was no way it was going to have prints, and no promise that the police would even try to ID them, if there were.

Shaking his head, Cole muttered, "She almost drowns, swims with sharks around her during the storm, gets hit by lightning, then barely missed the gators."

"How many lives they say a cat got?" Manny asked as they headed around the bar toward the front door.

"Nine, so I'd like to think she's got five to go."

Manny just grunted.

They ambled in and sat sideways at the bar so they could scan the entire front room, which was a lot busier than when Bree had been there earlier. From Bree's description, Cole could tell the bartender was the same guy. He could tell the guy didn't especially like Manny here, as if one Mexican would begin an onslaught of them here in redneck heaven. Just to get his attention, Cole ordered in Spanish. "*Dos cervezas aqui*— Mountain Brewed."

The man raised one shaggy eyebrow. "Don't sell many of those 'round here, but get in a case now and then for a special customer."

"That right? Maybe a friend of mine. Dark-haired, works out all the time?"

"Could be," the guy said, nervous now. "Never comes in, sends a friend." He grabbed a bottle opener and bent the first metal cap.

Cole considered playing dumb about the fact Bree had been here, but that probably wouldn't work. He decided to try a plain, old man-to-man approach and hoped he didn't have to get rough, even if he was ready to. He figured, one wrong move here and they'd be taking on almost every man in the bar.

"We're friends of the woman who was in here earlier today," he said, keeping his voice low. "the one you made a shandy for and sold the two Mountain brewskis."

"What's the deal with the guy you're all looking for?" he asked. "Swear to God, don't know his name or why a class act like her took to meeting him here—yeah, well, I guess I do," he added with a snicker.

"Did Bess get a good look at him?"

He seemed startled Cole knew the woman's name. "What's the prob, I asked," the guy demanded, still not raising his voice either. "He leave her and she wants him back? Or what?"

"Yeah," Cole said. "Or what. Can I talk to Bess just for a sec?"

"She's pretty busy, fryin' fish."

"You see, we've got other fish to fry, too. If I can just talk to her, I won't feel I need to make a police report that the woman you're referring to was attacked by a guy with a wrench when she walked out of here in the rain today. Her attacker might just fit the description of the man I'm trying to trace, but I can just let the police take over and come out here to snoop around, check your liquor license, question your customers, and—"

"Lay off, I hear you. Come on out in back. And we don't need no health inspector here lookin' at the kitchen neither, if you was going to bring that up next."

Bess's description of the mystery man was the same general, nondescript one the bartender and Bree had given. "But there is one thing I thought was kinda funny," she added, after the bartender had gone back out and Cole and Manny were about to leave.

"What's that? Anything might help."

"More 'n once, I think she met a different guy. Like maybe she was really getting around, meeting clients here or something. You know—johns. If you're involved with her, I'd try asking her about it."

Cole smacked his hand down so hard on the counter that her pile of knives jumped and clattered. She grabbed one and held it in front of her.

"I didn't mean nothin' by it, just telling the truth," she muttered. "If that don't do no good, just get on outta here 'fore I call Jerry."

Manny went way up in Cole's estimation when he automatically covered his back by facing the door, in case she did call Jerry in. Cole clenched his jaw and gritted his teeth.

"Can you describe anyone else she met?" he asked, trying to keep calm.

"Listen, mister, it's pitch-black out there at night. I'm standing here doing dishes or fixin' food. I just glance out, that's all. It wasn't the same guy all the time. There were at least two different ones, one taller and thinner than the other, that's all."

Cole raked his hand through his hair. "Thanks for your help. I appreciate your honesty," he told her as they went back out through the bar.

But he was considering lying to Bree.

After the rain stopped, Lucinda wanted to go sit on the lanai to watch what was happening at the marina, but Bree felt afraid. Until Cole learned something about her attacker, she was hesitant to even sit outside.

Such a feeling infuriated her. She was not going to become a victim or prisoner. Sure, she'd be more careful now, but whether or not her attacker's purpose was to scare her into silence or shut her up for good, she wasn't going to cooperate. The best defense was surely a good offense.

"Why don't you pour us both a glass of OJ from the fridge, and I'll be right back," Bree suggested. "But the furniture on the veranda will be soaked, so we'd better just open the doors to the patio and sit in here for now. The doors are locked, but I'd appreciate it if you unlock them so we can get the breeze and see out better."

As Lucinda headed for the kitchen, Bree went to the bathroom, popped into her bedroom to brush her still-damp hair, then hesitated in the hall to stare at the closed door to Daria's room. Manny had said he'd heard Sam had a sort of shrine to Ted, no doubt with cherished mementos and photos. Bree didn't want to become obsessed like that, nor would Daria want her to.

Still, after the funeral, she'd go through her sister's things again. She'd give some away to the church for their collection for migrant workers, keep precious things, of course, and offer some to Amelia. When Bree had searched the room so thoroughly yesterday, she'd noticed a few new clothing items of Daria's she hadn't even worn yet. Maybe she would keep a few things for herself. Wearing them would make her feel closer to Daria. How often they'd shared clothes over the years.

Something compelled her to open Daria's

door and glance in. She gasped, clamping both hands over her mouth so hard she felt her cut against her teeth.

True, Daria had left the room in disarray, and Bree had moved things around, but it was even more of a mess. No one had been here when she wasn't, so what had happened?

The pillow on the bed was out of its case. Other subtle changes caught her wide stare, a picture they had taken in Greece aslant on the wall, a sock hanging out of a drawer Bree had carefully closed. And two pairs of shoes, which had been under the bed skirt now peeked out.

Trembling, she glanced behind the door, then looked under the bed and into the closet, which looked rearranged. Bree opened the bureau drawers she'd gone through. She rifled through the top one, as she was certain someone else must have done.

The Gator Watering Hole coaster was gone.

She almost called Cole on his cell, but she remembered that she'd given Amelia a key to the apartment. It had been almost as if Bree had presented her with the Holy

Grail, she'd been so pleased. Maybe Amelia had wanted some remembrance of Daria and had just come over, though she didn't believe that was likely. At least she would have left a note. Of course, Manny knew where the extra apartment key was downstairs in Bree's desk. He'd been here all morning, while she was gone and Lucinda was sweeping the back room.

Shaken, she rejoined Lucinda, who had two glasses of juice waiting on the coffee table next to the orange orchid Cole had given her in the hospital. As Bree had asked, Lucinda had the veranda doors open to the warm breeze off the bay.

"Sorry I took so long," Bree said.

"No problem. By the way, the doors weren't locked like you said." She turned to Bree and smiled up at her. But her smile faded, and she went wide-eyed. "You okay?" the girl asked. "You look like you've seen a ghost."

14

"I'm not sure I want you to see the painting in my office," Cole told Bree as he unlocked the front door of his Turtle Bay shop, which had *Streamin'* and a yacht he'd been working on moored right out the back door. "I know the old pickup line is come have a look at my etchings, but this one may give you a jolt."

They had just returned from a Sunday brunch at Amelia and Ben's house where Cole had fallen in love with their two sons— in a much different way from what he was feeling about Bree. So fierce was his desire to protect her that he'd talked Manny into not telling her that Bess had insisted Daria had been meeting more than one man. There had to be a good explanation for that, and he wanted to break it to her gently. Maybe he'd find the right time once they were out sailing this afternoon.

It was a windy but hot, sunny day again, and he was going to take her out to leave a memorial wreath over the Trade Wreck site, where she'd last seen Daria. He knew she needed any kind of shoring up she could get. Not only was she grieving for the mysterious loss of her beloved sister, but Bree was deeply shaken by her discoveries that she hadn't known Daria as well as she'd thought.

"A painting?" she said. "What about it? Naked women or something? We thought about getting one of mermaids for our front office, but all the ones we found were top-less, and we figured it would give the wrong mess—oh, I see what you mean."

She stood silent at first, staring at the large reproduction of the painting as he closed and locked the door behind them.

"I've seen that before—in a book some-where, I mean," she told him, leaning lightly back against him as he put his hands on her shoulders. "Such wonderful movement and power."

"It's a great reproduction of my favorite painting of all time, a Winslow Homer done right around the turn of the nineteenth century. It's called *The Gulf Stream,* so I named the sloop and my business, Gulf Stream Yacht Interiors, for it. It's kind of my inspiration for my philosophy of life, especially in tough times."

His pulse picked up. Maybe he could break the bad news to Bree right here, but before he could say more, she interrupted. "Those are bull sharks swimming along with the sloop, right?"

"Right. But what I really love about it—the only reason I brought you through this way, when the sloop's out back—"

"Is because this is a sloop very similar to yours. And, like the day you rescued me, it protects the sailor from those sharks."

"True, but I always liked the way the sailor looks calm. The mast is broken, but the sloop's not sinking or even taking on water. Despite the looming storm and the danger in the water, he knows he'll get through it all."

Standing in his loose embrace, she turned to face him. He wanted to pull her to him, but he said, "There's one other thing I need to tell you about what Manny and I learned at the bar yesterday. Bess swears that Daria met at least two different men out in back there. It was dark, and she couldn't give a good description, but saw enough to know it was two men."

"What? But then—then there were two beers the bartender knew to give me. One shandy, two Mountain Brewed."

She didn't get the implications of what he was saying, Cole thought, and perhaps that was just as well, but he added, "Not two men at the same time—different times."

"Maybe she met a couple of guys from her class afterward," she went on. "I'd hate to go back to the school and make some general, public plea for information. Besides, why would both guys be so secret or taboo that she met them out in the dark in the boon-docks?" He could tell she was on a roll now, probably to keep from admitting Daria could have had an entire secret life built on lies. "Or, you know," Bree plunged on, "Viv Holliman's hair is really short. Maybe the Hollimans are the ones who met Daria there—to discuss business . . . at different times . . . but . . ."

Her voice trailed off. He saw her shudder. She must know she wasn't making sense.

"You think I'm clutching at straws," she said. "If—if," she stammered, "she was meeting more than one man and they found out and were insanely jealous or something like that, wouldn't they have gone after each other? You're thinking one of them might have wanted her to pay for two-timing him, then things got out of hand?"

He pulled her to him. Despite the fact she held the wreath she'd made, she put her free arm around him.

"I don't know what I'm thinking," he admitted. "So far we're still fact-finding and don't have enough to form a theory to act on. We've got a damn multiple-choice quiz going."

"I don't know if I can get through the funeral tomorrow," she admitted, her lips pressed to his shoulder, "especially with this new, dreadful possibility. I mean, if there was some sort of attack on Daria like there was on me . . . we'd have to convince the police of that. Cole, maybe she accidentally fell and hit her head during an argument with someone, but then, when he left the boat alone to drift and crash, it became sort of—of indirect homicide."

"Manslaughter."

"That's it. If any of that could be true, that it wasn't an accident, I've got to know, to get justice for her. And what if her attacker's at the funeral? I've heard that killers sometimes are drawn there or to the burial place of their victim. Who hurt her? Who hurt her and why?"

He cupped her face in his hands and wiped tears from her cheeks with his thumbs. "First of all, let's concentrate on getting through the funeral, and then we'll do what we can to find enough evidence to get the cops to open the case. Keep Daria's room sealed, and we'll try to get someone in there to take fingerprints, though if someone is truly clever and desperate, don't get your hopes up. Hey, the good news is that, when I agreed to do the job for Dom Verdugo, I talked him into moving his casino yacht from Miami to the marina here. That way I can stay around to help you. I suggested to him it would be good PR if he had the boat here for people to see. I think he's even planning a party cruise on it soon for influential people—without the gambling, of course."

"I know you want to keep the gambling from coming in here."

"I do, but I think he's also a good candidate if there was foul play in Daria's death, and I've spoken with more than one of his employees who could fit the description of your attacker."

"I'd put Sam's diver, Ric, on the list, too, even if he did make that dangerous dive to find Daria with us. All right, let's go, Captain. Bon voyage, ship ahoy and all that," she said, cradling the flower wreath to her. "Oh, I left the pelican float to keep the wreath in place in your car."

"I'll get it. Go on out in back and choose a piece of wood you like so we can float that better."

He kissed her quickly and headed back to his car. When he glanced through the front office window, he saw her still staring up at the picture of the sloop sailing toward the storm with the sharks chasing it.

"Why hasn't seeing more of Bree cheered you up?" Ben asked Amelia as they sat by the side of their screened veranda pool, watching the boys race little wooden sail-boats in the shallow end. "I don't mean that the loss of Daria is something you'll get over quickly, or ever, for that matter, but you've been spiraling down. Even Bree seems on a more even keel than you, and she's lost more than—"

"How dare you say that!" She shoved the book she'd been reading about the grieving process onto her chaise longue. Ben had been going over a stack of affidavits.

"I just meant Bree was her twin, lived with her . . . Honey, I'm going to call the doctor and have him prescribe something to get you through the funeral tomorrow."

"No," she said, reaching over to grab his wrist and trying to keep her voice down. "I won't be drugged so I say something I shouldn't."

"Like what?"

"I just mean your friends will be there, and a lot of important people, I'll bet. The Austins, maybe even Marla Sherborne. It's going to be a media event, and I won't have everyone staring at me because I look comatose."

Ben shifted his work aside and swung his legs down between their lounge chairs. He bent over his knees to lean closer as Jordan shouted from the pool, "Dad, my boat won that race. James says it didn't, but I did!"

"You two get along now or you're getting

out of there!" Ben told them. "I'm trying to talk to your mother."

"Trying to," Amelia noted. "Meaning, you're not being very successful at it."

"Let's not argue. I know you're under stress and I underst—"

"You don't. Not really. Ben, you're a lawyer and my husband. I have something to tell you, part of the reason I'm feeling so awful about Daria."

Instantly, his expression changed. His concerned gaze seemed more guarded, she thought. His shoulders tensed. But she had to tell someone some of it or she was going to go right out of her mind and be a raving harridan by tomorrow.

"I saw Daria the day she died," she blurted.

"And didn't say so? Why?"

"Please don't read too much into that. You know her birth caused my mother's death . . . ."

"Yes, but there was hardly any intent on her part."

"Would you just listen?" she said through gritted teeth. She wanted to scream at him, but the boys would hear. "I know you're used to firing questions at people, but just listen."

He nodded, curious now, but he looked like he was holding his breath.

"I made a date to have a late breakfast with her at the Grog Shop at the far end of Turtle Bay Marina that morning. I asked her not to tell or bring Bree. I guess I just thought I'd try to divide and conquer them, or something like that. Anyway, when we met outside on the dock, I told her I was tired of being shut out. That Dad had always shut me out, maybe because I looked so much like Mother, as if he couldn't bear to see a reminder of her."

"Go on," he prompted when she just gripped her hands tightly together.

"And she said, if anyone was the reminder of Mother's loss it was her and Briana, and they'd gotten along with Dad just fine."

"That's all?" Ben prompted when she said no more.

"I—I don't know what got into me, but I told her she was selfish—that I hated her. Then she got right in my face and said, 'Amelia, you've got to get over your crazy ideas Dad didn't love you and grow up.' Crazy ideas, she said. Then I—I shoved her and she shoved me back so hard I bounced into a mooring post and could have gone right into the water. I could have been crushed by one of those big boats tied there, for all she cared. And don't tell me I started it first, like I'm some kid. She—both of the twins are the ones who started all my problems, first losing my mother and then, in a different way, my dad!"

He stared at her a moment. She could see his wheels turning, assessing her story, probably looking for flaws, discerning motives. "There's no more?" he asked. "That's the last time you saw her, so you're feeling guilty about the way you parted?"

She nodded, kept nodding. Her entire body was shaking.

"I wouldn't tell anyone else about that unless it comes up somehow," he said. "You obviously didn't go in for breakfast together after that, so no one saw you eating with her. Amelia, you have got to find the strength to bury these deep-seated feelings. And don't argue with me when I make an appointment for you with a therapist I know. There's nothing else, is there?"

She realized she was still nodding. "No," she said, and shook her head side to side. There was more to tell, but she was hoping that bleeding out this much of the festering

poison would help her get through tomorrow. How ridiculous were those courtroom dramas or funeral scenes, where the guilty party shouted out what they'd done in front of everyone.

"Dad, Mom! He's looking at me really funny, and he's splashing me!" Jordan shouted. "Make him quit it! It's his fault."

"That's it!" Ben told them. "I'm coming in to play policeman and the first one of you who messes up is going to his room!"

He leaped up and cannonballed into the deep end to the squealing delight of their sons. Amelia stared at the big splash he'd made as her son's words—"It's his fault . . . fault . . . fault . . ."—echoed in her head.

"I picked this piece of dark wood since black's the color of mourning," Bree told Cole as he came into his back workroom with the pelican float from his car. She loved the rich smell of this well-lit workroom, piled high with various exotic woods in long trays. His workbench looked out over the far end of the marina next to the Grog Shop Restaurant. Cole had told her he ate a lot of his meals there, when he didn't get takeout or delivery.

A man who was dedicated to his work, she thought, just as she had been.

"African wenge wood," he said of the stark piece. "That's a good choice. It's very hard wood with not much grain." He took a minute to attach the peach and yellow hibiscus and blue plumbago blossoms to it so they wouldn't break up, then they headed out the back toward the *Streamin'*.

At least it was a cloudy day. Sometimes she thought her hearing was not as acute as it had been at first after the lightning strike, but she was still overly sensitive to light. Perhaps that helped her to see better in low-vis water—Briana Devon, the X-ray-eyed underwater superwoman. Maybe that was why she had spotted the broken piece of *Mermaids II* and then the wheelhouse with Daria inside, when the other divers didn't see things as clearly.

The *Streamin'* headed out into the bay at a good clip, as if she yearned for a race. Bree didn't doubt that Cole could make this sloop move, even if it was dead calm. Bree and Cole had life preservers nearby, but she didn't feel she needed one with him at the helm. Still, she warned herself, as the sails bellied out and they moved from the bay into the gulf, after all she'd learned about Daria since her death, she should know better than to totally trust anyone now. Love might never change but the trust at its foundation could.

The wind tugged at her hair and shirt; they were almost flying. She loved to escape the land and ride the waves, but she could hardly escape her grief at sea. In a way, her sister was and always would be a part of the deep and its mysteries. This great water had given Daria joy and purpose, but it had taken her life—or so the authorities said. She might have drowned, Bree thought, but she was becoming more and more certain that the sea was not the real killer.

She wondered if she should have let Daria's remains be buried at sea. She could have agreed with the Hollimans' Eternal Shells offer, but she couldn't trust them. Too much the shysters, but then, she wasn't certain who wasn't. Someone, maybe someone close to Daria, and to Bree, too, could have caused her death.

"You said you can find the spot by heart now," Cole called to her.

By heart, she thought. Yes, she'd always be able to find the spot she last saw Daria alive by heart, a broken heart.

"It's right about here," she told him. "Just a sec, and I'll eyeball the land coordinates."

She looked back toward shore and picked out the Naples pier and Gordon Pass to the south, then triangulated those by the reddish roof of the Ritz Carlton Hotel to the north.

"Yes, this spot is good," she told him, "but go a little farther south before you anchor so you don't catch the turtle grass meadow. Which reminds me, I'll have to get someone to come out here to check it with me Tuesday morning before my report to the commission that afternoon."

"You think you can handle the dive and the report alone—without Daria, I mean?"

"Yes, I can," she said, her voice strong. "I have to see that all through. Maybe it will flush someone out."

"Not with you as the bait! And I won't let you dive alone. I'll go down with you, if you promise to stay out of the wreck."

She nodded, but he wasn't looking as he furled and tied the sails and dropped anchor. As she readied the wreath, he came to help her. How sore she felt from the beating she'd taken yesterday. She was turning black-and-blue—even greenish-gold—in places she couldn't show Cole.

She appreciated how he let her guide the placement of the wreath, just lifted it to keep its weight off her hands as she balanced everything on the side of the sloop. When the boat listed a bit toward their weight, he leaned farther aport, leaving her to bend over the side of the sloop alone.

For one moment, Bree wasn't sure she could bear to let it go. How would she ever get through the funeral if she couldn't even let go of a wreath she'd made?

She gently placed it on the water, threw the pelican float's sixty-foot tether line in, then dropped the round metal anchor she had tied to the piece of wood. The float bobbed to the surface, its red Day-Glo rings bright and bold. The wreath looked lovely on the wood. It started away, then bobbed almost in place as it rode the waves.

She was grateful that Cole gave her this moment alone, yet she longed to cling to him. Staring down into the gray-green depths, she mouthed the silent words, *I love you, my Daria. I'll always love you, but what did you do? What did you get mixed up in?*

She remembered again that she hadn't heard a motor in the water that day. How had someone approached *Mermaids II?* Maybe in a sailboat?

At that thought, she jumped when Cole came close again. They sat on the floor of the sloop with his back against the stern seat. He'd been sailing that day of Daria's death, she thought. Others could have been, as well. That could be why she hadn't heard a motor.

When he pulled her into his arms, she leaned against him, grateful for his concern and strength. "Did you see any other sailboats out last Tuesday?" she asked. "Since the weather guys were really off that day, others—especially people with big sailboats—might have gone out."

"I saw a few, at least early. But they seemed pretty distant."

"From you or from this position?"

"I get where you're going, but I'm not sure how we'd check into that. Area marinas seldom keep track of when vessels permanently moored at their facilities put out, and a lot of sailboats, just like power boats, are in private berths up and down all the canals."

"I suppose," she said with a sigh, "I could inquire of the civil air patrol, but they already put in so many hours. When Dave Mangold, my pilot friend from the patrol, gets back in town, I can have him ask around if any planes were flying the day of the storm and saw any watercraft of any kind. It all just seems like such a long shot. Cole, she must have known whoever approached her. I'll bet whatever boat came up to her, she recognized someone and let them board our boat or get too close to her. It's creepy to think of her out here in this exact spot, while someone crept up or tricked her somehow . . ."

"Don't think about it now. You're here to honor her memory today. You need to relax before tomorrow."

She nodded fiercely and turned so she had her back against the inside of his knee for support. He had one arm around her waist; her bent legs were draped over his other one. It eased her lower back pain to lean into him, and it eased her heart just to touch him.

"Cole, my voice of reason," she said, putting her head on his shoulder. She knew she was setting herself up to be kissed: she hoped so, the cut on the inside of her mouth and sore muscles notwithstanding.

"I don't ever feel very reasonable about you," was all he said before he bent to cover her mouth with his.

It was their first real kiss of mutual, meshing needs and desires. He'd comforted her before; he'd protected her. Now she wanted more.

The boat moved under them in a rhythmic cadence, and they seemed to roll with it, first one way, then the other, their weight toward her, then him. He slanted his mouth over hers and his hard hands pulled her closer. As she wrapped her arms around his neck, his free hand skimmed over her, shoulder, arms, waist, hips, thighs, back up to cup her breast. She arched under him, breathing with him. His merest touch seemed to heal all her body's aches and pains, if not those of her heart.

The *Streamin'* yanked against its anchor and dipped its masts. The lines creaked and the waves rustled incredibly loudly.

A ship sneaking up on us? Bree thought. As she jerked bolt upright, her head bumped his chin. She twisted away from him to look all around.

"What?"

"I just—sorry. I thought I heard something, that there was another boat. Sorry."

"Yeah, me, too. I wasn't sure if that was the

boat rocking or the entire world. I'd better bring her around."

Bree steadied herself as he scrambled for the tiller. She saw that the wreath took the push of the waves but stayed firmly in place. That's what she would do, too, she vowed. Cole brought up the anchor and unfurled the mainsail. "Watch out, or you'll see where we get the saying, Lower the boom."

She ducked and he brought the ship about and headed them back in. He'd handled both the sailboat and her skittish behavior smoothly. Amazing that she'd only been with this man off and on for five days, and yet felt she knew him. The same mistake she'd evidently made with Daria.

15

It was a blessing that the day of the funeral was cloudy with a sea breeze, or it would have made the temperature in the little church where Daria's family stood in a receiving line unbearable. So many attended that the line came up the center aisle and snaked around the side, leading past the closed casket.

"This funeral brings back memories of someone lost too young," Sam Travers told Bree.

She instantly felt on alert. Ric and Lance were with him. Bree stared hard at Ric, trying to see if he avoided her gaze. He didn't, but his left cheek had a cut on the same side where she'd hit her attacker with the bottle. Of course, it could be from anything, and salvage diving was too often a contact sport.

"Yes," Bree said to Sam, deciding not to give in to his subtle badgering. "Very happy memories of my life with Daria, which I will always cherish. I wouldn't want to let bitterness consume me. And I do thank you for all your help in the search for her."

"Oh, so nice of you to come . . ." she said to the next people in line as she turned away before Sam could fire another salvo. As if she had sent Cole a mental SOS, he suddenly appeared, shouldering Sam slightly aside and offering her a glass of water.

"Thanks for being so thoughtful," she told Cole as Sam glowered and moved on.

"I heard," Cole said, speaking quietly and quickly, "that Sam's firm has taken a job in Sarasota to help demolish the supports of an old bridge, so he'll be out of town for the next few weeks."

"Good! Sam would go anywhere in the state for a demolitions job. Ted used to talk about how his dad was a Vietnam War hero, setting charges to destroy bridges and underwater barriers to troop movements. His specialty has always been combat or commercial explosives. That's probably made it much harder for him to accept that Ted's death was from a bomb. I wish he could let it go, but I am starting to understand his pain."

Cole took her water glass and moved away again. He seemed to be everywhere in the room, yet kept an eye on her. Anytime she looked his way, he was watching, even when he had her two nephews practically hanging on to him in their mutual admiration society, which they had formed swiftly. That had deeply touched her. Cole was good with kids. Everything about him seemed so good.

"Mayor Dixon," she said, greeting the next person in line, "thank you so much for coming. Daria would have been honored . . ."

During their wait to speak with the family, visitors viewed photos Bree had selected of high points in Daria's life. It was hard to find ones that she herself wasn't in, too. She made sure most of the early pictures had Amelia in them.

"Josh and Nikki, you've been a great support through all of this," she greeted the Austins as they exchanged hugs.

"It's the least we could do for an old friend

of Josh's," Nikki said. "And for you, too,
Briana. Oh, I'd like you to meet my father,
Cory Grann from Clewiston. And I believe
you've met his friend, Marla Sherborne."

Politics might make strange bedfellows,
Bree thought, but this was quite a crew. Cory
Grann was extremely handsome. He would
have made a good Marlboro man, and he
would have fit in a Clint Eastwood gritty
Western. Yet he was dressed like the captain
of a yacht with white slacks, a natty navy
blazer and an ascot, no less. More than anyone else here, he seemed to be cool and col-
lected as he gave his condolences. This, she
thought, was the so-called sugar baron ecolo-
gists loved to blame for pollution runoff.

"Oh," Nikki said, gesturing toward a thirty-
something man who brought up the rear of
their group, "and this is Mark Denton, our
campaign aide and pilot."

Bree shook his hand. His shake was so
firm she fought to keep from wincing. She
was still sore and had covered several
bruises with makeup today. She noted that
Nikki left out that Denton was also a bodyguard, but then others were leaning in, trying
to hear what the celebrities of the gathering
were saying.

"Sorry for your loss," he told her. His lips barely moved when he spoke, as if he was the master of the stiff upper lip. If he was skilled at PR, it was probably all in written releases and sound bites.

Surprised that Josh hadn't spoken, Bree turned to him. It wasn't like him to be so quiet. He looked ashen. Either he was ill or he was grieving for all he and Daria had once shared. Tears in his eyes, he clasped her hand until Nikki put her arm in his and he abruptly let go.

"We're staying for the funeral," Nikki told Bree. "And we'd love to have you visit us someday, especially if you want a change of scenery for a while. At our retreat near Clewiston, I mean—in Tallahassee we do nothing but run around in circles, both in different directions. But we have a house on my father's grounds near Clewiston and Lake Okeechobee. Nothing but boring sugarcane for miles, but it's amazingly relaxing. We could even send Mark to fly you over."

"It is just lovely there," Marla put in.

"That's very kind," Bree told them, deeply touched.

"Sure, no problem, picking you up," Mark Denton said as if to fill an awkward moment when Josh still didn't speak. "My employers' wish is my command." Marla and Cory Grann were already talking to Ben and Amelia, and the line moved on.

Friends and friends of friends went by in a blur. Bree had a chance to ask Daria's accounting instructor if any of the students went out together after class, but he said he didn't think so. She asked the same of Viv and Frank Holliman.

"We suggested it once—twice, didn't we, Viv?" he said.

"But Daria always had to get home and left very promptly, though we did spend time chatting with her before class, when she was there."

"I saw her copy of your brochure," Bree told them, still embarrassed she hadn't believed them at first. "Eternal Shells looks like a fascinating opportunity, but I really needed to pass on it for my sister."

"After all, our earthly shells are delicate and we need to think in terms of eternal ones," Frank said, quoting exactly a line from their brochure. "Well, keep it in mind for yourself—someday."

Bree could not shake her instinctively uneasy feeling around them. Despite what they had said about never meeting Daria after class, Frank was built a lot like her attacker—and perhaps like the man Daria had met out in the Glades. He could have worn a wig to help disguise himself, and he could have cheated on Viv. But surely Daria couldn't have been attracted to him—at least, the Daria Bree thought she knew.

After greeting guests, who must have numbered at least two hundred, and making sure that the reporters at the front of the church were kept at a distance, the family led everyone outside in back for the funeral itself.

It was standing room only, after the family and closest friends filled the chairs that church volunteers had set up. The view of the gray-green bay and gulf beyond the coffin, then the pewter-hued horizon, was magnificent. Bree had left the photos inside, for they would just blow away, but she'd placed some of Daria's favorite seashells and her diving mask on the casket next to the family's spray of white roses, with the ribbon which read *Beloved Sister and Aunt.*

James and Jordan were on Ben's far side, swinging their little legs and shifting in their wooden seats. Briana was on the center aisle at Amelia's right side, with Ben on

Amelia's left. Bree thought that Pastor Wallace said all the right things, comforting things, uplifting things. But she still felt so lonely and low.

"I'll read now from Psalm 107," the pastor said as his simple black-and-white robe fluttered in the breeze.

"Those who go down to the sea in ships,
Who do business on great waters,
They see the works of the Lord,
And his wonders in the deep . . ."

He went on reading about those at the mercy of the sea, who cry out in their troubles. He said everyone was grateful that they had not lost Briana that dreadful day, too. *Was* everyone grateful for that? she wondered.

The pastor segued into a message on Daria's too-short life, on the gifts she took from the sea and the gifts she gave the sea, including a mention of the report that would be made public tomorrow. "Daria's sea grass project endeavored to protect God's great and precious sea, just as God now protects her soul forever. Daria—with her twin sister at her side—loved God's creation, both above these waters we see even now and far below their surface."

When Amelia kept fidgeting more than her sons, Bree realized she should have asked the pastor not to overplay their twinship, but then, he knew little about the third sister. So many people had remarked about how much Bree looked like Daria, how it was as if she still moved among them, and Amelia had looked more shaken each time she overheard that.

The funeral director had asked Bree and Amelia if they would like to view the body before closing the casket, but they'd both declined. Bree wanted to shut out the horrid picture of how Daria had looked when they'd found her body, and Amelia just repeated, "I can't. I'm so sorry, so sorry . . ."

Bree tried to concentrate on the service, but she kept wondering whether her attacker—and maybe Daria's murderer—was here. Fred Holliman was the perfect height, but would a wig have stuck to his head after a fall in a ditch when his baseball cap came off? And that bruise on Ric's cheek. She had no doubt Sam Travers would give everything he had to see Bree suffer as he had since Ted died. No, she was going crazy, carrying everything too far. Where was the line between self-protection and paranoia?

Over Amelia's protest, Bree had insisted the Salazars sit just behind their family. Manny was deeply grieved today, and his wife, Juanita, kept crossing herself. Lucinda sat next to her older sister, Carianne. Their family was all in black and wearing large crucifixes, even Lucinda.

The members of the Clear the Gulf Commission were here and sitting together, except for Cole, who kept prowling the perimeter of the church and now was standing off to the side as if he'd been hired to keep order.

The congregation sang "Eternal Father Strong To Save," which Bree knew as the Navy Hymn, with its resonant, haunting chorus of "O, hear us when we cry to thee/ For those in peril on the sea."

Oh, yes, she could cry right now. Amelia was sobbing silently, her shoulders shaking despite the fact Ben had a firm grip of her left wrist. Bree clasped her other hand. Crying would do no good. It was finding out who had possibly hurt Daria and making that person pay that would bring some closure.

Bree would find a way to forgive, but only after truth and justice had its way.

She stared at Daria's favorite diving mask on top of the casket. The diffused sun glinted strangely off the plastic as if two bright, unearthly eyes stared out from behind it. Someone here was wearing a mask. Someone here might be pretending to be grieving and be staring at her even now. Had Daria's murderer meant to kill her, or was it an accident and he or she had simply fled before the boat was taken by the storm and bashed on the seawall? Had that same killer come after Bree? And the most terrifying thought of all: could the murderer have meant to kill Bree but mistook Daria for her twin?

The benediction was from a Bible verse Bree and Daria had always liked because it seemed to them it asked for the Lord's blessing on daily work. Starting out their business, they'd needed all the help they could get.

"So teach us to number our days
That we might have a heart of wisdom . . .
And let the beauty of the Lord our God be upon us,

And establish the work of our hands for us;
Yes, establish the work of our hands."

After a final prayer, Pastor Wallace announced that everyone was invited to stay for a luncheon served by the women of the church here on the lawn, after which there would be a private burial for family only. Everyone stood while the pallbearers carried the casket to the hearse for now.

Bree took Amelia's arm and walked her inside, with Ben on her other side and both boys keeping close. Amelia was trembling so hard that Bree's heart went out to her. She had denied coming into their apartment and searching Daria's room for mementos. Bree believed her, but even that inquiry must have shaken Amelia. Her older sister must also be mourning the times she had never had with Daria, and the lack of precious memories to cherish.

"I just can't face everyone right now," Amelia said, pulling away. "I'm going to ask the pastor if there's someplace I can lie down."

"I'd go sit with you," Bree said, "but someone besides Ben has to mingle."

"Yes, of course. Besides, everyone's feeling sorry for you, not me."

"Amelia, I—"

"It's all right, Bree," Ben said. "You boys stay with Aunt Bree until I get your mother settled down."

"Not much wailing and no kneeling, not like when Grandpa died," Lucinda told her family in English as they ate sandwiches and salads on the lawn between the church and the bay. "Feels funny not to have a mass, too."

"It is their way, and it's okay," Manny told her.

"Glad you can accept different ways of thinking and doing things," Lucinda muttered.

"Don't start!" he said, shaking a finger in her face.

"Don't either of you start," Juanita said. "She set you up for that one, *sí?* Let's just get along today, all right? This the United States of America, and thanks to Bree, we accepted here right with the money and power people."

Manny just glared at Lucinda as he finished his lemonade. "Maybe when word gets out I'm Bree Devon's partner, people 'round here won't like that," he said, wiping his mouth with the back of his hand. "When I went with Cole to that place I told you 'bout, if looks could kill, I be dead. And that backwoods bar not even up to Turtle Bay."

"Shh!" Juanita scolded. "It bad luck at a funeral talk about your own death. It mean, if you not die within the next year, the next of kin of this one buried today be dead."

Manny rolled his eyes. "Sometimes, *mi* Juanita, I see why our Lucinda want to run from our ways. Next you be telling me just 'cause this a sad day, our *quinceañera* for her be cursed. Let's say *adios* to my partner Briana and head home, *sí?*"

When they made their farewells, he was surprised that Bree and Lucinda hugged each other. And annoyed when he heard Bree say quietly to her, "Remember what I said, Cindi."

The ceremony at the grave site was blessedly brief, because Amelia was still a wreck and that was destroying Bree's hard-won poise, too. They all walked to their cars. Ben put Amelia in theirs—the boys had gone home with a friend—when Bree said, "I'm staying until they close the grave."

Ben turned to face her. "It will depress you even more. You don't have to do that."

"I know. But I came into the world with her, and I want to see her settled and at peace, as they say."

He took her arm and walked her away from his car. In the distance they could see the funeral director talking to the cemetery crew with their waiting backhoe.

"Bree," Ben said, obviously fighting to keep his patience, "she's at peace. Now you have to work on that, too, not keep causing waves."

"That's a good one," she said. "Not causing waves."

"You know what I mean. I can tell you're not really letting the dead be dead. I'm not the county prosecutor for nothing, and I can read between the lines about what you've been thinking all of a sudden. If you pursue a half-cocked murder scenario, you're only going to get yourself upset or worse, hurt."

She pulled away from his hand on her arm and turned to face him squarely. She was tempted to tell him she'd been attacked, but she didn't want him insisting she stay home or with Amelia. And what he'd just said almost sounded like a threat. "Hurt, meaning?" she asked.

"To use another cliché, you're going to stir up a hornet's nest if you go around suspecting people of some sort of wrongdoing, accusing them—"

"I *will* accuse them if I find out someone staged that so-called accident. I thought a county prosecutor might call a possible murder a little more than 'some sort of wrongdoing.'"

"Amelia said you think someone broke in and searched Daria's room. If I get a CSI tech to come out there and take prints, will you lay off?"

"I'd appreciate that. I was going to try to get the police to do that."

"I said, will you lay off then?"

"No. Someone clever enough to pop the lock on my veranda doors and desperate enough to climb up onto the second story to do that needs to be stopped. But if CSI does turn up a set of prints other than mine or Daria's, will you pursue it?"

"Of course I will. Look, I'll see if I can call in a favor and send someone over tonight. We wanted to have you come back to the house, but Amelia needs to take a tranquilizer and go to bed. She's never gotten over what she considered desertion by her mother, then her father."

"That's not the way it was."

"But if she thinks it's true, it's reality to her, and I can't risk her losing you on top of Daria. There's my bottom line."

So he wasn't actually threatening her. He was just worried about Amelia, and that was completely understandable.

"And another thing," he said, in what seemed a lame attempt to change the subject so she wouldn't argue about Amelia and their father, "is Cole DeRoca."

"What about him? He only saved my life and has been more help to me than anyone. Please don't tell Amelia that, but it's true. Jordan and James like him and—"

"I like him, too, but think about it. He's overly possessive and protective of you, and you've only known him a week. I'm advising, in the emotional state you're in, not to get either psychologically or physically involved with him."

That advice reminded her of what she'd just told Lucinda, but this was different. She was not some adolescent girl in rebellion against her parents.

"Actually," she told Ben, "I had met Cole once before. I even had lunch with him, but he was going through a divorce and nothing came of it right then."

"See, then he might be emotionally vulnerable right now. You know—the rebound effect."

"Thank you, Dr. Phil."

"I admit it's a blessing that he found you on the beach and saved your life. But he's too convenient. He's always in the right place at the right time. His office and workshop are right next to the Grog Shop at the end of town, right?"

"Yes. And?"

"Are you positive he didn't know Daria, if he'd bumped into you before?"

"What are you implying? He knew of Daria, because he's on the Clear the Gulf Commission. But we were given our assignment to observe and photograph the sea grass meadow without actually appearing before the commission. My report tomorrow will be the first time I've been there live, so to speak. Ben, you're wrong about Cole. If I can't trust him, I can't trust anyone."

But those last words tasted bitter in her mouth. If she hadn't known her own twin sister, her lifelong best friend, could she really trust a man she'd known only a week?

16

___

True to his word, Ben sent a CSI tech to Bree's place that night. Foolishly, she had been expecting someone like she'd seen on the various TV shows featuring forensic scientists, but it was a young, plain, overweight woman. Her ID card hanging on a bright blue cord around her neck read Marilyn Davis but she asked Bree to call her Mari.

"You'll see this makes a bit of a mess," Mari said as Bree led her toward Daria's bedroom, "but I want to lift a lot of prints, then eliminate yours. If you have something you're sure your sister touched—a glass in the bathroom you haven't cleaned yet, something like that, I'll eliminate hers, too. Oh, this place has really been tossed, hasn't it?"

"I'm afraid so. I had searched it earlier but someone else did, too, and those are the prints we hope to identify."

"Did you report the B and E—breaking and entering?" she asked as she tugged on latex gloves and got to work, leaving small pools of dark powder here and there.

"No, because several people had keys. Evidently nothing of value has been taken that I could report."

"Okeydoke," she said, her voice darkening with disapproval. Bree almost told her that Ben hadn't suggested reporting it either, but it was none of her business.

"You know," Mari said, perhaps eager to change the subject, "I've never dusted a place where identical twins were involved. A lot of people figure they have identical prints, but that's not so."

"We've been asked that more than once over the years," Bree told her as she leaned in the entry to the bathroom and watched her work. "The prints are supposed to have similarities, though."

"True. Identicals have the same genetic makeup and their DNA is virtually indistinguishable, but fingerprints are not completely a genetic characteristic. They're partly determined by each separate embryo's environment in the uterus. Their ultimate shape can be influenced by position in the womb and a few other things I can't recall from my forensic classes."

Bree went into the bathroom to get Daria's drinking glass and gingerly took Daria's mascara and powder from her makeup drawer. She could see visible prints on both plastic cases. Many more cosmetics were here than Bree had recalled her using, including seven tubes of lipstick, when she almost never wore that. But she was getting used to being surprised about her sister. There had been a man in her life she had not wanted to tell Bree about. She only hoped that she hadn't done something that kept Daria from confiding in her. Surely, it was something about the man himself that made Daria remain silent, and she needed to find out what that was.

She rifled through the rest of the cosmetics drawer but found nothing. Perhaps she'd find nothing, prove nothing. She was becoming more and more certain that someone had harmed—killed—Daria, and that now, somehow, she'd become a target, too. Her stomach fluttered in fear, but she beat the feeling down as she put the items in a towel and took them to Mari.

She stared at the thin white gloves encasing Mari's busy hands. Maybe the person who'd searched this room had worn gloves, too.

"I appreciate your taking care of this so quickly," Bree said, leaning in the doorway again. She couldn't stand the silence in the room as Mari moved about like a ghost.

"Orders from the top."

"My brother-in-law, Ben Westcott?"

"Him and some other big brass."

"Josh Austin?"

Bending intently over a brass pull of the dresser, she shrugged her shoulders, but admitted, "The whole CSI unit is amazed at how fast the autopsy report was completed and released. At least, most of it."

"What do you mean, most of it?"

Mari straightened. Her eyes widened, as if she realized she'd overstepped, however much Bree knew about Ben and Josh pulling strings.

"Probable cause of death was the key thing, that's all."

"But what else wasn't released yet?"

"Forensics differs with different situations. I'm sure you'll see everything in black and white soon."

She'd obviously clammed up. Was there something else about Daria's death? Surely she had not been beaten or assaulted, because no one could pass that off as an accident. What else could an autopsy reveal? Could she have been hiding some sort of serious, even terminal, illness? Maybe if word of that got out it might look like she'd committed suicide and neither Ben nor Josh would want that. No, impossible. People with fatal diseases didn't make appointments to get their teeth whitened. It all came back to the fact that Daria would never have left Bree alone out in the gulf. *But,* a little voice taunted her, *the woman who died that day was not the woman you thought you knew.*

As soon as Mari finished and left with her collection of prints, Bree locked the place up tight and drove to Ben and Amelia's. Good. Lights were still on in their spacious home. She hoped Ben hadn't gone to bed, because she planned to question him about the rest of the autopsy report.

She knocked instead of ringing the bell. The porch light clicked on, then off, and Ben opened the door. She gasped when she saw he held not only the evening paper but a pistol at his side.

"Don't mind this," he said, putting it down on the table in the hall. "When I answer the door late at night, it's just a precaution. In my position—"

"In your position," she interrupted, following him into the den, "you tend to play God."

"What? Did the CSI person come? What are you talking ab—"

"Don't blame her, but she let something slip about the rest of the autopsy report—you know, the rest of the story."

Leaning over the back of his tall, leather chair, he frowned. Hands on her hips, Bree faced him.

"What about it?" he asked. "You and Amelia didn't need to see all those chemical readouts of blood, bladder and stomach tests, ad infinitum, or diagrams of dissections. She wasn't on drugs, she wasn't drunk, she wasn't ill, so—"

"I want to see it, all of it."

"A lot of that stuff takes days. I thought it best if the family got her body back and had her laid to rest. The county medical examiner could have held her body for up to ten days when it needed to be embalmed, not just refrigerated, especially in this hot weather. There. You wanted the facts, you've got them. It was hard enough as is and didn't need to be dragged out."

"I'd like to drag the truth out of you!"

"Now look," he said, pointing at her and raising his voice before he lowered it again. "My goal in all this—to protect Amelia first, and then you."

"Amelia, fine, but you have no right to make decisions for me or for Daria. And, of course, none of this has a thing to do with protecting your reputation, especially with the election less than two months away."

"That didn't even enter my mind."

"Let's say I partly believe that, but I want to see the autopsy report. Do you have a copy here?"

"No."

"Then I'm going to the Collier County Medical Examiner's office first thing tomorrow, before I dive the Trade Wreck, and demand to see—"

"All right, damn it," he said, and finally came around his chair to slump in it. Bree was horrified to see how ashen and haggard he suddenly looked. It was as if he'd been drained of fight and energy. "You asked for this," he said, "so just sit down and brace yourself. Swear to me you won't spring this on Amelia, because she's really shaken— grieving for all she's lost over the years, as well as for Daria."

Bree perched on the edge of the smaller leather chair facing his. As she gripped her hands together in her lap, every nerve in her body tensed.

"The autopsy revealed Daria was about seven weeks' pregnant."

A great silence crashed into the room. Bree could hear her heartbeat, feel her blood rushing through her veins. Yet her mind went blank. At first those words seemed to bounce off her, as if they were in a foreign language. She didn't move, she didn't breathe. Strangely, the first thought she had was that she now knew why Daria had avoided diving these last few weeks— why she'd lied that she had a bad tooth- ache the day of the storm. It wasn't wise for pregnant women to scuba, since too much water pressure could harm a fetus. Daria had known she was pregnant and had wanted to protect her baby!

Bree wanted to scream, but she amazed herself by speaking calmly—it seemed to be another person's voice. "Can a DNA test ID the father?"

"A DNA test of the fetus would indicate paternity—if you had the father's to match with it. But I didn't want her body dissected in that way. And having Daria disinterred now that she's buried would be crazy and cruel."

She wanted to argue that he was the one pushing for a quick autopsy and burial, but she said only, "It might lead us to her killer."

"Bree, stop it! It would also make all the papers and stir up scuttlebutt. I—I take it you didn't know."

"Of course I didn't know! Not about a pregnancy and not about who could be the father. Why would I know something like that? I'm only her roommate, twin sister, life-long friend, the person closest to her in the entire universe—at least, I used to think so."

She was tempted to tell him that she'd been attacked at the Gator Watering Hole, but she was coming not to trust Ben. Even if he'd sent the CSI tech, he hadn't urged her to report the B and E, and now the report of the prints would go to him before Bree saw it. He had claimed that protecting his own reputation played no part in all this, but he'd just blurted out he was trying to avoid scuttlebutt. He must have realized that the unborn baby—her niece or nephew, who had died with Daria—was a motive for murder, depending on what the murderer had to protect. Ben was the county prosecutor, for heaven's sake! But he was trying to gloss this over, stonewall things. Just to spare Amelia and her, as he had said?

She glared at him, unable to hide her anger. "Ben, you know very well that whoever's child it was, whoever she was meeting secretly, could have killed her."

"In the middle of the gulf in a storm?" he challenged. "You said you didn't hear a motor. Maybe he walked on water or swam out three miles."

"I never thought I'd live to see you obstruct justice," she accused. She rose and started out of the den. Ben jumped up and grabbed her arm, swinging her back around.

"And you're going off the deep end!" he accused, his grip tightening.

"Last time you said I was making waves and now I've gone off the deep end. You've got lots of deep, rough water on the brain. Now let me go! I'm devastated and horrified and furious, yes, at her—and you—and at myself for not knowing. I'm going home to bed to sob my eyes out—again."

She shook loose from him. "Is there anything else I should know?" she demanded.

"Just that even the surprising fact of her pregnancy does not warrant your demand that this become a murder case. I'll let you know about the fingerprints, and I'm monitoring things."

"Oh, I see you are," she said, and strode for the front door. As he caught up and opened it for her, she added, "Will you tell Amelia?"

"Since you've taken it out of my hands, yes."

His pistol lay on the hall table. She had the strangest sense she should take it with her, for her own protection. Just like those sharks, something *was* swimming just below the darkening surface of her life, but she couldn't tell what.

When she finally fell into a fitful sleep that night, Bree sank into the sea. Its black depths reached for her, powerful and violent, and pulled her down, down.

At the bottom of the gulf, the stormy currents swept her into a glass coffin, where she held her breath and tried to fight her way out. She had no scuba tanks, no regulator, no air. Where was her mask?

Water filled the glass coffin. Her hair drifted in her face like her dying turtle grass. It stuck to the skin over her eyes, blinding her like the water in a ditch. She struggled to see.

She raised her hands to get out, to fight against being drowned, against being attacked by a man with a raised wrench. But the wrench was shaped like a concrete shell just outside her glass coffin. People waved from outside. Her parents. Ted. Daria, with a baby floating in her arms.

Someone else appeared on the other side of the glass. Sam, smiling through his mask, happy to see her trapped. He shouted at her, but her good hearing had gone and her hair half blinded her.

Daria, where are you? Daria . . . who scuttled the ship? Who drowned you?

Scuttlebutt. Ben was outside, too, shouting that he was trying to protect the family from scuttlebutt. He, too, wore a diving mask that hid his face, but she could see he had his gun. He was not pointing it at her, but at something in the depths, the dark depths of the sea . . . .

Where was Cole? Cole could come to save her.

Though she was trying hard to hold her breath—her last breath—she screamed Cole's name. A man in a black mask wanted her to drown, but someone was shaking her and she shoved her hair away and sucked in a huge breath.

"Bree. Bree! Sweetheart, you're having a nightmare," the deep voice said. "Wake up, it's Cole."

It was real. He was here, smoothing her hair away from her face, which was wet with tears.

Yes, she remembered now. She'd called him after she drove back from Ben's. Cole had come over and insisted on sleeping on her sofa. Last time she'd had a nightmare, Amelia had run to her, but this was Cole. Thank God, it was Cole.

He held her until she stopped trembling. "Want to talk about it?" he whispered.

"No, it's too bizarre. I just want it to go away, to forget it, forget everything."

He wore his shorts but no shirt. His bare chest seemed so broad with its expanse of muscled skin and crisp, curly hair. He felt cool compared to her.

"Running away," he said, "is not how you've been handling any of this. You know that would never work."

"I know. I know. I'm so glad you're here."

"After all this is settled, I'd like us to spend time together of a different kind."

She hugged him. "Yes."

"I'm trying really hard not to take advantage of the fact that you need me now. We hardly know each other under normal circumstances."

She knew he was trying to talk himself out of climbing into bed with her, but she didn't want to make that easy for him. She held him tight. Sure, she was insane, dancing on the edge of the same sort of desire that must have hit Daria so hard she had to hide things. She clung tighter to him.

"Bree, sweetheart, I can hardly breathe."

"That's the way it was in my nightmare. Sorry."

She loosened her grip on him slightly and sat up straighter, though they still leaned against each other. Since Bree had heard Ben say Daria was pregnant, nothing had sunk in. Even in explaining it all to Cole, it had not seemed real. The sister she would have sworn she knew seemed to slip further away than even death could take her.

Now Bree fought to clear her head. First thing tomorrow, she had to check the Trade Wreck sea grass meadow, photograph its sorry state one last time before she found the strength to give her report without Daria by her side. But Cole would be with her during the dive and there at the Clear the Gulf Commission. Why couldn't she clear her head and forget the nightmare that clung to her as hard as she had to Cole?

She shifted slightly away from him and swiped at her slick cheeks. He handed her a tissue from the box of them on her bedside table. Nodding her thanks, she blew her nose and wiped her eyes, then took a drink from the glass of water he handed her.

"A part of me," she admitted, "does want to run away. Take a cruise, drive down to the Keys and sit on the beach, but anywhere I could see the water would haunt me. Maybe

I should take Josh and Nikki up on their invitation to have Mark Denton fly me across the state and stare at nothing but boring sugarcane fields, as Nikki put it."

"Do you mean it?"

"No. I've got to see our sea grass project through, even if it will create a lot of fallout. That turtle grass is in worse shape than I am. For Daria and the future of everything around here, I've got to see it all through. The meadow is dying from toxic pollution— and that means the entire biological chain and this whole paradise are endangered. Sorry. It seems I'm delivering my report already." She tried to smile through her tears. "I'm sorry I woke you up."

"You didn't. Despite the hum of the AC, every sound outside jolts me awake."

"You're too tall for the sofa."

"I'm fine. You think you can sleep?"

"I've got to. I can't go into that meeting looking like a witch."

"Not you, not ever, even now. My mermaid is like those beautiful sirens that lured Odysseus's ship right into them."

"To crash into the rocks, you mean."

He kissed the top of her mussed head and slid off the bed, reluctantly, she could tell.

Yes, she needed him, and she was pretty sure she loved him, too. But had Daria thought that and made some sort of colossal mistake with a man she desired? A fatal error?

17

It seemed strange to dive without Daria, yet so comforting to have Cole with her, and Manny at the helm of the boat. The sea was calm, the water unusually clear. The flowers had washed off the memorial wreath she'd left, but Cole's piece of dark wood still floated in place. Perhaps they should retrieve that and the pelican float before they left. It would be no good to have a boat run into it, nor to have the site marked so that someone else could easily find and potentially damage the struggling sea grass meadow.

As she and Cole descended near the

anchor line, Bree held the camera tight, as if she could lose it again. They made a standard safety stop, gazing into each other's eyes through their masks, but even that reminded her of her nightmare again. Had her subconscious been trying to warn her? Against Sam? Against Ben's meddling? When the man with a mask raised the wrench in the dream, it was in the shape of the Hollimans' eternal shells. She'd been confined in a glass coffin, reminiscent of the way Daria had been trapped in the wheelhouse. Some people believed dreams foretold the future, but she would not let herself be trapped as Daria must have been. Never.

She fought to focus, because she had much to do today. Get these final pictures, prepare the rest of the PowerPoint presentation she and Daria had already done some work on. She was tempted to dig up a plug of the sea grass to show everyone, but she couldn't bear to harm the sparse growth that was already suffering below.

Cole reached out and took her free hand in one of his. She nodded she was fine, so they upended and swam down.

As usual, they'd dropped anchor away from the grass so it wouldn't get torn up.

Gertie the Grouper greeted them, a good sign this day would go well, Bree thought. The early-morning sunlight slanting through the water gave it a greenish tint. She wondered if it was this bright for Cole, or if it was her extra perceptive sight again. Was that permanent after the lightning strike, a strange gift—or curse—with her increased hearing ability, for surviving all that had happened since that disastrous day?

They swam past the Trade Wreck and headed for the familiar site of the meadow. When the findings were released, the media would hype everything, and both the pro-environment side and the economists who wanted increased business and tourism on shore at any price would be up in arms. The green earth activists would clamor for more stringent pollution and building construction controls, to return the gulf to its once-pristine condition; their opponents would argue that the demands of increasing population were worth temporary setbacks in nature. And she would be in the middle of all that cross fire.

For her presentation this afternoon, she would begin with a slide dedicating the report to Daria's memory, then juxtapose the earlier photos with these latest ones of the declining—

Bree gasped and almost choked. Up ahead—it couldn't be!

She kicked hard to get closer and stared down as Cole joined her. Hovering, she just gaped at first. The grass couldn't have flourished this fast. In one week, after being damaged by that rough-water storm, the meadow had come back from oblivion? It looked green, healthy, hardy. Surely, she wasn't at the wrong site, because the Trade Wreck was right there where it should be. Manny had put them in the same spot as ever.

She shook her head to clear it. Though this was the site she and Daria had tended for months, it was not the same sea grass. Turtle grass, yes, but it must have been planted here. The site had been resodded!

Cole was gesturing, asking her what had happened. She motioned to him that someone must have dug up the old grass and put this in. He shook his head, then pivoted to look all around them as if someone unseen could be lurking.

Slowly, careful not to disturb the bottom and kick up silt or sand, Bree upended again to get her face close to the edge of the sea grass plot. She swam its entire circumference. Then she crisscrossed it, back and forth, while Cole held her camera and just watched.

Too neat, too new, she thought. In a few places someone had tried to make the edges of the meadow look ragged. On the interior, large tufts of turtle grass had been planted with great care in random fashion to make it look more natural. And the bed of grass was a bit smaller than what had been replaced. This must have come from an entirely different area of the gulf, or perhaps even the other side of the state.

Where had it come from? More importantly, who had the know-how, money and nerve to plant it? Who had this much at stake in her report today? Their entire, precious project could become a waste and tarnish Daria's memory, as well as Bree's business and reputation.

She was tempted to defiantly ignore this, because, surely, the ends of her original report would justify the means. Whoever had done this would not dare step forward to challenge her. But all her claims could be easily disproved if someone dived here. Except for

Cole, though—and Manny, of course—she wasn't sure who would know the exact coordinates of the site. No, damn, they'd left that memorial wreath on the surface.

Shaking, she took the camera from Cole and began to photograph the grass from many angles, especially the tidy edges of the bed. As ever, she got macrophotography close-ups. With her diving knife, she cut out a six-inch square, which Cole cradled in his hands on the way up.

"Get what you want?" Manny called when they surfaced.

She yelled to him, "Not what I wanted or expected, but more proof that someone has a motive to want our report to be a good one. Practically overnight, that sad bed of sea grass looks as if it has resurrected itself. Whoever hurt Daria must have taken up deep-sea gardening when he couldn't stop me with a wrench."

Things got even worse back at the shop. "Manny, you haven't been using this computer, have you?" Bree asked as she tried to retrieve her earlier pictures of the turtle grass meadow. She had downloaded the new pictures with no problem, but her photo software seemed to be acting up.

"You know I hate those things. No way. What is it?"

"I can't believe this—or maybe I can. Someone has deleted the pics, even Daria's last shots that I just downloaded five days ago."

She frantically tried other folders, scanned lists of documents, did a search by key-words. Nothing. Had messing up Daria's room been a diversion for this tampering and theft? She hadn't been able to access Daria's new password, but had someone hacked into this machine—possibly without even being here? Still, the Gator Watering Hole coaster had disappeared, so someone had thought searching Daria's room was im-portant, too.

Though she had no more tears left, Bree felt sick to her stomach. Months of important work gone, her and Daria's legacy to the gulf they loved sabotaged. She leaned back in her chair. Manny hovered over her, speechless for once. Cole had gone home to change for the commission meeting. He wouldn't believe this. *She* couldn't believe this.

Bree ran to her desk to check the bottom drawer where she kept her backup CDs. Gone. Someone had been here in person. She raced upstairs into Daria's room to look in the drawer where her sister had kept her copies of backup CDs for the computer downstairs. Why hadn't she thought to check these before? When she couldn't get into Daria's e-mail, she had abandoned the idea of Daria's computer.

Gone. Not only Daria's SAV backups, but all her others.

Stunned anew, Bree bent over and hit her fists on her knees. Now she was even more afraid. Whoever was behind all this—and, no doubt, Daria's death—was clever, powerful and maybe wealthy. Dom Verdugo, as Cole suspected? He'd want a good gulf report. He had the motive and the manpower to try to stop a bad one.

"What you gonna do?" Manny asked, standing in the hall. His presence and question jolted her.

"I'm tempted to go dive to find some other sick sea grass to show the committee, so they can see what the Trade Wreck meadow actually looked like. But instead, I'm going to try to blow someone out of the water. I'm go-

ing to tell the truth, even if that angers someone dangerous very, very much."

"And now, the report we've all been awaiting," Marv Godwin, the chairman of the
Clear the Gulf Commission and member of
the local Visitor and Convention Bureau, announced to the crowded room with a nod toward Bree. She was sitting at the front table
with him, nearest the podium. She had been
trying not to stare at Cole, even though she
felt stronger when she glanced his way.

The rest of the commission members sat
in the front row. Looking at Amelia—who
seemed so haggard and nervous that Bree
was shocked she was even here today—did
nothing but make her more upset and uneasy. Ben sat in the chair behind his wife, as
if to keep an eye on her.

Sam Travers was here, sitting in the back
of the room, flanked by his divers, Ric and
Lance. Bree had expected them to be on
that job in Sarasota already, but Sam would
do anything to help protect the gulf he loved
and needed for his work. Josh Austin and
Marla Sherborne were in attendance, both
managing to sit in range of the cameras. Bree
was trying to ignore the hoard of statewide

media, with their microphones on poles that they thrust toward the podium. Several cameramen sat cross-legged on the floor in front, as if this were some presidential news conference announcing peace or war. In a way, around here, maybe it was.

"Of course, we are all deeply saddened," Chairman Godwin went on, "by the tragic loss of Daria Devon, and we continue to extend our condolences to the family. We are grateful Briana can be with us today at this difficult time with her findings on what is essentially the health report of our precious Gulf of Mexico. Briana?"

Applause, no less. She wasn't sure the chairman would be so grateful when he heard her report. Cole and Manny were the only ones who knew what she intended, because she thought Mr. Godwin might completely discount her report or try to stop her. After all, he wanted the outcome to be a healthy gulf that could handle more development and a casino yacht. Speaking of that, as she glanced at the crowd, she saw Dom Verdugo was here.

Standing in front of everyone, she teared up at first, picturing Daria here with her, wishing fervently this would still go well, even after some bastard had tried to pull the sick-sea-grass rug out from under her.

Her hands shook as she put her index cards on the podium and reached for the remote control that would run her now all-too-brief presentation. She put the first slide up on the screen. It was all black with the words in white: This Report Is In Loving Memory Of Daria Claire Devon, 1978–2006.

"Thank you, Mr. Godwin, and all the commission for your support and kind words about my twin sister. As you know, for the last six months, Daria and I have closely monitored and photographed the turtle grass meadow near the Trade Wreck, approximately four miles out in the gulf. Mr. Godwin is now passing around a handout with information on our fifty-eight dives and a chart indicating the health of the grass, a consistently downward trend.

"We used to call this our grassroots project, but later called it SAV for Submerged Aquatic Vegetation. I don't need to remind you that sea grass roots are key to the eco-health of the entire area. Sea grass roots hold the sea bottom in place, and the grass itself produces oxygen and shelters marine life. Yet our gulf sea grass is dying."

The occasional camera flash from the media bothered Bree. Even when she wasn't looking directly into the flashes, they bored into her brain. Her own voice over the microphone seemed much too loud, though no one was reacting that way. People were leaning forward, intense, listening to each word. Despite the icy air-conditioning, she felt herself start to sweat, but went on.

"Before I show you some slides, I want to make two major points. First, I want to reiterate that, in the six months Daria and I studied the site, the grass went from bad to much worse. As a result, other marine life is greatly impacted, even endangered. Life on shore suffers, too, and not just because we can catch fewer healthy fish to eat or swim in less clear waters. Secondly, I must tell you something else almost as upsetting to me."

She cleared her throat and darted a look at Cole. His big body was tensed up; he was frowning. He'd argued at first that she should not throw down the gauntlet, that she would make herself more of a target. She'd convinced him that, in a way, she was buying herself life insurance. How obvious would it look if something strange happened to the second sister who was making a stand against pollution, including that from a casino cruise ship, in this area?

"Someone," she said, "is out to sabotage the proof of our findings. Only this morning on a last-minute dive, I discovered—along with Cole DeRoca of your commission—that the shrinking, browning and fading sea grass meadow had been dug up and an area of much more flourishing grass put in its place."

Murmuring. A few gasps. A lot more strobe flashes. Bree gripped the edges of the podium and stared the audience down.

Josh Austin looked stunned. He whispered something to Mark Denton, who was madly taking notes. Mark nodded. Marla Sherborne's mouth had dropped open.

Sam seemed to register no emotion at all. It hit her then. One of the logical recommendations would be the necessity of deeper dredging to make more tidal cuts, which would induce seawater flushing. And Sam's business would profit from that, in a big way.

As for Dom Verdugo, he looked almost smug as he tugged the cuff-linked wrists of his shirtsleeves down under his blazer. Yes, he would want a healthy-looking sea grass meadow so he could insist the gulf was stable and could take the demands of his big boat and the people it would bring in. And he had the money and a jet to bring in more robust grass from across the state or even from the Caribbean.

"Also," Bree plunged on, though her voice sounded too strident to her, "someone hacked into my computer, which held six months' worth of photos, literally hundreds, so that I would have no visual proof and look discredited. Our triple backups were also stolen. But I can show you one slide of my sister and me that we had printed up *before* the digital ones were taken."

She put a slide on the screen of the two of them, hovering over the sea grass, smiling through their masks. Daria had used the camera's automatic timer to get that shot; it had the name and number of their shop underneath. They had planned to use this photo for publicity, but decided at the last minute that the sea grass looked too sick for their big smiles. How strange that hidden, rejected photo had saved the day. Was the person who was playing with their lives hidden, too? Was he someone she knew— someone here today?

"Please ignore the Two Mermaids promotion," Bree said, "and take a look at the sea grass just under us and behind the lettering. This picture is about three months old, halfway through the project, but you can still see how puny and brown the sea grass looks, compared to the excellent shape of this newly sodded grass, which would do a Naples golf course proud."

She ran a series of slides, calling attention to an especially straight edge of the bed and to a view showing that the grass had been planted below the level of the rest of the surrounding sand. "Note also," she added, "that you do not see tiny sea life, such as arrow crabs, clinging to the new, flourishing grass. When it was dug up and taken out of water, those creatures perished, and no new ones have had time to find a home here. In closing, just let me say that not only I, but also Cole DeRoca, can testify that these are two very different sea grass beds—the one my sister and I were hired to monitor and the transplanted one some enemy of truth has gone to desperate lengths to deceive all of you with. *Desperate lengths,*" she emphasized again, almost shouting, and sat down before she could blurt out her suspicions about Daria's death.

The room exploded in questions. Marv

Godwin jumped to his feet, holding up both hands to quiet everyone. "All right, we promised you a Q and A session," he said. "As for Briana Devon here, let's remember she's only the messenger . . . ."

And what, Bree thought, was the rest of that saying? Oh, yeah, don't kill the messenger. Had she protected herself today or set things up so someone would try to do exactly that?

18

Bombshell At Clear The Gulf Commission Hearing, the headline in the *Naples Daily News* read the next morning. A photo of Bree at the podium took up a quarter of the front page, with the slide of her and Daria underwater in the background. The article didn't accuse anyone but mentioned that the fallout might include temporary restrictions for onshore building and might "sway even more voters from backing at-sea gambling." If that was the ultimate fallout, Bree thought, and Dom Verdugo became a suspect in the turtle grass switch, he would be even more furious at her than before.

Bree's report about someone replacing the sea grass meadow was also the lead story in the local morning newscasts she checked. Mark Denton phoned to tell her the story was being carried statewide and he and "the candidate" admired her courage. An e-mail from Senator Marla Sherborne, one of nearly a hundred sent to the shop's Web site, said that "the ripples" were being felt even in Washington.

It was not, Bree thought, as she sat at the table with her head in her hands over her barely touched breakfast, the way any sane person who had been attacked in more ways than one should keep a low profile. But she'd decided to flush out whoever was hurting the gulf—and whoever had hurt Daria. Would that be the same person?

When Cole emerged from the shower after another night on her sofa, his hair was slicked to his head. He pecked a kiss on her cheek as if they were an old married couple and poured his own coffee. He'd already eaten.

"Any more phone calls?" he asked.

"I turned my cell off, and the TV. The e-mail count keeps going up. Everything's exploding," she said, turning the paper toward where he sat across from her. As he bent over the article, she pointed to the word *bombshell.*

It annoyed her that he looked so good, compared to the way she felt. She'd spent half the night awake again, afraid of bad dreams and going over and over candidates who might have substituted healthy sea grass for sick, and for possible fathers of Daria's child. Of course, there were many unknowns, but something Manny's daughter had asked about Daria kept sticking in Bree's brain. *Had* Daria gotten over Josh? Or had they run into each other somewhere and *boom!* Old passions had exploded? Even if that were true, it seemed the man was seldom alone. Nikki was on the campaign trail with him, and he always had Mark Denton at his elbow.

Yet Bree kept recalling that Daria had told her once out of the blue—no, they had just seen one of Josh's TV ads, where he and Nikki were walking the beach hand in hand—that Nikki had suffered two miscarriages and they were desperate to have children. How long ago had that been? Certainly, in the last seven weeks or so. At the time, Bree hadn't even wondered where

Daria had come up with that intimate information. Just gossip, that's what she'd passed it off as. But was it firsthand knowledge? And would someone like Josh, who seemed to have almost everything he wanted, need to prove he could father a child?

"A million dollars for your thoughts," Cole said, looking up from reading the article.

"I thought they were only worth a penny."

"Not anymore," he said, putting his coffee cup down. "Inflation plus your fifteen minutes of media fame's upped the ante. I can't wait to get working on the paneling for the *Fun 'n' Sun* today to see how Verdugo is reacting. He looked pretty smug for a while at the meeting, but I saw him storm out."

"Cole, remember how I said I'd like to get away?"

"You can't run now. Besides, I've committed to get that casino yacht project going so I can keep an eye on Verdugo and his boys. I couldn't go with you."

"I think I mentioned that Josh and Nikki Austin invited me to spend some time at their place in cane country? Clewiston's not far, and I wouldn't stay long. Maybe just for the day, if they'll fly me there like they said."

"Bree, Josh may not be as high on our

watch list for hiring your attackers as Sam Travers and his divers or Verdugo and his goons are, but he—"

"He bears watching, and that's exactly what I'd like to do. Or, barring that, since he's so busy, I'd settle for picking Nikki's brain."

"So you're thinking whoever fathered Daria's child might be a more important lead than someone desperate to stop your report on an endangered environment?"

"I don't know what I think, except that those are the two most obvious motives and I've got to keep pushing at possibilities. Even if Josh were somehow involved, I can't believe he'd ever harm Daria, especially if she was carrying his child."

"Haven't you ever heard the saying that absolute power corrupts absolutely? The man is a politician with big ambitions. Despite the Hollywood morals in this country today, an illegitimate child by his old flame could ruin his marriage, which is no doubt tied to big sugar money in his campaign coffers. It could sully his reputation, when he's built up this 'you can trust Josh Austin' facade."

"But I've known him for years and believe he can be trusted to . . ."

Bree covered her eyes and burst into tears. She heard Cole scrape his chair back. He came around the table and pulled her up into his arms. Then when she got up to head for her bedroom, he sat in her chair and tugged her into his lap.

She forced herself to stop crying. She got the hiccups but kept talking anyway. "I didn't know that was coming," she said, wiping her eyes with her napkin. "It's all I do lately, swing from heroics to hysterics. It's just that I was going to claim I know Josh well, when I obviously didn't even know my own twin sister."

"Just rest this morning, okay? Then walk over to the *Fun 'n' Sun* to meet me for lunch, and we'll go to the Grog Shop. Let Manny run things downstairs while you check the e-mail, in case there's anything there that would give you another lead. Call me on my cell if something turns up. And I'll try to psych out Verdugo."

"Aye, aye, Captain," she said, trying to sound in control again. She gave him a weak salute as another hiccup jolted her.

"Somehow, sweetheart," he said with a sigh, "I don't think you're the kind of first mate—or any other kind of mate—who takes orders well."

"Something here for you," Manny told Bree as she went downstairs to check the e-mail on the Two Mermaids Web site after Cole left. "That red-haired diver, Lance, the one brought back your flippers, just dropped it off. A sealed letter from Sam Travis, something to do with business."

As if it were a letter bomb, she took it gingerly from Manny. He sat at Daria's desk. Bree saw he'd put a new nameplate and his family pictures where her sister's things had been. His morning cup of yerba maté was in a mug Daria had always used for coffee. A screwdriver and wrench lay there, as if his realm of the back room had begun to migrate to the front office. Biting her lower lip, Bree went to her own desk and slit the envelope open. In Sam's bold handwriting, the note read,

I know you're still shook but think about this. It's a good time for you to sell out to me, like I offered last year. Remember your brother-in-law was all for it. Have your lawyer contact mine. I'll take Manny on, raise my earlier price, and buy out your property there, if you want to move and move on. S. Travers

She could not believe his gall. Red pulsating lights seemed to explode behind her eyes. With all she and Daria had worked for, did he think she'd turn tail and run? She had a good mind to rip this to shreds, but it might be evidence later of a motive for Daria's death if Sam was involved in any way.

"What is it?" Manny asked, getting up from Daria's—his—desk.

"Lock this place up. We're going to see Sam Travers in person. I take it that they haven't left for their big demolition job in Sarasota yet."

"His guy said tomorrow. What is that?" he repeated.

"Sam's second kind offer to buy us out and to hire you, too."

"No way. *Caramba,* I work hard to get this far here, and I'm not taking orders from him neither."

Bree bit her lip again. She didn't like the way Manny had put that. She was tired of giving him the benefit of the doubt because he was under so much family pressure. Damn it, so was she! But there would be time later to discuss who was the senior partner here. Right now she was going to give Sam Travers a piece of her mind and hope he didn't keep insisting on a pound of her flesh.

Manny locked up hastily and followed Bree out onto the street. "We not taking the truck?" he asked.

"It's not that far. I'm walking. Maybe I'll work off some of this anger."

She was surprised that so many people called her name, thanked her for taking a stand on keeping the gulf clean, or wished her good luck as she strode past. Yes, she'd done the right thing to tell the truth and take the sea grass plot public. Now, if she could only get a credible lead on what had really happened to Daria.

As she approached Sam's large, three-story building, which she used to know inside and out when she and Ted were dating all those years, the first person she saw was Ric, up a ladder. He was repainting the Travers and Son Search and Salvage sign. Sam had never changed the business's

354 Karen Harper

name after Ted's death. Even now, it looked as if Ric was just brightening the colors, not changing the wording. Ted had promised his father that when he came back from the service—if he didn't decide to make the marines a career—he'd work with him here, and Sam had immediately put up the sign as if they'd already sealed the deal.

She noticed something interesting about Ric, besides the fact that he was obviously adept at scaling ladders to second stories.

"Manny, how many guys do you know who paint with gloves on?" she asked. She noted they were diving gloves, which made it even stranger, because they were expensive to get splotched with paint.

"*Que sera sera,*" Manny muttered, evidently not following what she meant.

A ladder and a pair of gloves! After the commission report yesterday, Ben had told her that the CSI tech had turned up no "foreign" fingerprints. The intruder might have worn gloves.

"Don't walk under that ladder—bad luck," Manny said, and grabbed her elbow.

"Great. If I walk around it, I'm sure my luck will make a big U-turn for the good," she said, instantly regretting her sarcasm.

"Hey, Briana!" Ric called down. She was still so angry she was tempted to just keep walking, but maybe it would be a good idea to talk to this guy. Her dad used to say you could catch more flies with honey than vinegar.

"I thought you'd be setting off underwater detonator caps in Sarasota by now," she called up to him, shading her eyes in the morning sun.

For a guy who seemed so muscular, he came lithely down the ladder. Yes, she thought, as he stood on the pavement between her and Manny, he was just the height of her attacker at the Gator Watering Hole. Now to get some info, without giving her suspicions away.

"All of us are going first thing tomorrow," Ric said, his eyes assessing her. "We'll be gone a couple of weeks, blowing old bridge buttresses, then sinking or salvaging the debris."

He smiled at her, more a tight quirk of the sides of his mouth. He wore no sunglasses and she saw he had dark eyes—also the color of her attacker's. As he talked, he pulled off his gloves. He had manicured hands, no less, and a handsome ring on his right pinkie finger. Maybe that explained the gloves. Why hadn't she tried to memorize something about the masked man's hands? If Ric had been her attacker, why would he risk getting up close and personal with her right now? Maybe he planned to earn her trust, then get her off alone and finish the job he'd botched at the Gator Watering Hole.

"Sam's skilled at demo work from his years in 'Nam," Ric went on. "He's taught us a lot, Lance and me. Used to be part of a unit they called frogmen, the ones now called the SEALs. I think they should have named them sharks or barracudas."

"Pretty dangerous work, isn't it?" she asked as Manny frowned at them. "But then, I suppose that's part of the thrill."

"True, the adrenaline really gets pumping," he admitted, his eyes flickering over her again. "Pays better than regular diving, too, time and a half. Sam calls it combat pay. Listen, Briana," he said, turning his back on Manny, who grunted but shuffled a couple of steps away. "I'm really sorry about your sister, and I'm glad I could be there to help when she was found."

He twisted his gloves between his fists as he spoke, almost as if he were wringing someone's neck. He lowered his voice and leaned slightly closer. "After I come back, you want to go diving somewhere different, just for relaxation—for fun? Down to the Keys, maybe? I know it's been terrible for you, but you've got to start living again—for yourself and her, too, now."

Bree suddenly felt at a loss for words. The last thought, that she could enjoy life in memory of Daria, moved her deeply. She wanted to be angry, not to get conned into liking this guy. He ought to go moonlight for those super sales reps, Fred and Viv Holliman.

"That is," he went on, "if you're not tied in real tight with DeRoca. I don't mean to be pushy or poach on someone else's territory."

"Thanks for the offer," she said, trying to sound noncommittal. She wanted to get away or she was going to lose it again. She looked up at the sign he'd repainted. "It's strange to see a diver up a ladder," she said.

"Jack-of-all-trades, master of none," he said, with a shrug and a smile that made him seem self-deprecating and almost charming. Except, she reminded herself, his trades might include B and E and attacking women with a wrench, if not worse.

"Thanks again for your kind words," she said, "but I need to have a few unkind words with Sam right now. Good luck on your demo dives in Sarasota."

As she started away, Manny whispered, "Oh, you thinking he might be the one broke in—and almost broke your bones at the Gator Watering Hole."

She didn't have time to answer as he opened Sam's front door for her and they stepped inside.

"I can't believe you're home right now, the busy man of power lunches," Amelia told Ben. She'd heard the garage door go up, and had been surprised to see his car turning into the driveway. "Are you feeling all right?"

"Actually, I came home to be sure you were."

"I'm holding my own. Can I fix you something for lunch?"

"Sure. How about just plain old *PB* and *J,* like we used to live on while I was finishing law school?"

"It used to be necessity food, now I guess it's comfort food." She started getting things out on the counter.

"Actually, I need to tell you a couple of things," he said, getting two diet sodas from the refrigerator. "First of all, the fingerprint tech said only Bree and Daria's prints are in the bedroom."

She stopped unscrewing the top to the peanut butter jar and stared straight ahead at the cupboard, as if she could read something in the wood grain there. "Strange, isn't it," she whispered, "that Daria can be gone and her prints remain? There are so many places she touched . . . Sorry, I didn't mean to sound like some sappy greeting card. What else did you come all the way home to tell me?"

"There's more that turned up on the autopsy," he said, popping the tab on a soda, a sound like an exclamation point. "There was some mystery man in Daria's life. She was pregnant."

Amelia sucked in a sob. For one moment she had thought he was going to tell her that the report stated that someone pushed Daria shortly before she died or that they could tell who had pushed her into the steering wheel on her boat, but that was ridiculous. That was her guilt talking again. Pregnant! In a way, that meant there were two deaths, one of a niece or nephew she would never know. She fought to steady herself because she thought she might throw up right here in the sink.

"So Bree has no idea—who?" she asked.

"No, and I believe her. But she's on a crusade because she thinks whoever fathered the child might have harmed Daria."

Amelia gripped the counter. From behind, Ben put his hands on her waist. As if the kids were home and he didn't want them to hear, he whispered, "I got you an appointment late this afternoon with a good doctor, a kind of a family counselor."

"A psychiatrist, a shrink," she countered, not moving, feeling frozen where she stood. "How nice a doctor can see me at the snap of your fingers."

"Honey, I asked him as a special favor to work you in. The appointment's kind of late in the day, but I can take you there the first time. He'll be someone to talk to confidentially, like talking to a lawyer."

She nodded stiffly and tried to process all he had told her. Bree might have been right that someone wanted to silence Daria, someone besides her own, older sister, who'd wanted to shut her up for the cruel things she had said. A man now had a motive for wanting to get rid of Daria. But after all, Daria's death was by drowning.

"You're taking this much better than I expected," Ben said, sounding wary. "Much better than Bree did."

Amelia nodded. It was best if Ben thought she was doing better, and best if the psychiatrist thought so, too. She had no intention of telling anyone she'd gotten Ben's pistol out of his desk drawer in the den this morning and just stared long and hard at it, until she'd realized it was almost noon and heard the garage door. Or that she'd been desperate enough to rent a boat she hardly knew how to steer and go out to continue her argument with Daria, who had said she would not be diving with Bree that day the storm came up.

For Bree, being inside Sam's shop was always like stepping into a time warp. He'd kept the front office the way it was when she and Ted had been dating. They'd both worked here as kids, and, after his mother's desertion and his parents' divorce, Ted had lived here with Sam for a while, over the store. As far as Bree could tell, their private rooms—Sam lived somewhere else now—were still accessed by the same outside stairs she and Ted had sneaked up more than once.

But there were a few different things now. A new guy worked here, manning the phone and computer, one of Sam's concessions to modern technology, like his echo sounder and GPS systems on his boats. And a large poster—actually, just of a saying of some sort—hung behind the front counter. It read,

> For want of a nail , a shoe was lost,
> For want of a shoe, a horse was lost,
> For want of a horse, a battle was lost,
> For want of a battle, a war was lost,
> For want of a war, a kingdom was lost.

"Can I help you, Ms. Devon?" the guy behind the desk asked. She didn't recognize him, but everyone knew her face—or Daria's—lately. Before Bree could answer, Sam came in from the back room. Without another word, the man cleared the way for him.

"Like that sentiment?" Sam asked, jerking a thumb at the poster. "It means one little thing can ruin eternity for someone."

"I get the point."

Bree remembered Manny telling her that Sam's other diver, Lance, had said Sam had a shrine to Ted's memory in the attic here. Obviously, this poster, like everything in Sam's life, was tied to the loss of his son. Though she hadn't intended to start with him this way, she asked, "How easy was it for you to tell Daria and me apart, Sam?"

"What's that have to do with anything? Her smile was a little more lopsided, and she was jumpier than you, least till lately. As for looks, hard to tell. But I know she wouldn't have dumped my son the way you did."

She ignored the jab. Then it was possible Sam could have come after her on the water that day and hurt Daria by mistake. Or he'd sent Ric, who couldn't tell them apart. Would the slow engine on a barge register under-water?

"Then let's just pretend," Bree plunged on, "I'm here to speak for myself and for Daria. We turned down your offer of a buyout be-fore, and I'm turning it down for both of us again. Manny's my new partner and he agrees."

Sam didn't even glance Manny's way as his gaze burned into Bree's. "Suit yourself," he said with a shrug, though the frown that sliced between his narrowed eyes showed he was hardly shrugging this off. Her eyes widened when she saw Sam had a wrench in his pocket, protruding as if it were a silent threat. Thank God, she'd brought Manny with her, because when Ric came in the front door with his paint can, she felt surrounded.

"That's all I came to say," she told Sam.

"Far's I'm concerned, that's all there is to say," he muttered, crossing his arms over his chest. "I made that offer in good faith to help you out and get you outta the area where I don't have to hear, see, or think about you. Get on outta my shop then, 'cause you're trespassing and always were."

Bree spun and strode out, vowing silently that she'd be back when Sam, Ric and Lance were gone. Maybe there would be something she could use against him in that upstairs shrine, where he worshipped the memory of Saint Ted.

19

Bree stormed back to her office with Manny in her wake, only to find Nikki Austin getting out of a large, dark car in front of the shop. She was alone.

"Bree, I just wanted to see how you're doing," she said, and surprised her with a sincere hug that wasn't just a touch and a jump back this time. "Josh and Mark are at a Rotary Club breakfast in town, so I took the car to pop over. The news coverage on your report is amazing!"

Especially amazing, Bree thought, with Josh giving interviews about it right and left. She said only, "I ought to be running for office.

Everyone seems to know my face and name. Can you come in?"

"Actually, I was wondering—Josh, too—if you'd like to leave the media questions to the professionals and take us up on our offer to get away for a while."

As Manny unlocked the front door and went in, Bree hesitated. Nikki's arrival was like a sign she should pursue a visit with them, wasn't it?

"That's so kind, but I know you're both busy."

"Josh has a full docket today and won't join us until this evening, but Mark's going to fly me across the state in about—" she dug her cell phone out of her purse and glanced at the time on it "—an hour and a half. A change of scene might do you so much good."

Bree knew this would upset Cole, but the opportunity was too ideal to pass up. She had to take risks, just as Cole was doing by hanging tight to Verdugo.

"I'd love to, especially if it's just for the day and night."

"We'll be back here early afternoon tomorrow—for a rally at your and Josh's old high school, no less. Rah, rah, Austin for senator! Listen, Briana, you'll love sugarcane country, with its miles and miles of fields to get lost in. Believe me, there's something about the place that makes sorrows easier to bear."

"Looking good," Dom Verdugo's voice came from behind Cole. "That custom rosewood's gonna add a lot of class."

Ever since Bree had called and they'd argued about her going across the state, Cole had been furiously working on installing the paneling. He was so preoccupied that he hadn't even heard footsteps. He'd been almost listening at keyholes earlier, so the fact he hadn't noticed Verdugo's approach upset him even more.

"Glad it suits you, and we're still on for this deal," Cole replied without looking at him. "You seemed pretty teed off after the commission meeting yesterday. I didn't think you'd still be so optimistic that having a casino boat in Turtle Bay is going to go your way."

"I have a talent for working things out."

Cole finished nailing the baseboard, then stood and faced Verdugo. "So did whoever installed that all-new turtle grass meadow."

Verdugo's expression didn't change. "Meaning?"

"You realize some will point the finger at you."

"Let them. Nothing will stick, not when there's a list long as my arm could have done it."

Was that an admission of guilt? Cole wondered.

With a finger jabbing the air, Verdugo went on. "An entire coalition of store owners and builders are dying to develop this area, and this boat will bring in the tourists and dollars they need. No one can stop progress, not in South Florida. Besides, you think I'm the kind of guy who'd do something that blatant? Whose side you on, DeRoca?"

"I'm on Briana Devon's side, and she's distraught about her and her sister's work, not to mention the loss of her sister."

"I can understand that, sympathize. But tragedies happen, ones no one can explain, and don't forget it."

That sounded like a threat. Cole stared back at Verdugo, not letting his gaze waver.

"But, hey," the older man said, producing some of his ever-present caramel popcorn as if from up his sleeve, "I came to tell you I sent out invitations to the local powers-that-be, including the Clear the Gulf Commission members and some political people, to take a cruise on this baby Friday evening. It'll be a shakedown cruise, so to speak—no gambling, of course, but eats, drinks, live music. I want to explain the *Fun 'n' Sun*'s clean-water system, how all refuse is handled on board and unloaded later ashore."

"So you'd like the paneling done by then."

"Only if it doesn't push you. Actually, I'd like to invite you—bring Briana, too, if she's up to it. It'll be great PR for you, as well as me."

"Which do you prefer doing, Mark?" Bree asked. "PR, piloting, or escorting the candidate and his wife?"

Mark Denton was flying Bree and Nikki across the state in a white, four-seat Cessna pontoon plane. Nikki said she had a speech to write and had put Bree in the copilot's seat to enjoy the view for the one-hour flight. After they left the Naples suburbs with its tentacles of new housing projects reaching outward, the Everglades swept under them, the water reflecting the sky. Shortly after they'd crossed Alligator Alley, they had flown over the Seminole Indian Reservation, then fields of vegetables and citrus, and were now heading northeast toward Lake Okeechobee and cane country.

"I took up flying fairly late," Mark answered her question. "Media and public relations were my first love."

As before, Bree thought that for a man in his position, he didn't seem glib or especially friendly. But his real talent might be in writing speeches and press releases.

"Family?" she asked.

"Married to my work for now."

Though she made a point of staring out the windows ahead and beside her, Bree tried to study the man. His well-shaped head was covered with dark stubble; with his buzz cut, he reminded her of a marine. Slashes of brown eyebrows arched over brown eyes, now hidden by his aviator sunglasses, which reflected Bree whenever he looked her way. His nose was a bit crooked where it must have once been broken. Usually, he spoke without seeming to move his thin-lipped mouth. She had the feeling he didn't like her, but maybe he just thought the Austins should be sticking to business and not entertaining some bereaved friend.

Despite the drone of the engine, Bree knew that Nikki, sitting directly behind her, could hear what they said, for she occasionally chimed in. Now she leaned forward between their seats to say, "Mark's going to pilot the Austin machine clear to the White House someday."

"Graduate to flying Air Force One?" Bree asked, trying to go along with the joke. But she remembered Josh had told her Nikki was ambitious, her hopes set on going to Washington with him and climbing the power ladder.

"I thought maybe press secretary," Mark said, sounding entirely serious. "One who doesn't just parrot the party line but helps to make policy. What do you think, future First Lady?" he asked Nikki, and she playfully punched his shoulder. "Hey, that's Clewiston, America's Sweetest Town beyond, but this is the start of the Grann sugarcane fields," he said, pointing as he began to take the plane lower. Descending through the blue, blue sky and skimming over the waving green plants reminded Bree of diving the depths of some lovely underwater spot—not, unfortunately, off the coast of Naples.

She had seen sugarcane before but had paid little attention to it. The plants were tall and green with woolly beige plumes, but that was all she recalled. Now, she was in awe. Field after field of cane, swaying in the breeze, stretched for miles through rich, black soil. Train tracks glittered in the sun, ones she knew must lead loaded rail cars to the sugar refineries.

"Are those big machines harvesters?" she asked about the metal monsters parked near a tin-roofed shed.

"That and cane choppers, and you want to stay way clear of those," Mark said. "Most of the harvest starts in about two weeks, but some of it's ready now. Got to satisfy America's sweet tooth. Grand Sugar, which Nikki's father owns, is the third biggest sugar supplier in the nation after U.S. Sugar and Crystal. And beyond, on the horizon, Lake O," he said, sounding conversational now, as if he was loosening up a bit. "It's so close to the Grann property that we just land on the water, taxi to their dock and take a Humvee waiting there."

"I've never seen Okeechobee from the air," Bree said, marveling at the stretch of blue water that ran through the Glades to the gulf. She wondered if people ever scuba dived in Okeechobee. "What does that name mean?" she asked.

"Seminole for big water."

"Makes sense to me."

It was also starting to make sense to her that the wealth of King Sugar, as she'd heard it called, had a very long reach in the state. Not only to satisfy America's sweet tooth, as Mark had mentioned, but, as Cole had said, to fill political coffers. And maybe even reach deep into the gulf to erase evidence that would help prove pollution from these cane fields played a part in poisoning gulf water.

Bree stared in awe when Nikki and Josh's home came into view at the end of a lane, lined with live oaks, about a mile from her father's plantation home, which they'd already passed.

"It's beautiful," she told Nikki, who sat beside her in the backseat of the Humvee Mark drove. "Tara from *Gone With The Wind!*"

"Just don't be looking for Rhett Butler inside," Nikki said with a laugh. "You know, I always hated that movie for its unhappy ending. That stupid woman loved the wrong man."

"That's what I always thought about it,"

Mark put in, "but then, despite the fact that it takes place right in the middle of the Civil War, it's really a woman's movie."

Rolling her eyes at that, Nikki said, "Actually, I patterned this house, a wedding present from my father, after one Josh and I saw on our honeymoon in New Orleans. But to make it look right, I had to import live oaks and Spanish moss and get rid of a lot of palms and all those air plants that usually cling to trees around here."

A sort of phony Tara, Bree thought. If she'd gone to all that trouble with tiny details, Nikki Austin, like Amelia, was a control freak of the first, and worst, order.

As they pulled up, Bree saw that the big-pillared porch was a sort of false facade, too, for the house wasn't as large as it looked. With a promise to show her around after she rested, Nikki escorted Bree up the sweeping central staircase to the guest suite and left her alone.

Bree put her small overnight bag on the padded bench at the foot of the big four-poster bed and stared out the window. The view, probably the same on all four sides, overlooked miles of densely planted, twelve-foot-tall sugarcane, which began just across the small lawn and narrow garden. In a way, it made her feel claustrophobic. The sugar-cane had waves like the sea, but even from this height, she felt enclosed rather than en-raptured.

On the oak table by the bay window awaited a silver tray with a pitcher of iced tea, surrounded by small cut-glass bowls with packets of Grand Sugar, lime and lemon slices and extra ice. On a flat crystal plate, with a yellow hibiscus bloom in the center, was an array of exotically hued hard candies. Ah, the lifestyles of the rich and fa-mous, she thought, and wondered if the al-lure of any of this could have turned Daria's head while Josh flip-flopped her heart. But the money behind everything here was from Nikki's family, not Josh's. Even if he'd tried to leave his wife for Daria . . . no, she was be-ing ridiculous.

But that secret teeth-whitening appoint-ment. Nikki Austin had teeth that almost glis-tened. Did Daria feel the need to compete with her rival's beauty? What about those ex-tra cosmetics in her drawer? Did Daria dis-cover the only way she could win out over the stunning, wealthy, married Nikki was by having Josh's baby? And, if so, how was Bree ever going to get the truth of a secret liaison out of Josh?

To Bree's surprise, Nikki's father drove over in a golf cart to join them for a late lunch. He spoke again of her loss, asking if there was anything they could do to help ease her pain and grief.

"Nikki's been very kind and helpful—Josh, too," she assured him.

Despite the fact it was delightfully cool with the air-conditioning inside the house, the three of them sat out on the warm, screened-in back veranda and were served cold raspberry soup and crab salad by a middle-aged, Haitian-born housekeeper-cook named Lindy who spoke with a French accent. The table was set with linen and silver; the centerpiece was a charming combination of blue plumbago blossoms floating in a dish that had hard candies in the bottom, which Bree thought at first were marbles.

As Cory Grann played host in Josh's absence, Bree could certainly understand how Marla Sherborne had become involved with him, even though he must have started out as enemy number one to her beliefs and political platform. The wealthy widower was not only conversational and handsome, he focused his complete attention on anyone he spoke to, whether it was the housekeeper, Bree or his daughter. But it didn't take Bree long to wonder if she'd been brought here for a purpose, just as she'd come for one.

"Big sugar's been blamed for years for everything that goes wrong in the Glades, and now we're also the major whipping boy for gulf pollution," Cory Grann said, somehow working that into their conversation and looking intently at her.

"Which is ridiculous," Nikki put in, "since the cane farmers no longer use heavy fertilizers and toxic pesticides. There's big cattle farming north of Lake O, and they seldom go after them."

Cory nodded. "Lee and Collier county officials should stop blaming us for their poor river and gulf water health and tackle pollution sources in their own backyards. Same with the ecofr—folks," Cory amended. She was sure he was going to call them eco-freaks, as some of their opponents did. "It's just that we're an easy target for anything that goes wrong. And it's very difficult and dangerous to be a target," he added with a decisive nod at her.

Bree felt a slight shiver race up her spine, but she tried not to react visibly. Were those words a subtle threat, disguised by all this luxury, kindness and politeness?

"I know you've converted Senator Sherborne," she said.

"Marla knows how much money we've donated for cleanup." He leaned slightly closer across the table. "And for this state's other green causes."

Bree had read that big sugar had donated twenty-two million dollars to various Florida election campaigns and to fund lobbyists, as well as to sponsor some down-home television ads that were pro-sugar. Despite their lack of nutritional value, what would Americans do without their sweet fixes? She and Daria had always loved candy.

And then it hit her that, more than once, Daria had brought candy home she'd said she'd bought, and it was just like the citrus-flavored, brightly colored hard balls displayed in nearly every room of Josh Austin's house.

Yes, as pretty and sweet as everything seemed here, she was certain these people meant to play hardball with her.

20

Bree was surprised to find she'd fallen asleep on her bed.

"But," Nikki said when she knocked on her door to tell her Josh would be here in a half hour and they'd have drinks before dinner, "that's why you're here—to relax. Believe me, I know it takes a long time to deal with such losses. For me, it helped to get busy—to fight back, in a way."

Bree thought she would say more, but she darted down the hall.

Bree showered, changed into slacks and a carefully selected blouse and headed for the stairs. The door to the bedroom next to hers stood ajar. She hesitated a moment before walking past it and downstairs. It was—or was meant to be—a nursery, with pale yellow walls and rainbows on the wallpaper, and yellow carpet, too. But it was bare of furniture, an empty box of a room, like a present that was never opened however bright the wrappings.

Daria must have been right. Nikki and Josh had lost two pregnancies, and if they'd had a nursery ready, that might mean Nikki had been pretty far along. Was it as devastating to lose a hoped-for baby you never knew—twice—as it was to lose a sister who was the person closest to you in the world, even if you didn't know her as well as you thought?

Bree's stomach knotted as she went downstairs and heard Josh's voice mingled with Nikki's, but she couldn't tell what they were saying. When she joined them, she saw she'd interrupted a private moment, for he had his arm around her, though she had her outside arm propped on her hip as if she'd been trying to make some point.

"Bree, glad you could join us for some R & R." Josh greeted her and pecked a kiss on her cheek before stepping back. She saw his

eyes fill with tears he blinked quickly back as
he turned away. Either he was very glad to
see her, or he and Nikki had been speaking
of something emotional. Or maybe he was
taken aback by the fact she looked like
Daria. She had intentionally chosen a blouse
she knew her sister had worn more than
once, supposedly to her accounting class,
but evidently to meet a man at the Gator
Watering Hole. Bree was dying to challenge
Josh about that, but she had no idea if he
was the one with the information she
needed.

"All right, ladies," he said, rubbing his
hands together, "we are going to make our
own caipirinha drinks with home-grown
cachaça before dinner."

"Our own what, with what?" Bree asked.
"Something Mexican? My Latino business
partner—" there, she'd said it "—drinks a
pick-me-up called yerba maté all the time."

"This is the national drink of Brazil," Josh
said, taking each of them by the arm and
steering them outside and down the front
steps, "and it's catching on here, especially
in Miami. Who says exhausting statewide
campaigning doesn't have its perks?"

Bree could tell he was forcing his light

tone. He walked them over to a wooden table set up on the lawn at the edge of the eastern cane field. Several trays held three tall glasses, and bowls of lime wedges, sugar and ice. From the grass below, Josh picked up a thick stick, a sharp knife and a huge, curved machete with a wooden handle.

"It looks like someone's about to declare war," Bree observed, but her voice sounded shaky. She jumped behind Nikki when Josh picked up the machete and swung it in a wide arc. It whistled in the hot, humid air.

"This," he said, "is the way they used to cut cane."

With a tremendous swipe, he sliced through two cane stalks, toppling them toward the women.

"Timber!" Nikki cried, and Bree smelled liquor on her breath already. Each woman caught one of the twelve-foot stalks, despite being half-buried by its leaves.

"Man, using this thing makes me feel good," Josh said, and with a quick laugh, started to decapitate the heads of other stalks, then swung lower to make yet others crash down.

"Be careful, or you'll cut yourself!" Nikki

cried. "You don't need to be all bandaged up at your alma mater tomorrow."

That's right, Bree thought. Josh was speaking at Lely High School tomorrow. If she could just risk getting him alone, that might make a good entrée into getting him to reminisce about Daria.

Josh walked back toward them, the huge arched blade still in his hand. He bent down, took the cane Bree held and dropped it onto the ground, then hacked it into three equal pieces at its lowest joints.

"Sugarcane school, lesson number one," he said, holding up one of the joints for her to see. He dropped the machete on the grass and, with the knife on the table, peeled back the husk to reveal what looked like hundreds of wet straws inside the piece of cane. "Bite on this," he told Bree.

Keeping an eye on the machete and knife, Bree touched the severed straws with her tongue. Sweet juice flooded her mouth.

"Spit out the rest," Nikki said. "The chewy stuff is the bagasse. But the liquid's a great source of energy—and of sugar."

"Now, lesson number two," Josh said as he peeled another piece, then put it on a plate and chopped it even smaller before he jammed it in one of the glasses. He took the big wooden stick from the table—it was over a foot long and barely fit in the glass—and mashed the cane.

"Obviously," he said, "the best bartenders across America do not carry on like the madman demo you've just seen. The sugar-cane distillate we just made by hand comes in a variety of brands, some of which are aged in cognac barrels or oak casks in France, no less. But I think we should start bottling and aging our own cane into this *cachaça*."

He mixed three drinks with the ingredients and then tapped Nikki's and Bree's glasses before they drank. "To the future of cane and a great senatorial election," he said. "Now watch it, because this stuff can sneak up on you, just like rum. Here, I've got some extra made."

"Before dinner, let's show her our secret getaway from our big-house getaway," Nikki said as Josh took a swig of his drink.

"And she doesn't mean our little pied-à-terre in Tallahassee. Sure, let's go."

"Lead the way," she said. "Lindy will ring the bell for dinner."

"Onward! Ever onward! Josh Austin for

senate!" Josh cried, and raised the machete before him as if it were a flag they could follow. Nikki just shook her head and picked up the tray with more mixings for the drinks. Bree thought the caipirinha was delicious— sweet, yet tart and refreshing—but it had such an alluring kick that she silently vowed to furtively pour hers out along the way. She had no intention of getting drunk and then being questioned by Josh about how much she knew. No, she was hoping he'd have too much so she could set him up for a heartfelt talk and, maybe, a confession. Besides, she had to keep her wits about her, since they seemed to be leading her into the labyrinth of deep cane, and Josh still had that massive weapon.

Amelia was grateful that the doctor hadn't asked her to lie down on a couch, although there was one in the room. "So this doctor-patient information is entirely privileged, like with a lawyer?" she asked Dr. Scott Nelson. Ben had assured her of that, but she was double-checking. The man had a kindly face and soft voice that exuded compassion.

"Absolutely," he said, folding his hands on one crossed knee. They sat in facing chairs as if they were just here for a friendly chat, but she had no intention of falling for that. Oh, no, she fully intended to keep up her guard.

"I could be subpoenaed," he explained, "but I'd refuse to testify and my records would stay sealed. I'd go to prison before I would betray a trust from a patient."

Testify? Go to prison? His mere word choice evoked horrible images of his clients being arrested. And Ben was the prosecutor who would be responsible for bringing a murderer to justice.

Ben had not exactly answered the question of how close he was to Dr. Nelson, to get her an appointment this quickly. She decided not to ask the doctor if information was also kept private from a family member. More than once, she'd seen Ben worm things out of his own clients or other lawyers. She'd already told him too much. She could only pray that he—or Bree, in her crusade, as Ben called it, to find out who had hurt Daria—would not check around the marina and discover that Amelia had rented a boat.

Despite her fears of open water, she's gone out into the gulf until she'd spotted *Mermaids II.* She'd cut the motor and let the boat drift closer, because she figured if Daria heard her, she'd order her to keep away. The rental motorboat was almost on top of the dive boat when Daria had seen her and helped her grapple the two crafts together so Amelia could climb aboard, telling her off the whole time.

And then, it had all happened so fast. More arguing, the push that made Daria slip and crack her head against the steering wheel in the dive boat's little wheelhouse. Daria had said she'd been nauseous and a little dizzy, and now Amelia knew why. Daria shouldn't have slipped from that little push. She must have been dizzy from the first trimester of her pregnancy. Maybe the nausea was why she really hadn't dived with Bree. Everything was really Daria's fault, not hers, Amelia assured herself.

She had scrambled off the boat, back to her own vessel, panicked that Daria might be dead and she'd be blamed for what was an accident. Because she was afraid Bree might surface if she heard a motor, she let the boat drift away again before starting it. She had to get back in, because the storm was starting to kick up. Surely Bree would surface and help Daria. They had always stuck together, so let them take care of each other now.

But to the kindly faced, soft-voiced psychiatrist, she was saying nothing. Even if he were a trusted Catholic priest—and there were fewer of them than ever lately—in a soundproof confessional booth, Amelia would never tell him or anyone else. Despite the fact that Daria's death had been ruled a drowning, despite the fact she blamed Daria for her predicament, Amelia feared she had killed her own sister. And no one—not even Ben, trial lawyer extraordinaire—could ever defend that.

Although the sugarcane was planted in rich-looking, mucky soil, they followed a twisting, narrow gravel path. The song "Follow The Yellow Brick Road" ran through Bree's mind as she walked behind Josh and Nikki into their own land of Oz, hopefully one with no flying monkeys or wicked witches.

Bree felt curious but nervous. The leaves of the thick cane rustled and rattled; the field seemed to sigh as if it had a life of its own. As startled birds burst into the air, Bree startled in turn. She scolded herself that she was getting paranoid. Insects buzzed around her and she swatted them away. When she was certain no one was looking, she dribbled some of her drink, as delicious as it was, on the ground.

She'd argued with Cole that she was certain the Austins would not harm her. If Josh had not been involved with Daria, there would be no problem with her visit, she told him. And if Josh *had* been involved, he'd try to keep a low profile. That certainly would include winning Bree over and not harming her. Daria's death had become her life insurance. But where were they leading her?

"Fear not," Nikki called over her shoulder, as if she'd read Bree's mind while they walked the path between towering, endless stalks of sharp-shaped leaves. "We just want to show you our private waterfront property."

"You're kidding. In here?"

"And since it's not polluted," Nikki said, taking a big swig of caipirinha, "King Cane cannot be blamed for hurting your sea grass hundreds of miles away."

"Was that King Cane or King Kong, my dear?" Josh asked, his cleverness sounding too forced. "This reminds me of the scene where the big ape comes out of the jungle—"

"You're not getting another one of these,"

Nikki said, taking yet another swallow of her own drink.

Suddenly, the green cane curtain ended in a big circle. Before them lay a large pond edged by reeds, with ibis wading for fish and cormorants spreading their wings to dry.

"This day is full of surprises," Bree admitted.

"You ain't seen nothing yet," Josh said. "This is the hundred-acre detention pond, which filters out the phosphorus and nitrogen from the farm's runoff before it even flows through the Glades to the gulf."

"Mandated by the ruinous Everglades Forever Act in '94," Nikki added. "As wonderful as it sounds, its purpose was to punish cane growers for giving Americans exactly what they wanted. Sugar—so they could all get obese! And, over here, our Shangri-la away from home."

Bree looked left where Nikki pointed and saw they'd erected a screened-in dome, large enough for a table and four chairs. A hammock hung inside, too. The cane field they'd just come through backed up tight against it, but on the other side was a great view of the pond. As they headed for it, a distant bell began to toll.

"Damn, I told Lindy to hold dinner," Nikki said, pouting. "Do you have your cell, Josh?"

"Nope. This wouldn't be paradise if I dragged contact with the outside world in here. Bree?"

"Sorry. I left mine in the house. I had no idea we were going anywhere but to the veranda for a drink."

"I'll jog back and tell her not to expect us for a half hour or so," Nikki said as Josh opened the screen door and she deposited the drink tray on the table. "It won't take me ten minutes, and I'm carrying that machete with me. I'll bring a cell phone back."

"No cells!" Josh called as she hurried away. "No e-mails, no interviews, no statements, no press releases!" His voice trailed off as his wife disappeared around the twelve-foot-high, green corner of cane.

"Sometimes," he said with a sigh, "I'd rather be raising cane here than on the campaign circuit."

His pun seemed as flat as his earlier stabs at humor. Of course, he was tired, Bree realized, and trying to be a good host. But, like Nikki's false-fronted house, was he covering up something?

"That reminds me," Bree said, as she took

the wooden chair Josh indicated and he sank into the one next to her, "did Mark fly you here, too? Nikki and I could have waited for you."

"Yeah. He's back and forth a lot," he told her, rubbing his eyes with his thumb and index finger. "He has an apartment at Nikki's dad's house here, but he's on call to us 24-7 since I've been running." He looked over at her and forced a smile. "Like the Energizer Bunny, running, and running . . ."

"I'm sure the strain of being onstage all the time is grueling. Everyone watching, never any private time—except here with Nikki. You'd never get away alone with anyone but her or Mark."

He didn't answer but frowned out over the pond. Several red-beaked gallinules were fighting and others skimmed across the water's surface, half running, half flying, as if to cheer on their favorite. Bree wondered if this convenient time alone with Josh was just a gift from God—or orchestrated by the earthly deities who seemed to rule this cane kingdom. Either way, she was not going to let this ten minutes Nikki had mentioned go to waste.

"I'm sure it will be really emotional going

back to our high school tomorrow, especially after Daria's loss," she said. "You two shared so many good times there—so many memories and, once upon a time, plans for the future."

"I hadn't thought of the event that way. It all seems a long time ago. I'm in and out of the place in an hour and a half, with a speech to the whole school, then a Q and A with the government classes. Mark got some newspaper coverage."

"I know I'd be thinking of Ted—picturing him there—if I went back. And then, of course, recalling all that came later between us."

Josh shifted in his seat and took another swig of his caipirinha. The cane close behind them rattled its leaves, the sound almost like distant clapping. Bree's hands tightened around her sweaty glass, resting on the arm of her chair.

"But now Ted's dead," she went on, "and Sam blames me. It's hard to have that on my head and heart. Sam acts as if I actually physically harmed Ted."

Josh sat up ramrod straight. "Bree, I know you're grieving for her—I am, too, of course. But obviously, my emotions weren't tied to her like yours, except—ah, you know . . . from the past."

The silver-tongued Josh was fumbling for words. Had she hit a nerve?

"The truth is, I really, really regret," he said as every nerve in her own body tensed, "that Sam Travers has been such a jerk to you over the years."

That wasn't where she'd wanted the conversation to go at all. How could she get him back on Daria without giving everything away?

"I can handle Sam, but—"

"He's only happy blowing things up lately, but that's what he's always done," Josh insisted, "personally and professionally. He wanted to control Ted's life from the moment Ted's mother walked out. I shouldn't have spoken up for him to get that Sarasota demolition job, but I thought you might like him out of your hair for a while."

"You arranged that job? As a favor to me?" Or, she thought, as a ploy to get Sam's backing for your senate run.

"Yes, and he mentioned he'd like to buy you out. I told him it had better be a fair price. Had you thought about that?"

"He asked. I said no. I'm surprised both

you and Ben think you can try to push us into that, though."

"Who's us?" he said, ignoring her testy tone and veering off her chosen path again. "You're talking as if Daria's still with you."

She'd meant Manny, of course, but she saw another way to shake Josh up. "You know how identical twins are," she said, leaning on the arm of her chair to turn her whole body in his direction. She wanted to shriek at him, to demand to know if he'd had an affair with Daria and fathered her child, but then he'd surely clam up. And Nikki might be back soon. She had to do this quickly, quietly, but take a risk.

"How identical twins are?" he repeated her words, narrowing his eyes and staring her down. "Meaning what?"

"We always shared everything, no matter what we told others. We even knew what the other was thinking, feeling."

Lies, lies, she told herself. She'd learned that the hard way in the eight days Daria had been dead. But surely Josh didn't know that.

"You're not suggesting some sort of ESP with her, even now?" he asked, his usually assured voice gone almost breathy.

"I don't believe in ghosts, Josh, and yet I think someone could have harmed her. I believe she's at peace, but I can't let it rest."

She let her voice hang. She was starting to panic. Nikki would come back and she might not get Josh alone again, though she supposed his affair could be known to his wife. No, impossible. Not the way they carried on together.

She tried the only other tack she could think of. "Josh, did you consider that the autopsy might show more than just cause of death? Daria was pregnant—and I can't help but wonder if that could have, in a way, been the cause of her death. Not that the pregnancy went wrong, but that someone wanted to hush it up. I know you and Ben were trying to keep some things under wraps. I was going to mention it to you and Nikki later, but—"

He looked angry, but also puzzled. "Who was she seeing?" he asked.

"I don't know. Do you?"

"Are you crazy? You think it was me?"

"It was someone she felt she couldn't tell me about, for some reason."

"But you just said you shared everyth—"

"I know what I said."

"Are you trying to set me up? You *do* think she was seeing me! Well, she wasn't. And I don't need you mentioning that Daria was pregnant to Nikki. She's had two miscarriages, and I don't want her suspicions running wild when there is no basis in fact. Bree, damn it, I trust you, and I expect you to do the same. I am not the father of Daria's child. Hell, I'm not the father of any living child! And my only part in getting the autopsy results was trying to speed things up so you wouldn't have to suffer longer than you were."

That was the thing about golden boy Josh Austin—he always had the right answers, Bree told herself as she apologized to him and said she'd been grasping at straws. "I only know how much she loved you once," she said, looking out over the lake. "I had to know."

"Now you do. I repeat, I'm trusting you to be fair about this and not spread any sort of ugly rumor that would tarnish my reputation or Daria's memory."

Or your marriage or campaign, she thought. His voice had wavered, perhaps because she'd surprised and upset him. Before she'd discovered Daria had lied to her, she supposed she would have given Josh the benefit of the doubt, but now she wasn't sure. Did she really think he would have admitted an affair to her when that fact could ruin his marriage, his financial backing and tie him to a possible murder?

Then again, she had to admit, there was no murder investigation but in her own heart and mind. Ben passed it off as untenable; Josh hadn't made that leap when he denied the affair. Only Cole seemed to be in her corner, and he always played devil's advocate.

"I'm baa-ack," Nikki called, and Bree saw she had Mark with her. "Guess who I found, hoping for a handout at dinner?"

Josh didn't look any too pleased to have his aide here, but then, Mark Denton was the ultimate symbol of the campaign Josh had come here to escape, even if for a few moments.

As the sun sank and the tall cane cast long shadows across the pond, everyone chatted amiably, though she could tell Josh was seething. She knew she should regret that she'd abused her host and longtime friend with her fishing expedition, but she didn't. If she'd been careless or headstrong, too bad, because she was getting more desperate yet determined by the minute.

21

As soon as Mark Denton dropped her off at her apartment, Bree headed straight for Dom Verdugo's yacht to talk to Cole. It was just after noon, but she was exhausted. All night, she'd dreamed of Josh swinging machetes and cutting off heads, of sharks swimming out of waves of tall green sugarcane to devour her.

Did those crazy dreams mean something? Should she heed them and, despite the fact the Austins were crisscrossing the state campaigning, try to keep an eye on them? Cole was doing the same thing with

Dom Verdugo, and she'd have to watch what she said on his casino yacht, too.

The huge banner draped across the side of the boat read You Can Bet On It! Bree shook her head. There didn't seem to be much she'd be willing to bet on lately. She felt she was fighting the riptide again. Every time she thought she could get closer to answers, she was hit with another powerful pull of water trying to yank her under. And, in her worst nightmares, Daria still floated within the windows of the wheelhouse as if she were trying to escape from a glass coffin.

Bree was met at the bottom of the gangway by a young man with such bulky shoulders that he seemed to have no neck. Cole had said there were a couple of men here who, physically, at least, could be candidates for her attacker at the Gator Watering Hole. Her assailant had had a T-shirt mask covering his neck, but this man's build and height fit. Before she could open her mouth to tell him who she was and that she was here to see Cole, he said, "Ms. Devon, right? Mr. DeRoca said you might stop by. Right this way."

She followed him to an entry amidships. It was a beautiful craft with inlaid teak and

mahogany, polished rails, gleaming brass fittings, and velvet drapes covering windows.
She could hear music floating from somewhere aft and pounding, probably Cole's, just
ahead.

"Have you worked for Mr. Verdugo long?"
she asked, wanting to hear this man's voice
again. She'd like to put him in a lineup, along
with Ric, with black T-shirts wrapped around
their lower faces and wrenches in their
hands and have them all repeat the single
word *babe.*

"Not long, ma'am."

"Are you part of the crew?"

"Bouncer in the casino, once things get
going."

"Do you think the gambling vote will go your
way?"

"Never put anything past Mr. Verdugo."

He led her into a spacious area with several so-called one-armed bandits sitting in
the middle of the floor, crowding crap tables
and roulette wheels so that Cole could work
on the walls. She didn't see him until he rose
to his feet across the cluttered room and
their eyes met. As ever, clear down to the pit
of her belly, she felt the jolt of his stare, the
sensual impact of just being near him.

"See, you're a lucky man without even gambling, Mr. DeRoca," her escort called to Cole and left them alone.

She ran right into his arms. Lifting her off her feet, he held her tight and kissed her hard. They seemed to breathe in unison, both suddenly out of breath. Cole's body felt as hard as the wood he crafted with his callused hands, which skimmed her back and cupped her bottom.

"Mmm," he said finally, "I'm getting sawdust all over you."

"I don't mind."

"Yeah, but a little more of that and you'll be a walking giveaway of what happened in here, with sawdust all over your backside."

She felt herself blush hot. This was crazy. She was hardly a teenager like Lucinda, and when she had been, she'd never felt like this.

"Besides," he added, whispering now, "this place may have eyes and ears, for all I know, so save anything privileged for when we go to lunch. Let me wash my hands, and I'll get out of here for a while."

But the moment he returned, another man appeared with a quick knock on the door frame. "Mr. Verdugo told me that when the banging stopped—" Bree bit her lower lip and flushed again "—to tell you two that lobster salad and wine is waiting for you on the stern deck."

Bree was both touched and annoyed. She wanted to get away with Cole, to tell him things about her trip across the state that she'd been afraid to say over the phone, in case Josh could eavesdrop somehow. For one moment, she sensed Cole tense up and thought he was going to refuse the offer, but she was wrong.

"That's really nice of him," Cole told the man, who was also rather muscle-bound and the right height for her attacker. "I need to keep my nose to the grindstone here to meet the deadline for the party cruise anyway. Tell him thanks."

At least, Bree saw when they walked out onto the open deck, the table was set for only two. It was as beautifully arranged as everything in cane country had been, and spoke equally of money and power.

Cole signaled her to keep quiet, then picked up his plate and wine, motioning for her to do the same. They carried them off the boat onto the dock, down to the wooden stairs meant for boarding smaller boats without gangways. They put their food down and took off their shoes as she filled him in on Josh's denial he had anything to do with Daria's pregnancy. Dangling their feet in the water, they had their private, impromptu picnic.

"That *was* a nice table for two," she admitted as they kept an eye on the boat.

"For all I know," Cole told her through a big bite of lobster salad, "the table was bugged."

"We're both getting paranoid."

"Just careful."

"But we're eating Verdugo's food, drinking his wine."

"He's not going to poison anything except the gulf and people he hooks on gambling. He thinks he can buy anything. Tomorrow night he's invited the powers-that-be in the area—us, too, if we want to go—for a cruise party. If he could pay for individual pro-gambling votes, he would."

"How is your paneling deadline going, then?"

"I've had two holes in wood that I thought were just knots, but they weakened the entire plank as if I'd exploded a piece right out of it. I'll have to complain to my supplier."

"That reminds me, another thing Josh told

me is that he's the one who got Sam the job blowing up the bridge in Sarasota."

Bree thought again of how the newspaper headline had described her report to the Clear the Gulf Commission: Bombshell. Her eyes lifted at the sound of a commotion down the dock, and Cole turned toward it, too. Two young men in an old rowboat had somehow hit into the end of the dock and staved a hole in their hull. They were cursing, laughing and bailing madly.

"Need some help?" Cole called to them.

"No, we're okay!" one called back, still laughing.

Bree gasped. "That's it."

"That's what?"

"I know the police said they thought they'd found the place where *Mermaids II* scraped the concrete breakwater and sank, but the newspaper also said someone on the shore near Marco Pass thought they heard a bang. Of course, that could have been the dive boat hitting the wall during the thunderstorm. We saw that the stern had been broken."

"Yes. So?"

"I guess, in that storm, the stern could be heading in first. But what if a detonator cap was set to go off and that's why she—the boat and Daria—went down there? We should have looked more carefully, and so should the police. Once we found Daria, no one looked further at that piece of the stern to see if it was broken or blown in."

"And if explosives were involved, that would mean Sam Travers is, too?"

"Yes, or one of his men. I told you Ric could have easily gotten into my apartment with his ladder, then worn his diving and painting gloves so he didn't leave prints."

"So that Gator Watering Hole coaster could lead to him. But that's a stretch to tie him to being the father of her baby."

"I don't know. I just know that I have to dive Marco Pass again to look at that boat. If it hadn't been so tricky there, the police or someone could have salvaged it and then they would have seen what happened. Maybe Sam or Ric were banking on the fact they wouldn't bring the boat up."

"But Sam and Ric helped in the search when she first went missing."

"Searching where the boat wasn't until we asked for help at Marco and they had no choice."

"Bree, I dived with you twice when I didn't think it was wise, but—"

"If we can show an explosion happened on board, we can get the police involved."

"But there have been explosions from time to time on board boats for normal reasons, accidents. Someone poured in too much gas trying to start the motor, someone just—"

"I know! But I still don't think this was an accident!"

"Keep your voice down," he said, looking back toward Verdugo's yacht. "If we do dive there again, we should take some other divers, but hardly the two we took before."

"No other divers, just a lot of light power so we can see down there. We need to do this alone. If I'm wrong, we don't need someone else talking about it. If I'm right . . ."

"When would we dive?"

"Because of the low vis, we could dive after dark and see just as far. And there would be less boat traffic. We could even dive from the seawall and not from the boat."

"Not take Manny?"

"I'd feel better if he drove us to the seawall. He could keep an eye on things while we dive."

"Okay. Let me get a few hours of work

done, then I'll get my gear and meet you at Mermaids about six. I hate to say it, but the possibility of an explosion makes sense. The wind and thunder could have mostly covered up the sound. Give me your plate and goblet and you get going. I'm going to go find Verdugo to thank him. That way I have an excuse for sneaking up on him. I've managed to case most of the vessel that way, at least above the main deck."

"Be careful. See you at six," she whispered.

When Bree got back to her shop, she let herself in. Manny was out on a job, repairing a speedboat engine. She hadn't even unpacked. She had a lot to do, so she headed toward the stairs.

The front doorbell rang. She peered out and saw Manny's daughter and a tall, blond boy. Bree unlocked and opened the door.

"I know Dad's not here," Lucinda blurted. "This is my friend, Luke, and I wanted you to meet him. It's teacher conference day at school so we got off."

"Come on in," Bree said, though the last thing in the world she wanted right now was small talk with kids, when she had so much to get ready for their night dive. "Luke, it's nice to meet a friend of Cindi's," she added, shaking his hand.

"A good friend," she prompted, rolling her eyes behind Luke's back, as if Bree didn't get that this was the "friend's boyfriend" she'd talked about earlier.

"Sorry about your sister and all," Luke said. "Losing her like that really bites."

"Thank you, Luke. It sure does."

He was a head taller than Cindi and quite a contrast to her dark, cute looks. Thin, almost Nordic looking, a bit gawky and very serious. What would their kids look like? Bree wondered, before she caught herself and came back to facts. Manny would have a raving fit if he found these two here and knew Bree had invited them in. But, if she could control Manny, what would she want him to do in this situation? Definitely build bridges for these two, not blow them up.

Hoping Cindi didn't hate her for this, Bree said, "I'm sure looking forward to Cindi's *quinceañera* party. What a wonderful tradition, like a great foreign import. But it's also cutting-edge American these days. It's kind of neat to be setting new styles, don't you think?" she asked Luke.

"Oh, yeah, sure. I mean, I didn't think of it like that."

"My sister and I were asked to be some of the patrons for Cindi's big party, so I have a stake in everyone having a great time. You will be there, won't you? I know Cindi's looking forward to dancing with you. Cindi, if you want to ask some of your school friends over to learn some of the special dances, I'm sure your dad and I can clear out some of the back room for a practice area. We'll call it a combination of *High School Musical* and *Dancing With the Stars.*"

Cindi managed to smile and nod, but she almost turned blue from holding her breath.

"If I have time—and that's only if," Bree added, upping the ante when Luke simply stared at her, "I can give four or five of you a scuba lesson or two after practice." She was on a roll now, afraid to give the boy too much time to react or reject things.

"Luke," she plunged on, "the food will be fantastic with neat, new things to try, and Cindi will look like a fairy princess. It's better and bigger than any prom, you'll see."

"Well—yeah," Luke managed, looking as if he'd been hit by a tidal wave. "I'm cool with that."

Bree chatted them up some more, got them soft drinks, showed Luke Manny's desk, talked about him being a partner and his realm of motors and engines, which obviously intrigued the boy. She promised Manny would show him around the back room next time and got them out the front door just before Manny came back. With a sigh of relief for Cindi, if not for herself, Bree took that as a sign the rest of the day would go well.

But she didn't push her luck. Before she sat Manny down to tell him about Cindi and Luke's visit, she got him to promise he'd drive her and Cole to Marco later. She supposed she did make it sound a bit as if Cindi had come to introduce Luke to him. Now it was up to his Lucinda to play her part well at home.

Bree tried to take a nap but couldn't. She ended up pacing and looking at the clock. Three hours yet before she would meet Cole here for their dark-water dive.

She told herself that she had to get back to work on Monday. Clients understood a period of mourning, but her recent publicity had interested new clients. She had to get this place back on its feet. Back on its feet . . . she was dead on hers, yet she couldn't rest until she had answers. Manny had gone out on an emergency call, but her entire life seemed like an emergency since Daria had died.

The words—the reality—still staggered her. Daria . . . was . . . dead.

She leaned her shoulder against the double doors of the veranda and looked out over the harbor. Through the bare-boned forest of the masts and spars of moored sailboats, she could see the roof of Travers and Son Search and Salvage Shop. She'd love to look around in there, now that he and his staff were away. Had they taken that guy at the front desk, or was he still there to oversee things?

No matter, because she knew the back way to the upstairs, even where a key was hidden, if it was still in the same place after all these years. Since Sam seemed unwilling to change things, she'd bet it was. Sam, she was sure, had sent Ric to pilfer Daria's room, or else Ric had done it on his own. Turnabout was fair play. Besides, Sam didn't live there anymore, so she would only be trespassing in his shop—his shrine—not in his home.

Feeling bold, she locked up and walked the waterfront of Turtle Bay, just as she'd done yesterday with Manny in tow. This time she didn't even approach the front of the shop. Instead, she walked between the main building and the big boat-storage shed, as she and Ted had done years ago. A tall, wooden pole with a four-foot flat deck for an osprey nest, a nest rejected by the birds for years because it no longer had a clear view of the water, still stood there. Partway up the pole, in a chink, was a key to the third-floor attic entrance. The key had to be reached by climbing the outside stairs, which she did.

Yes. Sam really should have changed some things, taken down the *and Son* sign, moved this key. He should have admitted Ted's own decisions had put him in danger's way and have gone on with his life without hatred and revenge eating at him.

But as she leaned over the railing to reach for the key, she felt weak kneed. Could she go on without Daria? Admitting she was dead had been hell. And could she break and enter?

No, she told herself, she wasn't breaking in at all. She had a key, and it fitted quietly and perfectly in the keyhole. She had to do this.

The door creaked. Bree froze, but evidently no one heard her. These rooms were quite a climb from the office downstairs, even if Sam's employee was manning the desk there. She tiptoed in and closed the door behind her. The window slats were slightly open, casting thin bars of light across the floor. She jammed her finger under her nose to keep from sneezing. If Sam wanted to keep this intact, didn't he ever clean it?

This was the room that had once been Ted's, at least for several years after his mother left. Now it was a small museum, a long closed-up tomb. It reminded her of photos she'd seen of King Tut's tomb, the Egyptian boy king who had so many jumbled relics buried with him to take into the afterlife. Everything here was coated, not with centuries of desert sand, but with years of harbor dust.

Her wide eyes took in Ted's bed, desk and a chair with a pair of jeans thrown on it. An unlaced pair of dirty Keds. His catcher's mitt, tickets to Disney World, some favorite T-shirts tacked to boards—yes, she remembered that one from the Collier County Fair. Two big posters, one of them autographed, of football players from the Miami Dolphins. And everywhere, photos, photos, photos, ones Sam must have added.

She looked closer. In the early pictures of Ted, someone had been carefully cut out. His mother, of course. Bree hadn't known her, but she didn't think much of a woman who would leave her son, even if she did desert Sam Travers.

Awed, Bree looked further, past an array of Boy Scout badges, a lineup of bowling and Little League trophies. Then, tacked on a bulletin board, she saw some pictures she recalled. Like Sam's wife, Bree had been cut out of each one. She felt sick to her stomach.

Bree pressed her hands over her mouth, scratching her cheek with the key she still held in her hand. Did she now hold the key to who had killed Daria, either to make her suffer Daria's loss or because he thought he was killing Bree? He'd admitted yesterday they looked so much alike. But then why had Sam offered to buy her out? Why had he offered his barge to help search for Daria? It wasn't that he wanted to be there to see her pain, because he didn't arrive at the barge the day they had found Daria until they had discovered her body. Some things seemed to fit, but other facts didn't.

Ted's old stereo set was here, with its big boom box speakers. But it remained a boy's room. There was nothing of his days as a marine, nothing of his death—until she went into the next room, that had once been Sam's.

Bree gasped and jerked so hard she hit her knee on a chair. A life-size mannequin was arrayed in full marine gear, Ted's dress uniform, beret to boots. Its limbs had been bent into a near salute.

And on the opposite wall, a flag she recalled Ted had brought home with him just before he'd gone to Iraq. *Semper Fi,* it read, then in Ted's handwriting under it, *Always Faithful.*

Bree sucked in another big breath as she caught sight of something in the dull, dusty mirror behind her. She swung around. It was a picture of her and Daria. Written across Bree's face, in Sam's writing, was *Never Faithful.*

She started to cry. She couldn't help it. Sam hated her that much. Whether he felt she had deserted Ted, as his wife had deserted him, didn't even matter now. He'd been eaten up by revenge.

Sam had wanted to make Bree suffer, and he'd succeeded. He must have killed her sister, either by design or mistake. There was no reason to search this room for some other kind of proof. The room itself was proof enough. Somehow, she was certain she'd find that one of Sam's detonator caps had blown a hole in the very heart of *Mermaids II*—and her own heart. Did he think the bomb would bring him justice for the bomb that had killed Ted?

But perhaps she could find what sort of detonator caps they used now, then match whatever they found diving to that. Sam used to keep his explosives separate from everything else that was in his big storage room downstairs. There had always been a room on the second floor she and Ted were not to enter, which Ted jokingly called the "boom room."

She tiptoed along the tiny attic hall past the bathroom and opened the door to the stairs. She could hear the muted voice of a man but couldn't tell what he was saying. So Sam's front office man was here. No problem, because she wasn't going onto the first floor and if he kept talking, she could tell exactly how distant he was.

The stairs to the second floor creaked, so she walked down the edges of the cracked plastic treads. But she was only partway down when a voice came much closer than the other. She froze, pressing herself to the shadows on the wall as someone walked below into the very room she'd been going to enter.

Ric! It was Ric. Why wasn't he in Sarasota? Had Sam come back, too?

He was on his cell phone, talking to someone. Thank God he didn't glance up the flight of stairs when he walked past.

"Yeah, I'm on-site, getting more blasting caps and primacord. That bridge is one mean bastard, but these babies will work great if I just get them calibrated right."

He must be talking to Sam. They hadn't taken enough demolition material, and Ric had to come back for more.

"Yeah, a detonator, too, don't worry."

Should she go back upstairs or might he hear her? He was making some noise in there and, of course, his own voice or Sam's might cover any sound she made. Slowly, carefully, she started to go back up the stairs.

"Okay, see you later with everything you

need. And remember that little raise you promised this time."

Sam could be bribing Ric for his silence on Daria's killing! Or for doing his dirty work, like trying to scare her away from solving Daria's death. If she testified to what she'd just overheard, would it be admissible in court? Probably not. But none of that mattered. She and Cole would find evidence underwater now, because they knew what to look for in the broken, blasted body of *Mermaids II.*

22

They dove at dusk. Boat traffic in the Marco Pass was lessening, though vessels went by from time to time with their running lights on, coming in from the gulf. The wind was gentle, the waves a light chop.

They'd walked half a block from where Manny had parked Bree's truck in a visitors' spot at a large, beachside condo community. He seemed more nervous than Bree and Cole as he rolled their tanks and gear along in a two-wheeled shopping cart.

They would each take two battery-run dive lights down with them, tethered lightly to their wrists to be sure they didn't get dropped or float away in the murky dark. Bree carried the penetration line, which they would lay down as they went in so they could follow it out. A pen line made for slower swimming, but they could surface where Manny was waiting and not make the mistake of ascending in the channel.

They had all been quiet, but Bree spoke as they neared the concrete seawall. "I still consider *Mermaids II* my property, and I intend to try to bring up any evidence of explosives we can find, so I've brought two lift bags."

"You should have called your brother-in-law to check whether that would be tampering with evidence," Cole said, "especially if we can get the police to open this as a murder case."

"And let him know we're doing this? I've had enough of his lectures and taking over things he had no right to control. He should take care of Amelia, not worry about me."

"But I can tell Amelia worries about you. She wants the two of you to be closer."

"I know. I think we can be, but right now, I've got to do this. I used to think that Daria couldn't rest in peace until I could prove who hurt her, but I'm the one who can't rest until this is over."

"I checked the fill in these tanks two times," Manny told them, as he helped them gear up. "You should dive at dawn," he muttered, half to himself. "Not many boats then neither."

"By dawn," Bree told him as she tightened the straps on her weight belt, "I hope to be knocking on the door of the Naples Police Department with proof of a murder."

They eased into the night-dark water side by side, tethered to each other's weight belts by a ten-foot rope. That was the only separation they would allow themselves, they had vowed as they'd kissed for good luck. But now there was no more talking, only the sound of bubbles and the hiss of their breathing. They had not even brought slates to write on. Hand signals and a common purpose—and having been here before—that's what they were relying on.

Yet as they descended, Bree found the low vis suffocating, as if the solid walls of a coffin were closing in on them. Still, her eyesight was acute; the dive lights worked well, giving them about a four-feet radius of sight, and they both had compass watches to take them approximately to the spot where the dive boat lay. The day they'd stumbled on

Daria and *Mermaids II,* neither of them had thought to take a compass reading.

This time they located the main body of the ship before the stern, which had been— Bree was sure now—blasted out. How strange it must have been for Ric to see what their explosives had done that day he'd helped to recover Daria's body. If she'd not been so distraught, Bree could have noted how they reacted. Cole had only spoken to them before the dive, while they were cleaning and loading their spearguns.

From the dark depths loomed the majority of the sunken boat, as if it were a ghost ship sailing straight toward them. But that was just a trick of the swift current, lit by their lights. They peered into the wheelhouse where they'd found Daria's body.

It struck Bree that the glass was still intact. Wouldn't a blast have shattered the windows? No, Sam or Ric would know to use whatever strength it took to blow a hole in the hull without creating debris that would float in as evidence. More than one person had told her Sam Travis was skilled at sinking an old boat or a bridge and leaving everything else around it amazingly intact.

Bree heard a boat's slow motor whisper

past in the channel overhead. Her hearing was still sensitive from the lightning strike.

As they started away from the wheelhouse, her light caught something, and she turned back. Cole felt the tug on their rope and came back. It was only a grouper hovering near the wheelhouse, one that looked to be the size of their old pet Gertie from the Trade Wreck. She'd like to think that Gertie had come here to keep watch over the place Daria had died.

They swam lower, right along the bottom, still laying the pen line toward where they were certain they had spotted the piece of the boat before.

Yes! There it was! The grayish glint of metal, the curved aluminum handrail that pointed toward the broken stern. Bree was confident that piece of white metal should show up in their lights. But where was it? Could the shifting sand and silt here have buried it already?

Bree motioned to Cole that she was sure it must be here. He nodded and started to brush the bottom away with both hands. Ordinarily, that would lessen visibility, but it hardly mattered where they could only see four feet anyway.

Then, there it was, the piece of *Mermaids II* that had borne its name and now read, *MA D I.* They quickly uncovered more to see if the edges were jagged or pierced.

Yes! Something from outside the hull on the stern had blown the metal inward into a gaping hole the size of a watermelon. The first time she'd seen this, that section had been under sand and silt. She supposed, even if the police took a look at this, they could insist it was caused by a collision with the concrete seawall. No, surely they could tell it had been caused by what she'd over-heard Ric call a blasting cap.

Chills raced through her. She blinked back tears to avoid fogging her mask. Somehow this hole had been made below the waterline. Perhaps the perpetrator had placed the de-vice on their boat while it was docked, hoping the small, attached bomb would not be seen. Or perhaps the bomb had been placed when the boat was at sea by someone under the surface. Was another diver in the water be-sides her that day? Or had the explosive been attached after the boat either drifted or was towed away? If it was towed, why didn't Bree hear the motor or the craft doing the towing?

She looked at Cole, who nodded. He understood! Answers at last. Evidence which would lead straight to Sam Travers and his men. It all fit now, but first they had to retrieve this big piece of metal, get it up to the surface. It was so heavy that she might need both lift bags. Then she had to hope it didn't surface where a boat was going through the pass—

A barbed shaft from a speargun zinged off the metal inches from her hand. Cole's big body jerked; he pushed her away, yanking their tether taut. As he turned to follow, another stainless-steel spear raced past them in a blur of bubbles.

They'd been followed. By the killer? Now she knew who and why.

They could see no one, but someone could see them. Or were there two shooters down here, both Ric and Lance? Maybe the strong currents warped the speargun's trajectory.

They turned off the dive lights that made them targets. Utter blackness closed in like a trap. Keeping the ten-foot rope between them taut, Bree kept shifting her position. She was certain Cole was doing that, too, however much he kept putting slack in their tether.

Bree's breathing, her clicking regulator, her heartbeat and pounding pulse were like drums beating in her head. She couldn't so much as see her own bubbles now, let alone Cole.

Suddenly, someone gripped her upper arm and pushed her up, up. *Cole.* It must be Cole. Yes, they had to surface, then wait to see who else came up. But she hated to leave this evidence down here. It might disappear like her sea grass meadow. She reached down to touch the metal piece from her lost boat again before Cole yanked her away.

For one moment, she feared it wasn't Cole, but if she couldn't see him, she could sense him. To her surprise, he forced her fingers below his mask. His regulator and mouthpiece were gone, and air gushed out of his torn hose in a blast of bubbles.

A spear must have cut through his breathing gear. She took a big breath, then pulled her mouthpiece out and pressed it toward his lips. He pulled her closer as he evidently took a breath. They could buddy breathe, but that was difficult under the best of circumstances. They'd have to ascend fast. At least they weren't so far down that they'd get the bends. Two reasons now to get out fast.

But as Cole thrust her mouthpiece back at her, a big light blinded them. Now that their lights didn't make them targets, their attacker needed his.

Cole shoved her one way and went the other as a spear slashed between them. Their tether pulled loose or broke, or had Cole cut it? Someone came at her—not Cole—as she started away, struggling to get her bubbling mouthpiece back in her mouth.

Up. Up! *When in doubt, get out,* but there was no doubt about this.

The man grabbed at her, got a fin. She kicked at him, hit her ankle on his dive light, so it went off. Was she down here alone with the enemy? Cole was out of air, out of time.

Bree jackknifed and kicked the man with both feet, hitting him in the chest. She dumped her weight belt and kicked hard, clawing at the water, fighting for the surface. She came up closer to the gulf than she wanted, but not more than twenty yards from where Manny must be.

Cole. Where was Cole?

She spun around. Nothing. Without a light, how could she go back down? She had no idea where he could be now.

In a whoosh of white water, Cole surfaced, sucking in air.

She spit out her mouthpiece. "Cole! Here!"

"Get out! I lost him!"

Yes, Bree thought as they both swam toward the seawall and Manny came running toward them, but the killer had lost them, too.

Manny grabbed under her armpits and helped pull her out. She was gasping like a beached fish, but she tried to explain what had happened to him. "A diver down there— shot at us—speargun. Hit Cole's hose. Tried to buddy breathe, had to surface but—found a hole blasted in the hull—below waterline."

Still sucking in huge breaths, Cole climbed out beside her, then staggered to his feet and stood to look out over the inky stretch of water. Bree scanned it, too. Nothing. No boats, no diver surfacing—nothing.

"I can't even spot bubbles in this dark," Cole muttered.

"It's got to be the same guy who attacked me at the Gator Watering Hole. And the same one who blows holes in boats and bridges for Sam. At last, we know Daria's killer! I wonder if Ric could be the father of her child."

Bree heard Manny grunt then swear under his breath. In all the chaos, she should have told her new partner about that, but now it would have to wait until later.

"Manny," she said, noticing his bare feet and the pool of water where he stood, which could not have come from her or Cole, "you're soaking wet."

"Fell in," he said, his voice gruff. "*Caramba,* I think we all got in over our heads."

Here came Bree, down the stairs. Manny had been expecting her.

After she had fed both men, Cole had fallen asleep on the sofa, where Manny heard him say he was going to spend another night. At first light, Bree and Cole were going to call the police to see who they could go talk to about retrieving the piece of bomb-blasted metal—if it was still there, Bree had said. They'd waited over an hour, pacing up and down the seawall, but no one had surfaced and they saw no boat nearby from which someone could have dived.

Manny insisted on eating at his desk downstairs while he got ready to close up and go home late. He'd called Juanita to tell her not to worry. She'd said that Lucinda wanted to bring her friend Luke over to meet them on Sunday and he was to keep his temper and be kind to the boy.

"What did you mean earlier by 'we *all* got in over our heads'?" Bree asked him bluntly.

He'd been sitting at his desk, chin on his hands, staring into space. He guessed if Bree could turn Lucinda around, even a little, he owed her some of the truth, at least.

"And I'm sorry," she said, sitting on the corner of the desk so she seemed to loom over him, "that I didn't tell you earlier that I'd found out Daria was pregnant."

He cleared his throat. "I knew that."

She gasped. "Since when? Who told you?"

"Not sure when. A month at least. Daria told me—more or less."

Bree looked as if someone had slammed her in the gut.

"Overheard her take the call. From her doctor," he went on. "She stepped into the back room 'cause you at your desk, I guess. She didn't know I was there, working on my knees on some stuff. *You're sure? You're sure I'm pregnant?* I hear her say."

"But she never knew that you had overheard her secret." Bree said that like a statement, not a question.

He sighed and shifted on his chair, suddenly aware it had been Daria's. "Nah, dropped a wrench."

"So you said you'd keep her secret. Did you ask who the father was?"

"She just tell me it very complicated. Yeah, that's the word she used."

Bree's hands slapped her thighs. "Damn it! Why didn't you tell me earlier, when she was missing, at least?"

He shrugged. "Honoring the dead, her last wish to me, in a way. If she was gone, nothing can be done about the baby."

Bree jumped up and started to pace with her arms folded over her chest. Thank the blessed Virgin, he thought. She'd assumed he'd simply volunteered to keep Daria's secret. Truth was, he'd suggested to her that he'd keep quiet if she'd turn more and more of the running of the business over to him during her pregnancy. She'd told him she was having and keeping the baby. He admired her for that, but he'd still blackmailed her, in a way. He hadn't asked for money, but she'd offered it. As ashamed of himself as he was now, he'd taken it, a couple of hundred dollars, which he was pretty sure she got from her lover. But if Bree learned all that, she just might find a way to kick him out of here.

Cole sat on Bree's veranda drinking coffee the next morning as she made the call to the police. He could catch occasional things she said, her voice impassioned.

That's how he'd felt about her from the beginning, impassioned. Had it only been ten days since he'd found his mermaid washed in on the stormy shore? He felt as if he'd known her—wanted her—for years. Since their mutual drive to find what had happened to Daria might be over now, would she need him less?

He did not feel the relief she did. Yeah, everything pointed toward Sam and Ric, and Cole was glad the investigation would soon be in official hands. He still didn't trust Verdugo, but maybe that was because he hated what he stood for, escape from reality and easy money through gambling. It had ruined his mother's life, his dad's and his, leaving a legacy of only loss.

He frowned in the direction of Verdugo's yacht, where he was going to finish the paneling today so the place would look good for the shakedown cruise—the PR party, as he'd heard Verdugo call it. Cole agonized that he had sold out to Verdugo. He'd only wanted to help Bree by keeping an eye on the man, and the paneling deal had fallen into his lap as the perfect way to do that. But he still longed to chuck it all and start up a boatbuilding business of his own.

He'd agreed to go out on the casino boat tonight, but only so he could search an off-limits storage area he'd noted below decks yesterday while Verdugo was distracted by his guests. Now, he was also looking for diving gear and spearguns. The police could focus on Sam Travers and his divers, but Cole could not shake the gut feeling that Verdugo was dirty, too.

Bree came out and sat across the little table from him. She was almost smiling. That tilted the corners of her gray-green eyes and made her look less exhausted.

"Finally," she said, and sighed so hard her shoulders rose and fell.

"They're going to open the case?"

"A Lieutenant Mike Crawford is going to get a search warrant for Sam's house and shop and put in a request that the police dive team retrieve the stern piece from *Mermaids II* in Marco Pass. I told them I hoped it was still there, because of what happened with my sea grass report to the commission. I said I'd dive with them, but they said absolutely not, that my description of the layout would be enough. And that they would interview both of us at length tomorrow morning."

"Great!" he said, reaching over to clasp her bare knee. "I hope that now you can relax a bit."

"For the first time, I admit I feel totally wiped out. I couldn't let up before, not until we found Daria, buried her, then found her killer."

"But if it *is* Sam or his divers, the question remains whether he meant to kill you."

"If that was his plan, he could have done it several years ago, probably closer to when Ted died."

"Maybe it took time for him to get to the point where he'd risk it, time to lay plans."

"Maybe time to realize he'd get more vengeance not by eliminating me but Daria. I believe he wanted me to suffer for her loss as he had suffered with Ted's. Then, when Daria and I dared to open a business that was competition to him, even though he could almost buy and sell us—and tried to—he just bided his time until he could make it look as if Daria had an accident. Maybe he came upon her in the storm and took his chance, maybe he stalked her. I don't know, but I hope the police can get it out of him."

In a way, he wanted her to go with him on the casino boat tonight, but he wanted to be alone when he searched the storage room he'd seen Verdugo's men go in and out of.

"Verdugo said I can bring you tonight," Cole reminded her, "but I thought you might want to just crash—sorry I put it that way. Are you okay with being alone?"

"I've already decided not to go. Don't worry, Manny's coming over to play body-guard, since we have a lot to discuss about our new partnership. And," she said, sounding lighthearted for once, "I'll wait up for you, and you can tell me all about it. Besides, Lieuten-ant Crawford promised to call me here with an update this evening."

"I like the sound of that, not just the police being on the case, but you waiting up for me."

He pulled her closer and kissed her, linger-ingly at first, then intensely. Her lips opened; a jolt of desire nearly shot him off his chair. Her fingers moved across his temple and through his hair, stroking it. He felt swept away, as if he was sailing full blast, skimming over the water to parts unknown but deeply desired.

When they finally broke the kiss, with her mouth moving along his cheek, she said, "I realize I've said this before, but I don't know what I would have done without you through all this. Take care of yourself tonight. We might have survived by being in your boat when the sharks were in the water, but I'm afraid on that yacht, you'll actually have some sharks on board with you."

23

Manny was late. He'd called to say he'd had a flat tire on Golden Gate and had spun off onto the berm. Bree realized she was still suffering from the residual effects of paranoia. She should have asked him if he was all right, but instead she blurted, "You're sure it was just a flat? No one's tampered with the truck?"

"I know tires like I know motors. Be there as quick as I can."

"Make sure you're far enough off the road so no one hits you."

"Yes, boss."

"'Yes, partner,' will do," she said as she punched off on her cell. She was hoping to use tonight to patch things up with Manny and set out some mutual rules for working together, because they had to get the business back on its feet. She was pretty sure a lot of Manny's problems with his daughter and with her and Daria had been that he was from a culture—and a gender—that didn't like taking orders from women. They'd have to really talk that one out, or else their partnership would never work.

Bree decided to call Amelia to update her on Lieutenant Crawford taking Daria's suspicious death case, but knowing Ben, he was probably already up on the latest developments. For all she knew, the judge who signed the search warrant had reported right in to him. But the voice who answered the phone was not Amelia's.

"I'm Mrs. Westcott's sister," Bree said. "This is the Westcott residence, isn't it?"

"Oh, yes. This is the babysitter, Johanna. I thought it might be my mom."

"Please tell Mrs. Westcott I called and I'll phone again tomorrow."

"No problem. They went out on a big boat

at the Turtle Bay Marina tonight. The boys are being really good," the girl added, as if she had to give Bree the parent report.

"Tell them 'hi' from their aunt Bree, and that I'll see them soon."

She should have known, she thought as she put her cell on the table, that the A-list of movers and shakers around here would include Ben Westcott. She was glad Amelia was well enough to go. Patching up things with Manny was one thing, but Bree knew she had a long way to go with Amelia. She hoped she could help her believe that she was loved and had always been loved. She hoped they could help each other.

As much as she was finally starting to relax, Bree jumped when the downstairs doorbell rang. Maybe Lieutenant Crawford had stopped by in person. Deciding not to turn on the inside office lights until she saw who it was, she hurried downstairs.

It was Nikki Austin, dressed to kill, as usual. Mark stood behind her, looking pretty natty, too, leaning against the car as if the part he would play tonight was chauffeur. Snapping on the main office light, Bree unlocked and opened the door.

"Wow," she said, admiring Nikki's jade-green, strapless, silk cocktail dress. "You look fabulous."

"We're going to meet Josh on board the casino boat for the big show-and-tell party, where Verdugo *shows* the powers-that-be how he's lily-white in the pollution department and *tells* us to get the voters to see things his way. Marla Sherborne's attending, too."

Bree almost told them Ben and Amelia would be there, but she decided to stick with Verdugo. "At least you're on to the casino king," Bree said. "Cole will be there, but, as you can see," she added, gesturing at her shorts and T-shirt, "I'm staying put."

She considered telling them about the police taking the case, but she decided she'd wait on that, too. It still was possible that Josh, not Ric, was the father of Daria's baby. Then again, Daria could have met Ric on a diving job and not told Bree about their developing relationship because he worked for Sam. Even in their brief encounter, Bree had seen how charming Ric could be.

Mark came closer behind Nikki. "We saw your lights and thought we could give you a lift over," he said.

"You know," Nikki added, pointing to her

stiletto-heeled sandals, "no one can walk far
in these things. We'll wait for you to change.
Mark can drop us both off."

"Thanks, but I'm really not going. Enjoy
yourselves."

Bree's office phone started ringing. She'd
had it on speaker earlier and forgotten to
take it off. It might be Cole, and she didn't
want everyone to hear what he said.

"Excuse me a second," she said, but she
didn't get to the phone in time. A man's
voice—not Cole's—spoke. "Bree, Dave
Mangold here. I'm so sorry to hear what
happened with Daria and that I wasn't here
to fly with the civil air patrol for the search."

It didn't matter if Nikki and Mark overheard this, Bree thought.

Dave's voice went on. "I've been to visit
my daughter in Memphis and I didn't even
learn Daria had been lost until I got back today. I got your messages on my phone here.
I did see something strange when I was flying out that afternoon. Racing ahead of the
storm, I saw a pontoon plane towing a boat
that could have been your dive boat—not
sure, but it was really weird. They were
heading toward Marco Pass, I think . . ."

His message continued, saying he'd call

back later. The reality of what he'd said hit Bree like a rogue wave out of the dark. A pontoon plane, no doubt the very one she'd been in. She'd heard no motor when she was underwater because an amphibious plane's motor was above the water.

The timing could not have been worse. Nikki and Mark had heard everything, so there was no faking her response with them. Her stomach went into free fall as she turned to stare at them, standing close to each other now, intimately so.

"Too bad we can't convince you to go to the party, then," Nikki said, her voice now solemn rather than solicitous. "The entire Clear the Gulf Commission will be there, I hear."

"My sister and her husband are going, so I'll get a blow-by-blow from them," Bree said, trying to find a way to brazen this out. "They're stopping by to say hi any minute now."

"Nice try," Mark said, aiming a small gun at her. "Nikki just talked to Josh on board and the Westcotts are already there, though he hadn't seen your watchdog, Cole, yet."

Could Cole be coming back for her? How long would it take Manny to get here?

Bree's mind raced over possibilities. Were these two working with Josh or against him? She was furious with herself for not reading things right, for being sucked in by the Austins and their so-called bodyguard. And what was the real relationship between Nikki and Mark? Bree's voice came sharper than she intended; it didn't sound like her.

"Have you decided to stoop to using a gun now instead of your more bizarre weapons, like a wrench or speargun—or a detonator cap?" she asked Mark. "You've set Sam up to be a suspect in Daria's death, and with my help."

Mark's grimace was more of a grin. "We were still trying to just scare you off at the Gator Watering Hole," he said, his voice calm and controlled as he walked closer, hit the play button for Dave Mangold's message again, then deleted it. "By the way, the piece of blasted stern from your dive boat has gone the way of your sad sea grass meadow. The same way you're going to have to go now— bye-bye."

"Then after killing me, you'll merrily go sailing with everyone?" Bree challenged.

"You're way off base again," Nikki said as she pulled on a pair of white gloves and walked away to lock the front door. "Since you've missed the boat, so to speak, I'm afraid you're going to commit suicide by drowning yourself out by the Trade Wreck where you last saw Daria. And we're not going out on the casino yacht because in—" she glanced at the time on her cell phone "—less than sixty minutes, an underwater explosive attached to the boat is going to take it and everyone on board to the bottom of the gulf."

"You mean Bree's not on board?" Amelia asked Cole. He'd been busy showing people his woodwork, especially after Dom Verdugo had pointed it out to everyone in his opening remarks. "I thought I'd get to spend some time with her."

"She's really anxious to do that, but she's exhausted," Cole told her, raising his voice to be heard above the buzz of conversations in the main salon.

The man certainly cleaned up well from the time he'd waited with her in the hospital, Amelia thought. He'd looked like a sea captain that night at their house, but he had stepped right out of the pages of *GQ* magazine tonight. If she were Bree, she'd have come along just to beat the women off. It certainly would do Bree good to have a man in her life—but then, maybe she wouldn't need her older sister any more than she ever did. Bree and Daria, Bree and Daria—she could almost hear the way they'd chattered to each other from the moment they could talk.

When other people came up to talk to Cole, Amelia took a shrimp appetizer from the circulating server—the shrimp had a small edible orchid perched atop it, no less—and wound her way through the crowd and out on deck. Ben was so busy talking to Josh Austin he wouldn't miss her.

Josh's wife had just phoned him to say she had a terrible headache, that she was just going to lie down at their local campaign headquarters. Word was that the Austin power couple hoped to emulate Bill and Hillary Clinton someday. Now wouldn't that be something? Maybe Josh would put Ben in his cabinet.

As the boat left the harbor, Amelia ate her appetizer but saved the orchid. With a pink cosmo in her hand, she leaned against the wooden railing, then edged around the back of the yacht. As they left the shore lights of

Turtle Bay behind, the stars popped out overhead, but she preferred looking down mesmerized, into the white wake in the dark water.

This gulf had swallowed her sister, drowned her. If Daria had not been unconscious, would she have died or saved herself? And then, would she have blamed Amelia—hated her even more? If she told Bree what had happened that last day, would Bree ever forgive her? How did it feel to slip under the sliding waves to die?

The buzz of voices and laughter floated to her, mingled with the murmur of the sea. Her drink glass slipped from her fingers and disappeared into the silvery wake.

"A toast to Daria," she whispered, and tossed in the tiny orchid. They seemed to be heading in the direction of the Trade Wreck where Bree and Daria used to dive together.

Why had she always been so afraid of the waves and water? Amelia asked herself. But she'd been brave enough to go out in a boat to talk to Daria, who had told her to grow up and get over things. Dr. Nelson had said the same, in a more convoluted, quiet way. He'd said her perceptions might not be reality, at least for other people.

Amelia leaned out even farther, looking down, down into the silken surface of the sea. Again, she assured herself that the coroner's report stated that Daria had actually died from drowning, not from the blow to her head. And that had been an accident— she'd slipped, just slipped in the heat of their argument. But guilt pressed Amelia down, down, drowning her . . . .

Bree's eyes darted to the clock on the office wall. A bomb to go off on the hull of the casino boat—no doubt under the waterline— in less than sixty minutes. Cole gone. Amelia and Ben. Verdugo. Josh and his opponent, Marla. All those others. Yes, these two had to be lovers or else Nikki would not let Josh die.

Somehow, she had to do something, and fast. The minute hand of the clock was moving so quickly. If she could keep them talking, Manny might come, but how long would that take? She had to get to a phone and get the coast guard out there to intercept Verdugo's boat.

Bree said to Nikki, "I'm shocked to think you're planning to get rid of Josh, your ticket to Washington and the halls of power."

"I would have been behind him all the way,

before he betrayed me," Nikki said as Mark handed her the gun and went into the back room, clicking on the lights. The man knew his way around here, but then, he'd probably been downstairs, as well as upstairs, searching Daria's room.

"But it was best that Daria be eliminated," Nikki went on, "and now Josh, too, for what he's done. Haven't you heard about the widow's sympathy vote platform? Congressman Sonny Bono dies in a tragic, publicized skiing accident, and his widow gets elected in his place. Years before, Congressman Boggs goes down in a plane crash and his widow takes his office. The third time's the charm."

Bree's jaw dropped. Her gaze met and held Nikki's. The woman looked rock steady and icy cold. Forget the tactic of trying to work on her emotions or sympathy.

"If you're thinking the explosive on the boat will make Sam a suspect, you're mistaken," Bree insisted. "He's in Sarasota, so he has an airtight alibi."

"Wrong again," Nikki countered. "He's been called back by Josh to speak at a luncheon tomorrow about saving the gulf. Briana, I know you and Sam don't get along, but you should know he's spoken out for your sea grass stance. But I'm glad you suspected him as the mastermind behind Daria's death, just as we had hoped."

Bree just gaped, stunned anew. She'd tried to blame him for all of this and now she might not be around to testify when he took the fall for Nikki and Mark. "Then Ric's working for you?"

"Oh, yes, he's working with us and for us. He's worked closely with Mark."

"Shooting a speargun at Cole and me. Helping Mark break into this place and search Daria's room—and tamper with our computer?"

"It *is* quite a list, isn't it? But we have to end it all now. Ric won't talk, because he's an accessory. Besides, Mark's going to be my chief congressional aide—at least until we can find the appropriate time to get married. So I'll need a new strong arm, and Ric's agreed to become that."

Bree could have sunk through the floor. She'd assumed Ric was talking to Sam about a detonator cap and explosives on the phone yesterday. But if Nikki and Mark had killed Daria, were they purchasing those items from Ric on the sly? Josh had said he'd arranged for Sam to get the job blowing up a bridge in Sarasota. He'd probably told Mark or Nikki how Sam had a vendetta against Bree, or maybe Ric, their supplier, had filled them in on that.

A damn spiderweb, but one that looked like it would hold. Bree felt not only helpless but furious. Think! Think, she told herself.

"How did it happen—with Daria? Did you and Mark know she'd be alone on the boat?"

"She brought it on herself—with Josh's help, of course. I don't totally blame her. Blame fate, if you must. I just happened to overhear Josh take a call at our home in Tallahassee when she called him on his business phone. She probably thought I'd never intercept a call coming into his office. But I picked up on the line and heard her tell him she was pregnant—pregnant with his child, when two of mine had died!"

The gun shook in Nikki's hand; she gripped it so tightly her fingers went white. Bree could hear Mark in the back room. What was he doing? She almost wished he'd come back to calm Nikki down. Surely they didn't want to shoot her, at least not here. But Nikki seemed to get hold of herself as she spoke again.

"You were such a smart girl to grill Josh at our little getaway in the cane field by the pond. You were on the right track."

"You didn't go back to the house," Bree accused. "You eavesdropped from that thick cane. It was all a setup."

"*You* were trying to set Josh up. Mark and I both heard every word you two said. Well, you can guess why I got off the handsome, the clever, the *lying* Josh Austin's bandwagon, when he lied to you. Believe me, he's lied to me for months. And, in the middle of a key election, managed to spend time with your sister. Looking at you right now makes me sick—Daria revisited, Daria déjà vu."

"I may look like her, but I am not my sister. I didn't even know her as well as I thought." Bree meant every word she said. Daria had not deserved to be killed, but she'd made a mess of things.

"Mark had told me of Josh's affair earlier—or let's say, I managed to entice it out of him," Nikki went on, as if she had to rid her soul of her guilt in this defiant confession. "But neither of us knew about Daria's pregnancy until I overheard that phone call. Daria told Josh she was going to make up a story to get you to dive alone while she just stayed with the boat. Here's a good one for you— the rocky sea didn't make her ill, but Josh's baby did. Anyway, she was surprised that it was me in the plane, with Mark, instead of Josh. She thought her lover boy had come to surprise her. Mind you, she'd fallen and hit her head and was barely conscious when we arrived. Mark set the detonator and we towed her into Marco Pass before it went off in that fierce storm. I knew she wouldn't resist our plans when she called me by your name and said she was glad you were there."

Tears blinded Bree. If Daria thought her twin sister was with her at the end, maybe it was some comfort to her. It comforted Bree, though it came from the demented woman who had caused Daria's death. Bree hugged herself around her waist as if to hold herself up. "But when you and Mark became lovers, that was the same deceit you detested Josh for."

"His was worse! He deserted me because I can't have children. Mark and I joined forces to clean up the mess Josh had made."

"I can understand how you felt betrayed— especially because of your two losses."

Stunned by all this and desperate to warn those on Verdugo's boat, Bree knew she was struggling for words.

Mark came back out into the office, carrying a big salvage net with a long handle and a length of cord he must have cut off a lift or buoy. "That's not going to work," Nikki said, pointing at the rope. "We can't have ligature marks on her if she went out in her boat and drowned herself. Take off your shirt and tie her wrists with the sleeves of it."

Bree's mind seemed to clear. She kept a dive knife under the backseat of *Mermaids I,* but it would do her little good with her hands tied behind her. After Mark shed his sports jacket and stripped off his shirt, she thrust her wrists out in front of her.

"Turn around," he said, and shoved her toward her desk. She had no choice but to obey, though she knew it might be better to take a bullet here that could be traced. A shot from the distance Nikki was standing couldn't be construed as a suicide, whereas her drowning would. She could see the headline now: Despondent Over Sister's Loss And Failure Of Sea Grass Project, Briana Devon Drowns Self Same Night Casino Boat Is Blown To Pieces. And there would be no one—Cole, Amelia, Ben, even Dom Verdugo—to say different about her.

Then Bree heard the distinctive sound of Manny's old truck. He was here! Could she warn him, or would they shoot her to shut her up? Her heart pounding, she strained to hear his footsteps and his key in the lock. What was taking him so long?

When Bree heard him approach, she opened her mouth to scream. Mark must have heard something, too, for he jammed a handkerchief in her mouth and shoved her to the floor.

"Get over here—cover her," he ordered Nikki, and darted out from behind the desk. Nikki knelt behind Bree, pressing the gun to her neck. The woman's hand was shaking. Bree dry heaved, choking into her gag.

Manny unlocked the door and the familiar bell rang.

"You upstairs or in the back room, partner?" he called out. "Light's on back in th—"

With a sickening thud, Bree heard Mark strike Manny and his body crumple to the floor.

It was hard to slip away, but Cole finally managed it. Verdugo probably expected him to keep pretending to be part of the *Fun 'n' Sun* team, but he was done with that. He wondered if the guests were swallowing Verdugo's promises of no pollution from this boat half as easily as they were swallowing free drinks and the lobster and lamb entrées.

Keeping an eye out to be sure none of Verdugo's lackeys were on the lower level, Cole went below decks. As far as he could see, the coast was clear.

A glimpse out a porthole he passed revealed a calm night. Stars, no moon yet. He wished he was with Bree to enjoy it and wondered what she was doing. Waiting for Manny or Lieutenant Crawford's call? He was tempted to phone her, but he needed to check out this storage room first, then decide if he was going to search further. He'd have to calculate the timing, the risks.

The storage room was locked, but there was a closed flat cabinet on the wall with keys. Yes, this one was for that storage space. Twice he'd seen Verdugo's goons take keys from here and go into the room. Glancing up and down the corridor, he unlocked the room and darted in. Even when he found the light switch and clicked it on, the small, windowless room was dim. It took a moment for his eyes to adjust.

Not a storage room, but a bedroom. And a naked, Latina-looking young girl was gagged and tied to a single bed, her eyes wide with fear.

24

"Her man coming in here is an unfortunate complication," Mark told Nikki.

Bree strained to listen. As far as she could tell, Manny hadn't moved. Was he unconscious or dead?

"Since we're eliminating anyone who might get in our way, what's one more?" Nikki said, standing and taking the gun barrel from Bree's neck. "It's still best if she commits suicide. Maybe he tried to stop her, and she hit him over the head?"

"Let's go with that. Or maybe Sam came back, stumbled onto this guy and knocked him out."

This was all her fault! Bree had to get them talking to her again, but they ignored her muffled protests as they dragged Manny behind her desk and relocked the front door. Bree tried to catch a glimpse of him as they pulled her to her feet. He lay facedown, a dark pool of blood spreading under his head. When he'd come in, he'd called her *partner.* They would have worked things out, and he would have worked things out with Lucinda.

Mark pulled Bree to her feet. When she balked, he dragged her through the back room, out the door and down the dock toward her boat slip. Nikki followed, carrying the large net and the key to the boat. Bree had finally put *Mermaids I* in the dock space where the larger, newer boat used to be, the one that had become Daria's coffin. She was the last mermaid left, and *Mermaids I* would be the hearse that took her to her grave.

"Say goodbye to Nikki, because she's not coming," Mark told her, shoving her into the boat on her belly. She saw he was going to pull the dinghy behind them so he could get back in after staging her suicide. "She's going to campaign headquarters to lie down with a raging headache, while I get rid of its cause for her. A few volunteers are working late tonight, so they'll be a good alibi. I'll walk over there later, and everyone will assume I was with the car the whole time."

Bree was barely listening. She was near enough to see the knife, but she'd never reach it with her hands tied behind her back. Why didn't someone come along the dock? Nikki kissed Mark passionately—"for good luck," she whispered—and hurried away.

Everything they did went off like clockwork. Clockwork, like the timed bomb they must have put on the hull of the *Fun 'n' Sun*, where no one would see it.

Cole covered the trembling, naked girl with his suit jacket and carefully pulled the masking tape off her mouth. Despite all that, she spread her legs for him and he had to shove them together. He whispered to her in Spanish that he was here to help her.

Tears filled her eyes. *"Cuidado! Cuidado!"* Careful, she kept whispering.

She was afraid to say anything at first, evidently thinking he was another of Verdugo's guys who had access to her. Finally, he coaxed out of her that she was from Guatemala, where he knew most of the women involved in the human trafficking trade had been taken from their homes or sold by their destitute families. She'd been promised a job as a waitress in a Miami casino, but *Señor Verdugo, he bring her here for his boys.*

It was enough to make Cole throw up, but at least it proved he'd been right about Verdugo. Sam might be behind everything else, but Verdugo was dirty, too. He'd get years, not on a luxury yacht but in the state pen, for this.

Cole explained in Spanish that there were some important people on board who could help, but he would have to leave her here for now.

"No, señor! No, por favor!"

Thank God, no one was in the hall, because he could kill Verdugo and his men with his bare hands for this. Wait until he told Bree he'd found a way to stop Verdugo and it had nothing to do with gambling.

Wearing gloves, just as Nikki had, Mark took *Mermaids I* out of Turtle Bay toward open water. As she lay facedown in the boat, Bree felt the vibration of the motor, the rush of water against the hull as they cut through the bay.

Back to the place where this horror began, she thought. The Trade Wreck, where

Daria's and her life was wrecked. If he'd just untie her and throw her in, she could swim in again. Piece of cake—no storm, maybe no sharks. But she knew, with the way he and Nikki had set everything else up, he would not just toss her into the water.

And then, as she saw the handle of a large, long-handled retrieval net he'd brought, she realized his possible plan. Maybe he meant to keep her underwater with that net until she drowned. Could she hold her breath long enough to convince him she was dead? If he untied her hands before he threw her in, could she yank him in or swim down and away from him? Did he have the gun or had Nikki taken it? If only she could get control of the boat, could she make it out to the casino yacht in time to tell everyone to get off? How much time was left? It had to be less than half the sixty minutes Nikki had mentioned.

Too soon, they reached the site of the Trade Wreck. Mark cut the motor and let the boat drift.

"Sorry about this, really," he said as he hauled her to her knees. "If you had just let things go, not played detective after your sister was dead, this never would have happened. You should have taken the warning at the Gator Watering Hole, but we couldn't have you running around knowing what Josh did, because that could point to Nikki in Daria's death. Soon, everyone will point to her as the next senator from Florida, then on to the stars."

Bree looked up at the stars through her tears. So beautiful but cold and distant. He finally pulled the gag out of her mouth. Her throat was so dry she could hardly talk.

"If she turned on him—she'll turn on you," she rasped. "In D.C., a stunning and ambitious woman like that, she'll meet someone who can help her move up more than you. Her father won't want her to marry a mere—"

"No," he interrupted and gave her a shake. "Everything we've done together bonds us for good."

"She got someone to get rid of him, didn't she? She'll get—"

"Just shut up. That's it."

He *was* going to use the net to hold her down, and he did not untie his shirt from her wrists. He planned to take it back later, when he was sure she was dead. Could she twist out of the shirt in the water? Could she get free from the net to swim down instead of trying to come up for precious air?

The boat rocked as Mark half picked her up, half rolled her in. She hit backside down and fought to right herself so she could dive, but he put the big net over her. It was a strong-webbed one, meant to bring up large, heavy items. He yanked it down over her and twisted it to entrap her so she couldn't dive or escape.

Then, he shoved her underwater and held her there.

"Amelia, are you all right?" someone asked. She jolted back to reality and jerked away from the rail. It was Cole DeRoca. He looked upset.

"I'm fine."

"You don't look fine, any more than I do. Would you do me a favor and get Ben out here without drawing attention to it? I have something I have to tell him."

"Sure," she said, and started away, then gripped the railing because she felt un-steady. "Is it—not something about Bree?"

"No. Hurry, would you?"

She was back with Ben in less than a minute.

"I was checking a storage room downstairs," Cole told them, "and stumbled on a young woman tied up there. She's been abused, she's naked and she's terrified. Says she's from Guatemala and Verdugo's keeping her here for his guards—for the whole damn crew to rape, for all I know."

"Got him!" Ben said, smacking his palms together. "I don't care what kind of lawyers he pays for, I'll get him at least ten years for harboring a sex slave. And we get rid of the casino boat at the same time. Bingo!"

"But so we don't have a knock-down dragout fight when they realize we've found her," Cole said, "we'll have to leave her there until we get back to the dock or get the coast guard out here."

"You can't leave her there for one more second!" Amelia cried. Both men had obviously forgotten she was here. But how dare Verdugo or anyone else treat a poor girl like that!

". . . so let's come up with a story," Cole went on, "that someone's ill, and Verdugo needs to head back in early."

"I can do that," Amelia told them. "I'll claim an appendix attack, but I'd like to help that girl afterward. Yes, Ben," she interrupted as he started to speak again, "I know she'll be handed over to the authorities, but someone's got to be her advocate. You'll be busy with media interviews galore when all this hits. Cole," she added, patting him on the shoulder, "you've saved another woman from destruction. Wait until Bree hears this. That young woman must be traumatized, maybe suicidal, and I know I can help her."

Bree fought. Grabbing the metal frame of the net with both hands tied behind her, she tried to yank him in. Is this how a netted fish felt, pulled from the realm of the sea where it could breathe only drowning air? *Daria, is this how you felt in the wheelhouse when our boat went down?*

Cole. She'd wanted to have a life with Cole. She wanted to build bridges with Amelia, teach the boys to dive.

Should she not struggle, save air? Just accept this? Needed a breath, save air . . . save herself.

Strange colors pulsated before her eyes, blues and greens, bright gold. Like a lovely underwater dive. Like the sun in the sky with the sea beckoning beyond . . .

Going to suck in seawater now . . . going

to die . . . just hold Daria's hand and sink into the soft earth under all the sea grass with her . . . Cole, smiling, sailing away with Cole . . . The bright colors in Bree's brain were fading, fading to gray and black. She had been certain she could fight death below the surface. The sea was her friend, but it had taken Daria, and now . . . now . . .

With a whoosh, someone pulled her up. Her head broke the surface. She sucked in a huge breath of air.

Had Mark changed his mind? Was she hallucinating? Was she dead?

Bree blinked water from her eyes, took another deep breath into her burning lungs. Not Mark, but Sam Travers. He hauled her over the side of his dive boat, scraping her belly, but she didn't care. If Satan himself had saved her, that was just fine.

Bree lay on her back, gasping in blessed breaths as Sam unwound her from the sopping net.

"Where—you—come—from?" she got out.

"I wanted a quiet boat ride, and I saw the bastard take your boat. Thought he was stealing it, so I followed him. When I figured out he had you in that net, I yelled at him.

The SOB took a shot at me, so I shot him with a speargun someone stupidly left loaded here in my boat."

Perfect justice, she thought. Her head cleared in a flash as she sat up and saw Mark Denton's body, sprawled against the prow of *Mermaids I* with a spear in his chest.

"I should have let him drown you, of course," Sam went on as she was finally freed. "Here I come back to help Josh Austin with your cause and find out I've been served with a search warrant. If you had anything to do with th—"

"Sam, I know we've had terrible times, but you have to help me," she said, getting to her knees and then her feet. She was dizzy, but she scanned the horizon beyond the Trade Wreck site. Thank God, Verdugo's big yacht was heading in, not out.

"What time is it?" she asked.

"What?"

"Time! I can't explain now but to say the guy you just shot has planted some kind of bomb—the same kind that blew a hole in Daria's boat—aboard that ship. He got the supplies from Ric."

Sam swore only once, then seemed to go into combat mode. "It's nine twenty-three," he told her, glaring at the luminous dial on his watch.

"Then we have twelve minutes to get the explosive off the hull."

"Twelve minutes? They put a timer on it? Even at full speed, they won't make it in. And I'll never get a diver, let alone the bomb squad, out here by then."

"Sam, I'm the diver and you're the bomb squad," she said, grabbing one of the two tanks she saw on board and seizing a mask someone had left near the speargun. She spit in it and started wiping off the plastic to clear it. "And we have to catch that boat while you tell me how to get rid of a demolition cap with a primer cord, like you use to blow up bridges."

"It's Primacord," he said. "Just pray we catch that yacht." He started his motor, leaving *Mermaids I* with the dinghy Mark had planned for his escape in their wake.

"I'll bet you had assignments harder than this in Vietnam!" she shouted. "And I'll bet Ted did in Iraq, too! No matter what you think, Sam, I was proud of him and what he did there."

Their eyes met. She thought she might have made a mistake mentioning Ted, but

Sam nodded fiercely and revved the motor on full speed. "Wish I could have gone after Ted's killers the way you did Daria's!" he shouted.

Fighting tears, Bree nodded and braced herself in the bouncing boat, struggling into the unfamiliar gear and checking the gauge on the tank. Not much air in the tank. "Lights?" she yelled at Sam. "Do you have dive lights?"

"Portside storage under the seat!"

Bree knew she was exhausted and yet energy poured through her, as it had the day she swam through the storm. Sam had taken an angle where they were closing on the boat, but surely two more minutes must have gone by. Why was the yacht coming in earlier than expected? Could they have learned about the bomb?

She tried to concentrate as Sam shouted instructions to her.

"If it is one of my detonator caps—"

"It is!"

"It's actually a form of TNT. It's stable, relatively insensitive to shock, so don't be afraid to pry it off. But do not jimmy the Primacord if it's visible. It will be stuck on the hull by what looks like kid's clay, in a bright color, maybe blue or red. It will have metal end caps and one end will be threaded for insertion of the detonator. For a boat as big as that, they may have used a booster of tetryl."

"At least that's a fairly new boat. It can't have a lot of barnacles yet to obscure the cap. I'm going to look near the hull, since that's where they blew up *Mermaids II.*"

"Who did?"

"Later. Look! Someone's outside on the deck!" She saw two men, one as tall as Cole. Yes, it was Cole!

Sam buzzed the port side, blowing an air horn she hadn't seen. Bree was screaming but it drowned her out.

Cole saw them. He leaned out. Josh was outside, too. Poor Josh—poor everyone, in about seven minutes.

"Stop the vessel!" Sam was commanding through a bullhorn. "Bomb aboard! Bomb!"

Josh disappeared. It seemed to take forever, and the big waves from the yacht kept pushing them away, but the yacht finally stopped dead in the water.

Dead in the water, Bree thought, as Sam took them closer, under the higher deck of the larger vessel.

"Bomb?" Cole shouted down. "Has Sam changed his mind and told you—"

"He's here to help!" Bree shouted up to him.

Sam reversed their direction and motored them back closer toward the stern. Cole ran along the railing to stay over them. Bree had so much to say to him, but it would have to wait.

"Not much time," she told Sam as she fitted her mask and stood up to jump in. "Get as far away as you can, just in case."

"No, I'm backing you up. Just get it off and drop it into the depths, because there's no time to defuse it. You'll do fine."

The entire world had gone mad. Sam Travers was backing her up and telling her she'd do fine and she believed him. Sam had given her her life back once already. At least that was one good thing to come from this terror.

"Get all the deck lights on!" Sam was yelling through the megaphone to Cole and Josh. "Get everyone up on the decks or front of the ship! And don't let anyone jump off."

The last things she heard as she descended into the water were, "Bree, be careful!" from Cole and Sam bellowing, "Tell everyone to brace themselves and call the coast guard, just in case . . ."

Bubbles and her lights gave her vertigo at first, but she righted herself. The sea around her lit up. They must have turned on more deck lights. How far under the surface would Mark have put the bomb?

Her dive light skimmed the newly painted dark blue hull, up and down. It was so shiny she could glimpse a muted reflection of herself, as if Daria dove with her.

How much time left? No one usually knew how much time was left in their lives. Daria had not known, Mark either.

Nothing here at this level. Try the starboard side, the one that would have been toward the dock. Yes, the dock would have sheltered Mark when he planted it.

Time ticking away. At Daria's funeral, the words, *So teach us to number our days that we might have a heart of wisdom* . . .

Everyone's days were numbered. How many would die here if she didn't find the bomb?

Then, there it was. Two small, circular metal things, close together and stuck firmly to the hull. No cord was visible but it had to be here. With her dive knife, she pried the red adhesive off, not touching the detonator or the booster or whatever she was looking at. She'd seen movies where people had to cut the correct colored wires to stop a timer, but this seemed so primitive, so simple.

Yes, one was loose. Despite how cool the water felt, sweat was stinging her eyes within her mask and it was fogging up. Time must be gone. It was going to go off with her right on top of it, but she had to try. Try to save Amelia and Ben so their boys would not be orphans. Save Cole, even Verdugo. Josh, though, when everything came to light, might wish he was dead.

When she got the second metal piece off the hull, Bree let go of her dive knife rather than resheafing it. Then she dropped her dive light so it wouldn't hold her back or bump the pieces. She was trembling so hard she might set them off herself.

She jackknifed and upended, taking the pieces, one in each hand, kicking down, down.

Then she let them go—somehow letting all her fear go, too—and kicked and clawed madly for the surface.

She saw the lights above her and was almost to the surface when a muted boom and a fist of water thrust her upward. The sea roiled, and she thought she was back again at the day this all began, fighting to make it to shore.

Her ears hurt. Then hard hands grabbed her and Sam hauled her up and over the side of his boat as Cole jumped, feetfirst, into the water and clambered on board, too.

Dizzy but delirious with relief and joy, Bree stripped off her mask, while Sam unstrapped her tank. Holding tightly to each other, Cole and Bree sprawled, soaking wet on the floor of Sam's boat, while Sam patted her on the back, saying, "You all right? You all right?"

Despite the fact that she kept shaking, Cole's embrace was rock steady. She was definitely more than just all right.

25

Two months later

Bree dived cleanly into the swimming pool on the patio of their new house. Cole knifed in behind her. Though she knew the chlorine in the water would make her eyes burn, she opened them anyway and reveled in the sight of him swimming with powerful strokes beside her, his hair rippling.

They had been married for three weeks but had been back only a few days from a trip to the Cayman Islands. Cole reached out and pulled her against him as they surfaced, rocking the water against the tiles. The pool was a small one, the villa just two bedrooms, but they had their businesses to build and they were insanely happy. Bree and Manny were running Mermaids, and Cole was transitioning out of rare wood paneling to building sloops and teaching others how to build them, too.

"Easier to float in salt water," he said, "but this is a heck of a lot safer. Nothing to get cut on, no storms, no sharks, no bombs." He was kidding about not taking risks, since he still dived with her on jobs from time to time, even sometimes with the new guy they'd hired.

She pressed herself against him with her arms around his neck, and he clamped her even harder to him. They always melded perfectly, chest to breasts, hips, thighs, though her feet dangled partway up his calves. He slid his hand along her sleek, arched back and pushed her bikini bottom down to cup her with both hands.

"We've got a while before Ben and Amelia and the boys show up," he told her, his voice a delicious whisper.

"Mmm. But we've got to finish dinner and put up the Congrats On Your Reelection sign for Ben."

The election had been three days ago. Marla Sherborne had won back her senate seat by a landslide. Josh had withdrawn from the election. His party had put some-one else up to oppose her, but to no avail. Ben had said Josh had turned down an offer to write his story and was starting up a *cachaça* business to produce bottles of caipirinha for a cane company that was in competition with Grand Sugar. Josh had also started divorce proceedings against Nikki, who was awaiting trial in the Collier County jail along with Ric—and Verdugo, for human trafficking. His desire to bring gam-bling to Southwest Florida had gone down with him.

"Oh, yeah," Cole said, playing her game as he unhooked her bikini bra. "We've got to set up the snorkeling game for the kids. And wash our hair . . ."

Bree laughed as they came together. Cole swore when the doorbell rang. "Why is Amelia always early?" he muttered. They both knew if they didn't get out of the pool now, James and Jordan would run around to the back of the villa and look in through the netted cage around the pool. "Batten down the hatches, matey, 'cause the kids are here. Just when I thought I'd make a kid of my own."

"At least you're not sleeping on the sofa anymore," she told him, trying to sound normal as she looked for her bikini bottom and bra in the water. Every time Cole DeRoca looked at her that way, touched her, it was as wild as a lightning strike. After being in the water during the distant bomb blast, her hearing and her sight seemed to have returned to normal, but nothing was ever normal with Cole in her life. She would always miss Daria, but her husband completed her, even as her twin sister could not.

Cole threw on a robe and left her scrambling to get back into her suit while he answered the door. He loved the boys and they him. Amelia had even let the two of them take the kids to the Swamp Buggy Races and didn't scold anyone when they came back looking like they'd been playing in the mud. Much of Amelia's efforts were now focused on spreading the word about human trafficking. She'd taken care of the Guatemalan girl the night Cole found her, and she was going to testify against Verdugo at his trial.

Now where was that terry-cloth robe? If Cole had taken it, he'd look like a giant in it. Bree barely made it back into her suit and wrapped a towel around her waist as the kids arrived.

"Aunt Bree, Aunt Bree, can we do that snorkel game now, where we find the coins in the pool?"

Both boys hit into her with hard hugs. "If your mother and dad say so."

"Not only do we say so," Amelia said, putting down a tray of cookies and brownies, despite the fact that Bree had told her she'd fix everything this time, "but—ta-da!" she cried, and produced a snorkel and a mask, both of which still sported their price tags.

"You're going to join us?" Bree said, walking over to hug her, however wet she was. Amelia didn't seem to mind. Ben was off in the corner already, talking to someone on his cell, but Amelia didn't seem to mind that, either.

"Leftover desserts from the fund-raiser luncheon," Amelia said. "And, yes, I want to join you. It's better than fighting, I hear."

When Cole hustled the boys off to change into their suits, Bree and Amelia stood arm in arm. Amelia had explained everything that had happened the day Daria died. Bree had been furious at first and blamed Amelia for leaving Daria vulnerable to Nikki and Mark.

But it was Daria's own mistakes and lies that had made her vulnerable. And perhaps, Bree had told herself, it was the morning sickness from the pregnancy that made Daria slip, not anything Amelia had done. Amelia had believed that Bree would surface soon and, as ever, care for her twin. Bree's conflicting feelings of love and hate toward Amelia had made her understand the torment Amelia had lived with most of her life.

The first month of Amelia's psychiatric appointments, Bree had gone with her. They'd worked through the past. When Bree had hugged her even then, Amelia said she knew that she was loved for sure.

"In the pool," Cole shouted, clapping his hands as the boys jumped in the shallow end. "Lots of fun things can happen in the pool, and we don't even need to be afraid of getting in the deep end," he said, with such a funny look at Bree that Amelia laughed.

"I have a feeling we interrupted something," Amelia said. "Maybe that's really why I want to get in the water. Ben and I have a very nice, big pool, and he's been much, much too busy lately. Maybe the wide-eyed honeymooner can give me a few tips."

The two of them giggled together, as if they were just silly, happy girls again.

A salsa beat shook the walls of the Garcia Party House in Immokalee. Nearly three hundred people crowded the food tables and the dance floor. This *Mexicana quinceañera* celebration with family and friends touched Bree deeply. She was proud to have been one of Lucinda's financial supporters to help pay for this beautiful party marking a girl's "sweet fifteen" transition to womanhood.

And it turned out that Daria had helped to pay for it, too. Manny had admitted that she had given him money to keep quiet about her pregnancy—and that he had spent it on a partial payment for the party house. Bree and her new junior partner had been through a lot of discussions on how they would run things at Mermaids, and they had come to a much better understanding of each other. Bree felt she'd been in the forgiveness business full-time lately, and was a much better, stronger person for it.

The Salazars had selected a Cinderella theme with pink and white bunting, and a Disney Cinderella, no less, on the five-tiered cake. Cindi—she'd asked Bree to call her Lucinda today—looked half bride, half prom queen in her white gown and upswept hair with her gold tiara.

Manny had said that she'd taken five required hours of pre-*quinceañera* counseling classes at her church about everything from family responsibilities to sexuality and religion. Besides that, the Salazars' meeting with Luke and his family had helped a lot. Manny had thanked Bree for her part in that and for visiting him every day in the hospital while he was recovering from being hit over the head with his own wrench.

"And now," Manny announced proudly over the tinny PA system, first in Spanish, then English, as his wife and even his ill, rake-thin mother beamed, "you all invited to dance to this Mexican waltz. Its name, *Mi Linda Hijita,* for our non-Latino friends here, means *my beautiful daughter.*"

After Lucinda's teenage supporters demonstrated the steps and everyone applauded, Bree and Cole left their *padrones* table to join others on the dance floor. Luke was partnering Lucinda this time, and she took his hand and led him over to Cole and Bree, dancing cheek to cheek in a corner.

"Thanks for coming, both of you," Lucinda said. She looked radiant. Luke, bless him, looked proud. "I just wanted to show you this bracelet, Bree. Every *quinceañera* girl gets one, 'cause it stands for the unending circle of life."

For a moment Bree wondered if Manny had told his family she was pregnant. Bree had shared that with him, not only because she'd need more help soon with the business, but because she didn't want to shut him out as Daria had both of them.

Lucinda went on. "Look close. I put names on the charms of people who are gone, but still with us in our hearts. Here are both my grandpas' names, and I put Daria's here, too, see?"

Bree's eyes filled with tears. Cole's arm came around her waist as if to steady her. Wordlessly, but mouthing *thank you,* Bree hugged Lucinda, before she and Luke danced off together again.

"You okay?" Cole asked. "Want to stay?"

"Of course I do. I don't want to miss what she has planned for Manny next. The look on his face will be worth the price of admission."

One of Lucinda's friends carried a chair out into the center of the dance floor, and she pulled her father out and sat him down in it. Another friend brought out a huge pillow, which Lucinda sat on at his feet, amidst the puffy softness of her full skirts. The band quieted and, looking up into her father's nervous face, Lucinda said in Spanish, her voice wavering, "I want to especially thank the main man in my life for sticking with me through tough times—and for this happy day and others to come."

On cue, the band began to play some song Bree didn't know, but it made Manny, macho no more, cry.

Bree turned to Cole and whispered, "I want to especially thank the main man in my life for sticking with me through tough times—and for this happy day and others to come."

Cole looked as teary-eyed as Manny as he put his arms around Bree and patted her belly. Bree put a hand down to link her fingers with his. She liked to think of her baby inside her, swimming already, safe in her own little sea.

Author Note

Since I live in Southwest Florida for part of each year, I know and love the area; I have, however, created the fictional Turtle Bay. The book's characters are all fictional and not based on or inspired by actual persons.

The day I completed this novel, the *Naples Daily News* carried an article with the headline, Dying Sea Grass Has City Council's Attention, so I felt validated I had chosen the right "hook for the book" a year earlier. For research, I am indebted to the newspaper's excellent series of articles called *Deep Trouble: The Gulf In Peril.*

The City of Naples is currently working on

water quality "to better manage water as it flows off yards and streets . . . and then into coastal estuaries." The local watershed for the gulf in Southwest Florida used to be ten miles but there are 120 miles of runoff. "The bay has also taken a hit from the . . . destruction of sea grass beds to make way for high-priced subdivisions along the bay." [*Naples Daily News,* Eric Staats, Feb. 2007] Needless to say, government funding for this is a continual challenge.

Another article of importance to my re-search was Jeff Klinkenberg's feature story on sloop-building and sailing, which ap-peared in the *St. Petersburg Times* and was syndicated in other papers. Since I do not sail or scuba dive, I am indebted to our friend John Hawkins, who does both and who kindly read the sections of the book dealing with these sports. Any mistakes in description are mine, not his.

There are some casino gambling ships in Southwest Florida, but none in the Naples area yet. These luxury pay-and-play yachts must go out beyond the three-mile limit to international waters before their gaming is legal.

For anyone interested in the fascinating

tradition of *quinceañera,* there is a book, published in August 2007, called *Once Upon a Quinceañera: Coming of Age in the USA.* The phenomenon of the Latina "sweet fifteen" celebration is quickly becoming an American event. The Latino culture is an increasing part of Southwest Florida life, as it is on the east coast of the state. As my husband speaks Spanish, we have had a glimpse into these people and customs, through our trips to Mexico and South America as well as by speaking with Latinos in Southwest Florida.

Also, special thanks to my Florida and Ohio friend, Mary Ann Manning, for her very own brand of PR for Karen Harper books.

For those readers who like South Florida settings, my two earlier books, which take place in this area, are *Black Orchid* and *Hurricane,* both from Mira Books. Please visit my Web site at www.karenharperauthor.com.

Karen Harper
Naples, Florida
April 6, 2007